ALSO BY JERRY JAY CARROLL

Top Dog

Dog Eat Dog

Inhuman Beings

PRAISE FOR JERRY JAY CARROLL

"A stylish, funny combination of parable and moral tale...Imaginative, seductively written, and a pleasure to read. *Top Dog* is a first rate entertainment."—*Richard North Patterson*

"A witty, adult, and imaginative fable."—*Martin Cruz Smith*

"If Kafka and Tolkien shared an office on Wall Street, this is the novel they might have written."—*San Francisco Chronicle*

"The Shaggy Dog meets J.R.R. Tolkien in this entertaining debut effort. The premise is wildly silly and metaphorically transparent and has absolutely no right to succeed on any level, but Carroll—through a combination of reasonably swift pacing and gruffly funny internal monologues—pulls it off."—*Kirkus Reviews*

"Carroll's tight, colorful prose proves zesty and absorbing. His characters ring oddly true. And his plot has touches of that Tolkienesque irresistibility, that thing that keeps you up past bedtime turning pages to learn what happens next."—*San Francisco Chronicle*

"*Top Dog* is one of those books I keep buying for myself (because I give it to people who never heard of it) and for others. It's one of the most creative and entertaining books I've ever read. In fact, it can be read as pure entertainment, so it's easy to overlook how deftly the writing and plotting are done."—*Amazon review*

"The writing is witty and original, the hero is certainly not the classic hero type, and the book ends before you realize it, it's that good!"—*Amazon review*

"I stumbled upon this gem while wandering the shelves of a half-price bookstore. I'm so happy I picked it up. Love finding random awesomeness!"—*Elise at Good Reads*

"*Top Dog* is an excellent example of what great fiction should be: creative, amusing, completely immersive, yet containing the seeds of some very serious ideas."—*Amazon reviewer*

"These two books are sheer pleasure, and if you can't separate that from reading great literature, shame on you. I am so sorry Mr. Carroll didn't write many more books, not sure why. Anyway, if you're a good story junkie like I am, get this and its sequel. You won't regret it."—*Amazon review by Lao T. Sue*

"*Top Dog* is one of those books I keep buying for myself (because I give it to people who never heard of it) and for others. It's one of the most creative and entertaining books I've ever read. In fact, it can be read as pure entertainment so it's easy to overlook how deftly the writing and plotting are done."—*Amazon review by Richard Best*

"Vastly entertaining tale."—*Amazon review*

"The writing is witty and original, the hero is certainly not the classic hero type, and the book ends before you realize it, it's that good!"—*Amazon review by Dr. Zoidberg*

"A roller-coaster ride through an astonishing world. Jerry Jay Carroll effortlessly plants you in the middle of a breathtaking adventure—completely implausible and yet thoroughly believable and engaging, thanks to his gifted writing. It reminded me of the opening moments of the film *The Fugitive*—you begin on the edge of your seat and never get off it through the rest of the book...His sequel *Dog Eat Dog* is even better. *Inhuman Beings*, while written in an entirely different genre, is also outstanding. I say, order everything Carroll's written and take them all on vacation with you. You won't be sorry."—*Amazon review by C. Bef*

"After reading (and very much enjoying) this author's book *Inhuman Beings*, I had to go out and find more of his writings. *Top Dog*, the prequel to his current *Dog Eat Dog*, had me smiling and reading with a sense of glee. The story may be one we've heard before, but never quite told with the hero (anti-hero?) having such a unique perspective. And Jerry Jay Carroll is one of the most entertaining storytellers to come along in the past few years."—*Amazon review by Edward Alexander Gerster*

"This is a witty book which delighted me from cover to cover. I found myself missing Big and the other characters in the book long after I finished. I'm thrilled Jerry Jay Carroll has come out with a sequel."—*Amazon review*

"I started reading this in a bookstore, and before I knew it I was three chapters deep. Had to buy it then. I've thoroughly enjoyed it, and have loaned it to several friends. Not a single person's come back and said they didn't like it."—*Amazon review by Dectra*

If you're looking for a fantasy that stands out for its originality, I would recommend *Top Dog*."—*Evelyn C. Leeper, New England Science Fiction Association, Inc.*

"When I read Jerry Jay Carroll's genre-blending *Inhuman Beings* earlier this year, he jumped immediately onto my list of favorite new authors. Even so, when I saw that *Dog Eat Dog* was a sequel to *Top Dog*, Carroll's debut novel, I was doubtful. Could that weird mix of satire and fantasy be pulled off a second time, without seeming stale or self-derivative? Yes, it turns out: *Dog Eat Dog* is every bit as fresh, entertaining and funny as its predecessor."—*Victoria Strauss*

"As ever, Carroll's prose is what keeps the readers coming back for more. He's so darn funny and endearing, it's almost unnerving. He's no slouch when it comes to wrangling a bang-up plot, either."—*Rick Kleffel, the Agony Column, Bookotron.com*

"A thoroughly enjoyable book for those fans of fantasy that have grown up (if not matured). We're not dealing with high literature, but with a storyline based on a Wall Street type turned into a dog, what do you expect? Still Carroll writes well and has produced a very fluid read. I'm looking forward to reading *Dog Eat Dog*."—*Amazon.co U.K. review*

"This was a good fantasy fable about learning what's important in life and what's not. I liked the main character, William Bogart Ingersol, aka Big the Dog, even when he recounts his past behavior. I also liked the interactions between Big and the creatures and people of the Fair Lands."
—*Krin5292@LibraryThing*

"*Inhuman Beings* is published by a science fiction imprint, and doubtless will be marketed as science fiction. Really, however, it's a genre-blender, a dizzy melding of one of the most cheesy of pulp SF concepts with hard-boiled shoot-'em-up detective fiction. There is absolutely no reason why it should work, but it does—wonderfully."—*Victoria Strauss*

"Jerry Jay Carroll is the reigning master of recombinative fiction, a refreshing voice. He not only makes everything old new again, but knows how to plot, develop characters and heat things up. *Inhuman Beings* is what *The X-Files* should be, with a little *Dr. Strangelove* thrown in for good measure. Hey, somebody should get this guy to write for television."—*Amazon review*

THE GREAT
LIARS

JERRY JAY CARROLL

This book is an original edition, and has never been previously published.

Cover photograph by John Collier, Jr., (1942) Library of Congress, Prints & Photographs Division, FSA/OWI Collection, reproduction number PLC-USF34-080555-E

Back cover photograph U.S. Navy, (1941 Dec. 7) Library of Congress, Prints & Photographs Division, Miscellaneous Items in High Demand Collection, reproduction number LC-USZ62-104778

Book design by Valerie Bellamy, Dog-ear Book Design, **dog-earbookdesign.com**

The account of his public school experience from My Early Life by Winston S. Churchill is reproduced with permission of Curtis Brown, London, on behalf of the Estate of Sir Winston Churchill © Winston S. Churchill.

Library of Congress Control Number: 2013923578

ISBN: 978-0-9898269-0-7

This is dedicated to Judy. It would take volumes to say it all.

I WOULD LIKE TO THANK TWO OLD FRIENDS FOR THEIR HELP AND ENCOURAGEMENT over the course of writing this book. Clint Reilly, a modern phenomenon, stole time from interests that range from real estate through media, politics, art, religion and philanthropy, to read two versions of this manuscript, and made many helpful suggestions. Kevin Leary spurred me on to the finish line. Most of all, I thank my wife, Judy, who is both anchor and wind in my sail. That's trickier than it sounds.

THE GREAT
LIARS

CHAPTER 1

WHAT I TOLD YOU ABOUT NOT KNOWING FRANKLIN OR ANY OF THE OTHER big shots back then was a crock. I knew him, but not well—a mile from it. I don't think people even close to him knew the man, not even Eleanor. He'd throw his head back and laugh, and you'd think he was your best friend. Then if he didn't like what you told him, or the way you said it, or even the way you combed your hair, he'd slip the knife in as soon as you walked out the door; pick up the phone or dictate a memo and that was it—your ass was in a crack, your goose was cooked, or whatever way you want to put it. Your district didn't get the dam, your career in government was done, or your name went on one of Hoover's lists for special attention.

That machine must be heavy. I can't picture a slip of girl like you hauling that big thing around for hillbillies to sing into. I never heard of oral history; I always thought it came in a book. That's progress, I guess. I've always been for it as long as I don't have to change. A-hawr, hawr, hawr. A little joke there.

I checked with the Smithsonian. Someone with your name works there, not that it proves anything. I was in the spy game myself, so I know things aren't always what they seem. I thought I'd write a book about that time and the other things that happened, even the bad stuff. Hire somebody to look up the dates and put in the flowery words and footnotes and the rest of it, but I never got around to it. It's one thing or another in life; you think you've got all the time in the world, and next thing you know, the sands are running out.

Would you do me a little favor? Open the drawer in the night stand. Under the Good Book, you'll find a little bottle with nerve tonic. The nurse was supposed to give it to me a half an hour ago, but I suppose she got held up. Some old duffer draws his last breath every other day here. No, I don't need the spoon. An inch off the top is close enough. Now, if you would be good enough to put it back. The Bible on top.

There are people here who forgot everything they ever knew, including their names, but my memory is excellent—too good, in fact. There are things you'd rather forget; Christ, the stuff that happens in war. Most guys don't want to talk about it, but in your dreams it's like you're there again.

Getting back to Franklin, I was practicing card tricks in the little room in the White House where we sat around like bellhops waiting for somebody to snap their fingers. My job was running orders that said "by hand of officer" to and from the Main Navy Building at 18th and Constitution. But there'd be days when time crawled and I spent considerable work on my card tricks; I got to where I could pick an ace of spades from behind your ear. Couldn't do it today, not with these stiff old fingers.

Major Jack Bolton gives me a sour look one day and asks, "Why don't you find a better use of your time?"

He was studying the manual on the Army's new eight-inch howitzer. Always nose to the grindstone was Jack. Even Captain R. F. Bellows of the Marines—we called him Windy—eased up when there was no danger a general or admiral would stick a head in.

Pick a card, I told Jack, any card.

He gave me a sneer and went back to his manual. I heard years later his battery was the last firing at Corregidor. Fine men, both of them, and I never blamed either for hating my guts. They finished at the top of their class while it looked for a time like I'd be the anchor in mine. Then I cheated in the finals and the disgrace fell to Al Billingham, known to us as Cement Head. Don't give me that look. A man does what he must.

Jack and Windy had first-rate careers while mine was on the mediocre side, and maybe even that's gilding the lily. The difference was I had juice through my step-daddy Josepha Brady, the blind Senator from Georgia as he was known. He wore dark glasses because those milky eyes of his gave people the willies. Mother made him pull strings to help my career along. He hated it and wasn't shy about letting me know.

"You'd be nothing without me."

He told me that a thousand times. But being somebody thanks to him beat being nobody, so I never complained. Call it taking the high road. I prefer the low road as a general rule, but that choice is not always yours. People on the low road aren't so quick to judge because they're not pure as the driven snow themselves. Let whoever wants take the high road with the saints among us. They'll arrive about the same time as me, but guess who will have the better time.

Because he was struck blind when he got snake bit, the Senator believed the Lord gave him second sight to make up for it. One night he had a dream where the world blazed up in the fires of war. He cried out so loud the servants came running and Mother had to pull his hair to wake him up. After that, he switched to the finance committee and was the Navy and War Department's steadiest vote to get us ready for war. That's how I landed that job at the White House. If I'd known what was to come I would have begged to march men on the parade ground seven days a week regardless of weather. I was sinful proud back then, but I wasn't above crawling if it meant saving my hide.

What about you, I said to Windy Bellows. Pick a...

Admiral Chester Nimitz picked that minute to breeze in, and he blew his stack at catching one of his officers with a deck of cards. He was chief of the Bureau of Navigation at the time, which put him above everybody except the Chief of Naval Operations himself.

"Wipe that shit-eatin' grin off your face, goddamn you," he told me, pardon the language.

Nimitz was a square-headed German from Texas, as salty as they come, and he lit into me with more choice language outside. Meanwhile, I'm thinking how to throw the blame on Major Bolton. The Navy would believe anything about the Army in those days, and it was the same on their side. Lord, we hated one another.

"Never mind," he said as I was telling him I was holding the cards for Bolton so he could get out his handkerchief to blow his nose. "You know a man name of Winston Churchill over in England, is that right?"

Yes, sir, I said.

I went with the Senator to London in 1936 after that dream of his and held his elbow as we walked through a gale to pay a call. Churchill was a short, fat man with bright blue eyes and a pink face. He was famous on his side of the pond, or maybe notorious is a better way to put it, but nobody I knew had heard of him on our side.

"Fine," Nimitz said, "the president wants to see you." He walked me to a part of the White House I'd never been before.

Even with a senator in your corner you walked on eggs around Nimitz. He wouldn't shove you out of his way like some of those old crocks with flag rank—I believe many were sorry flogging went out—but he could put you in the engine room of some oiler in the tropics where it was hot enough at noon to fry bacon on the quarter deck. They said he was kind to young officers, but I never saw that side. He had called for my records when I was assigned to the White House, and I guess he didn't like what he saw. Then to catch me with playing cards.

Mad as he was, he knocked timidly on the door and Franklin roared for us to come on in. He was behind his desk and a seedy-looking man smoking a cigarette twisted around in his chair to look at us.

"This would be Lieutenant Brady," the president said, waving off my crisp salute. "We're not big on ceremony in the Oval Office. Right, Admiral?"

"No, *sir*," Nimitz said.

If Franklin said nothing was bigger than ceremony in the White House, Nimitz would have agreed with that too. The higher the rank, the more fanny you kiss—fact of life. If you were too good to press your lips to someone's backside, the door opened to being shot at, blown up, or sunk by torpedo. Later on, it was kamikazes flying at your head. When bullets fly, give me a job shuffling papers behind the lines and you have a friend for life.

I've had a few bits of ribbon and metal pinned on me, but the plain truth is it was for actions I did my best to avoid. A reputation for bravery brings you as much grief as glory. When things go bad, all eyes turn to you, the hero with the medals to prove it. You can't leg it out of there like you want. If you do, they charge you with cowardice in the face of the enemy. That's the firing squad or a dance at the end of a rope. Oh, you run into men who say they want to be "tested" in battle, but don't pay any attention; ignorance explains the greater part of that. Being in a situation where heroes are made is damned poor planning in the first place.

But I'm getting ahead of myself. The peacetime Navy was a good life, though I dreaded fleet exercises. Higher ranks were always looking for ways to show they didn't let anything get past them no matter how triflin'. I sweated like a whore in church from reveille until my head hit the pillow at night. But that was only once a year, thank God.

It was fine work when you went on cruises to show the flag. You lolled on the beach, and the embassies laid on receptions in the evening where you rubbed elbows with the local big shots. They were a corrupt lot, but it wasn't my money they were stealing. There was plenty of time for the beautiful ladies or the plain ones if the others weren't willing—excuse me, ma'am, but I'm a simple sailor and you asked me to speak freely.

Back home you spent the nights at the officer's club, where you could count on a decent whiskey being poured. You had to listen to a lot of bilge, of course, and smile if the man was above you in rank. But if you can't do that you're not going to get ahead no matter the line of work, and I learned young it's better to give orders than get them. You can bet men shaped up when it was me cracking the whip. I might be easy-going, but it was all business when I was in command. Whoever says he doesn't prefer doing the bossing around is a hypocrite or a liar. Unfortunately, there's no shortage of either in this wicked world. And there are plenty worse sinners than them.

Is this the sort of thing you want to hear, stories of how it was back then?

A naval officer's pay and allowances let you live pretty well between the wars, not that I had to worry with Ma's money. That's why the Senator married her. Without her fortune he would've been just another crooked politician. But with it he could put on his hard face when other politicians got caught stealing, which was pretty frequent down where we came from. He wanted them put to work improving rural roads in the summer sun. He had a speech about how service to humanity was what he cared about most. You'd laugh yourself sick if you knew him. You'd fall down and pound the floor.

I figured I'd get a staff job pushing paper if we ever went to war because you don't put someone in harm's way that is related to a powerful politician, not if you want to get ahead in the Navy. The country got its fingers burned in the Great War and we were back to not giving a good goddamn about the people across the sea, which still seems like a good idea if you ask me. I never gave personal safety a thought back when I was a midshipman or ensign. We might have to steam down to Latin America and bombard greasers for the banana companies, but that was as far as it went. Those were golden times, the peacetime Navy. Jesus, I'm wiping away a tear.

I'm just talking along like you said; give me a hail if I wander off course.

Most of the big names you meet aren't what you'd expect. They're little twerps for the most part, but not Roosevelt. He was a big fellow before he got sick and still was from the waist up. The papers and newsreels never showed those iron braces he strapped on to stagger a few steps or being pushed around in his wheelchair. Jack Dempsey said the president's biceps were big as his own from using crutches. Republicans said he was crazy from syphilis and you could hear him screaming at night. He had to be tied down on Eleanor's orders, so the story went. But they steered clear of saying he was a cripple because that wouldn't be cricket. Politics is a strange business.

"This here's Harry," the president said with a wave at the scrawny guy.

My God, I thought, this bag of bones is the Harry Hopkins people talk about? He was Roosevelt's right hand man, but not for much longer if I was any judge. He looked like he already had one foot in the grave, yet years later he was to save me from certain death. Life's a funny thing; you'll learn that when you get a few more years on you. Harry's suit looked like he had it on loan from someone twice his size and his tie had a stain. Some said he was a damned Communist, Uncle Joe's agent in the White House. He's a forgotten man now but...oh, he's not? Well, I don't keep up much.

Hand me that there handkerchief, would you? I feel a sneeze coming on. *Achoo-ee.* Thank you for the blessing, young lady. It's drafty in this old dump; a regular gale blows down the corridors in the winter. No doubt it's on purpose. We old veterans are a burden on the taxpayer and every man laid in the ground from pneumonia eases the load. It's a hard world.

Franklin wanted to know how well I knew Churchill.

Pretty well, I said.

That wasn't the truth square on, obviously, but sometimes you have to bend it some. The man who can't do that better get used to looking up at assholes higher on the ladder because that's the view life has in store for him.

"These are grave times," Franklin said to me.

I guessed he meant how the Krauts were stirred up again and we best keep an eye on the Japs. Indeed these are grave times, I said with a sorrowful shake of my head, very worrisome to the thinking man.

"I'd like to ask you to go over to London on a secret mission for me."

"He will do as he is ordered," Nimitz rapped out.

"We want you to be our channel to Churchill," Hopkins chimed in. "You'll give him messages and pass on his answers."

"Messages we don't necessarily want the State Department to see," Franklin said, whipping off his eyeglasses for a sharp look. "Or anybody else, here or there."

I'm your man, I said. I'm thinking who wouldn't trade London for Washington with summer coming on?

Franklin said well and good and asked Nimitz what happens when a Jew with an erection walks into a wall.

"Beats me," the admiral said, already grinning.

"He breaks his nose."

When a president cracks a joke, you slap your knee or hold your sides like they're splitting. I see you're shocked, Miss…say your name again; some of my hearing went at the Battle of Savo Sea. Harriet Gallatin— maiden name I'm guessing. You heard a lot of nigger and yid jokes at the White House, Harriet. Franklin liked Catholic ones too, especially about the pope.

One he liked to tell was about the hillbilly with the nagging wife. His mule kicks her in the head one day and kills her deader than a doornail. At the funeral the minister notices the hillbilly nods when the women come up to him, but shakes his head when the men do. The minister goes up when it's over and asks why. Hillbilly tells him the women were saying how nice his wife looked in the coffin, and the men wanted to know if the mule was for sale. Got a smile out of you, didn't I? Franklin got a new crop of hillbilly jokes when he went down to Warm Springs for his legs. He did a country accent better than Will Rogers.

Franklin told me the Germans never would get over the Versailles treaty, which had been mighty rough on them. They didn't think they were licked in the Great War but got knifed in the back by poltroons back home and were dead set on revenge. The rest of Europe was in a bad way, the president said; couldn't bring themselves to think about another war. The French didn't know night from day, the English had their heads in the sand, Poles were as fascist as the Italians, and so on and so forth. Joe Stalin was as evil as Lucifer. The key to the situation was us and the English.

I was giving wise nods even though most of this was clear over my head. But that was his job wasn't it—seeing the big picture and moving us little pawns around this way and that. He said Churchill knew how important we'd be when war broke out and sent word he wanted to liaison with us outside official channels. After we'd been talking a while, a waiter with white gloves came in with stale pastries and coffee that was barely warm. You didn't want to bring an appetite to the White House back then. When our little chat was over, Nimitz marched me back to the Navy Building, and I got the feeling he was disgusted but trying to hide it. He knew dozens of officers more worthy of this job, but orders were orders.

"Not even naval intelligence is going to know about this," he said. "It's top secret, more than top secret. Your stepfather is in on this, which is why you were picked. This town leaks like a piss pot with a bullet through it. You'll pass on what Churchill gives you straight to your stepfather and he'll take it to the president. You won't be in uniform, of course. You'll stay at Churchill's home pretending to be a cousin from America."

I said I would do my best to make the country proud, et cetera, et cetera, the bilge brass hats expect even though they don't believe it themselves. Passing on what I was told to the Senator, what could be easier? The letters didn't even have to be in code. Nimitz must have been thinking along the same line.

"Why, a child could do this," he half muttered, "except for going to the cocktail parties." He rounded on me. "I've heard stories about you and women. There'll be none of that in London."

I think you mean a Lieutenant Brady out on the West Coast, sir, I said meekly. The man is quite the womanizer according to what I hear.

You see, Harriet, there was a Lieutenant Louis Brady with docks and harbors in San Diego, an upright family man and pillar of the Methodist church. I always put the blame on him when some story was put around by my enemies, otherwise no decent woman would have anything to do with me, and a lot didn't anyhow. He must have wondered about the hateful looks the ladies gave him, decent man that he was. Terrible gossips, those Navy wives. It was much smaller in those days; if you didn't know somebody yourself, you knew somebody who did.

"There's another Lieutenant Brady?" Nimitz looked suspicious but he couldn't rule out the possibility; anyhow the president had spoken.

I've suffered because of his reputation, I said. I put a little catch in my voice.

"You're dismissed."

I went off to New York to buy a wardrobe that set Uncle Sam back an admiral's pay. It included a midnight-blue dinner jacket; a striped, double-breasted banker's suit; country-house suits; checked jackets with side vents and hacking pockets like what the Prince of Wales wore. I looked so good the tailor wanted me as a model for high class magazine spreads, *Esquire* and so forth, and offered a nice price. The Navy is stuffy about that sort of thing, so I had to say no.

I also bought fancy leather luggage and had them scuff it up so it didn't look new. I knew I was going out on a limb, but to play a role you have to look the part. If I asked for permission, the green-eyeshade boys might have coughed up a chit six months later for a new shirt and an extra pair of trousers. There was a big uproar when the bills came in, and talk of a letter of reprimand. Kiss your career goodbye if you get one of those for your file. Fortunately, somebody put a stop to it, probably Nimitz himself after he swallowed hard.

On the trip over on the *Normandie* my thoughts kept returning to a fine young lass named Bridget. She was a maid in Churchill's home that I got friendly with on that first visit.

She wrote letters saying she loved me, but I never got round to writing back as I'm not much for *billets doux,* as the French say. "Hi, how are you? Things are swell on this end, how about yourself?" That's about my speed. Women used to write me page after page and got mad at the postcards I sent them, if I remembered when we reached port. They'd tear into me next time, and I'd have to work to calm them down. I'd say words on paper can't do justice to my true feelings and et cetera. Hell, you're a gal. You know women rattle off a hundred words for every one a man does.

CHAPTER 2

WHEN I MET LOWELL BRADY (THOSE ARE HIS WORDS ABOVE) IN 1953, he resided at the Fillmore Soldiers' Home in Washington, D.C., under an assumed name. It seemed at first it would be one of those glancing encounters that are soon forgotten. Instead, he was to wrench me from moorings in quiet scholarship and launch me on a perilous journey whose end is yet unknown.

He was known there as Kermit Crockett, a retired naval officer fallen on hard times after an unexceptional career in naval supplies. I was to learn in reality his career included secret wartime missions to Churchill and Stalin. He was at the center of events before Pearl Harbor, was with MacArthur at Corregidor, and at Guadalcanal when the issue was in doubt, and was a party to other major events. How could obscurity so completely claim such a man?

It was at the suggestion of Benton Broadbrow, PhD., chief deputy archivist of our section at the Smithsonian, that I began the oral history project upon my return from field work to Washington, D.C. Brady's room was off the beaten track in the sprawling facility, and I would never have found him if a gnarled janitor with a "fresh off the boat" accent had not taken an interest.

"Mr. Crockett, 'ee da mos' interestin' of 'eem all." Alessandro Manzoni pointed the way with a dripping mop. "He got stories he tella you all day long and inna ta da night."

I had spent my first hour recording the recollections of an older veteran who had lost fingers, toes, and the tip of his nose to frostbite after a night of drunken revel that ended with him passing out in a snow bank. His disfigurement left him remote and uncommunicative; nor did his job firing artillery shells at an enemy he never saw have intrinsic interest. Manzoni volunteered Brady as someone who might be of greater interest.

"He's a bigga man," he said. "Da biggest."

Lugging my cumbersome reel-to-reel recorder, I followed him to Captain Brady's room where a group of older men lounged on such familiar terms with each other that several had slipped out their false teeth for greater comfort. To judge from the bawl of laughter, an off-color story had just concluded. (I grew up with brothers and am well acquainted with male conversation.) Brady lay on a bed in a shabby robe and pajamas smoking a cigar. Something made me think his was the comment that inspired the hilarity.

"Hel-*lo*," he said when I stood shyly in the doorway. Astonished eyes turned to me, a small female suddenly interjecting herself into their rough company. I was aware false teeth were being stealthily retrieved from pockets, and heads ducking as they were inserted. "What have we here?"

"She's-a da history lady!" the janitor cried as if announcing royalty to a flourish of trumpets…

To digress, I owed my position at the Smithsonian to the many opportunities opened up to women when the men were away during the war. Through the help of my uncle Mayor Curtis Shultz of Helena, Montana, I went to work in 1938. Beginning as a secretary, I worked my way up to the rank of field researcher. I had the use of a jalopy to travel dirt roads in the rural South to record the folk songs of poor Whites and Negroes before the spread of radio should eradicate all trace of their origin and regional variations.

If that work is remembered it will be for the discovery of eleven versions of *Ole Dan Tucker* (first popularized in 1843 by the Virginia Minstrels troupe). Ole Dan was generally depicted as a manic figure of anarchic impulsiveness. This alienation from social norms is on vivid display in the final verse of a Negro version:

I come to town de udder night,
I hear de noise an saw de fight,

De watchman was a runnin roun,
Cryin Old Dan Tucker's come to town.

(Chorus)
So get out de way! Get out de way!
Get out de way! Old Dan Tucker.
You're too late to come to supper.

Tucker was a hardened sinner,
He nebber said his grace at dinner;
De ole sow squeel, de pigs did squall
He et 'hole hog wid de tail and all.

(Chorus)
Old Dan Tucker was a fine old soul,
Buckskin belly and a rubber ass-hole,
Swallowed a barrel of cider down
And then he shit all over town.

Not all versions were so scatological. Indeed, the jaunty air had an elasticity that lent itself to polemical appropriation, as seen in the political campaigns of Lincoln, Clay, and Fremont among others:

The balky horse they call John Tyler
We'll head him soon or burst his b(o)iler
His cursed 'grippe' has seized us all
Which Doctor Clay will cure next fall.

After my monograph was published, *Ole Dan Tucker: a Consideration* (Public Affairs, 1951), the Smithsonian brought me back and I met Brady. Upon hearing that I was interested in stories of wartime service, he rose and cleared the room. This dismissal was repeated on subsequent visits until my arrival became a signal for the old men to shuffle away with nodding heads and trembling limbs.

"First World War guys, most of them," he said. "Hard luck cases, alone in the world or their families threw them out for some reason. Christ, you ought to hear the mustard-gas cases cough at nights."

It was easy to see why, as I was later to learn, he had enjoyed such success with the opposite sex. He was a big man with dark brows and thick salt-and-pepper hair. You could see he had been extraordinarily handsome as a younger man, but now he was like a fine structure in a stage of noble ruin. His light baritone fell pleasingly on the ear. From the beginning, he had a playful, roguish charm.

He sometimes contrived to be arch as if my visits were a pretext for what I was really after. "Who'd you say you were with again?" he would suddenly say, hoping, as I thought, to surprise me into an honest answer. "How many minutes did you say it takes to drive here?" He called me at work once. "Just checking," he chuckled. "The switchboard operator sounds genuine, but then they wouldn't foul that up would they?"

Mistrust was not new for me. Rural people have a suspicion of government not easily overcome, particularly if the illegal distilling of alcohol is concerned—"moonshine" is the popular term. I would approach a remote farmhouse, my backfiring car giving plenty of advance notice, and see shabby men making for the woods at good speed. Hollow-eyed wives, worn thin by hard work and poverty and with small dirty-faced children clinging to their legs, came to the door to explain that their husbands had "just stepped out for a minute" or had "gone to borrow a mule."

I described my previous assignment for the Smithsonian to Brady, mentioning how fragile and perishable native song and folklore were and how great the tragedy to our culture when they were lost. I showed him a copy of the monograph I had written as an example of how they can be preserved for future generations.

"Who gives a flying fuck about Ole Dan Tucker?" he said, giving it the barest look. "Seems like the government could find a better use for tax money than recording hillbilly caterwauling. Give me a pencil and I'll give you a list, starting with tearing down this dump."

Although he spoke in a cultured southern accent, that comment shows it was sometimes in contrast to the crudeness of his utterance. If I should register an objection to his language or my countenance was perceived as disapproving, he would remind me he was a simple sailor and if I didn't like it, there was the door and I was free to use it.

After a few interviews he suddenly confessed that he had "borrowed" the name Kermit Crockett. "But tell your bosses I'm going to take my time answering their questions. You know, you wouldn't be bad looking if you didn't wear those thick glasses and did your hair different."

A neutral manner is best for an oral historian, however difficult it may be to maintain. I felt my face redden at his compliment, but I did not respond. I include comments such of these to give a flavor of the man. Such veers in conversation occurred often. I attempted once to draw him out about Harry Truman's views on naval power when he was in the Senate, and Brady was reminded of the former president's skill at poker.

"I wrote him an IOU and damned if he didn't have the CNO himself send a reminder when it slipped my mind."

Or he would break off a thought to say "a razorback hog wouldn't eat the slop they called breakfast today." This in turn might trigger profanity about some petty housekeeping rule about ashtrays imposed by bureaucrats. Or jungle rot on Guadalcanal.

"The rain roared down for hours, day after day, and you never got dry. Playing cards got so limp and mildewed you couldn't shuffle them. Some guys got feet so eaten away by fungus you could see bone. It took away your appetite more than K-rations. I was never so glad to get out of a place."

As his story came together amid many of these wandering asides, I was able to place him in the flow of that just-passed period of history, surely the darkest ever. Entire societies were uprooted or utterly destroyed; I don't suppose we'll ever know the toll except in round numbers. War once waged by professional soldiers on each other was visited upon civilian populations with a ferocity never before imagined. The collision of ideologies that brought about this calamity is for future historians to elucidate. My modest role for the Smithsonian was to contribute a small tile here and there to the mosaic.

The Spanish Civil War was in full spate when Brady accompanied his stepfather to London. "To put you in the picture," he told me, "that war was the Reds against the king's men."

This observation unfortunately was typical. Captain Brady had little curiosity at the time—or insight later—regarding those world-engulfing events, and he had only the most pedestrian opinions about the great personages with whom he had come in contact. Roosevelt had a big head; de Gaulle's was shaped like a pineapple. Churchill was not the great man summoning his people to the fight for their survival. To him, Churchill's most notable quality was a capacity for drink that was as amazing as it was admirable.

"The man had a wooden leg, I kid you not."

General Douglas MacArthur was "a four-flushing phony who never smoked that corncob pipe unless a photographer was around." General George Patton "had a voice like a girl." Josef Stalin "was like a fireplug in boots, and he had the meanest eyes you ever saw."

I could not help reflecting on what a misfortune it was that fate had cast such a man to witness these great men and mighty events. Why not a Herodotus or Macaulay?

But he had an excellent memory, as he said, and I soon saw it amounted to total recall. He would tilt his head back, close his eyes, and repeat entire conversations verbatim. Such people are rare, but sadly their gift is not to be confused with analytical power. I resolved to draw out what he had observed to add to the written record and thereby provide a "fly on the wall" perspective for future historians.

For example, my search of the written record showed it has not been revealed that General MacArthur, in Brady's words, "puked every color of the rainbow day and night" when carried to safety from Corregidor on a PT boat, or that Admiral Halsey "didn't have the brains to avoid a typhoon coming straight at him." He claimed to have had "a fling" with Eisenhower's mistress and resisted amorous advances from Clementine Churchill.

"Her mother had nine lovers on the string at one time, so I suppose it was in her blood. She was a bit long in the tooth for me, though. Her daughter Sarah—now that's another story."

I asked easy questions to begin with in keeping with the technique Dr. Broadbrow (whose protégé I was) schooled us in to establish rapport with a subject. But I found this unnecessary as Captain Brady liked few things better than talking about himself.

"You want to go back *that* far?" he said when I asked one of my warm-up questions. "Okay, I was a kid just like all the rest, except smarter. I hated school, but I was good at it. I could run my eye over a page and it stayed right up here in the old noggin. I drove teachers nuts. Here was this kid more asleep than awake while they jawed away at the head of the classroom; or I was flicking the kid's ear in front of me, dipping pigtails in inkwells—that sort of boy thing. They thought they'd get their revenge at test time, but I always was top of the class. I'd laugh and wave mine around when they gave the papers back, and that made them madder."

As we practiced oral history, you asked questions, had the answers transcribed by the Smithsonian's secretarial pool (in whose humble ranks I once toiled), checked the transcript for accuracy when it returned, and then sent it off to the archives. If it was felt there was falseness in a subject's account, it was permissible to disallow his narrative in a footnote. Disbelief understandably was my reaction when Brady said most of the recent history I knew was bunk; and that he had personal knowledge Franklin Roosevelt schemed to bring us into war with Japan, and even knew that their fleet was en route to Pearl Harbor. My face must have showed the shock I felt at these allegations.

"Isn't that why you're here?" he said with a wink. "They're cleverer than I thought, sending a woman. Well, tell them I'm tired of running. Let them do whatever they want, I'm past caring."

I am from the Smithsonian Institution, I said, as I have told you several times. I displayed the credential that gained me admission to the building where I worked.

"The boys in the OSS could make up one of those with an hour's notice," he said.

"It's your decision whether to continue or move on," Dr. Broadbrow said when I discussed it with him. He speculated that perhaps this was a case of lingering battle fatigue. Scholarship was thin on that subject, he said, and perhaps I might use Brady for a deeper exploration of that phenomenon.

He was a sweet little man in thick glasses who was only an inch or two taller than I. He had a toothbrush moustache and a pot belly which he had the habit of patting as if it was in need of steady reassurance. He was kind to everyone; truly he was one of nature's gentlemen. He and his wife Anne often had me over to dinner and to listen to the NBC Symphony Orchestra radio concert on Sunday.

If the fantastical things Captain Brady told me in a matter-of-fact manner were true, it would be an earthquake that would profoundly alter the conventional understanding of our times. I transcribed the tapes myself, an arduous undertaking I did at night when the office was empty. The four single young women I roomed with assumed I was having an affair, even though I told them not to be silly. Oddly, it had the effect of raising "Plain Jane" in their estimation. They were wild to find husbands, whereas that was never my sole ambition.

I wanted to disbelieve Captain Brady because I was as much under the late president's spell as everyone; I was tearful the entire day his death in Warm Springs was announced. For him to be swept away when victory was so close was heartbreaking. But the richness and abundance of detail in the captain's stories compelled belief. Just as a small example, he mentioned that Stalin doodled at meetings. "And it was always the same thing, wolves."

Dr. Broadbrow would occasionally ask how my battle fatigue research was going, and I always answered "fine." He said he looked forward to reading my monograph and then passed on to other matters. I realized I had to learn more about the background Brady claimed for himself, and this required travel. I explained these trips as visits to sanitaria where mental cases from the war were confined. Dr. Broadbrow was near the end of his career and subject to memory lapses. It pains me that I took advantage of this weakness with my white lies, but otherwise I could not have done the research.

CHAPTER 3

CHURCHILL WAS PAINTING A PICTURE WHEN THE SENATOR AND I GOT THERE in the fall of 1936. The umbrella I carried was turned inside-out in the strong wind, and the Senator got riled because his hair was whipped around. It was white and as thick as a Palomino's mane, and he was terrible vain about it. He cursed and struck out with his cane where he guessed I was standing. You had to be nimble when his dander was up or take a pretty good lick. Luckily, the butler opened the door before he found the range.

Churchill and the Senator retired to his study to talk, and cake and tea were brought by the pretty maid Bridget that I mentioned. She had cupid-bow lips and red curls under her cap. When I got to know her better, she sang sad Irish songs about lads that went a-sailin' away ne'r to return. That's the words to the song. I'll sing it for you if you like. Or they were hung by the British. They're a melancholy people, the Irish, though they liven up with whiskey.

I was a handsome dog as you see from that photograph on the table; damned good looking in my uniform if I do say so myself, but many an ugly officer looks good in tropical whites. Later that night after the Senator retired, I made my way back to 11 Morpeth Mansions—it's near Westminster Cathedral where the bells toll the quarter hour—and tapped as arranged at the servant's entrance and…well, no need to go into that. I was thinking about her the other day. She'd be a toothless old granny by now, or more likely dead.

The painting was Blenheim Palace where Churchill was born, a big fancy place out in the country. Right, you want lots of details. Let's see, he was writing a book about Marlborough, that ancestor of his, and proofs were stacked everywhere. He smoked a Cuban cigar and had a glass of Red Label and soda. I don't believe I ever saw him without a drink in his hand or at least close by. They said he had an eye-opener before he got out of bed in the morning. We liked our grog in the Navy, but not straight off the bat. Noon was where I planted my flag ashore. Eleven if it was a special occasion. Never any earlier than ten.

He took on a considerable load through the day—whiskey, champagne, port, brandy—but he never seemed drunk. He had a lot of those old Raj ways though. "Boy!" he'd yell at some servant bent over from old age.

That was one of the questions Hopkins wanted answered. "Is he a drunkard? A lot depends on it."

It seems Winston insulted Franklin at a party when he was sea lord and Franklin was assistant secretary of the Navy. The English were high and mighty and we were pretty low in the pecking order at the time; even Chile had a bigger navy. I never got to the bottom of what was said, but it seemed Franklin still had his feathers ruffled. I can tell you Churchill had a mighty sharp tongue when he cared to use it. The president and Harry didn't think much of Chamberlain and that crowd, but didn't want to put all their eggs in Winston's basket if he was a toss pot—Franklin's words. And the president wasn't one of your bluenoses, by the way. He was proud of his cocktails; mixed them himself at the end of the day. He'd pour anything within reach into the shaker and mix it all up. General Marshall always shuddered when he took a sip.

"My, that's good," he'd gasp, but he always turned down a refill. Needed his head clear for work, he said. Bad as they were, I never said no to seconds. It never hurts to be polite.

The Senator told me afterward he and Churchill mostly talked about the Krauts; Mussolini and the Japs were thrown in at the end. Hitler was rearming Germany faster than anybody knew and trying out his new weapons in Spain; he was even building an air force in secret. Winston had his own spy service as good as any in the world. Generals and admirals were in on it, and diplomats and big-shot businessmen who traveled in Germany. They tipped him off to stuff the Chamberlain crowd shut their eyes to. They were ostriches, like Franklin said. As the Senator talked away to help him remember because he couldn't write notes on what they talked about, I'd put in "Is that so?" Or "You don't say." I was waiting for him to drink his glass of warm milk and go to bed.

"You worthless cur," he said, flaring up. "You're not listening to a word. You want to go off and lay with diseased whores."

That's not true, Senator, I said, moving out of range as his hand went for the cane. You were saying Churchill doesn't think the Maginot Line will stop the Hun.

"Well, yes," he admitted grudgingly, "he thinks the next war will be fought with mobile armies and airplanes. Everyone on the German general staff is reading a book by a French colonel named de Gaulle that prophecies that's how it will be."

If he had asked for my opinion, I'd have said give me a defensive line like the Maginot and I'll stop whatever comes my way. It had forts, artillery, pill boxes, and underground tunnels connecting everything. What were the Germans going to do—go around? Well, as it happened that's what they did after beating the tar out of the Poles; tanks against men on horseback, that one. In my defense, everybody had egg on their face. To calm him down, I asked if he'd told Winston about his vision.

"He wants to hear more of my views tomorrow," the Senator said, puffing up. "He well understands my importance in the Senate."

When they came out of the study after that first talk, Winston apologized. "I hadn't realized you were the Senator's stepson as well as a serving officer."

I said think nothing of it, sir. Bridget here has been making me feel right at home. We talked about the weather while the Senator struggled into his coat.

"Great days are ahead the way the navies are expanding," Winston said at the door. "You'll have your own ship!"

I look forward to that, sir, I said smartly.

That's what he expected. People think that all young naval officers want is the command of a ship, but they couldn't be more wrong. The truth is anything smaller than a battleship is damned uncomfortable. Destroyers are noisy and hot unless you're on the bridge, in which case you're freezing in winter. There's a lead weight gets hung around your neck the minute you step aboard and salute the ensign. If anything goes wrong, you're who they blame. If the navigator misreads a chart and the ship goes aground, it's your career that is finished—and don't give me that rigmarole about life being unfair. Everybody knows that.

The next day we go back to Churchill's house—it's still raining but the wind's not so fierce—and I'm invited into the study this time. The Senator made it plain beforehand not to say anything unless asked, and to keep it short in that case because he didn't want people to think he was traveling with the village idiot.

Churchill was painting away on that canvas again when the old servant called Boy led us in. "According to the standards of the time," Winston told us, "Blenheim should have geometrical gardens and paths with sharp angles, but Capability Brown laid out the landscaping for a balance between man and Nature."

"Is that so," the Senator said with a false smile, pretending to be interested.

You could forget about talking to him about anything that wasn't politics; that was all that interested him. When I was a boy, I'd show him frogs and grasshoppers, and he'd get this mean look and say, "Now why in blazes would you think *I'd* be interested in that?"

Even that vision of his was political because he reckoned a grateful nation would show its thanks for sounding the alarm by putting him in the White House.

"Yes," Churchill continued, "Brown's partner was the architect of Blenheim, John Vanbrugh, a spy and Restoration playwright before he went into business with Christopher Wren."

"Looks like Nanking is fixing to fall to the Japs," the Senator said to change the subject. "Terrible atrocities, they say."

"They're a warrior race," Churchill said, "little chaps, but a fierce foe as the Russians found out. Their main weakness is a tendency to hysteria that comes from the Malayan strain in their blood."

"They had a mighty big empire in South America, so I'm told."

"I think you mean the Mayans, Senator. The Malayans are in the Far East, a different breed of cat. The Japanese were a valuable ally against the Hun in the Great War, and it's too bad you forced us to choose between you. Our situation in the Far East today would be less...shall we say fragile?"

"It had nothing to do with me," the Senator said, "I was but a junior member of the agriculture committee at the time."

Winston thanked the Almighty that the Senator was placed where he was at such a critical time for civilization, and that put a smile on the old man's face. "I am half American on my mother's side, did you gentlemen know that?" We said we sure didn't. "This is the window of the small bedroom where I came into the world. My mother fell walking across a field with a party shooting birds, the result being I was two months premature."

"I was born at home myself," the Senator said, "and so was everybody I know. They say these days women prefer the hospital if they've got the wherewithal."

Winston said his mother's great-grandmother was an Iroquois, making him something of a wog. The Senator asked what that was and it was explained.

"We have laws against race mixing in the south," he said, "but squaws can get a pass if they ain't too dark. Still, there are some back home that would look down at you if that got out, though I wouldn't myself now that I've met you."

Winston thanked him for this courtesy, took a sip of morning whiskey and started up on the Civil War. "I'm a great student of that tragic conflict and have trod those battlefields with map in hand. At Spotsylvania, my guide was a man who was just eight at the time and well-remembered that great battle. The world learned much about mass killing in those campaigns."

"We call it the War of Northern Aggression," the Senator said firmly.

"Yes," said Churchill, "wounds are slow in healing, as we in Europe know all too well. Wars often go by different names according to the side you are on." He paced back and forth as he gave us the benefit of his considerable knowledge of Civil War battles until the Senator began to tap his cane and hum to himself. "But to return to yesterday's discussion," Winston said when he noticed, "our greatest problem is to conquer the isolationism in your great republic in light of the gathering perils."

"Gathering pearls or diamonds nor any other jewel has nothing to do with it," the Senator said, hand-to-ear—his hearing was beginning to go. "It's my prophetic vision that brought me all the way over here. Fire raining from the skies, cities in flames, and lamentations rising from the people..."

"Danger," Winston broke in, "I meant to say gathering danger. Ways must be found to entangle America in Europe's fate lest the continent fall under the dominion of German militarism, or worse, the Communist enchantment farther east."

The Senator looked thoughtful. "I don't think *entangle* is quite the word you want, It sounds..."

"I meant *involve*, of course; it seems this is my day for misspeaking. Influential personages must be informed of the risk even to you in far off America of the Continent united in malign purpose. Committees must be formed, information collected and proga...educational efforts begun. I stress that it's best that this be done discreetly, a quiet word here and there. I achieve much at private dinners and lunches."

"Stalin and his crowd have a lot of support back home," the Senator said. "So does Hitler for that matter."

"A gentleman to see you," Bridget said.

"Tell him I'm not in."

"Yes, sir."

"Who is it?"

She brought a card on a silver tray. "Leo Amery is a man you should know," he told the Senator when he looked at it.

Amery was a little man, quick and dainty as those birds that run back and forth at the shoreline. There's detail for you, by God!

"Hello, Amery," Winston calls out to him as he comes in, "a rum day to be out."

We all shook hands. "Senator Brady is a very influential member of Congress," Winston said. "Leo and I were boys together at Harrow. I was thinking of those years the other day."

"A wretched time of life," Amery said. He looked at us, very sniffy. "I understand your country has made plans for war against us."

"Eh?" the Senator said. "Why...is that so, Lowell?"

I said not that I know of.

"I heard it last night at my club," Amery said.

"You couldn't expect a lieutenant to know of such matters," Winston said, "but I can tell you every country plans for war against even friendly powers. It keeps their staffs occupied."

"I've just come from breakfast with Neville," Amery said, taking a chair. He was so short his shoes didn't reach the floor. I coughed to hide a snicker.

"He ignores all my requests for a meeting," Winston said. "It is Horace Wilson, of course. No one has been that powerful behind the scenes since Cardinal Wolsey. I believe he hates me."

"I don't believe Wilson feels any deep emotions," Amery said. "He's a cold fish like the prime minister himself. I urged Neville again to increase the military budget—implored him. He will not listen. Stanley Baldwin was at least willing to entertain the remote possibility that he might be wrong."

"I don't have any memory of you being caned at school like the rest of us." Winston was looking at Amery over the cigar he was firing up.

"Of course I was."

"My first school was St. George's in Ascot. I was a month short of my eighth birthday when I entered. The headmaster was the Rev. Sneyd-Kynnersley. He was a tall, thin man with red whiskers like bat wings."

"What a way you have with words, Winston," Amery said in a dry way.

"How much satisfaction his whiskers afforded him was evident from the way he fondled them during lessons. He was as high church as was consistent with being very much the gentleman. He took us on jolly outings and enjoyed them as much as we did. It often felt like he was one of us in an adult's body. But Mr. Sneyd-Kynnersley explained to us the first morning of the term that he reserved to himself the right to flog us when warranted. Every Monday morning the whole school assembled and reports on conduct were read aloud. After a bad report from a form master, Mr. Sneyd-Kynnersley would stop and after a moment's awful silence say 'Harrison,' or whoever it was, 'you will come up to my study afterwards.' And so afterwards the culprits were led up by the two top boys.

"In the middle of the room was a large box draped in black cloth and the culprit was told to take down his trousers and two head boys held him down. The rod was brought down with the master's full strength. It took only two or three strokes for blood to run, and it continued for fifteen or twenty strokes. Sometimes there were scenes of screaming, howling and struggling which made one almost sick with disgust to hear. There was a wild, red-haired Irish boy, himself rather a cruel brute, who whether deliberately or as a result of the pain or whether he had diarrhea, let fly. Instead of stopping at once, Sneyd-Kynnersley went on with increased fury until the whole ceiling and walls of his study were spattered with filth."

"Really, Winston, this is a most unpleasant story," Amery said. "I'm sure these gentlemen agree."

"Spare the rod and spoil the child," the Senator said. He looked over to where he guessed I was sitting.

"I tell you this," Winston said, "because a harrowing experience at a young age leaves a deep sense of the evil that can lurk behind appearances."

"I suppose you mean Herr Hitler," Amery said. "It is my belief the man has been done an injustice. Unlike you, I have actually spoken to him."

"I have no wish to at this point."

"Then you don't have an open mind."

"I once believed he was a sincere patriot and respected him for that. But I believe now is there is question as to his sanity."

"Ridiculous," Amery said, "don't rely on speeches for a domestic audience to discover his true intentions."

"Oh," said Winston, wasting a wink on the Senator, "the truth is reserved for distinguished foreign visitors?"

"I admit we didn't discuss his views on Jews, Austria, Germany's former colonies, or other such matters."

"What did you discuss then, the weather in Westphalia?"

"Hitler is willing to guarantee the integrity of the British Empire in return for a free hand in Eastern Europe. He doesn't care about the return of Germany's African colonies. He says that's an issue stirred up by the Jewish press to poison relations."

Winston puffed on his cigar. "I was staying at the Regina Hotel in Munich a few years ago. An amusing man I knew named Putzi Hanfstaengl was a favorite of Hitler for his singing and piano playing. He told me Hitler came to the hotel every day at five, and he would be happy to arrange an introduction. My son was very high on Hitler at the time, so I was willing. I told Hanfstaengl I could not see why Hitler was so violent toward the Jews. When my words were reported back to Hitler, he stayed away from the hotel the rest of the time I was there."

"There is no doubt in my mind," Amery said, "that he is a man whom we can do business with and Neville feels the same."

"I pray they never meet."

"Why do you say that?"

"As soon as Hitler sees that old man he will recognize him for what he is, a bourgeois pacifist. It would be like giving a wild beast a taste of blood."

"Your point is he would take away an entirely different impression from a meeting with you?"

"I doubt very much that Herr Hitler would suffer any misapprehension about pacifism. You are not troubled by his treatment of the Jews?"

"There are excesses after every revolution and perhaps the press exaggerates them."

"The *Times* does not, Winston said. "They keep anything critical of Germany out of its pages at the request of the government."

"This violence directed toward Jews will pass. Neville believes with me that it would only make matters worse for them if official notice was taken."

"The Nazis bring out the worst traits in the German character, a mean spirit of revenge and a tendency to brutality."

"They are an intelligent, hard-working race," Amery said. "They are people one would want on his side."

"The Germans are the most tractable, fierce, and martial race in the world. In spite of all their brains and courage, they worship power and let themselves be led by the nose."

It looked to me like Amery saw he couldn't change Churchill's mind and wasn't going to waste any more breath on it. We all shook hands again.

"Seems like a nice fella," the Senator said when he was gone.

"He wants to bring back high tariffs," Winston said. "He thinks the commonwealth will substitute for when England was the workshop of the world and other countries were content to supply us with raw materials. Times have changed, but he doesn't realize that."

"High tariffs would leave us out in the cold," the Senator said. "That would stick in craws back home."

"Bismarck said the fact that the British and American people have a common language was the most potent factor in the world. Raising tariffs against your goods would throw away that advantage. That beggar-your-neighbor thinking is the very reason this Depression persists. I was in New York when Wall Street crashed and standing at a window on the fifteenth floor when a man flew past. His eye caught mine for an instant."

"Good Lord," the Senator said.

"I often wondered how long it took for him to regret his decision; I suppose less than a second. What a terrible mess bodies make on the sidewalk when they fall a great distance."

"I don't want to think about it," the Senator said.

"They had to bring a fire truck round with a high-pressure hose. He was a financier ruined by the Crash, the newspaper said. Your dream, Senator, leads your mind down the same path as mine. There will be another war."

"Such was vouchsafed in my prophetic vision which is what I prefer to calling it a 'dream.' Anybody can have a dream. They're a dime a dozen."

"Very true. Five a ha'penny we'd say. The common chimney sweep can dream, but a vision betokens something of finer quality and greater amplitude."

"I'm a modest man, but I'm glad you see that."

"We will need you Yanks to help us once again. But England cannot pay the butcher's bill while you conduct a leisurely debate as before over whether to dirty your hands with our Old World quarrels. The cream of a whole generation is gone in my country. The first battle at Ypres alone claimed six peers, sixteen baronets, six knights, ninety-five sons of peers, eighty-two sons of baronets, and eighty-four sons of knights. The male line ended in families that had led the realm for five hundred years."

"Well, you folks are going to have a problem," the Senator said. "The last time you laid it on pretty thick with those nun-raping and baby-bayoneting stories. Not even my stepson would fall for it again. Right, Lowell?"

I knew if I said something back he'd remind me in front of Winston I'd be nothing without him, so I just smiled

"We must identify who our friends are in your great republic and bind them to us more closely," Winston said. "And we must know our enemies to render them impotent."

"You better start with the Hearst press," the Senator said.

"I'm aware of their malignant influence and also how it might be neutralized."

"How's that?"

"Have you ever been a guest at his castle in California?

"Can't say that I have."

"A vulgar place, but impressive in its way. His company makes enormous amounts of money, but he spends every penny and then some. As a result, Hearst finances are very wobbly. Canadian pulp mills extend him a great deal of credit. It amounts to ten and a half million dollars in demand notes renewable every six months. If that credit was withdrawn his newspapers would cease publication."

"And you could do *that?*"

Winston snapped his fingers. "As easily as this. If you don't have paper you can't put out a newspaper."

The Senator was speechless with awe.

"This is just between us," Winston said with a pull on his cigar.

"The silence of the grave has nothing on me."

"There are a great many British actors in Hollywood. C. Aubrey Smith, Cedric Hardwicke, Charles Laughton, David Niven, Basil Rathbone. Do you know those names?"

"One or two."

"Leslie Howard, Robert Donat, Ronald Coleman, Cary Grant, Claude Rains, Boris Karloff."

"What about them?"

"Americans are mad for moving pictures. Hollywood could create a climate of opinion in our favor. We could suggest themes or even supply scenarios for the screen. Charlie Chaplin tells me they are always looking for subject matter. The Americans love costume dramas and stories of court intrigue. Having very little history themselves, they dote on ours. And I'm confident the Jews in Hollywood will give every assistance."

"You know Charlie Chaplin? Well, I declare." That impressed the Senator even more than being able to put Hearst out of business with a snap of the fingers.

Winston gave him introductions to a few other big shots we paid calls on, politicians and so forth; business leaders, the Archbishop of Canterbury. I won't bother telling you about them unless you really want to know. Sightseeing was out for obvious reasons, so we spent a lot of time in our hotel room while the Senator made telephone calls. I had to be available to lead him around when he wanted to go downstairs to the restaurant or get some fresh air. I was glad when it was time to go home.

CHAPTER 4

LOWELL BRADY'S MOTHER, ELIZA BARTLEY, DAUGHTER OF A WEALTHY businessman, was a dark haired beauty and prominent figure in Savannah, which I visited in the course of my research. His father, William Travis, was a wastrel or adventurer depending on the account. Mary Henderson, a contemporary of both, wrote that Travis "was a handsome, dashing rogue with a roving eye who enjoyed drink, cards, and other forms of gambling." Judge Orlen Jenkins, a leader in the state's General Assembly, reckoned him "an amiable fellow good at horseshoes."

After his father disappeared while looking for gold in South America, his mother married Josepha Brady, a landowner and hog grower elected to the 69th Congress, and the young boy took her new husband's name. Brady, who still had eyesight then, was later appointed to a U.S. Senate seat after the death of the incumbent, Isaiah Blaggett, known as "Whoop 'n' Holler" for his style of speechmaking. It appears the marriage was not happy because of the clash of ambitions. Hers was to rise in society against powerful female rivals and his was to advance his promising political career. Some of the lawmakers needed for the coalition he built in the legislature were colorful rural folk scorned for their rustic ways in the lofty circles in which Eliza moved.

State Senator James Backus, a powerful figure in the General Assembly known as "Baccy" for the lump of tobacco always in one cheek, was a source of contention between them, as were Israel "Coughin'" Coughlin and Clement "Swampy" Severson. The former suffered from a respiratory complaint and the latter wore boots caked with dung as proof of his promise never to "put on fancy airs" no matter how high the world might exalt him. Severson had a folksy manner that was much admired. "I haven't seen you since the pig ate your brother," he'd say in greeting a constituent. Eliza refused to invite Severson to her fancy levees, but did permit him to attend garden parties "if a good wind was blowing."

As her only child, Lowell received lavish attention when he was in sight. But her busy social life resulted in queer periods of neglect when she appears even to have forgotten his existence, and she left his rearing to nannies and tutors. Josepha at one point objected that Lowell was becoming spoiled, stating that his insolence was all the proof a reasonable person needed.

"Withhold not correction from a child," he read aloud from the Bible when they quarreled over a window Lowell had broken with his slingshot, "for if thou strike him with the rod, he shall not die. Thou shalt beat him with the rod, and deliver his soul from hell."

Josepha accused her of blasphemy when she replied that she did not care what the Bible said; nobody was going to beat her child with a rod or even a willow switch cut from down at the creek. "If you lay a hand on him," a witness quoted her as saying, "I'll shoot you down like I would a rabid skunk." That she could bring down a deer from a distance of a hundred yards gave weight to this threat.

More slingshot incidents occurred, culminating with a hematoma the Rev. Raymond Millbrand of St. Joseph Episcopal Church suffered to a buttock as he bent to pick up the hat knocked from his head by an earlier missile.

"He's just getting warmed up," her husband warned. "He'll be going for the vitals next."

Whether because of this or the pneumonia she developed—Reverend Millbrand had come on a pastoral call in that connection—the decision was made to send Lowell to the Ironwood School for Boys in Michigan. A servant saw Josepha chuckling to himself as he read a pamphlet that set forth Ironwood's philosophy. The school, situated in a dark pine forest on a remote peninsula, was run on the lines of a penal colony.

It was housed in a gloomy castle built by a wealthy landowner named A. E. Crocker, a man who held peculiar beliefs including the redemptive power of suffering. Ice appeared on the insides of dormitory windows and water froze in pipes during winter, meaning the two hundred boys went unwashed unless icicles were knocked from the chapel ceiling and melted in a cauldron in the castle's sally port.

The boys were issued single blankets and slept on beds each made from primitive tools on the day of their arrival. They stuffed pine boughs in burlap sacks for mattresses, the likely source of the fleas and other insects that infested Ironwood School. Their diet consisted of hard biscuits, root vegetables, and, twice a week, stringy cuts of meat from wild animals shot by a hunter employed by the school.

Crocker wrote in *Bending a Boy's Will to a Moral Purpose* that "short rations and the lethargy that ensues are the surest path to taming turbulent young spirits in conjunction with a three-foot length of leather belt that we at Ironwood call The Lesson Giver."

The staff, called Friends, included retired circus strong men and former animal trainers. Although lacking even the barest formal education, their presence enforced the long silences mandatory in study hall and the many pages of rules the boys had to memorize. Lowell was able to recite them backward and forward on the first day, bringing him to the favorable attention of Crocker, who ordinarily maintained a distance from his charges.

In winning the patronage of the Founder, Lowell gained a second blanket for his bed and a standing invitation to the Friends dining room. The tables there groaned under the plenty required to satisfy the appetites of the former circus men. Already big for his age, Lowell flourished while the other boys were wan from the "turbulent spirits diet" and the heavy physical labor required of even the youngest. So the qualities his mother and, more particularly, his stepfather wished curbed, paradoxically seemed to have been encouraged.

The school contracted its students out as laborers to farms and mills when work was available. When it was not, they were kept busy carrying heavy stones a long distance one day and returning them the next to their original location. It appears Lowell was excused from these duties and rode a pony as a junior overseer.

"They gave Brady a riding crop he used pretty freely," one classmate recalled. "You'd hear hooves drumming and then came the whistle and sting across your back. 'You're going too slow,' he'd say. Or, 'That's for making a face at me at vespers.'"

It might seem that parents would object to the harsh regimen, but on the other hand they had sent their unruly children to Ironwood to be "shaped up," as Crocker put it. It is by no means certain complaints or pleas to come home would have been heeded, even if they had survived the censor's scrutiny: letters were not sealed until the staff had read them.

"I heard they closed up Ironwood after I left," Captain Brady told me. "It was a damned shame—some lawsuit or the government stepped in. It was a great place, and old Doc Crocker was good as gold to me."

Eliza's diary and letters in this period record social events hosted and attended and a long trip with her husband to the capitals of Europe in 1912, but do not mention Lowell. A flirtation with Count Luigi Barcarole in Venice resulted in her husband kicking the nobleman down the stairs. The following night a coiled adder bit Josepha on the ankle as he stood on the balcony of their hotel room and yelled "pipe down, you idiots" at gondoliers singing on the Grand Canal.

A servant of the count was seen hurrying from the hotel, but investigators focused on suspicions that the gondolier's guild had hired an assassin in response to Josepha's shouts from the balcony. The serpent's bite took his sight after nearly killing him. A priest summoned to administer last rites was driven from the bedside by Josepha's strong views about Catholicism.

Even with the attempted murder of her husband, Eliza's regret for having led the count on, and the long journey home with frequent stops for spells of hospitalization, it is difficult to explain her lack of parental attention. It was Josepha himself who first remembered the boy, idly asking Eliza after their return to Georgia what trouble he had been up to lately. His blindness prevented him from seeing her stricken look.

"They don't have a telephone, and he's never been one to write," she answered.

She had somehow managed, as she later told a friend, to hide the emotion in her voice. "And for Josepha to be the one who remembered was the worst." His mild curiosity satisfied, her husband returned to complaining about the damnable summer heat, a subject that preoccupied him during his convalescence.

Eliza's diary said on that very day she sent a telegraph to Ironwood asking about her son. It was Crocker's habit to reply to messages on Saturdays when he was driven to town in state with students in their smart school uniforms and feathered drum-major hats riding on the running boards of his charabanc, ostensibly as an honor guard. But it appears they served as a human screen against objects thrown by townsfolk. Crocker had made himself unpopular as a result of his lofty airs and penchant for cheating local merchants.

"Your boy tip top," he telegraphed to Eliza as he did to every inquiry from parents.

This was not always true as Ironwood was swept by contagions year around and injuries were common during the planting and harvesting seasons when the boys worked around dangerous farm machinery. Parents who came to pick up their boys for summer vacation were horrified to find they were on crutches or missing fingers. Crocker's explanation was that "experience was a hard teacher, but a good one." It was rare for those boys to return for the next quarter.

But in Lowell's case "tip top" was accurate. He was elected student body president and the power derived from his mentorship by the Founder put him in the position to grant or deny favors. When Eliza and Josepha visited Lowell at Ironwood they found him "swaggering with arrogance," as his mother wrote in her diary. He did not want to leave the school, but Josepha had decided to run for Congress and advisors believed a stepson at the Naval Academy might make the difference in a close race.

CHAPTER 5

MY ORDERS WERE TO SEE THE SENATOR OFF AND RETURN ABOARD THE next Navy ship crossing the Atlantic. That was *Kramer*, an old four-stacker laid down in the Taft administration. It should have gone to the breakers long before, but thanks to our penny-pinching Congress it was still in service. You probably couldn't count the things wrong on a ship that old. Salt water is a terrible corrosive and you can chip and paint all you like, but it's just a holding game until it becomes a losing game. Vibrations loosen bolts or metal fatigue sets in. Oh, a million things can go wrong on those old ships.

A day out of Portsmouth, one of the side-fired boilers blew out the firebox and we limped back at eight knots. Lube oil built up in the port sumps and that increased the sickening roll you get on destroyers even in a small sea. She had weakness in the stem, looseness in the bilge keels, and damage to the cutwater.

Commander Harold Mayhew was the skipper, and he took a dislike to me on sight. It might have been the short man thing. Having to look up at people all the time gets in their craw. He had slits for eyes in a round face with a taffy nose. They were suspicious, shifty eyes. Below decks he was known as an ape with a frozen pan, meaning real gloomy. I would've kept clear of the bridge except for the vomit men were spewing below decks. My gorge comes up just thinking about it.

A British warship came out of a line of squalls. "Looks like the *Minotaur* class," Mayhew said as he looked through binoculars.

She slowed and signal flags went up asking if we needed assistance. It might have been a genuine offer of help—I'd have given 'em that myself—but not Mayhew.

"I wouldn't put it past the Limey bastards to pipe the band on deck and play *Rule Britannia*," Mayhew said. "Friendly enough to your face, but laughing behind your back; that's the English for you. I got a bellyful when I was in the Grand Fleet. Quite a few of us would've liked the chance to knock the Royal Navy down a peg or two, but it would have been pretty one-sided. They finished up the war with sixty-one battleships to our thirty-nine and ninety cruisers to our nineteen. Tell them no."

"Shall I add thanks, Captain," the bosun asked.

"Just say no," Mayhew said.

He was the kind of commander who wanted orders followed to the letter unless they got him in trouble with higher-ups. In that case the poor bastard who had done what he was told caught hell for not knowing what Mayhew really meant. I liked subordinates to hop to it myself, but clamp the pressure on too hard and they plot behind your back. Being on guard for that wears a man down. Know when to look the other way—my philosophy in a nutshell.

The reply was hoisted, and Mayhew looked over the shoulder of the officer of the watch hoping to catch him in a mistake on the rough deck log. *HMS Glasgow* bent on more knots that put our wallow to shame. We didn't say much because Mayhew didn't like unnecessary talk on the bridge. Then shots of black smoke came from *Glasgow's* stack.

"Just like a tramp steamer," he said. "If it was my ship I'd tell the engine room to adjust those burners and be quick about it. Have you noticed how many British warships are paying calls lately, Brady?"

No, sir, I said.

"You must be blind. You can't walk into an officer's club without running into them being matey. What do you suppose is behind it?" He didn't always follow his rule about unnecessary talk.

Before I could answer, Ensign Fox, a young pup fresh from Annapolis, said the Royal Navy sees trouble coming and wants us in sooner than last time.

"Do you think we'll be with them if there's a war, Brady?"

We were last time, I said cautiously. It's best to feel your way with his type. I was a guest tradition said he was supposed to be nice to, and he'd probably got wind of my connections, but sometimes the Mayhews of the world lash out blindly against their own self-interest.

"Congress would never let us get into another European war, sir," Lieutenant Connors said.

"So we'll let the Europeans fight it out among themselves?"

"What's in it for us? They didn't pay back the money we loaned them in the last one."

"That's a damned good point, Connors. What about the Pacific then?"

"That's different. We're going to lock horns with the Japs, you betcha."

"Mind the rudder. You're swinging right."

The steersman was a young fellow named Costas. If dumb was dirt he'd cover an acre. He spun the wheel. "Aye, sir, minding the rudder."

"Meet her now."

Mayhew had a short fuse when it came to ship handling. Is this the kind of nautical stuff you want, Harriet? You call it flavor, do you? I don't see the interest myself. Fine, where was I?

"Costas is trying hard, Captain," Connors told Mayhew.

"He uses too much rudder, goddamn it. Have Bostick at the helm when we reach Portsmouth. I don't want us reeling in like Paddy on payday; we've given the English enough to laugh about."

"Yes, Captain," Connors said.

"Nothing says a smart ship better than how she drops anchor. The same time the hook goes down I want the colors run up, the jack hoisted, and the booms out smartly. You've tested the windlass? Good. That anchor better not bob like a yo-yo. Make sure the side boys are presentable; one of them had a dingy brassard in Halifax and another had brown shoes with his leggings. I've also seen some green buttons. See that the men wash them with vinegar. And too many people hang around the quarter deck in port. That reminds me: the steward served canned peaches yesterday at lunch. I ordered them taken away and then they were chopped up in dessert at dinner. You know what I think of canned peaches."

Connors said he'd find the man responsible and punish him.

"No liberty for anyone on deck in a mismatched uniform. Be aware that some snoop from one of the bureaus might show up hoping to find us slacking off. I want all the engine room maintenance records in apple pie order, and everything down there better shine like a nigger's heel. Now, get on with your paperwork."

They don't tell you about paperwork at the academy. A lot of midshipmen would look for another line of work if they did. Just for an example, there's something called the S and A Form 84 for inventory of leftover stores. It had three long rows for items and twelve for quantity, unit price, and amount. One time there was a difference of twenty-seven pounds between leftover potatoes on Form 84 as opposed to Form 335, the stock ledger. To make them match meant going through requisition forms, invoices, vouchers, mess files, order books, storeroom records, the monthly ration memorandum, and what have you. Hours of work. Instead, I dumped the potatoes overboard when nobody was looking. In wartime that's showing initiative. In peacetime it's a court-martial offense.

Anyhoo, when we got back to Portsmouth I caught a ride on a cruiser heading back home. We arrived back at Newport after the bars closed. It was so quiet the crack of billy clubs on heads carried across the water. The years come and go, but your ordinary seaman never changes. He blows his money on paydays as fast as he can. When they commenced brawling with others, the city of Newport expected us to drive them back to the ships by any means at hand. I led many a shore patrol as a young officer, and I count them as some of my most educational experiences. I learned something new about stupidity every blessed time.

Do you know Newport? Admiral Mahan was superintendent of the Naval War College there in the 'Nineties. You might have heard of him. Well, that's will-o'-the-wisp fame for you. He said wars are won by big naval battles where one side beats the stuffing out of the other. Everybody believed his theory for a long time. Lucky for us, the Japs believed it longer than anybody.

Newport has a big Episcopal church I went to so as to gain a reputation for piety. That's important if you want to rise as a naval officer, at least it was in my time. I generally dozed off during the sermons and back then

I didn't snore, so nobody was any the wiser except for a few of those nosy old biddies every church has got. They don't miss much, do they?

It was a lively place in season, some gala or other every night. They had cotillions featuring Claude Thornhill's orchestra in mansions as big as palaces with ballrooms to match where we danced the Cokey Okey and the Bumps-a-Daisy and the rest of them. There were tea parties, lawn parties, jazz parties—every kind of party you can name. Naval officers from good families, and that was a fair amount of us, got invites on stationary so creamy it looked like you could wring out enough for morning coffee. Most had the same idea I did, and that was marrying into old money. The problem with that plan was the competition.

Every whelp from a rich old family—the du Ponts, Whitneys and what have you—had the same idea. My family on Mother's side was well enough off, but a long way from that league. The rich don't marry people with less money if they can help it. Sure, mistakes get made. Somebody gets pregnant or falls in love with the riding instructor. But generally speaking everybody wants to move up the ladder not down. I learned pretty fast that charm and good looks don't count for much when put up against money.

Only one woman was within my reach and she was the daughter of Morris Stanhope. At one time a third of the country had a Stanhope sofa or chair in the parlor. They began as New England farmers but went into business. You'd think money is money, but old money looks down on new money unless that's the only kind available.

That's what Angela Brewster—grand old woman, Mayflower stock—told me one afternoon as we had tea and cucumber sandwiches. She took a shine to me because I reminded her of a beau when she was young. She said that as the Stanhopes scratched their way up the children got fewer and sicklier. Blood thins unless you bring in new breeding stock. The Senator grew hogs on his farm—he called it a plantation until he ran for Congress—and could talk your ear off on the subject.

You'd think old Stanhope's daughter, Penelope, would be in the top rank of heiresses until you saw her. She was tall with a crooked back and a lazy eye and not much of a chin. A mouse on stilts somebody said. Stanhope didn't want to lose her because he was a widower and she ran his home, but he also didn't want the family line petering out. That didn't mean he wasn't choosy.

"I won't buy a pig in a poke; I don't care how good a man looks in a uniform." His very words as reported to me by Penelope herself.

Mrs. Brewster said she had suffered many a romantic disappointment—look, seriously, who cares about this? An old salt like me wants things simple. A war going on in Korea and the government's paying you to listen to me? Things must be better than they say. Okay, so Penelope had many a romantic disappointment.

My pal Al Dillingham who was from a Main Line family in Philadelphia—a great guy who went down with his ship in the Pacific—pointed her out to me at a lawn party. I introduced myself and she looked so scared it was like I was going to drink her blood and wanted to get started. Once we got acquainted, we got on well enough even though making conversation was heavy going. Filling up the silences tired you out.

Nice ring on your finger there, I said.

"It was my mother's. She's dead."

Sorry.

"Oh, it's not your fault."

I know. Long pause. Well, it's a nice ring.

"Thank you."

I just have my academy ring.

"It's nice."

We looked at my ring.

Delicious sandwiches, I said when it looked like we were done with that.

"The wasps seem to like them."

You don't?

"Mayonnaise turns when it's warm."

I think I heard that somewhere.

"People can get awfully sick. I had a friend who—well, she ruined her dress and shoes."

They'd be baloney sandwiches on a ship.

"Do you like baloney?"

I can take it or leave it.

"I never liked baloney."

I don't know who could've done much more with that conversation. I took to reading the newspapers for things to talk about, but the murders, tragedies, and whatnot didn't always interest her.

"Why's the news always bad?" she asked.

That's a good question, I said. I put a frown on like I was thinking it over. Long silence.

As the social season went on, I got a better idea of the competition. One was a red-haired lawyer named Mark Finch and the other a captain in the Army named Sid Meister. Each of us got invited for dinner and a cross-examination at the Stanhope mansion that looked haunted even at high noon. Old, bitter-looking servants crept around the dark corridors. Stanhope must have saved a fortune on lighting. It was so spooky I had to keep myself from running for the car at the end of the evening.

Stanhope was as welcoming as a rocky coast with a strong blowing wind against you. He was pinched and bony, all sharp angles, and was as dry as salt. After pouring us a miserly thimbleful of sherry, he led me to the library where family ancestors stared down from oil paintings. Each Stanhope looked like he'd just smelled a fart and someone was going to pay for it. I would've turned them to the wall or hurled them down to the basement for the rats to gnaw. They had a terrible problem with them running around in the walls.

He might not be a sailor on familiar terms with the whorehouses of the world, old Stanhope tells me, his meaning clear, but give him credit for being smart enough to understand my kind of man. He rubbed thumb and forefinger together.

"The others sat in that chair you're in and insulted my intelligence by saying they loved her. The lawyer even began sniveling that he couldn't live without her. I said I'd have him thrown out if he didn't stop."

Well, sir, I like being around Penelope. That was as far as I felt I could go with a shrewd character like him.

"You might and you might not."

He came to the point. His fortune went to Penelope provided she remained a dutiful daughter, and that included picking a husband he approved of.

Any son-in-law of his would be expected to work in the family business, and work damned hard, too. Both Meister and Finch were willing to sign a contract agreeing to that and such other terms as he might think up.

The point of marrying Penelope was not to end my Navy career but to move me forward. Getting him around to this wouldn't be easy. I said I'd want to think about it before I signed anything.

"I'll pay a good wage to Penelope's husband, whoever he is, and set them up with house and car. She'll have a monthly allowance he can't touch without me knowing it."

Very generous of you, sir, I said.

I thought of the looks other officers and their wives would get when they drove up with the servants lined up on the front steps in powdered wigs and buckle shoes. Brady's done all right for himself they'd say, envy chewing at their guts. Entertaining in the peacetime Navy was as important to promotion as how well you played polo. The war changed all that, and I'm one of those who say not for the better.

As I toyed with my empty glass hoping Stanhope would take the hint, I wondered how I'd bring Penelope around once things were settled between us. She told me she could sometimes get her way if she pecked away at him long enough.

I coached her on what to say. "Dearest father, I wish my husband to remain a seafaring man." She gave me the story afterward blow by blow.

He raged and kicked at furniture until he ran out of breath and had to sit down. Then when he thought the point was decided, she started up again in the whiney voice he hated and there was another explosion. But he was old and she was young. In the end, she wore him down.

Stanhope said in our man-to-man talk that whoever she married would have to hire a good cook as she had zero know-how in the home arts. She could boil water, but he wouldn't trust her to toast bread. What he expected his son-in-law to do for the company made pick-and-shovel work sound easy. He'd go on the road to beat down suppliers on price and keep the unions out of the factories. If he was caught hiring thugs to rough up the organizers, which Stanhope strongly hinted was what worked best, he'd be on his own as the company had its good name to consider. And I shouldn't fool myself that he'd let his daughter stay married to a jailbird, that being legal grounds for divorce.

"Penelope hasn't said which of you she likes best, and I don't give a damn. What's important is whether I can work with the man."

The dinner was overdone roast beef and mushy vegetables, every bit of flavor boiled out. It had to be the cook getting back for her beggarly wages. But Stanhope probably didn't notice. Food for him was coal shoveled in the furnace. A little dish of prunes was dessert.

The meals were silent unless I brought up something I read in the papers. Amelia Earhart must be dead; the terrible floods along the Mississippi with farm animals stiff from rigor mortis bobbing like corks, and trees ramming boats and people drowning; you know, the regular stuff they have. Stanhope and Penelope stared like I had grown a second head. What did that have to do with them, that was their reaction.

Someone pointed out Captain Meister to me at the officer's club. I introduced myself and after a while he asked did I have my talk with the old man yet. He was a small fellow with hurt-looking eyes; reminded me of a spaniel.

Just the other night, I said.

"Stanhope all but accused me of being a fortune hunter."

There was no hinting around with me, I said. He came straight out with it.

"He reminds me of Pershing. If he took a dislike to you, it was a just matter of time before you were blowing the whistle and leading your men over the top with maybe a minute to live before you were mowed down by machine gun fire. You're serious, I suppose?"

About marrying Penelope, you mean?

"If you were the one she picked."

I said I suppose so. The old man let on he has a heart condition.

"That's just a story. The Stanhopes live as long as a tortoise. Did he ask if you're willing to sign a contract? It sounds like you'd be on the road all the time."

There or in prison, I said.

"I get the impression he thinks the other man is a grifter. Has she said anything about...you know."

I didn't tell Meister, but up to that point I hadn't even kissed Penelope and I doubted he had either. She turned her head away the one time I tried. When I got back to bachelor's quarters, I blew my breath at Bill Phipps and asked does it smell bad.

"What have you been eating, garbage or shit?"

I told him his so-called sense of humor would get him in trouble someday.

"Looks like you already are," he said. "There was a captain around an hour ago looking for you, and he's coming back."

Captain Eric Weismiller knocked at my door an hour later. I was told to deliver these orders personally, he said, not looking very happy about being a messenger boy.

"Report to the White House next Monday at 0800."

CHAPTER 6

CHATTING IN A NICE RESTAURANT LIKE THIS SURE BEATS WHERE I LIVE, don't it? White tablecloths and a snotty Frenchman at the door. It's sad but after a while you get used to the old fellows taking their teeth out at meals when something gets stuck. Let's order a bottle of wine. Quite a nice list they've got.

I know you're itching for me to get to Pearl Harbor and the rest, but I'm in no hurry as long as the government's picking up the check. The *Château Cheval Blanc* looks good. I drank enough of that in the old days to float a Higgins Boat, and Winston always said this was its best year. You don't care for white wine? Then we'll have a bottle of red as well. That *Château Lafite Rothschild* is mighty fine. No, no, I insist. *Garcon*, if you please.

The Churchills put me in Sarah's old room overlooking the back garden. She had disgraced the family by dancing almost naked in a revue in the West End, and married a Jewish comedian to top it off. I saw the show quite a few times.

My theory is to know a foreign country you have to understand their customs. So I spent a good deal of time in pubs and going to music halls and the revues and so forth, probably as much as I did playing cards and billiards in the fancy clubs where Winston got me guest memberships. My hope at the clubs was to pick up some chance remark that might interest Washington, but all you heard was "A pox on the man that dealt these cards" and "Curse the luck, by Jove." I won quite a bit until they began to catch on to my, ah, style. I made the mistake of mentioning to Winston's son, Randolph, that I was a pretty steady customer at the revue.

"I would think one visit would be sufficient. Why go more—to ogle my sister?"

I admit he had me there, but I claimed there was a singer I liked. Sarah did have a pretty good figure. "Now, now," Winston said to Randolph, lifting a glass of this very wine to toast British-American friendship.

By the way, you're going to have to be creative when you turn in your expense account; I just noticed the price. It's a crime what they get away with in places like this. Look at that Frenchman smirking. I bet he doesn't sell a bottle of this from one year to the next.

Back to business and Randolph glaring at me over his glass. He was as nasty a drunk as you'll see if you live to be a hundred. Winston told him he had to pretend we were cousins, but hadn't explained why. He had to keep a lot of things secret from Randolph because he had a loose tongue. He was a terrible snob on top of the rest of his faults; even others in the upper crust thought so, and most steered clear of him. We didn't hit it off; jealousy was my guess. He was good looking enough, but didn't stand a chance when I walked into a room. I know it sounds conceited and all that, but the ladies made a bee line for me even if he had his mouth open to say something. Winston put the word around that I was a rich American, but it wasn't just that. I don't look half bad even today, wouldn't you say?

There were plenty of places besides Sarah's revue for ogling. Nude women posed on stages in clubs where they called them living statues to get around the law. Undercover police sneaked in to make sure they didn't move a muscle. I got to know one of the living models; an art student named Wanda. I squired her around Fitzrovia for a while. That's where writers and artists hung out. They're not my type; fairies and humbugs as Randolph pointed out. He was generally wrong on any subject you could mention, but not in this case. Sometimes you put up with people you wouldn't dream of when Wandas are what's at the end of the rainbow.

We spent a lot of time at the Wheatsheaf on Rathbone Place where you sat at tables so close your nose was in somebody's ear if you turned your head. Hot as hell. It was full of people who looked unhappy enough to kill themselves as soon as they finished the pint somebody bought for them. And after listening to them for a while, you wished they would. The ones not fed up with life were miserable as hell about other things.

A lot of Communists and anarchists were regulars. There were plenty of lower class accents as well as the toff kind; it was unusual for the classes to mix like that. Have you ever heard someone from Yorkshire talk? They might as well be those aborigines that grunt and whistle. At least with the Scots you can pick out a word here and there, usually enough to get the general drift.

There was a lot of talk back and forth about poetry. How can anyone take that guff seriously? And politics; if it wasn't poetry it was politics. They passed around cheap-looking magazines without a single picture, not even a drawing. Just tiny columns of print you had to hold close to your face. Wanda said the articles blasted people from other cheap magazines for being lackeys and stooges of the bosses.

She hung on every word so I had to pretend I was interested myself. People shook their fists in each other's faces and fights broke out. Tables and chairs got thrown over. Women screaming bloody murder, of course, and then the bobbies were blowing whistles. It reminded me of the glory days—plowing into drunken crowds with a shore party at my back, swinging billy clubs like they were going for the fences. You had to hold onto your glass at the Wheatsheaf if you got up to look at the fighting. If you didn't, some sneak finished your drink before you sat down again. You looked for who did it, but we were stuffed in so tight it could have been any one of a half dozen moochers.

One night someone sat down at our table with a look that said we should feel honored. Somebody whispered he was the genius poet from Wales. He had tousled curls, and looked as proud as Lucifer. He said nothing, just stared into his pint. I was guessing he must be thinking poetic thoughts, but it turned out he was just mean drunk.

He said to me, "You don't look like you belong here, mate. A suit like that belongs on a banker's back."

"He's my friend, Dylan," Wanda said. "He's from America. Lowell Brady meet Dylan Thomas."

"I'd throw this pint in your face if I thought you were a tool of Wall Street," he said.

Then I'm glad I'm not, I said nice as pie.

"So what do you do then?"

Hogs, I said.

"What? You're a pig farmer?"

Laughter around the table.

In a manner of speaking, I said with dignity.

I was aware of Wanda's pleased look. No pub brawls if you wanted on her good side.

"What? I can't hear you in this infernal din."

I said that I was in the livestock trade. That's the story Winston and I agreed on, as I'll tell you later. I said it might be that the shoes on your feet were made from a hide I raised from a piglet.

"I need some new ones."

He scraped his chair back and put his dirty, rundown shoes on the table. "Whoops, sorry. Looks like I stepped in dog shit."

More laughter from the crowd. Wanda smiled at my gentlemanly behavior, and I'm thinking things are looking up for later that night. For someone who sat naked on a stage for men to stare at, she was slow to allow admirers to handle the merchandise.

Then Dylan Thomas started to heckle me. Why did America claim to win the Great War when millions had been slaughtered before we got off our big arses? Why didn't we forgive England's war debts—weren't we rich enough already? You're a culture of barbarians, worse than the Germans in some ways, and so forth into the night. I just smiled and he pushed off after a while.

Later, I had to go to the gent's room and he was crouched before a toilet bowl reciting poetry and heaving his guts out. "The socket-free lone visionary eye soaring reflectively..." He reared forward for more puking.

I pushed his head all the way in.

"Bloody hell..." he said on the way down. His gurgle made up for all his insults. I was out the door before he came up gasping for air and back at our table looking innocent by the time he stumbled out with his fists doubled.

"Look at Dylan," someone said. "It looks like he's been in a downpour."

"There's lumps of stuff in his hair," Wanda said.

I slipped her away before Dylan could put two and two together.

Life with the Senator had given me a pretty tough hide, so I overlooked Randolph's cutting remarks about "my Yank cousin." He liked to quote some Frenchman who said America is the only nation to go from barbarism to degeneration without the usual interval of civilization.

After hearing that at a party in Mayfair for about the tenth time, I fired back. "Who cares what some rotten frog said?"

The ladies laughed and clapped and the men said "Hear, hear!"

He threw dark looks around the room and left. He hoped to follow his father into politics, but my opinion was he had no future in any job where people had to like him. Time has proved me right.

I think I'll start with the lobster bisque and then the lamb chops with truffles. What about you, young lady? Not much of an appetite again? To think I ate like this every night in London. Live it up while you can, that's my motto. Not that I didn't when I had a chance, but it seems to me I could have wrung more out of it if I'd put my mind to it. All that time I trailed after Churchill could have been put to better use. I doubt Roosevelt looked at the letters I sent even though I spiced them up with plenty of gossip. He liked that, the Senator wrote me; he was only human like the rest of us.

So I wrote about a Foreign Office big shot named Lord Halifax. The man was famous for his piety but was having an affair with Baba Metcalf, one of Lord Curzon's daughters. A real stunner, that one.

"They say it's platonic," Clemmy told me, "but she gets every man she goes after. She turned down Jock Whitney for him, and you know how rich he is."

Everyone in the upper class knew everyone else, extremely well in many cases. Wink, wink. I heard all the gossip. Baba had an affair with Oswald Mosley who started the British fascist party. She cuckolded her husband, Fruity, the Duke of Windsor's best friend. Oswald had another even more beautiful mistress, Diana Guinness, who dumped her rich, young husband for him. Like her sister Unity, she was a friend of Hitler.

To give it another twist, Mosley was married at one time to Baba's sister. This is the kind of stuff Franklin loved; we don't have anything like it over here.

You'll stay scrawny if you don't eat more, Harriet. Men like something to hang onto. Now I've gone and made you blush again. Sorry, salty sailor and so forth. This bisque is damned good. Yes, pour a little more wine, waiter. A little more, you're looking at a thirsty man. Not quite to the top. There, that's fine.

One day Winston was at the table where he stood to write and I was playing solitaire waiting for him to say something to put in a letter when a boy started whistling on the street below.

"Damn that noise," Winston said. He went to the window and called down. "You there, boy! It you must make that racket, go somewhere else."

Just then a car pulled to the curb. "That's Mountbatten's Rolls-Royce." A minute later a tall man in a naval uniform was shown in by the new maid. Bridget was gone, did I tell you? Caught stealing silverware.

"Hello, Dickie," Winston said, "meet Lowell Brady my cousin from America."

We said hello and shook hands. Commander Mountbatten, as he was at the time, was as tall as me and a handsome dog himself. We got on right from the start.

"One of Dickie's claims to fame is he can undress, bathe, and dress again in two minutes."

Get out a here, I said.

"It's true," Mountbatten said. "My best time is a minute and forty-eight seconds."

"He has ready-tied elastic shoelaces, braces permanently stitched to trousers, a buttonless waistcoat he pulls over his head like a jumper, and zippers instead of buttons," Winston said.

"I'm always looking for ways to speed up getting dressed," Mountbatten said. "A few seconds getting to battle station might be the difference between life and death."

"I have been working with Dickie to get the fleet its own air arm," Winston said.

"I have great news," Mountbatten said. "The RAF will do the training, but our fliers will be attached to naval shore establishments. The Admiralty are so happy they're promoting me to captain."

"That calls for a glass of champagne." Winston rang for a servant. "A bottle of the 1918 *Grand Cru*," he told him.

I'm not much for champagne, but I can tell you that was damned fine stuff. I'd order a bottle to show you if they had it here. The two of them crowed over how they'd stuck it to the old battleship crowd. I was a battleship man myself at the time, but I didn't let on. Flimsy airplanes versus the thick armor and big guns of a battlewagon? It didn't seem much of a choice. We were to learn better, of course.

"You are how old, Dickie?" Winston asked

"Thirty-seven."

"This will not make you more popular. The average for a captain's rank is between forty-two and forty-five."

"They already think I'm too rich and too royal and a second rater who lacks sea sense; I've heard it all. And now they'll say I'm too young, but I'll bear it somehow. What a pity you're not PM, Winston."

"The same thought occurs to me not more than a dozen times a day."

"You are the fittest, everyone says so."

"Thank you, Dickie. I am not entirely immune to flattery."

"Damn it all, it's the plain truth."

"One makes enemies in politics but relies on time to thin their ranks. Mine cling to life with great tenacity; some from my father's time have transferred their hatred to me. What is this business in the Pacific?"

"The Admiralty are furious over American claims to some flyspeck island in the Pacific. We put a survey team ashore and built a radio transmitter to keep an eye on Japanese activities in case they expand from the Mandates. We left the Union Jack flying on an aluminum pole. Then the Yanks put their own party ashore and say the island is now under the jurisdiction of their Interior Department, and if we want to do any further construction we must apply for a permit."

"What fools to quarrel with the Americans over trifles."

"The Admiralty's point is we're being squeezed out in the Pacific.

Their shipping companies already carry more cargo than ours out there. Our ambassador says Australia is beginning to look more American than English."

Winston waved that away. "That is no more than a mere vapor in some nebulous future. There is much more danger closer at hand."

"I quite agree, Winston. I'm merely reporting the opinion at the Admiralty."

"The Admiralty must no longer regard the Americans as naval rivals but as allies. If you ever have the opportunity, Cousin Lowell, I hope you convey these sentiments to your fellow citizens. Perhaps a word to the Senator?"

Consider it done, I said, raising my glass.

"Changing the opinion of the Admiralty will take doing," Dickie said.

"If men cannot adopt new ways of thinking, they must be put aside."

"Are you coming to Adsdean this weekend? Bring Lowell with you. He'll enjoy meeting Edwina."

"I have not yet decided," Winston said.

"Try to talk him into it, old chap," Dickie said to me. "Charlie Chaplin is coming and so is Douglas Fairbanks. You'll have a jolly good time."

I didn't know what Adsdean was—a regatta, a fox hunt?—and Dickie was out the door already. He went everywhere in a hurry. I've never seen the point of rushing; it's the Southerner in me I guess. Wherever you're going will still be waiting when you get there. You can make exceptions, like if a Jap is coming at you with a bayonet as happened on Guadalcanal. Ah, the lamb chops. I could eat a horse, saddle and all.

"Their country place," Winston said when I asked what Adsdean was. "They always have an interesting collection of guests—they're mad for film people—but you're constantly hectored about activities. A questionnaire is left in your bedroom every night asking which you plan to do the following day, riding, shooting, motoring, tennis, picnicking, and so forth. They get offended if you don't promptly fill out and return it. You'll go with me, of course. You might pick up something to interest Washington."

The problem was I was so far out of my depth I never heard much that I thought Washington would care about. Winston was usually dictating to his secretary or talking to visitors about Parliament business.

"If I let slip a state secret here and there," he said, "it is because I want your president to know I am opening my heart to you without reservation. We English-speaking people must set a common course in the parlous seas."

Let me know when you let one slip, I said.

I dozed off once in an easy chair after a big lunch and when I woke up he was still talking, not having noticed. He stood looking out the window and shaking his head.

"So there you have it, David wants to chuck it all and marry his mistress."

My thought was if a man makes his mistress an honest woman, where's the harm? Yes, waiter, you can top that off. You're just sipping, dear. We don't want to leave any for the kitchen staff; they'd guzzle it without any feeling for the quality.

Well, it turned out this David was King Edward and the mistress was Wallis Simpson, who I saw with him at Adsdean that weekend. Putting two and two together, I realized Winston was worried that he'd want to marry her. That was trouble because she was a divorcee and American on top of it. No way was that going to fly with the English.

Winston's chauffeur brought the big black Daimler over from Chartwell on the Friday and we drove through rain to west Sussex. Adsdean? Okay, it was a stone mansion covered in ivy. A long drive leading up to it. A nine-hole golf course is part of it.

"On a clear day," Winston said, "you have a view of the harbor and the Isle of Wight. The house is supposed to look Tudor, but it was built in the 1850s. I don't suppose I told you that Dickie traces his line all the way back to Charlemagne."

The man with the empire, I said.

That was all I knew about him. Have you ever thought about how much useless knowledge gets pounded into the heads of defenseless kids? Hannibal and Shakespeare and all those Caesars—what good does knowing about them do?

"He's related to all of the crowned heads of Europe," Winston said, "including the czar before he and his family were murdered by the filthy communists." Winston had known some of the Romanoffs. "The czar sadly was not an intelligent man, but he was not unkind."

We stood there watching the chauffeur struggle with the luggage. Winston looked around to see if anyone was in earshot.

"Do you remember how I said I'd let slip a secret now and then for the Senator to convey to the president? Tell him the French agree with my sources that in the event of war the Germans will be able to produce three times as many airplanes as we can. With an expected wastage of eighty per cent in combat, this would very quickly tip the scales in their favor."

I'll get that right off to the Senator, I said. Is there a post office near?

Churchill took me by the elbow and we walked toward the door. "Next week is soon enough to send off your dispatch. Perhaps you will learn more this weekend of interest to your government."

What I learned straight off was what a knockout Mountbatten's wife was. She was better looking than Betty Grable, who I met later. Edwina had been out riding and met us in boots, jodhpurs and a green sweater that matched her eyes. She fussed with her wind-blown hair and gave me the eye. Hang on, I'm thinking, here comes some fun. Everybody in the upper class seemed "randy," as they called it, and slept with everybody else. I suppose they still do unless the war changed things. That was the real reason for those house parties, to let people screw somebody new.

There was always some attractive young thing—and not so young sometimes—slipping me a note asking me to drop anchor after lights out. When you passed people tip-toeing in the hall the thing was to pretend you didn't see them and never mention it the next day. During one weekend in Cornwall, the high water mark for yours truly, I was called on for *amore* by five ladies, nineteen to thirty-eight in age. A stallion in a paddock of mares doesn't get that kind of workout. My arches hurt from tip-toeing, and another part did too. Not that I'm complaining, mind you. But there, I've got you blushing again, sorry.

They had a houseful of guests, people with titles, members of Parliament, admirals and generals, cabinet officials, also landowners from neighboring estates. Ruddy men and big, horse-faced women. There were hounds underfoot or sleeping in chairs; you got hair on your clothes if you sat down.

Most belonged to a crusty old squire who had the local fox hunt; they said he never went anywhere without his pack of dogs. Fights kept breaking out with Dickie's dogs until the squire went home.

We wended our way through the people and dogs with Winston introducing me as his cousin from the New World. "He's a hog grower from the south of the United States."

If there's one thing I can do well it's get along with people. I can walk into a room of strangers and act like I've known them forever. I came by this naturally this as a kid watching the Senator at the county fairs. He acted like there was nothing he'd rather be doing than shaking hands and slapping backs when the truth was he hated it.

"Why do all these children they lift up for me to kiss have snotty noses?" he asked my mother. "What's wrong with the parents?"

He saw a hypnotist at one of those fairs who was so good he could make a man take off his pants and not remember it afterward. The Senator was not above blackmail and saw potential in this man for bringing some of the duller-witted Republicans around to his point of view on some bill he wanted passed. He tried to talk him into joining his staff, but the man was a wanderer at heart and didn't care to give up the circus life.

The English have a different style; faster talkers for one thing, and they're not as loud as us folks in the south. After a couple of drinks at one of our parties you can count on somebody cuttin' loose with a rebel yell. People hug and kiss and carry on. I'm trying to think what you'd call the English. Standoffish—yeah, that's it. They don't like somebody throwing an arm around their neck. Meet their eye, comment on the weather, and Bob's your uncle, as they say over there.

Charlie Chaplin came through the door right after King Edward and Mrs. Simpson and it was hard to say who impressed people more, though I'd give Charlie the edge. He was a dapper little fellow in a blazer and silk cravat, not at all like the tramp in the picture shows; quite the cultivated gent in fact. The checkered motoring cap he swept off his head when he bowed to us wasn't quite right, but that's the flashy movie crowd for you.

"He is the most lovable, shy and pathetic little man and yet so full of humor that he can keep one amused by the hour," Mountbatten said.

"The clown in literature is often a tragic figure, Dickie," Winston said.

I'm pretty sure Dickie's thinking ran along the same lines as mine. How could somebody funny be tragic? But far from me to contradict Churchill. He was a great man, no doubt about it, although few knew it at the time. Oh, they'd give him credit for spunkiness, but that was as far as it went. Some say Roosevelt was great, but I don't for reasons you and your bosses well know.

The king was a shrimpy guy himself; and as for Wallis, I didn't see the attraction. She knew how to dress, but that was it. I'd actually say she was on the homely side. Big hands for a woman; somebody said she could strangle a rabbit with those mitts. Nobody liked her much except the king's paid ass-kissers—a faggy lot they call courtiers—and my guess was they were just pretending to stay on his good side.

"What happened to his old mistress?" I heard a dowager say.

"Thelma Furness called the palace one day," another lady answered, "and was told the prince wouldn't be taking her calls anymore. Seventeen years together!"

Wallis was standoffish in a crowd. When it was just the two of you—different story. She sniffed out all there was to know about a man in sixty seconds flat. Just looking you in the eye she figured out your strength and weaknesses, mostly the weaknesses. They said her tricks were picked up whoring in the Far East. That explained her hold over the king. Oh, I bet she made him squeal. I came close myself on one occasion.

I think we're ready to run our eye down the dessert menu, waiter. Bring me a balloon of brandy while we're looking. Make it a cognac, a double to save you steps. A little something for you, dear. No?

Adsdean was cold as a tomb. Every bedroom had a fireplace, and they had to keep them roaring day and night just to take the edge off the chill. You wore heavy sweaters and kept your hands in your pockets except when eating. The butler put me in a room up on the top floor a few steps down from where the servants lived, but I didn't mind because each step up got a little warmer.

The breakdown was the social people Winston said he didn't have time for and serious types in dark suits who came from London and drove back after dinner. Winston drew me aside as I was telling a pretty young woman her dress matched her eyes and necklace. Her earrings as well, now that I noticed.

"Really?" she said, batting her eyelashes. "What luck."

"Some of us will be going into the library," Winston said in a low voice, "for discussions I want you to listen to from behind the yellow silk screen sent here for this purpose. Don't make a sound after we come in."

I hoped to wiggle out of it because of the young lady and also to shake Chaplin's hand and thank him for all the laughs he'd given me, but it wasn't to be.

"Beautiful, isn't she?" Winston said. "Araminta Hallam-Peel will be a fine catch for some young man. She's the daughter of an earl, and the family has bags of money. Now is a good time to steal into the library."

Winston could get a look that said "Don't cross me," and this was one of those times. A word from him and a telegram from the Navy Department could come tomorrow ordering me home. I didn't think the White House would be my next billet in that case. It would more likely be the Great Lakes Naval Training Center or skippering a refrigerator ship.

I waved at Araminta and mouthed, Wait. Then I ducked into the library and behind the yellow screen. A few minutes later, the men in dark suits trickled in with Winston bringing up the rear. By shifting positions, I could take in the whole room through the peephole.

"If this rain keeps up, we will have trouble getting our cars out of that field," said a man who Winston later told me was Anthony Eden, the foreign secretary. A nice looking fellow except for his teeth.

"The cars can't be seen from the road," said Brendan Bracken, a friend of Winston who was Randolph's age; they were so close people said he must be a bastard son. "Winston believes his telephone is tapped by MI5. He hears clicks on the line and once heard someone breathing."

"Who would be doing that?" Eden asked.

"You'd have to ask Neville. Or perhaps MI5 are doing it on their own."

"I don't care who knows I'm here," Eden said.

"Where is Admiral Sinclair?" Winston asked.

"His deputy Stewart Menzies is coming from his car," Bracken said at the window. "He's stepped in something nasty."

"They let the neighbor graze his cattle there," Winston said. "They get a well-aged side of beef in return; the rural economy at its best."

Stewart Menzies came into the room looking annoyed. He was an Army colonel with a hush-hush job in the intelligence service.

"I expected Admiral Sinclair," Winston said.

"He had a doctor's appointment," Menzies said. "He asked me to stand in for him."

Okay, I'll describe him. Late forties, I'd guess. Pale face and light-colored eyes, silvery-blond hair thinning on top. Snappy dresser. He wore a three-piece tweed suit with a handkerchief in the breast pocket, a regimental tie, and a gold chain at his vest.

Winston told me later the family fortune was from Gordon's gin, and he was a member of the Beaufort Hunt. That put him at the top of what they call the mink and manure set. The Menzies country estate is just south of the royal castle at Balmoral to give you an idea. Winston gave me the low down on everybody in the room over brandy. Sadly, by then the young woman in green was long gone.

"Wigglesworth is back from the Far East," said Sir Peter Harmsworth, some sort of senior civil servant. "It's a shambles out there. There is utterly no coordination between the services, none. Our attaché in Tokyo, a General Piggott, appears to have gone native. He refused point blank to have anything to do with setting up an intelligence network. It seems he admires the Japanese."

"Who is Wigglesworth?" Bracken asked.

"Deputy director of intelligence for the Air Ministry," said Dickie.

"He's not the only one who should be put out to pasture," said Harmsworth. "Henry Steptoe is the head of SIS in Shanghai with the cover of vice-consul. He wears a monocle and has a furtive manner that gives the most ordinary meeting a clandestine air. He is so obviously a spy that some believe it cannot possibly be."

"How long has General Piggott been out there?" Winston asked.

"Off and on since 1904," Harmsworth said. "He is nearing retirement."

"The process should be hastened. Piggott, Wigglesworth, and Steptoe. They sound like characters in a Wodehouse novel."

"The general is entirely ignored by the Foreign Office," someone said. "His cables are called Piggottry."

"They've been so busy infiltrating the communist cells out there," Harmsworth said, "that very little attention has been paid to Japanese espionage. Security is shocking. During flying boat layovers, diplomatic and secret mail is kept on the plane under the floor or taken ashore and put in a cupboard. In Bangkok a junior officer literally sleeps on the pouches. We have a post in Hong Kong for listening to Japanese navy radio traffic that is so overcrowded that some poor fellow has to work out of the WC. He has to stop his work when a colleague answers nature's call."

"Disgraceful," General Edward Spears said from his easy chair. He had a moustache and sucked on a pipe.

He and Spears went back a long way, Winston told me. He had wanted him as his adjutant when they were in the trenches, but Spears spoke such good French the higher-ups kept him for talking to the frogs.

"Chinese cooks work a step or two from the room where decryption is done," Harmsworth continued. "The code room is shockingly under-manned. Wigglesworth met a man who has worked three years without a single weekend off."

"We might as well throw in our cards there," someone said. "We have our hands full with the Hun."

"That would mean an irrecoverable loss of face for the white race," Winston said. "The independence movement in India would be immea-surably strengthened, and it would be a matter of time before the crown jewel of the empire was lost. Rivers of blood would flow between the Hindus and Moslems. Australia and New Zealand would turn to America, and we would be an empire in name only."

There was quite a bit of back and forth I won't bother you with. Nobody seemed to think much of Chamberlain because he had been in trade.

"England was great only when led by its great aristocratic families," Winston said. "They were people of spirit and courage who gave little thought to the cost of things. The middle class has invaded parliament and the civil service, and their first instinct is never risk anything that might jeopardize their jobs and pensions. They cannot think on a grand scale or rise to great occasions."

"The prime minister does not understand Hitler because he does not understand Germans," said Robert Vansittart, another Foreign Office big shot who looked down a long nose. "One of the things I have learned in life is that eight out of ten Germans think it not only legitimate but laudable to take every advantage, however unfair. There is no such word as gentleman in German, for this denotes some consideration for others. There is only the word Herr, the substantive of the verb *herrschen*, to dominate others."

"You cannot blacken an entire people for the actions their government takes," said Alexander Cadogan, another FO big shot from an ancient family. He was as small as a jockey.

"People seem shocked that I am anti-German," Vansittart said, "but what else could I be? The Germans have killed and tortured too much to be misjudged. They count on conquest to raise their standard of living. Prince Bulow was one of many Germans surprised at how little the English understand them. 'They aren't prone to suspect really evil intentions'—he wrote that in 1899 and it was published for all to see, but naturally we've paid no attention. Horace Rumbold told me when he was ambassador in Berlin that the leaders of the Nazi party seemed mentally ill."

"Robert does not believe," Cadogan said, "that the Versailles Treaty had anything to do with German anger and resentment."

That got Vansittart up on his high horse. "It is the most astounding thing that the Germans have been able to persuade the world they were badly treated by a treaty whose reparation and disarmament clauses were never enforced and which took from them nothing which they had not acquired by robbery and murder. It is actually worse. Germany's victims extracted a thousand million pounds from them while we and the Americans were lending them two thousand million pounds. Their war criminals were steeped in atrocities, but the Allies renounced the right to try them. They allowed the Weimar Republic to conduct the trials and in consequence, the very few that were brought to trial were acquitted or lionized. In every war since 1860 to the present, Germany has been the wanton aggressor. The leader and his ruling clique are irrelevant as the character of the German people will always produce bellicose leaders with an ideology of force, and it does not matter if he is called Frederick, Wilhelm or Hitler, or the people around him are Junkers or Nazis."

There was a silence and I had to freeze so I didn't make the chair squeak. I got the feeling Vansittart had been carried away and people were embarrassed for him.

"I have just obtained from a source I shall not name," Winston said finally, "a copy of our new manual for cavalry training which emphasizes the importance of the well-bred horse. Twenty-three pages were devoted to sword and lance exercises. Do you want to know how much was devoted to mechanized movement?"

People shuffled their feet, expecting the worst.

"Three paragraphs," Winston said.

"Good Lord," said someone I couldn't see from my peephole.

"This manual was approved by several committees," Winston said. "How is such stupidity ever to be rooted out? Even the ostrich does not drive its head so deeply into the sand."

Churchill gave a glance at the yellow screen like he wanted me to pay special attention now. "Bill Stephenson has made a good start at identifying people in American who can be persuaded to use their influence on our behalf."

"Don't give me too much credit," said a small, fit-looking man with a Canadian accent standing by the fireplace.

"Some of you don't know Bill," Winston said. "He fought in the trenches as a teenager straight from high school, won a battlefield promotion for bravery and was a captain by nineteen. He got gassed and was invalided back to England. He could have rested on his laurels, but instead he joined the air force and became an ace. He was shot down, captured by the Germans, and escaped. Bill is now a businessman who travels often in Germany," Winston said, "and has brought me many valuable impressions about how rapidly it is rearming."

People clapped and Stephenson turned red. I would have gripped my hands overhead or taken a bow. Moments like that don't come along all that often. I say milk them for all you can.

"We are subsidizing the Overseas News Service," Winston said, "which is owned by the Jewish Telegraph Agency, itself a subsidiary of the New York Post. The money will allow the news service to add correspondents to increase its attractiveness to American newspapers. We will plant articles and photographs with them and we also have high hopes of obtaining control of the Herald Tribune, a very influential New York newspaper. By hidden hand we are purchasing a very powerful shortwave radio station on the East Coast that was established to build friendship among nations. It has a reputation for purity of motive and broadcasts to more than thirty countries in twenty-two languages. I am told it receives a thousand letters a week from listeners."

"Do you know the damage that could be done if America's isolationists learned of this?" asked Eden. "Or that priest with the radio program, Father Coughlin."

"We have taken precautions," Menzies said.

"CBS, one of the major American radio networks, has appointed a new European director," Winston continued, "a man named Edward R. Murrow. Advances are being made privately to this influential gentleman. Radio people in America are allowed more independence than the BBC grants, so he may prove very useful."

"Our efforts in Hollywood are beginning to pay off," Stephenson said. "Working through a producer named Walter Wanger, we have created an Anti-Nazi League."

"This man Wanger's movie Blockade," Winston said, "was banned in Spain, Italian, Germany and other fascist countries."

"I saw that one," said Mountbatten. "A thumping good thriller. Put us in a very good light."

"Alfred Hitchcock, one of England's most promising directors, has agreed to take up full time residence there to gain a more favorable representation of British characters in their movies," Stephenson said, "and the producer Alex Korda is already doing good work for us. To give you an idea of the possibilities, fifty million Americans go to the movies every week. Hollywood makes four hundred movies a year to satisfy the demand."

"How does one go about gaining a more favorable representation?" General Spears asked.

"By how the characters are written in the screenplays," Stephenson said. "The lines they speak and so on. The English will be portrayed as plucky while Germans wear monocles and have sinister dueling scars. Think of Korda's *The Lion Has Wings* where the English are symbolized by inoffensive donkeys at the seaside and the Germans by champing war horses in Berlin."

"We could use fewer donkeys and more war horses," Spears said. He touched a match to his pipe. "To change the subject, I've come across a book by a French colonel named De Gaulle called *The Army of the Future*. It claims static defenses like the Maginot Line are a thing of the past. Mechanized armored units will maneuver and attack instead. I'm told it's required reading for the German general staff."

"People are always coming up with fanciful theories about what form future wars will take," Winston said. "Artillery would make rubbish of mechanized forces trying to force the Maginot Line. You know, I met a French military officer named De Gaulle once. He was extremely tall with hips like a woman. I wonder if it's the same man."

"It's a pity we have to sneak around like this," said Major Desmond Morton. He was a neighbor of Winston's with some job in intelligence. "It would simplify matters if our government and theirs were able to cooperate without the world knowing."

"The Americans couldn't keep a secret to save their souls from eternal damnation," Eden said.

"Lindsay's the wrong man to have as ambassador in Washington in times like these," said Vansittart. "He is too much the aristocrat; his very appearance puts them off. That walrus moustache and those bulging eyes. After ten years he still makes no effort to mix socially with anyone but the Newport and Palm Beach sets. He's nearly seven feet tall, so it seems he's always looking down at people. We need someone there with the common touch."

"There is still resistance to be overcome," Stephenson continued. "The Hays Office is against politics in motion pictures. Although they are sympathetic to us, Jewish producers don't dare challenge the censors for fear of being called warmongers. As we shape public opinion over there, we hope to create conditions where more direct messages can be put into the movies. Symbolism is all well and good, but the ordinary person doesn't always get it."

Then they turned to grousing about "that American woman" the king had taken up with. They really do look down on us colonial mongrels.

At dinner afterward I was put between an old duchess who got it in her head I was Australian and the squire who had come back without his dogs. He told a story about his pack ripping a fox apart before he could whip them away.

"The badgers will get her pups," he said. "Better that way; they won't die of starvation."

I was about to say our razorbacks eat people given the chance when the duchess asked what Queensland was like. It took a while before I could get her to understand I wasn't an Aussie, and then she wanted to know why I'd claimed I was in the first place. Afterward, Churchill and I had our night-cap in his room.

"You heard a lot tonight that His Majesty's government would rather was not known. Please emphasize to your president the pains I have gone in the interests of complete openness."

I said 'deed I would and went to my room.

I was dozing off when Edwina slipped into the bed. Considering the present company, no details. She blew me a kiss from the door as the rooster crowed and at breakfast acted like she barely recognized me. Like I said, that was the way it was done.

That was a splendid meal, *garcon*. My compliments to the chef and the bill goes to the little lady here.

CHAPTER 7

THAT MEAL WITH DRINKS BEFORE AND EXPENSIVE WINES WITH THE MANY courses became the pattern. Captain Brady was willing to discuss his experiences, but meant to take as long as possible. The recording machine with its slow-turning spools was like a silent guest at the table. Sometimes he directed his stories as much to the microphone as to me.

There was no chance federal auditors would approve the expenses incurred in wining and dining at the smart restaurants he chose, so I footed the cost myself from private funds. I felt I had a sacred obligation to History.

President Roosevelt is now regarded as the God-like figure that steered us safely through the storms. Rural electrification was one of his mighty New Deal accomplishments, the fruits of which I became very familiar with in my travels. Likewise, the Civil Works Administration, the Civilian Conservation Corps, the National Recovery Act, Public Works Administration, and all the others. But if he secretly shaped events to trick us into the Second World War, that would require a radical reassessment of his presidency, however right the decision may have been, with vast if unknowable political consequences for the future. The glorious nimbus that surrounded his name and works would be dispelled to reveal just another politician who differed only in the magnitude of his ruthlessness and treachery.

I was always rebuffed by Captain Brady when, hoping to conduct my questioning less expensively, I revived my effort to convince him my interest was only that of a humble scholar and not part of a government conspiracy.

"You want to talk over a cup of coffee in some greasy spoon?" he said scoffingly. "They're not getting off that cheap. How about we go to the Palace de Paris next week? The *Post* says their salmon stuffed with white truffles is the greatest. Who knows, maybe it's even good enough for you. I don't see how you settle for those little salads all the time. Women as scrawny as you shouldn't be dieting."

The letters Captain Brady mailed weekly to his stepfather for transmittal to the White House have vanished. But I discovered circumstantial evidence favoring their existence when a clerk in the Navy Department happened across a file of memoranda between the Bureau of Navigation and the Bureau of Supplies and Accounts concerning his expenses in England.

"It seems this was misfiled," the clerk said with a shake of his head. "It's the women who worked here during the war. Nobody trained them right."

Captain Roy Howard queried his counterpart at the Bureau of Navigation about reimbursement Brady requested for a dinner at the Savoy. "Five bottles of expensive French champagne were consumed," he wrote. "Admiral Prescott said he will not pay this from Bureau funds, nor the attached expenses that include a gelding bred in Ireland, and saddle and 'accoutrements for riding to the hounds.' Other irregularities include the rental of a yacht for three months and the purchase of a silver-headed walking stick for a costume ball."

Captain Howard added, "This officer appears to be living the life of a rich lord. The Bureau of Supplies and Accounts considers his spending unconscionable." Even though money—"a large sum," as Howard wrote— had been transferred from a contingency fund not subject to Bureau audit, that fund was now exhausted.

In reply, Captain Morris Tucker of the Bureau of Navigation conceded that Brady's mission was not known to ONI (Howard had queried that department), but had been "authorized at the highest level." A meeting of the admirals in charge of the bureaus was arranged to adjudicate the matter. A series of memos showed the meeting was scheduled and cancelled several times, but finally it occurred and the Bureau of Navigation prevailed. The minutes showed the Bureau of Supplies and Accounts would continue disbursements to Brady and cease questioning expenses.

* * *

I think it was the cane with the silver knob that made them blow their stack. I bought it for Lady Grisham's masked ball. I went as Louis IV before the revolution. Satin breeches, powdered wig—the works. I hired a coach and four with a trumpeter in the box. The horses reared and nearly run away with us when the flash bulbs went off. That was a big hit with the photographers and the crowd that watched us swells arrive. The pictures of Gwen Westcomb with her mouth open in a scream at the coach window were in all the papers the next day.

What Supplies and Accounts never got was I had to pass as a Yank with a load of dough. That meant throwing it around like it was water. Sure, I stayed with Churchill and that cut down on expenses, but when you're in high society you have to look like you belong. Otherwise people don't open up because you're an outsider, what they called a parvenu. That's French for "nobody," I think.

If I got invited to dinner, I had to pay it back at one of the exclusive clubs Winston got me into. A roasted ox costs an arm and a leg, and what they charge for liquor borders on crime. The clothes I bought in New York were good enough, but I didn't have enough. Some days you have to change three or four times or it's the same story, people don't think you belong. So I started buying new stuff at a shop on Saville Row that Dickie recommended. The Bureau blew another gasket when those bills came in.

If you're in fox-hunting circles you don't show up with some rented nag; you're judged by what you ride. I don't say it's right, just how it is. The world just about ended when I sent them the bill for Drummer. He was a cob seventeen hands high; incredible bloodline. No better horse in the Beaufort Hunt; Menzies himself told me that.

That cane with the silver knob saved my ass by the way. In Russia my boots wore out and I had to wrap my feet with rags. Christ, you wouldn't believe how cold it was. People lost their fingers, toes and noses from frostbite. Men fell down because they couldn't take another step and they were blocks of ice an hour later. Even though it was like a lucky rabbit's foot by then, I traded the cane to a general who ordered a soldier to take his boots off on the spot. We left the poor devil in the snow in his stockings. Now, don't give me that look. I thought General Sablukov would order the man a pair from the quartermaster's wagon, and I'm sure he would have except German rounds began dropping again and we had to run for it.

* * *

Captain Howard was a tall, thin man with a dry, laconic manner who lived in retirement in leafy suburban Maryland. "Lowell Brady," he said icily after I explained my research. "I haven't thought of him for years." He had been clipping a hedge in front of his house and paused to stare off into the distance. "Lord, the bureau hated that man."

"Why was that," I asked.

"Every month or so we'd get a big envelope stuffed with bills and receipts. Some were for enormous sums—I remember one for twenty-five hundred pounds for 'overhead.' A few of us thought the only way a man could go through that much money was gambling. Much of the paperwork he turned in had been crumpled up and smoothed out at a later date. Some had wine stains.

"It was clear he thought he could pretty much do as he pleased, damn any rule or regulation to the contrary, and it turned out he was right. Our chief went over to see Admiral Nimitz in a towering rage about a cane with a silver knob. 'I won't pay it,' he told us, 'satin breeches are as far as I go.' He came back from that meeting and said henceforth he didn't want to know how much Brady spent or on what."

We went inside and had tea with his wife, a heavy woman with a sarcastic manner and eyebrows plucked to give her an arch look. She was one of those critical women who see little good in others. She quickly decided that I was the kind who would never marry. Too small, too lacking in sex appeal; a lonely woman who would abandon any hope of changing that if she were smart. I knew what was going through her mind as much as if she had spoken aloud. What was sad was she had every reason to believe that.

"I met Brady once," Captain Howard said. "A conceited ass, full of himself. If his mother wasn't married to an important senator he would've been run out of the Navy long before the war."

On one of my trips I went to the library at the University of Georgia at Athens where his stepfather had donated his papers. I hoped to find the letters from London or at least some mention of them.

"They have been removed," a curator told me with surprise as she looked at the file. "And, most unusual, this note says we are to obtain the name of anyone asking to see them."

"I don't think you can ask that," I said.

"I don't either. It's very strange." She was a pleasant matronly woman in her fifties. "Let's pretend you never walked through the door."

* * *

We had to go to the best restaurants or Captain Brady showed his balky, sulky side.

"I'm not going in there," he said with scorn. "Look, a couple with two little kids. That tells you all I need to know. Take me back to the old soldiers' home."

He had suggestions from time to time, but mostly it was up to me to choose where we ate, and I knew little about fine dining. I asked friends at work and subscribed to a private newsletter for gourmands. I drove us to the Maryland shore for seafood and Virginia for ham dinners. He wouldn't talk about his experiences when we were on the road; that was reserved for the table. He sat silent on the passenger side except for comments about other drivers or events of the day such as:

England had the atomic bomb; the announcement had been made by his old friend Winston.

Seventy-three inches of rain fell in a single day on a city in Brazil. "I've been in a foxhole with rain coming down like that."

If Harry Truman was smart he wouldn't run for reelection.

A plane landed at the North Pole for the first time.

UFOs buzzed Washington, D.C. and jets were scrambled. "I think there's something they're not telling us."

A huge earthquake struck Alaska.

The head of the cooking staff at the old soldiers' home was arrested for stealing. "Let's see if the chow improves."

You have to dress up for nice restaurants, and that meant more expense. I went shopping with my coworker Elise who kept up with fashion. She talked me into outfits I wouldn't have considered on my own. I had to pay more attention to hair and makeup.

Captain Brady noticed the change. "You're looking good," he said at one of our interviews. "I like your hair."

I felt my face get hot. I know my strengths—good mind, hard worker. There is nothing that would make you remember me unless it was my legs are too short and my arms too long. A girl in high school said I was put together by the same committee in charge of the camel. I don't know why I'm going off in this direction.

* * *

Man, this shrimp is out of the world, as good as they've got in New Orleans. Okay, where was I? Oh yeah, Winston had a fit over Chamberlain's government rolling over for the Krauts. They were honorable men with good records in the Great War, he said, when did they become such lily livered cowards?

"I'm sure you don't mean that personally, Winston," Lord Halifax said, throwing me a sad look.

He was the foreign secretary, a tall, lean fella born with a hand missing. He wore a glove with something stuffed in the fingers to make them look real, but nobody was fooled. We were standing around with drinks in the smoking room at Parliament with a crowd that included Inskip, Professor Lindemann, Boothby, Lord Salisbury, and a bunch of other Conservatives on the outs with the party. Everybody was talking about Munich. Peace in our time, Chamberlain said.

"It is sordid, squalid, subhuman, and suicidal," Winston said. He was really worked up, his face red instead of pink.

"I paid a visit recently to the Vale of York," Halifax said in a dreamy way. "Looking from an elevation at its lovely prospect that is so typically English, I felt that it was my duty to preserve it in any way I could."

"At what cost?" Winston snapped at him. "Seeing it possessed by the Germans?"

Halifax looked guilty, but stubborn too. "Some accommodation must be made with reality. The Germans are developing a powerful war machine."

"I have warned of this for years."

"Yes, yes, Winston, as everyone knows. But we need two years before we will be ready for war, may God forefend."

"As the Germans are arming themselves faster than we are, their advantage will be even greater at the end of that time."

I'd heard plenty of that talk and anyhow the Senator said he got the picture and was pressing me to get him something new. I caught the eye of the young mistress of an earl and drifted her way.

I had met the young lady on one of those country weekends and—well, the truth of the matter is she found me irresistible. I had her first under a hedge and then we passed many a pleasant hour in the conservatory, the floor of the conservatory if you want the truth. I moved the potted ferns around to make a little nest.

Portia had the whitest skin and the blackest hair, a raving beauty. Ruby red lips, green eyes, and all that poetic stuff. If that wasn't enough, only Mrs. Simpson had more bedroom tricks. We would have, ahem, found a room and carried on in more comfort except Winston wanted me to listen to what he was going to say at dinner.

He always held forth when the plates were cleared, and people were expected to listen. The Poles, he said, were mistreating the Jews as bad as the Germans, driving them out of the big cities and so on. But London must not protest it for fear they would throw in with the Italians and maybe even the Nazis. He talked for an hour. Looking around the room, I saw some eyes half-closed and a few shut all the way. I wasn't feeling all that bright myself.

I hadn't seen Portia since that weekend—I learned later she'd had quite a few boyfriends and they kept her busy—and we were just getting catching up on things after dinner when Randolph butted in.

"I'm surprised you're not over there sucking up to my father," he said to me.

It seemed he had his eye on Portia himself. This made him even nastier, hard as it was to believe.

Hello, Shorty, I said. Have you met Portia?

"Long before you," he said coldly. "I came across a funny saying by Oscar Wilde the other day," he said to her. 'America was discovered before Columbus got there, but it had always been hushed up.'"

Who's Oscar Wilde? I said without thinking.

"My God," Randolph said, "the man doesn't *know*."

"Of course he does, silly," Portia said. "Everybody does."

I know now because I looked it up; he was a queer writer a long time ago; but I didn't at the time, and it made me look kind of slow. Portia liked the, um, physical side, but she told me under the hedge that brains were just as important to her.

Stupidly, I tried to be funny— Are you talking about Oscar Wild and Wooly? and so forth—thinking at the time he might be a music hall comedian. But squirm as I did, I couldn't hide I didn't know who the man was. You wouldn't think life turns on such small things, but you'd be wrong.

"It's a waste of time asking pig farmers about literature," Randolph said.

"Pig farmers?" Portia said, wrinkling her nose.

Hog grower, I said with dignity. There were lots of times I was sorry that was the cover story.

"You know what the difference is between the two?" Randolph sneered. "More pig shit to shovel."

I couldn't think of an answer to that, and Portia took his arm and they strolled off laughing.

The very next day Morris Stanhope arrived in London and called from a hotel in Bloomsbury. He told me to join him for dinner at four o'clock sharp.

That's awfully early, I said.

"I didn't have lunch."

Winston and Clemmy hardly ever ate before eight and lots of times it was nine; sometimes dinner wasn't over before midnight. What with cocktails before and all the wine with dinner and brandies afterward to settle the meal, as Winston put it, there were times I plowed into bed with my clothes on and sometimes even my shoes. Not him, though. He went to his study and put in three or four hours writing books and speeches or articles for the newspapers.

You matched his schedule or went hungry. The cook, an old cow with chins down to her bosom, didn't care for outsiders in her kitchen. She threatened me with a big spoon once when I came downstairs looking for something to eat.

The butler apologized later. "She didn't know who you were, sir."

I said never mind, my man. That's how you talk to the lower classes over there. They wouldn't put up with it here.

Stanhope led me to a fish and chips joint a long ways off where every-one had dirty hands from work and wore a cloth cap. "I asked a man in the street where you could get a decent meal and not be robbed and he said this was the place." He hadn't changed a bit, still mean and hard-faced as a statue. "When are you coming back home? My daughter's not getting any younger."

They haven't told me.

"What do you do here?"

I'm afraid I can't say, sir.

"Why not?" His eyes got narrow.

It's secret.

"Secret—humph. I see a lot of people in uniform over here. I suppose the fools are getting ready for another of their wars. Well, they won't trick us into it a second time."

The waitress brought fish and chips wrapped in greasy newspapers.

"That suit you're wearing looks expensive," he said, pushing a chip into his mouth.

He leaned forward for a closer look. "How much was it?"

I don't know, I said.

"They let you walk out the door without paying?"

The bill went to the Navy.

"A silk lining! That probably cost as much as any five I've got in my closet."

He groused about the waste of tax money, one of his favorite subjects. I gave a nod or shook my head now and then to show I was paying attention.

"Well, there's nothing to be done about it under this president. Power has driven him mad. I'm meeting tomorrow with some people who want to distribute my furniture in India. Want to come along and see how I squeeze 'em? It'll give you an idea how to operate."

The truth is I was cooling off on Penelope. A few widows sitting on huge fortunes had given me encouragement at various balls and parties, and I was feeling my way with them. A couple had older sons who might be troublesome.

"Old turkey-necked coquettes wearing too much rouge," Randolph sneered.

Their vintage bothered me not a whit; wine's better aged in a barrel. I suppose word was getting around that I was a tiger 'twixt the sheets. Your average Englishman's not much in that department, or so I was told by more than a few of the ladies.

Winston had warned there was muttering about my "crude fortune hunting" in the clubs, and I should watch my step in light of the sensitive nature of my mission and so on. You might not like hearing this, dear, but we're all sinners in a wicked world.

I'd like to see a top-notch businessman work his magic, I told Stanhope, but unfortunately I have to meet a man at the embassy.

"All day?"

Our lives are being shortened by overwork, I said. A committee is going to the ambassador to complain.

"Hard work never hurt anybody. I'd turn that committee out of the office and give them more to do. They wouldn't try that trick again."

My plan to marry Penelope might have been on the back burner—I'm letting the chips fly where they may no matter how it makes me look—but I didn't want to shut off the possibility. You never know what's going to happen next in this old life, and you don't want to burn a bridge you might need in the future. Waiter! Another bottle.

"How much longer will you be gone?" Stanhope asked me.

You'll have to ask the Navy.

"I warn you that attorney is slinking around. Penelope might like you this much better"—he held thumb and finger a smidgeon apart—"but I wouldn't count him out if I were in your shoes. It would help if you wrote real letters. She showed me a couple from you; big handwriting on small bits of paper that said you're all right and how's she? I'm not much of a hand at letter writing myself, but then I'm not scheming to marry a rich woman." He waved a gnarled finger back and forth. "A word to the wise."

I made a show of being humble and grateful for his advice, but he was a hard man to fool. Two months later I got a letter with a newspaper clipping about Penelope being engaged to the lawyer. "You missed the boat," he wrote. I never did hear from her.

But by that time I was courting the widow of a baron with a stately home in Norfolk, a hunting lodge in Scotland, and a grand twenty-room apartment in Mayfair. Lady Cybil Hemingford was twenty years older than me, and had more than a little gray in her hair—beautiful hair by the way that she put up in combs—but she could still kick up her heels. She knew everyone in London society where, by the way, Winston was about as popular as ants at a picnic.

"Even though you're cousins, I don't know see why you spend so much time with him. Everyone thinks he's a bore and—what's it called?—a war monger. No one cares a snap about Czechoslovakia or those other awful foreign places that are in the papers every day." She and her set wanted to bury the hatchet with Germany, and the rest of Europe could go hang as far as they were concerned.

"Hitler is the only man who can keep Stalin's Asiatic hordes in check," Sir Aubrey Barnswallow told me at a cocktail party. It was one of those affairs where men in tuxedos fiddle high-brow music nobody listens to, but people talk louder to be heard over their racket and soon they're roaring away.

"My understanding from a private source high in the government—we went to Harrow together—is they'll agree to leave the empire alone for a free hand in Eastern Europe. We'd better accept the offer while we still can." Barnswallow was a big shot in trade, tons of money. He wore a monocle like a lot of the older gents did back then. You don't see them much anymore.

I reported what he said to Winston at lunch the next day, and he got a thoughtful look. "Have you noticed how many women these days wear bracelets with Nazi charms?" he said.

Can't say that I have, I said.

"They seem to dangle from every other wrist in Mayfair, and young men wear their hair in that slanted way across the forehead, like Hitler. I suppose they will be giving that stiff-armed salute before long."

Along about this time the abdication crisis blew up and Winston was busy night and day so I didn't see much of him. First he was trying to find a way the king could marry Wallis and keep his job. When that didn't work out, he tried to grease the way for him to leave the country with enough jack to live in his usual style. Winston hoped they could ease back home one day without a lot of fuss.

"Time is a great healer," he said.

"The president is very interested in this," my stepfather wrote in the middle of it all. "He wants more detail if you can spare the time, but do not take away from your official duties."

They thought I was working my tail off, though the truth of it was it was often dawn before I got home from playing cards or...[Here he winked.] The British press kept a lid on, which meant Franklin suspected there were plenty of juicy details he wasn't getting. Like I said, he loved gossip he could pass on before anyone else.

The problem was that fighting for the king put Winston on the outs again with just about everybody else in the country. People said he'd thrown away all the credit he had finally built up after all of those years as a pariah with the crowd that ran England.

A book was published that said, and let me think until I get it right. "Those who came out as King's champions were an unprepossessing company, an unstable politician, flitting from party to party, extreme reactionary, and himself first fruit of the famous snob-dollar marriage; half alien and wholly undesirable."

Winston gave me a sad look when he put the book down. His hide is a thick as an alligator about politics, but he's a softy about his family, especially his mom. "My parents were a love match if ever there was one, and there was very little money on either side. In fact they could only live in the smallest way possible to people in London society."

I couldn't say whether my own folks were a love match. My real pa went off to the Amazon to look for a gold mine and was never seen again. I sometimes wondered if he was swinging in a hammock with a gang of little bastards underfoot. He wasn't the most reliable man, from what I heard. My mom didn't talk much about him, but sometimes she'd say he made her laugh. I think she missed that. There weren't many laughs with the Senator.

Winston asked my opinion about battleships. This was something I knew about for a change. He said the Royal Navy was planning to build more of them with ten fourteen-inch guns on four turrets.

I told him we liked nine sixteen-inch guns on three turrets. Forty percent more striking power that way.

"Our experts say there is the possibility shells interfere with each another in flight."

That doesn't worry us, I said. That extra turret adds weight, and the Royal Navy has to make up for it with lighter armor plating. So less punch and a thinner skin.

I said the Royal Navy's new battleships, *Hood* and the others, were already obsolete given the bottoms the Germans had laid down, not to mention what the Japs were up to. The Senator told me an enormous hemp curtain hid something they were building in one of their shipyards. He must have got that from Harry or the president.

Cybil was a great one for suddenly lighting out for her lodge in Scotland to fish or shoot. Servants were sent ahead and we followed in her Bentley. She wore a chinchilla cape and we had a tartan robe across our laps. Lord, that's a cold place, wind and fog day after day. My theory is that's why everyone is so sour. It's no place for a southern boy, that's for sure. You wolfed down all the groceries you could for enough body heat to keep from freezing. That probably explains haggis, which is guts cooked in a sheep's stomach. Makes your own churn to think about it, don't it? Nobody but a Scot would go near it.

Cybil talked me into wearing a kilt from her father's clan—"To get at you faster, my boy," as she put it, meaning they didn't wear underwear. She was a stickler for tradition; insisted on it. Sometimes she'd catch me unawares and take a playful grab for my goolies. Quick as a snake she was. Her hands were so cold I'd jump like I was shot.

Her place up there had a full staff of servants, even though she only made a handful of visits in a year's time. We slept in a Chippendale four-poster with a blue silk canopy. The bedroom had a Chinese lacquer secretaire that Cybil said was worth a fortune. I was in the lap of luxury and enjoying every minute.

One afternoon the postmaster bicycled up from Ardersier on the Firth of Moray, a miserable little place that was the closest town. He said there'd been a telephone call and come quick as they'd be calling back. I rode on her crofter's motorbike with my kilt flapping. My balls were the size of walnuts when I got there. Pardon the off color, but it's true.

"Brady," a voice said when I was put through to our embassy in London, "you're ordered to report back to Washington ten days from tomorrow."

It'll take at least two weeks, I said.

"Not my problem."

To say it was a shock shoots low. I was in a good setup, and it had gone on so long I was sorta thinking there was no reason why it couldn't stay that way. That's the thing about grooves; you think you're in solid but one good bump and you're knocked on your rear. Sometimes it's for the good and sometimes not. There's no way of knowing at the time.

Cybil was a grand old gal, high spirited and all that. A lot of fun. If she hadn't been killed in the Blitz, we probably would have married and I'd be rich today.

CHAPTER 8

W E BOWLED THROUGH THE VIRGINIA COUNTRYSIDE BOUND FOR A PLACE praised in the gourmet newsletter for meat rubbed with special spices of a secret nature and roasted to perfection. Brilliant orange Butterfly Weed and yellow Black-eyed Susan growing alongside the roads were profuse and heavy-headed from the spring rains. I was nervous, hoping the restaurant lived up to its billing. He was cross when they didn't measure up, and was already in a bad mood because his knees and feet were troubling him. They had worn out from all the miles he had walked as a fugitive.

"A long way to drive," Captain Brady remarked, "not that I mind. It's a beautiful afternoon, not too warm and not too cold." He looked over at me. "Nice dress."

I felt myself blush as always when he paid a compliment; at the same time I was nettled. I strive to rise above the shallow and the superficial, but praise from him undermined that goal. The poets say beauty is fleeting. Plainness is not, alas; it lasts a lifetime. I mention this to demonstrate the effect even the captain's casual gallantries had on someone not accustomed to hearing them.

He liked to eat early, and we were usually back at the old soldiers' home by eight o'clock. "I saw in many a dawn in the old days, but now I need my beauty sleep. It's the damned insomnia from my years on the run. I never knew when one of your assassins would bust through the door."

I had almost given up trying to convince him. "I've said..."

"Yeah, yeah," he said, waving me to silence. "But pretty soon the bosses are going to start pressuring you to work faster. I know how the system works."

A few minutes later his mood lifted and he remarked on all the newer cars on the road—it seemed everyone was buying one—particularly Oldsmobiles and Buicks.

"Streamlined is the word. Back in my day, cars were as square as a box of crackers and they came in one color, black."

The chicken masala with small red potatoes at Enrique's was excellent, and I breathed a sigh of relief. Captain Brady praised the Pinot Noir from France as "damned good." I always brought him an expensive cigar as it made him more expansive *après le diner.* He lit the cigar from the candle on our table.

"This reminds me of the ones Winston smoked, always the finest Havanas; ten or twelve a day. Clemmie said he stank of tobacco, but Winston didn't give a damn. "Let those offended by my cheroot not approach my person."

Calling for another balloon of cognac and more coffee, he grinned. "You don't really mind me drawing this out. You enjoy listening to an old sailor with his locker full of yarns."

I couldn't deny that I did. To my surprise, he reached across the table and put his hand on mine. It was like an electric shock went through me.

"But transcribing all those tapes; what a job! There must be miles by now, and the best is yet to come."

* * *

Winston went off to the south of France with Clemmie to paint and then they were going on to Monte Carlo to gamble, so I didn't get a chance to say goodbye. When I told Randolph I was going home, he said, "About time" and went back to his newspaper.

A run of bad luck had left me a little on the shorts—a lot if you want the truth—but I judged that hitting Cybil up for a loan wouldn't go over very well. She was death on the gigolos hoping to get their hooks into the widows in her set. Parasites, she called them. Leeches.

So the voyage home was quite a comedown. The Bureau of Supplies and Accounts was on their high horse, and my proceed order didn't come with travel money. That was a violation of naval regulations, and I could cite you chapter and verse. You would've thought the bastards had to dig the money out of their own pockets and their kids needed shoes. But the trouble they made about the mix-ups in expenses made turning the other cheek the better part of valor. If you work in government you know there are a thousand ways to screw you. They could claim they couldn't find authorization because I was outside the chain of command, or there was some paperwork missing that had to be countersigned a dozen times, and so on into the night. Long story short, I had to ask the Senator to use his connections to get me a berth home and told Cybil that seeing me off at the dock would be too rough on me.

"Oh, my dear boy," she cried, "I didn't know you had these hidden depths."

I told her I didn't like people to know how soft I was down deep.

Women like mush like that from a man. The strong, silent type? Forget it. Your average woman wants nothing to do with them. Oh, they'll settle for one if the other choice is talking to the wall, but they won't be happy about it. Most men don't see that because they don't know women. They turn on the radio when they come home or dive into the sports pages. Not saying it's right or wrong; just the way it is. You have to work hard to know what makes women tick and keep updating yourself because they can change in a minute. Of course, I don't have to tell you.

I didn't want Cybil to see the Greek steamer the Senator's office booked me on. It was a scow hauling stinking hides to New York and a few passengers who couldn't even afford steerage on a better class of ship. You could smell her a hundred yards off. I had a cabin just big enough to turn around in. The smell got into your hair and clothes and took away your appetite, not that the food was much to speak of.

"This meat, it is bad," said a fellow I met named Samuel Grossman.

We sat at dinner the first night. He was a small Jewish businessman from Berlin with a heavy accent. Good clothes but they hung on him like he'd lost plenty of weight. He had the saddest eyes, and I didn't like to look in them. It was like a sad violin began to play in your mind.

He was glad to be out of Germany. "I'm the last to go," he said. "It took every pfennig I had, a fortune if you must know, but my whole family I got out."

I heard it's bad, I said.

Winston's network of spies told him that all the time. He asked the *Times* to write about it, but like I said before, they had agreed with Chamberlain to keep it hushed up. Ten Downing thought publicity would only make things worse.

Grossman was right about the meat, and I passed on it. The other passengers didn't, though, and you could hardly sleep that night from them heaving their guts out in the head. It sounded like feeding time at the lion house. Sorry, dear, it's not the nicest thing to talk about at dinner.

"The world has no idea," Grossman told me. "Jewish men on the Prater in Berlin were made to take their clothes off and walk on all fours. This happened two weeks ago. Jewish women were made to climb ladders into trees and like birds chirp. Many commit suicides, whole families. Worse will come." He shook his head. "Far worse."

I offered to show him some card tricks, but he said he didn't feel up to it just then.

"I'm thinking of the Jews who thinks this passes and life goes back where it was. They will not see what to me is clear as windows."

Next morning we stood at the fantail talking through handkerchiefs held to our faces. "How do you come to be on such a ship as this?" he asked.

Connections, I said.

"Some connections."

The Senator used that shipping firm for hog hides he sent around the world. He had a sense of humor, but it was a mean one; you had to take what he dished out and come up smiling. Let him know he got under your skin and he came at you all the harder.

A deck hand told me you got used to the stink after a couple of days and he was right. The captain, a fat Greek, got sick like the others. He sent the chef below to shovel coal, and we never saw him again. The food didn't get better, but at least people weren't busy at both ends.

A car was waiting when the ship docked in New Jersey just as twilight fell. The driver honked and waved from behind rolled up windows. He was a guy in a porkpie hat and a cigar in his teeth.

"Put your luggage in the trunk," he shouted through the window. "I don't want to open the door. Christ Almighty, I smelled you guys five minutes after I saw you. Whatever you brought, please take it back."

When I got in he said he was from the Hotel Pierre where I was booked courtesy of the White House. We pulled away and a minute later he rolled down the window.

"Hope you don't mind the wind back there, pal," he said, "but I can't breathe."

After a few days you don't smell it anymore, I said.

He said something I didn't catch. He hung his head out the window and drove with one hand.

The hotel lobby was crowded and people shot me hard looks. The desk clerk covered his nose and two couples left the elevator when I got in. I would have been turned away if the White House hadn't made the reservation. I'm not the thin-skinned type, but I admit I was feeling a little sensitive. It was a real nice suite with a good view. As soon as the bellboy brought my trunk up I had a long, soapy shower. I was just drying off with a towel when the telephone rang.

"Lieutenant? Harry Hopkins here. Welcome home."

Thank you sir, I said.

"Come to my room and let's have a talk."

Aye, aye, sir.

"Aw, you can knock that stuff off, Lowell. I'm just a civilian for cryin' out loud."

He just about lived in the White House at the time and actually moved in not long after. But if that's the way he wanted to play it that was okay with me. When I got to his room he offered a drink and said the Senator had passed on every letter to him.

"Maybe a little too much about the royal family for my taste, but the president liked the stuff about Wallis Simpson. A pretty hot number I take it."

That was all they talked about for months, I said.

"You gave us some valuable stuff about the German flying clubs."

Even the RAF underestimated them. Winston's figures shook everybody up.

"He's stiffened spines; that's for sure. Will Chamberlain give him a spot in the cabinet? A man can only do so much from the back bench."

A lot of Conservatives hate him, I said, and the Labour Party remembers him wanting to mow down workers with machine gun fire in the general strike.

"You're satisfied he's not a drunkard? Franklin brings it up all the time. I think it's because of Eleanor; she's got a thing about drinking. Christ, as if any of us are teetotalers."

Winston likes his grog, I said, no question about it. But it doesn't get in the way.

Harry had a glass of milk in his hand and rubbed his stomach like it hurt. He looked the same as the first time, sick and skinny as a rail, a suit too big for him and his tie twisted and pulled down. But he had a winning way, and I wasn't surprised to learn he had been a student body president in college. What's the word—debonair? Yeah, that's it. He might look seedy, but definitely a man of the world.

"The trouble brewing over there is what's finally pulled us out of the depression," he said. "We were sliding backward again until the Germans started up. Franklin even went back to Hoover's way of doing things, and they didn't work any better for him. Don't quote me, but thank God for Europe's troubles. Factories are hiring and the wheels are turning. We're rearming them and us at the same time. I can see the time coming when a man who doesn't have a job is a lazy son of a bitch. Do you smell something bad in here?"

If you're around a strong smell long enough, breathing it in and out, it must come out your pores. A lot of sailors smell like a bottle of cheap gin after a leave. I sweated every drop of booze out of them the next day, you can bet your bottom dollar on that. I had drummers and trumpeters practice ruffles and flourishes alongside while they chipped paint. Not exactly what you want with a hangover. Hopkins got up and looked around in corners.

"Something's rotten in here. For twenty bucks a day you'd think they'd give you a room that didn't smell like a slaughterhouse."

I said it was another example of how the country was going to the dogs.

"I ought to complain to the manager."

I went to the window and pretended to look at the view. When I came back I took a chair farther away.

"Did you read that I decided not to run for president?" he said. "Health problems."

I gave a nod to say I had even though I hadn't.

"I thought about running after I left the Department of Commerce, but the chief decided he'd go for a third term. I was toying with the idea of going back to Iowa and running a movie theater, but he talked me into staying on as his assistant. That means I get all the hot potatoes."

I said I hoped I wasn't one of them.

Roosevelt knew thousands of people, but people in the know said he had only five friends, Hopkins being one of the closest. You don't want to be near power when something is in the wind. The candle gives off light, but the moth gets burned. Waiter, this glass is emp…

Hold on, you know who that is over there? Bill Donovan! He started up the OSS. Hey, Bill! Bill! How ya doin'? Lowell Brady. Good to see you again, buddy. He looks like we caught him at something. The man's a better Catholic than the pope, yet I wonder if that's his wife. She looks a little young, but she could be a second wife. I've got a few stories about Bill when I get around to it. Waiter! This glass is empty. So Harry goes on complimenting me on my work in London and I start to relax, even puff my chest out.

"The chief was tickled that he had someone telling us what's really going on over there. He thinks you're a master spy."

Strange as it seems, people seemed to have forgotten Churchill was feeding me all that stuff. An entire intelligence agency would only get a fraction of what I passed on to the Senator. Churchill was playing his own game, of course. He was already thinking ahead to when he'd be prime minister and wanted Washington to see how great it would be to have him as a partner. I didn't let on, of course. Why should I? Modesty never helped any career, like I told you before. Nobody beats the drum for you because they're too busy trying to push ahead of the crowd themselves. Take credit for other people's work if you can get away with it because that's what they're doing to you. It's the way of the world, darlin'.

"He's jumping you up a couple steps," Harry said, smiling through his cigarette smoke. "You'll be a full commander."

I snapped off a salute. Give the Commander-in-Chief my thanks, I said. I'd be up there with the whiz kids and grinds from my academy class, the guys who kissed me off as a plodder. I could hardly wait for the look on their faces.

"Give it to him yourself," Harry said. "We'll see him tomorrow in Washington when you get a letter of commendation. I saw your mother last week at a reception. A powerful woman; I guess it takes someone like that to keep your father in line."

He's my stepfather, I said.

"She's a friend of Eleanor, so the chief steers clear of her."

Well, I guess I'll be going back to London in a week or two.

Harry shook his head. "We called you home because Franklin has a hunch it's just a matter of time before Winston is in the cabinet. You're going to work at the White House."

Not that old job! I blurted it out.

Harry winked. "The president thinks you're a born spy. He's wants you to work as another set of eyes and ears for him. Got plans for dinner tonight? We want you to pick somebody's brain, an English newspaperman named Hector Bywater. He just might be as good a spy as you. They sent him over here back in 1916 to find out who was planting delayed-action bombs in their ships. He found out it was Germans working out of a liner interned in Hoboken. There were big headlines in London and plenty of red faces over here. The man's a bloodhound. He discovered that Italy was building fourteen new warships in secret, and was the first to tell us about Germany's pocket battleships."

What am I supposed to find out, I asked.

"Hell, you're the spy not me. He knows more than anybody what the Japs are up to. We can't lose sight of them while we're concentrating on Europe. Just get him talking, milk him for what he knows." He looked at his watch. "You're meeting him at Dario's across town. You'll just make it if you leave right now."

He peeled a couple of twenties off a roll when I said I only had British currency in my wallet. A single pound note if you want to know was all that stood between me and beggary until I talked to Mother.

"Tell Bywater the chief is one of his biggest fans," he said. "One other thing. This is just between us; the president doesn't want you to tell the Navy. If Bywater gives you anything good he'll spring it on the admirals just to enjoy their amazement. It's a kid's game, but that's the boss."

Bywater was waiting for me at the bar, a beer and shot man from the glasses in front of him. A flower was in his lapel.

"Glad to meet you," he said, giving me a big paw to shake.

He was a hulking guy who looked like those plug-uglies promoters hire to tune up good fighters. Mashed-in nose and a thick brow. The funny thing was he had a high voice like George Patton. The sergeants had to warn the troops not to laugh when George started talking. That girly voice didn't fit the blood-and-guts image.

Bywater wore a baggy tweed suit and shoes that never saw a lick of polish if I was any judge. You come across people who don't care what they look like. I never pass a mirror without checking things out. He dropped the flower on the floor and ground it under his heel.

"Made me feel like a fairy," he said. "The only man in the room with a flower, for crissake. Tell Harry that's not on in the future. I'd rather be the man in the corner diggin' in his nose to the second knuckle."

I ordered a round and we made small talk until a waiter said our table was ready. Bywater was in the country calling on newspapers to find buyers for his articles.

"Bloody 'ell," he said all of a sudden, "that's a bad smell even for a dago joint. Didn't notice it before; it's enough to put you off your feed. Other people are looking around, too."

I asked how he got into the writing line to get him off that. As you know, it's the rare man who doesn't think he'd make a story for a magazine. Some think they'd be good for a whole book. Makes you laugh.

"I was born Trafalgar Day in 1894," Bywater said. "I think it's why I've always had an interest in naval affairs. On my birthday they opened up the Royal Dockyards, the closest thing to heaven I could imagine. Big ships and men in smart uniforms; everything spic and span Bristol fashion. Sometimes the royals came out. Oh, it was glorious. The war kicked the stuffing out of us, but back then the empire was at its height. I was quite the scholar for my years. I wrote an essay when I was ten about the Battle of Yalu River. It would have been published except the editor found out my age.

"The Chinese sixteen-inch guns should have carried the day but the Japanese cruisers with fast-firing six-inch guns sank or drove ashore five ships to one of theirs. Chinese shells were ten times heavier, but the Japs fired ten times faster. It ended up a slaughter. Not as bad as the pasting they gave the Russians, but bloody enough. Mr. Hopkins said you wanted to ask some questions."

I didn't have a clue what to ask. Luckily, he didn't prompting.

"A showdown with Japan is inevitable as I said in *The Great Pacific War.*" He paused. "You *have* read it, haven't you?"

I quote it everywhere, I said.

"Did you read my earlier work, *Sea-power in the Pacific: a study of the American-Japanese naval problem?*"

A powerful work, I said. I hadn't heard of that, either.

"It's the same book except one's a novel. I wrote the second for the chap who'd walk a mile out of his way to avoid a fact. The publisher wanted me to put in a female character and some love tripe, but I told him to bugger off. The Japs were mightily upset that I wrote they'd lose a war with you Yanks."

I remembered to tell him the president was a fan.

"There was a time when he wasn't. He thought the last war was so bad there'd never be another, and anybody who thought different was old-fashioned. He wrote that drivel in a magazine as an answer to my first book. New or old-fashioned, makes no difference. Neither changes the fact Japan wants China, Australia and New Zealand for her surplus population. The other two will get the same treatment China's getting when the time's right. I take it you're a back shop man."

I asked how he'd know that.

"You're too handsome for field work," Bywater said. "I know what you're thinking: people notice my sort, too. How can someone as ugly as me blend in?"

I guess I should have disagreed out of politeness.

"Looking like an ape is as good as not being noticed at all. People think you're stupid and their mind moves on. It's my pa's fault, curse his black soul. He was a Welshman who liked his drink. He knocked all of us kids around, and Mummy got her share as well. Pa was the rolling stone type. He could talk some in eight languages, was a traveling salesman, engraver, a jack-of-all-trades. He came over as an ordinary seaman and jumped ship. There wasn't anything he couldn't do. He rode for the Pony Express and was mixed up with Buffalo Bill Cody's shows for a time. Before that, he was a secret agent for the Union Army. He knew a lot, but nothing real deep. He didn't like to be corrected, especially by snot-nose kids. That's where most of my beatings came from. When he'd make a mistake about a naval matter, I'd say so and show him in one of my Brassey's Naval Annuals. *Whack*, I'd get a backhand for being right. I got stubbornness from him, so I didn't back down, especially after he burnt a stack of my Brasseys in the fireplace. He twisted my arm behind my back and made me watch them burn. We engaged in fisticuffs when I was older and he bested me every time. He got hit by a trolley and died, otherwise who knows what I'd look like today." He tapped his skull. "Fortunately, nothing up here got damaged.

"From seventeen to nineteen, I worked as a streetcar conductor for the Union Railway in New York. We carried German immigrants to work and back, and I picked up their lingo, which was to help years later. You probably heard how I discovered the German saboteurs. They sent forty-two British ships down to Davey Jones' Locker before I tipped off the New York City Bomb Squad."

Yes, I said, we were aware of it. I lifted an eyebrow to say we knew a whole lot more than that. He called my bluff without a blink.

"Right," he said, "it only took your lot sixteen years to find out I was working over here for the British secret service. I got a job with the *New York Herald* selling papers and worked my way up to reporter where I got noticed by Gordon Bennett himself, the publisher. You've heard of him?"

I hadn't, but of course I said yes.

"He was a man with a vile temper who insisted that people call him Commodore. But give the man credit, he got things done. He paid for the

Stanley expedition that found Livingston. He did it to build circulation, but still. There are dozens of stories about him. When he was engaged to be married he arrived drunk at her parents' mansion and pissed into the fireplace in front of everyone, though some say it was the piano. Engagement over! He was sailing his yacht on the Aegean and was on a collision course with an American warship. It wasn't the Commodore's style to give way to anyone, and they would have rammed if an editor hadn't grabbed the wheel in the nick of time. Gordon Bennett—you always said both names— was so furious he put the man off on an uninhabited island and sailed away. It was only after others convinced him he could be charged with murder that he sent a boat back."

It got tedious—there were far more stories than I've told you—and I was sorry I got him started. I pity you having to listen to all those old-timers rattling away. There might be one in a hundred who isn't a bore, and chances are he's crazy or a liar.

"The Commodore is who got me started on Japan," Bywater said. "He was convinced they'd attack America because they were mad you took Hawaii. They'd had their eye on those pretty islands themselves. It's why he was against the Spanish-American War; he thought the Nipponese would use the opportunity to spring upon your fleet at San Francisco. They're fighting in China because they need her natural resources for a major war."

I said wouldn't most people consider China a major war?

"It's just a warm up for the main event. Some say they'll fight the Soviets next, which is what the Imperial Japanese Army wants. But their navy says it's you Americans who stand in the way the most."

Not as much as the English, I said.

"I'm afraid we're clapped out. We've got as much as we can handle with the Germans. It's up to you Yanks to hold the line out there."

Bywater began to draw a map on the table cloth. "Your admirals believe if the Japs attack the Philippines the garrison will hold out until your fleet steams to the rescue. But think of it. Your Atlantic fleet has to assemble and transit the Panama Canal to join the Pacific fleet. Port facilities in Honolulu are third rate and there are no fuel depots en route, meaning your ships have to carry everything they need to get there and back. Like a bullet, a fleet becomes weaker the farther it sails. And slower—a fouled bottom slows a battleship to fifteen knots. Distances are enormous in the Pacific, and there are no repair docks to fix what breaks down. You agreed not to fortify Guam—big mistake. When the Japanese attack, they'll have it under control by the evening of the first day."

The waiter asked him to stop drawing on the table cloth. Bywater glowered but put the pencil away.

"If you remember Admiral Mahan's doctrine, command of the sea is the key to military expeditions against hostile territory. We abandoned amphibious war after Gallipoli: half million casualties, three battleships sunk and three badly damaged—a disaster. But the Japanese have been practicing landings against a hostile shore for years, and must be pretty good by now. They got a forty-nine-foot landing craft with a bow ramp that can make eight knots carrying a hundred and twenty soldiers. Their way of training is brutal, but it works. If you survive, you're already battle hardened; the enemy can't dish out much worse. Their families get a letter saying they should feel honored their sons are serving the emperor, and from now on the army or navy is their family."

Why take Guam knowing it means war, I said.

"They have Formosa, they have the Carolinas. When they have Guam, they close the gap in the defensive perimeter around the home islands. A third of your ships would be sunk by the time you closed with their fleet."

I laughed and said we didn't think much of Jap fighting ability. That was true enough at the time.

"They think you're like the Romans under Caligula, corrupted by vice and luxury. They believe they'll win any war because of *issho kemei*, which means total commitment. Fanaticism is what we'd call it. They are a very confident race, your Nipponese. Cunning, too. *Hagakure*, the book of the samurai, says, 'Walk with a real man a hundred yards and he will tell you at least seven lies.' They believe lying to the outside world is the intelligent thing to do."

Who might your source be for all this, I asked casually.

It had popped into my head I'd score points if I could cut out the middle man. Bywater saw through me like window glass.

"A newspaperman worth his salt never gives up his sources." He took a careful look around. "The buggers are building a whole fleet in secret, more new ships than the rest of the other powers put together. I figured that out from their national budget. A fourth of it goes for naval construction."

Ridiculous, I said. They're poor as dirt.

I knew because I was as an ensign aboard *Nevada* when we sailed there to show the flag. Men wore straw clothes and rags for shoes: it was a country of scarecrows.

"Japan is starving itself to greatness," he said. "It's the only way they can become a first-class power on the schedule laid out in the time of the Meiji emperor. General Arthur MacArthur said a long time ago they were planning to attack you chaps."

You mean Douglas MacArthur, I said.

"No, his father, Arthur. He wrote that in 1908 when he was in Manila in charge of putting down the insurrection. A few years later, there was talk about Germany, Japan and Mexico forming a secret military alliance to keep you busy while the U-boats starved us to death. Nothing came of it because British intelligence deciphered the Zimmerman telegram that laid out the whole scheme and gave it to you. That's German arrogance for you; they couldn't believe anybody could read their codes. Pride goeth before the fall.

"The Japs are planning a fleet of three hundred ships with a displacement of 1.1 million tons. You Yanks expect to build 1.4 million tons for a *two-ocean* navy. Japan is building at least two and quite possibly four super battleships. They're far bigger than the five King George V Class bottoms we laid down and the two new battleships you'll have ready in 1941. So yours and ours will be obsolete the day they're launched. Care for a night cap?"

I was going to drop by the Stork Club—I always had good luck with the ladies there—and I didn't want this ugly brute scaring them off. So I suggested the restaurant bar.

"I'll give you an example of *issho kemmei*. School children go without coats in the dead of winter to share the suffering of Jap soldiers in China. Women gave up dresses and kimonos for gray pantaloons, and they aren't allowed to wear lipstick or makeup. No more than three curls in their hair. People don't speak English anymore because it's the language of the enemy.

Fortune tellers can give only happy predictions. Get the idea? It's harder than ever to get information out of Japan. If you're a foreigner, you're always watched. The Reuters man in Tokyo, a friend of mine named Melville Cox, was arrested on espionage charges. They said he jumped to his death from a window, but the embassy man counted twenty needle marks on his arms."

The bartender was a young man with a look that said he was above it all. We kick that out of them in their first week in the Navy.

"There it is again," Bywater said. "Young man, that odor—don't you smell it for God's sake?"

"Not before you sat down."

I followed Bywater outside. "Cheek of the fellow," he said.

As we parted, he fished a stogie out of a coat pocket. "One last thing," he said lighting it with a kitchen match. "Tell the president when the Japs attack, it'll be without warning. That's the code of Bushido."

That was the first and last time I talked to Bywater. When I passed on what he said to Harry, I mentioned that he looked like a caveman and I wouldn't put much stock in what he said. I know what you're thinking, dear, you shouldn't judge a book by its cover. He was certainly right about things. He died later under mysterious circumstances, and some said he was murdered. Here's the dessert cart. Looks like some hard choices, but we don't have to limit ourselves to one do we?

Memorandum

March 27, 1953

To: The Director

From: T.E. Hawley, SAC

Subject: William Donovan

Background:

Mr. DONOVAN, a prominent Wall Street lawyer and head of the Office of Strategic Services (OSS) during the war, contacted our Washington office regarding Navy CAPTAIN

LOWELL BRADY. Believing him deceased, Mr. DONOVAN was
surprised to be greeted by that person at Morgan's Chop
House in Arlington, Virginia. He was with an unidentified
female. He gave us three of the six numbers on the Maryland
license plate on the car she was driving. Mr. DONOVAN said
this information would be of personal interest to the
Director and should be conveyed to you as soon as possible.

/T.E. Hawley

Tolson _____

Simmons _____

Appleby _____

Coronet _____

Blivens _____

Gaskins _____

Jaspers _____

Kingsley _____

CHAPTER 9

A WEEK AFTER THAT DINNER I WAS CALLED INTO THE OFFICE OF ARNOLD Pettigrew, the assistant secretary of the Smithsonian Institution, whom I had only seen speak at staff meetings about upcoming exhibitions. Sleek as a seal, Pettigrew had a reputation for shrewdness in bureaucratic politics and finesse with Congressional committees. This last made him more valuable to the Smithsonian than for any scholarly competence he might possess. With him was a stern man who made Pettigrew nervous to judge from the rapid way he smoked his cigarette.

"Harriet Gallatin," he said, "this is Ted Hawley. He'd like to ask a few questions."

"What about?"

"You've been talking to a man named Crockett?" Hawley was broad as a door, had short hair and had a square jaw that looked as heavy as a ship's timber. His pale eyes glittered like an alpine lake in high summer. He wore a dark suit and white shirt with a quiet tie. His physical presence was heavy and intimidating, and it felt like there wasn't enough oxygen in the room for all of us.

"Yes, I have." My heart was sinking.

"May I ask what about?"

"He's one of many veterans I have been interviewing about wartime service."

"Oh, yes," Pettigrew said. His eyebrows jumped and he ran fingers through his thin blonde hair. "I've heard about that; lingering effects of battle fatigue. An interesting area of study, entirely legitimate."

Hawley's glance said he'd be the judge of that.

"Why did you pick him?" he asked me.

"A janitor told me he was the most interesting man at the old soldiers' home. So, naturally…"

"What's the janitor's name?" He took out a gold pen and a small notebook.

"Why do you want to know?"

"Tell him!" Pettigrew's nerves seemed ready to snap.

"He said his name was Alessandro Manzoni."

"It sounds like you have doubts," Hawley said.

"He was a man with a mop and a bucket. Why would I doubt him?"

"Mr. Hawley is just trying to get at the facts," Pettigrew said.

"The facts about what?" I said.

"How has this man described his service?" Hawley said.

"We haven't actually got into that."

"What have you been talking about?"

"The commodore"—I plunged on knowing I was getting in deeper—"has been telling me his complaints about the old soldiers' home." I turned to Pettigrew. "I'm using Dr. Browbrow's technique of gradually warming the subject up."

"Dr. Broadbrow," Pettigrew explained to Hawley, "believes there is a better chance at gaining the truth by befriending a subject and drawing him out."

Hawley favored faster means, I thought. It wasn't hard to imagine a rubber hose in his meaty hand.

"What is your interest in Mr. Crockett?" I asked.

"I can't tell you that." He took a leather wallet from an inside pocket and showed me an FBI badge. "But I can tell you it's not idle curiosity."

My mind froze. *So Captain Brady was telling the truth.* I refocused again as he was saying, "…would be kept in strict confidence."

"I'm sorry," I said. "Would you repeat that?"

"I said any information will of course be kept in strict confidence. No worry about that."

"What information?" I asked.

"You're asking Crockett questions, right?" he said patiently. "We want to know what he's saying."

"About what?"

"Just tell us what he says."

"What does it matter what he says?"

"We wouldn't be asking if we didn't think it was important."

"He thinks the food is terrible and the beds aren't changed often enough. The workers aren't respectful toward these men who..."

"I don't mean petty complaints," Hawley interrupted. "Is that all you talk about?"

"So far."

He looked at Pettigrew. "Maybe the pace can be stepped up a bit."

A dagger turned in my stomach. This was exactly what Captain Brady predicted.

"Are you cold?" Pettigrew asked me. "I can close the window."

"I don't think what you're asking is ethical," I said to Hawley.

"What if I were to tell you it's a national security matter?"

In a corner of my mind a voice said it was not too late. Swallow hard and tell him what he wanted to know. I stamped on the thought like it was a spider.

"I wouldn't believe you," I said.

Hawley stood. "I know I hit you with this all of a sudden. I'd like you to think about it. I'll be in touch." He shook our hands perfunctorily and left.

"I suppose it has something to do with the House Un-American Activities Committee." Pettigrew lit a cigarette from the end of another. "You're not a communist?"

"Of course not."

"And never have been?"

"No."

"Has Crockett ever said anything about Stalin? Capitalist masters and workers throwing off their chains—that sort of thing?"

"Not so much as a word."

"I hope to Christ they're not hunting Reds in the Smithsonian. You read about people losing their jobs. Men with PhDs are washing dishes for something they said in the 'Thirties."

When I got back to my office, fortunately empty, I shut the door and sat down. My heart was beating fast and my hands were shaking. I took several deep breaths to steady myself. I needed no further confirmation of Captain Brady's veracity. But how had the FBI connected him to Crockett?

"I shouldn't have waved at Bill Donovan," he told me next time we met. "Don't know what came over me; the wine, I guess. He probably stood behind a tree and wrote down your license number when we left. The FBI tailed you to here. Simple as A, B, C." He smiled in an apologetic way. "It looks like I was wrong about you, not that it matters now."

"But what do they want?"

"What they've always wanted, my trap shut for good. That's why I was on the move all those years. My mother and stepfather died after the war, God bless her but not him. I was a tramp with holes in my shoes when I walked up the dirt road to Crockett's barley farm. He was a cantankerous old guy, a widower without family or friends. Civilians don't like being ordered around like ordinary seamen, but he never adjusted after he left the Navy and took over the family farm. He got it in his head I was a holy man wandering in the wilderness like John the Baptist. I think it was my beard and hair; I had to let them grow because I didn't have money for a barber. Or maybe he'd lived alone for so long he got peculiar. I strung him along with a story about seeking the Lord in the lonely places, and we fell to our knees and he prayed aloud. The man didn't have a skeptical bone in his body when it came to religion, not one. He was a hard-core Old Testament man. Noah and the Ark and Jonah and the whale—he believed it all. All his neighbors were mad at him for one reason or another, and nobody would work for him. The farm was too much for him at his age, and he took me on as a handyman. He paid in cash from a shoe box, having little faith in the banks. He took out plenty for my room and board, but I didn't mind. I was wore out and glad to drop anchor in a safe harbor. I worked in his fields for five years. At night we'd sip cider and discuss the Bible. He knew it backwards and forward, chapter and verse. I put in a comment here and there from what I remembered from chapel at Ironwood School when I wasn't making fart sounds for the other boys. You put your hand in your armpit and bring your arm down like this. Always got a laugh.

"The commodore died peacefully in his sleep. After I found him in the morning, I removed such personal records as I needed to take on his identity, as well as the cash he told me was buried in a tin box by an apple tree. Unfortunately, he didn't tell me which apple tree, so I dug up the ground around a dozen before I found it. I drove his Chevy to the train station, left the keys on the seat, and bought a ticket to Las Vegas.

"It was a sleepy place full of bored women waiting for their divorces to come through. I doubled the commodore's money playing poker and lived high on the hog. Those divorcees didn't like their ex-husbands, but that didn't mean they had sworn off men. I could have married a dozen times if I wanted. Then I lost everything during the worst spell of luck in my life. I held when I should've folded and vice versa. It was a vicious cycle; every gambler has them at some point. That's when I came back and checked into the old soldiers' home for a roof over my head. Then you show up with that recording machine of yours. Now, you're getting all upset. It's not your fault, so don't start crying.

"They were probably surprised I'm still alive. The people who worked the case must be retired or transferred so they have to dig back in the files if they can even find them. Shutting a fellow American up for good isn't so easy in peacetime. This new crowd will know they have to cover their ass every step of the way in case some watchdog committee gets wind of it. They'll come for me in their own good time."

"And *kill* you?"

"Or lock me up until I die. That can't be long now because of my ticker." This was the first time he mentioned a medical problem. He looked off in the distance. "I'd like to get these stories out, but I'd understand if you want to call it quits."

I told him I'd never ever quit, that we owed a duty to History and Truth.

"You might be in danger yourself."

"I'm not afraid," I said. "This is America."

"It may be America isn't what you think it is."

Memorandum

March 28, 1953

To: To T.E. Hawley

From: John Edgar Hoover

Subject: William Donovan

Contact WILLIAM DONOVAN by telephone and inform him that his information was received. There will be no further reply, and you are instructed not to initiate discussions with him regarding this or any other matter without prior approval. Do not discuss this with others in the Bureau or the Department of Justice without permission from this office.

It is unlikely that DONOVAN saw CAPTAIN BRADY as stated. Sources thought to be reliable indicated at the time that he was MIA, and probably killed, while attached to Soviet forces on the Eastern front in 1944. No body was ever found, but this was not unusual under the conditions that prevailed. The Bureau kept his file open until 1947 when it was closed and removed to the storage facility at Bethesda.

To be sure he has not returned to the country after all this time, you are instructed to search through government records kept by the Veterans Administration, Social Security Administration, Navy Department, departments of motor vehicles, etc. Pursue the partial license number. Do not involve others in this work without my approval. If you have difficulty with your supervisor, inform me at once.

Make this your highest priority.

Remove all names from your routing list concerning this subject with the exception of Assistant Director Tolson.

/Hoover

Memorandum

March 31, 1953

To: The Director

From: T.E. Hawley, SAC

Subject: Harriet Gallatin

Background:

WILLIAM DONOVAN notified the Washington Office 3/27/53
that he saw LOWELL BRADY, previously believed deceased, in
Maryland. Through a partial license plate number I was able
to trace the car to HARRIET GALLATIN (born 7/23/1926 in
Hamilton, Mont.) She is a researcher at the Smithsonian who
lives on Harvard Street in the Mount Pleasant neighborhood
of Washington, DC. She has several female roommates.

GALLATIN conducts interviews of veterans for an "oral
history" of the world war. She previously published a
monograph on Old Dan Tucker. She is considered a good worker
by ARNOLD PETTIGREW, an official at the Smithsonian. She
has spent considerable time at the Fillmore Soldiers' Home
with KERMIT CROCKETT, an alleged retired naval officer who
resides there. However, records show that individual died in
1947, so that is an alias this person is using. He generally
matches the description given by DONOVAN. It is uncertain
whether she knows the true identity of CROCKETTif it is
him.

I cannot find any trace of BRADY in the records of
the agencies you mentioned. You said there is a Bureau file
on him, but the records division could not find it. Please
advise of its whereabouts if you have that information.

/T.E. Hawley

Tolson

* * *

So I reported to the White House on Monday morning and they parked me on a bench under a portrait of Grover Cleveland. I worried I might still smell even though I'd drunk gallons of water to flush out the pores. The Secret Service guys hadn't said anything, but they overlook personal stuff. They'll take away a ceremonial dirk or dagger for safety, but somebody who rubs goat piss in his hair for his religion gets passed along same as a Rotarian wearing aftershave. After a few minutes, a guy in banker's pinstripes joined me on the bench.

"Adolph Berle, State Department," he said, sticking out his hand, "Been waiting long, Lieutenant?"

Half an hour, I said. He didn't wrinkle his nose or pinch it shut, so I was starting to relax.

"They telephoned my office to say he was running late."

Nothing new there, I said. Everybody knew Franklin liked to talk.

He looked at his watch. "Will your business take long?"

I said his guess was as good as mine.

A colored servant brought us coffee and Berle and I made small talk. I mentioned that I'd just come from London.

"What's it like over there?"

Cold as a well digger's ass, I said. Foggy, too.

"I mean what's the mood?"

So-so, I'd say.

"Were you attached to the embassy?"

No.

"Something secret, I suppose; I won't ask about it. That was a nasty jolt, the Germans demanding a Polish corridor. Munich just fed their appetite. Peace in our times, what a laugh."

I put on my thoughtful look.

That tramp steamer had inched across the Atlantic, and the captain didn't pass on the wireless news if he even listened to it. I didn't want to look like an idiot, so I said yes, a nasty jolt—couldn't put it better myself.

"These won't be the last demands on Poland."

Bound to be more, I said. No question about it.

"I'd like to be a fly on the wall in the Kremlin." Berle stretched his legs out like he was used to long waits at the White House.

He was a very smart guy. He graduated from Harvard when he was eighteen and got out of law school at twenty-one. That's impressive, but we're leery of eggheads in the Navy. You want people who follow orders instead of thinking up better ways. That sows confusion in the ranks, which are not always sharp as razors. If the tried and true works, why fool with it? To give him credit, Berle came across as a regular guy. He used a few big words I pretended to know, but not all that many considering his background.

"There's no reason to prefer a British empire over a German one other than they treat people somewhat better," he said.

I often say so myself, I said.

"The world situation has a suspicious feel about it. It was New Englanders who went to Harvard who got us into it in 1917, and now the same group is doing it again," he said.

I asked what he thought of the Grover Cleveland portrait.

"A fair likeness I would say."

There were more people going to and fro in the White House than I remembered from before. They humped files up and down the hallway like they were already an hour late. I mentioned this.

"How long have you been away?"

Two years, I said

"You'll see big changes. When I first came, it was a typical Southern town, slow as molasses. It's more like New York by the day. Your own service is adding a thousand new officers on top of the four hundred you got this year."

I had gotten out of the idea of thinking about my career to tell the truth. This would bring the Navy to more than ten thousand officers, meaning a big jump in shore billets. I didn't know what Harry had in mind for me. I was hoping I'd be sent back to London, but if that wasn't in the cards something easy. Mother could always twist the Senator's arm to get me assigned to a base with regular hours and a light work load; palm trees would be a plus. Cybil was snobbish about America—"I don't care for the place or the people," she said—but maybe I could talk her into relocating for the duration.

Pa Watson came out of the Oval Office and beckoned to Berle. "You're next," he said to me. "Adolph's in a hurry."

Berle was in there for only a few minutes and gave me a friendly nod when he left.

Pa was the president's appointments secretary, but only the civilians called him Pa. If you're a junior officer you don't call a lieutenant general Pa unless you want to be in charge of a latrine detail in fly and mosquito country.

I marched in behind him, came to attention and saluted smartly. As before, Franklin waved and said they weren't big on ceremony and take a load off. Harry was smoking and smiling from a chair opposite the president's desk.

"Good morning, Lowell," he said. "How'd it go last night?"

"Before we get down to business," Roosevelt said, "this is yours." It was the letter of commendation. "A copy to your personnel file."

I gave it a quick scan. I was praised for "invaluable work" on a foreign assignment. No details for some clerk to pass on to a spy.

Thank you, sir, I said.

"Okay," Harry said, "shoot."

I gave them the run down on Bywater as Franklin fiddled with a ceramic donkey; he had all kinds of them on his desk.

"We didn't fortify Guam after the war because of the treaty," the president said.

"That doesn't mean we can't start now seeing as they're building ships in secret," Harry said.

That made sense to me, but looking back it's obvious Franklin was like those chess masters who figure the game out a bunch of moves ahead.

"Japan isn't what I worry about most," he said, "it's Germany. They've already got spies in South America mixed up in the politics. Those tin-pot dictators like what they see in Adolph; the bastards are all cut from the same bolt of cloth. If the British make a deal to save their empire, and I wouldn't put it past perfidious Albion, we'll be in the crosshairs. Throw the Italian navy in with the Kriegsmarine and they're equal to us."

"Most people want us to go it alone with Fortress America," Harry said. "They're sick of Europe and its troubles."

"Our people need someone to do their thinking for them," Franklin said. "You know that as well as I do."

"Never repeat that outside this room," Harry said to me, grinning.

"Hell, *Commander* Brady knows that," Franklin said, winking at me. "The man's one of our best spies. The question is whether they'd fight if Adolph backed them into a corner. Joe Kennedy says they'll fold like a deck chair." He pushed a button on the inner-com. "Tell Bob to come in."

Bob was a big Secret Service agent who wheeled Franklin into the bathroom when nature called. He came in and they went into the john.

"How do you think he looks?" Harry asked.

Same as before, I said

"He's working harder than ever."

That's a nice tan he's got.

"We just got back from fishing in Florida. The Navy flies the stuff down daily he needs to read or sign, so it's not like a real vacation. Churchill sounds like the type who doesn't back off from a scrap, but what about the English people?"

They don't like the Germans, I told him; I learned that from talking to thousands of people. I dropped that in just in case my expense account came up. But I'll tell you this, nobody buys that old 'For King and Country' stuff anymore.

Bob wheeled the president back in. "I heard that last bit," he said. "So Joe Kennedy's right that the English have lost their gumption?"

I wouldn't say that, Mr. President.

"What would you say?"

Back 'em into a corner and they'll fight hard.

"The upper class thinks that way, too?"

There are some that don't, I said.

"What about the Labour Party?"

They don't want anything to do with war, I said.

"So Joe Kennedy *is* right."

I wouldn't go that far.

I walked that tight rope about as well as anybody could have. I didn't say yes or no about the English will to fight so it couldn't be thrown in my face if they ran up the white flag. Never give a straight answer if you can get away with it. Tell them on the one hand and then give them on the other hand. Don't let them pin you down. *No straight answers!* Follow that and you'll climb every ladder. It took me my first four years in the Navy to learn. Write it down and put it on your mirror so you see it every day.

Franklin picked up another of his toy donkeys and fooled with it. "Senator Brady is working with the isolationists in spite of his strong feelings about Republicans." He threw his head back for a laugh. "I'd rather lie down with my hogs," he told me. "But I've got him snuggled up to the other side of the aisle. The time might come when I need a vote from Wheeler and Nye, and your stepfather is my bridge to them."

I never heard the Senator say a good word about a Republican, so it shows how persuasive the president was. I reckon the South might get over the war after a couple hundred more years go by, but then I'm an optimist.

"The question is what to do with you," Harry said, squinting at me through his cigarette smoke.

Should I bother to unpack, I asked, or just catch the first boat back to London? Harry could put things right with the Bureau of Supplies and Accounts.

"Not to leave this room," the president said, "but we've established some very quiet contacts with the British government. They'll be sending people over to give us advice, so I think we'll keep you close for liaison work. It's not everyone who can put the cuckold's horns on the king of England."

There was no hiding my surprise.

We had waited until past midnight in Eaton Hall. That's the Duke of Westminster's country estate, a huge place built in the Seventeenth Century. HRH had gone back to his room after what Wallis said was his usual poor performance—she had high standards between the sheets—and I had tiptoed through a quarter mile of corridors, stopping at points to turn my flashlight at the map she gave me as we left dinner. A couple of hours later I was tottering back to my room like I'd gone ten rounds with the Brown Bomber. Wallis said in the right mood she could wear out the best man and she sure was that night. You'd think nobody would be up at that hour to see, but there are eyes everywhere.

"Let's just say a little bird told me," the president said. "Well?"

With apologies, Mr. President, I said, a gentleman never talks about a lady.

Franklin liked me the better for that. He loved gossip but also believed in gallantry toward the fairer sex.

"Well said; right, Harry?"

"Right, chief."

They put a desk for me in a room next to the telephone switchboard where the operators hung their coats in Coolidge's time. I shared it with an egg-shaped political aide named Jamie Garrison who had a pink face from sun or whiskey. He bragged he was from the Bronx, but I never saw anyone who looked impressed.

"Christ's sake," he said as the movers arrived with my government-issue desk, "there's hardly room for me in here."

You had to turn sideways to squeeze between our desks. His rear end was always knocking over my pen and pencil set.

"Sorry, handsome," he sneered the first time.

An ass that big is bound to do some damage, I said.

"Oh, a wise guy, huh?"

That pretty much set the tone. Lucky he had to travel around the country putting the fix in with the governors and mayors or we might have got on each other's nerves. He had been proud he had his own office in the White House and then to get stuck with me.

"The chief wants you to know who's who at the Navy Building," Harry told me. "He decided a long time ago that official channels are useless. He tells the State Department in plain language what to say to another government about something or other. When it comes back after two dozen people have read and revised it one paragraph contradicts another. Sometimes it ends up saying the opposite of what he wanted. He's always looking for ways to get around the bureaucracy."

At first my duties were so hazy I could have gone in every other day and nobody would have noticed; and don't think I wasn't tempted. The people at the Office of Naval Intelligence wondered why I kept drifting by to shoot the shit. They were busy men and didn't like to take the time from their work.

It made them nervous that I was from the White House, and the word about my double promotion was all the more reason to be suspicious. The impression got around that I was a rising star in the world of ass-kissers sent to spy on them. The president's reputation for that sort of thing was well known. He'd give one job to several men and let them fight it out, or one man would get several jobs and Franklin would sit back and see if he sank or swam.

Nobody knew how much clout I had, and I didn't either. But I got the feeling I could throw my weight around up to the vice-admiral level. I saw fear in the captains working on promotion to flag rank. I was someone to be careful of until they figured out my place in the scheme of things. The names I dropped—"Harry" and "the Big Boss" had them shitting bricks. The vice admirals were another story. They had either hit the ceiling or knew promotion was locked in and no new guy was going to change that.

Everything was political in the old Navy Building, and I bet it's no different in the Pentagon; people spend most of their time defending their patch of ground or cutting the legs out from under someone else. The fighting men look down their nose at desk jockeys, but that's a mistake. The guys who move the paperwork up and down the chain have the juice, not the crazy guys who think nothing could be better than closing with the enemy with all their guns blazing. Of course, you want them out front when the shells are flying, but a great deal more time is spent not fighting than the other. At least, that used to be the case.

Bit by bit I learned who the bottlenecks were, the ones who thought the old ways were plenty good enough, the seat warmers and time servers. I fed the names to Harry and what he did with them I don't know. Not all of the deadwood got tossed overboard—the Navy doesn't work that fast—but a lot of new blood was brought in and thank God for that. A man doesn't get recognized for that kind of work, but he ought to. I'd have medals from neck to waist like those South America dictators.

My mother and the Senator were back from his annual tour shaking hands at county fairgrounds. She had been watching for me from the window and began crying at the front door as soon as I stepped from the cab. She was a grand dame in long black gown and ropes of pearls.

"There he is, Senator," she cried. "Our boy is back. Look how gorgeous he is in his uniform."

I didn't hear what he said, but she snapped back. "You keep a civil tongue in your head."

Mother always made a big fuss when I came home and gave me the guest-room with a fireplace. Next to Perle Mesta—"the hostess with the mostest," the papers said—nobody threw more parties than Mother. And what better excuse than her darling son's homecoming? After loud smacking kisses she led me past the Senator, who smiled coldly at where he thought I was, and introduced me to the guests.

It was the usual passel of back-slapping, elbow-grabbing politicians and wives. There was also a bunch of diplomats, society people, and big-shot newspapermen like Joe Alsop and Walter Lippmann. Lobbyists, too, with flashy young tarts. They're everywhere in Washington, the lobbyists. Some were in Congress for decades until the voters up and threw them out. They made more money in their new jobs, but you could tell they missed the power.

Clare Booth Luce, a damned attractive woman who somebody said was smart as a whip, tickled my palm when we shook hands. Her husband, Henry, a guy in the magazine field, looked like he had been chipped from granite and acted like it hurt him to part with words. He said "Hello" and that was it for me.

"And this is our new Canadian friend, Mr. Stephenson," Mother said as she guided me to a short, well-dressed man as alert as a bird dog on point. "The British ambassador was kind enough to bring him along."

I last saw Stephenson when I was behind the yellow screen at Winston's home explaining how Hollywood could help England. He told me my parent's home was charming and admired the colored butler's dignity. You didn't have to be Sherlock to know he was still spying. I wondered if I could put that to use. That's called staying on your toes.

"He's a great man, your president," he said. "We Canadians admire him enormously."

He's going down in the history books, that's for sure, I said.

Stephenson asked what I did in the White House and I gave a vague answer. If I hadn't known he was a spy and therefore pretty well briefed on

Washington, I might have hinted I was called on by the president to settle a question when his other people couldn't agree. He said let's have lunch and I said fine and dandy, Andy. That was a saying back then.

I'll spare you what Mother said about me breaking up with Penelope. She had been thrilled about a family connection with the Stanhopes even after she saw Penelope's picture in the paper.

"Oh, my God," she had said, putting a hand to her mouth.

That one doesn't do her justice, I said.

"I pray that is so," she said. "Look how much taller she is than the others even though she's hunched over. She doesn't have a crooked back, does she?"

The Senator made a comment about a dark room and a pillow case that earned him two days of icy silence from my mother.

"Oh, it was just a joke," he begged. "I hear ten worse before lunch every day of my life."

Mother said that might very well be, and she felt sorry for him if it was, but she wouldn't have him bringing that filth home.

A giant man was moving slowly through the room with two much-smaller men at his sides. It made you think of a passenger liner with tug-boats minding it.

"That's Sir Ronald Lindsay, the British ambassador," I heard a Southerner say with a chuckle. "He shore don't think his shit stinks."

I saw why they were talking about firing him. He had a thick mous-tache and eyebrows and a monocle on a ribbon. I knew his type from the fancy clubs where I spent many an hour drinking and gambling. Those old gents cursing their newspapers were young bucks back when the empire was at the peak. They had men flogged or even hung if the mood struck them. Who could blame them for having fond memories of those golden times? If you wanted someone at the top of the upper crust, Lindsay was your man. The wogs begin at Calais—that type of Englishman. He was so tall his noggin barely cleared the chandelier. It gave him another way to look down on the rest of the herd.

"What ho!" he said when they hove alongside Adolph Berle, who had to throw his head back like he was gawking at King Kong on the skyscraper. Sir Robert relaxed a muscle and the monocle dropped to the end of its ribbon.

"Charming party," he said. He said it like we colonists never ceased to amuse him with how we aped our betters on the other side of the pond.

Berle had given the impression at the White House that he didn't much care for the English, and I didn't think their conversation would be worth eavesdropping on. I'd gotten that habit, you see; it's hard to shake even now. Mother came over to pull on my arm to introduce her darling boy for her friends to simper over.

As I was on my way out for a rendezvous with a young lady named Adele who had a jealous husband that made meetings in out-of-the-way places necessary, the Senator wanted to talk to me. I was expecting more of how I'd be nothing without him.

"I'm told you've been useful in London and the president says he likes the cut of your jib," he said. "The jackasses in G2 underestimated the air force the Germans are building and so did your ONI. Keep up the good work."

He was softening me up for something. You seldom went wrong thinking he had a hidden motive when he twinkled at you.

Three days later I had lunch with Stephenson at the Mayflower Hotel. It was raining and I had to out-leg a woman with a little kid for a cab. I told the driver to step on it as I didn't want her spewing her curses at me. Cabs in the rain—it's the law of the jungle.

"You and I have a friend in common," Stephenson said as we studied our menus.

They used to put out a good feed at the Mayflower, and maybe they still do. We'll squeeze it in while there's still time. I'll think about these meals when they have me on bread and water, but probably they'll strangle me in a basement. Not that I'll go without a fight. Who would that friend be, I asked Stephenson in the same casual voice.

"Winston Churchill."

Great man, I said.

I wondered if Winston had told him about the yellow screen, but I wasn't going to ask. That's spy craft, you see. Don't give anything away unless you get something back worth more.

"Actually, Mr. Churchill wondered if you would give me help in seeing President Roosevelt."

Hmm, I said. Not as easy as all that.

"I appreciate that he's a busy man."

What's it about, I said.

Stephenson took a look around and leaned closer. "It's about establishing communication between Mr. Churchill and the president, secret communication. Informal liaison won't work anymore."

Isn't that what Lindsay is for?

"The ambassador is responsible here for government-to-government relations under the direction of the Foreign Office. Mr. Churchill is not in the government at this time. He said his friend Senator Brady, your father, might be able to help."

Stepfather, I said. That always hacked me off.

"Sorry."

I don't need his help, I boasted.

Stephenson leaped like a panther. "Oh, well, if you can do it on your own." He looked relieved.

I couldn't think of a way to climb down without looking like I'd puffed myself up to impress him.

It was useless trying to go through Pa Watson. He was as jealous of Franklin's time as a wife who suspects something. He said no twenty times for every yes, and that included people like Bernard Baruch.

"Not much is riding on this," Stephenson said as he spooned pumpkin soup. "Only the future of Western civilization."

I laughed.

"Oh," he said putting down his spoon, "I'm being very serious. Have you read *Mein Kampf*? It's Hitler's plan to conquer Europe, and why stop there— why not the world?"

I've been meaning to get around to it, I said.

I'd heard of it, of course; how could you not? But I hadn't stuck my nose in a book since my Annapolis days, and you'd win money betting I wouldn't start up again with Herr Hitler.

"We didn't want to believe it for the longest time, and maybe now it's too late, but we're awake at last. You Yanks are still asleep. Your army amounts to nothing more than a mounted border constabulary."

That too-late stuff was pure Churchill, what he'd been saying for years. It had become like a kind of nagging, and people had learned to let it roll off them like water from a duck's back. "It's just Winston," they said.

"You will understand the need for secrecy," he whispered. "No one; repeat, no one can know about this. It would land Mr. Churchill in hot water, and he got in enough of that over the abdication. He can't afford more notoriety or his usefulness will be over. What's worse is it would be fatal to our hopes of stopping Hitler if your isolationist element got hold of this."

He was right, of course. Lucky Lindy was a hero to the people, damned close to Roosevelt in popularity. People today forget what a big name he was; a lot would've taken him over Clark Gable. Pearl Harbor put an end to that, but up to then you didn't mess with him or the America First crowd. Even the Senator walked on eggshells around them. He showed his false smile and told them he respected their views even though he might have a minor disagreement here and there.

I went back to the White House after lunch and telephoned Pa Watson's secretary. She told me he was booked solid for the next ten days; in short, the kiss off. Then she asked if I'd gone through the chain of command as Pa would blow his cork if I hadn't. A friendly warning, she said.

If I couldn't even get an appointment with the president's appointment secretary, what chance did I have with the Big Boss? I'd only got ten minutes to talk about my two years in London, and some of that was used up by a hillbilly joke about the deacons deciding not to buy a chandelier for the church because nobody knew how to play one. Harry and I laughed and pounded our knees.

If I let on to the secretary, Miss Heard, why I had to see the president that would be two people knowing what Stephenson told me to keep secret, the other being Pa Watson because she'd tell him straight off. She would ask for Stephenson's name and who he was, knowing that Pa would ask. The Secret Service, ex-cops with faces like boiled tomatoes, would find him quick enough. And then what was to stop Pa from calling him up on his own?

I'd be cut out of the action and credit if there was any. Said straight out it sounds calculating, but what's wrong with that? I was who spent all that time behind the screen nearly dead from boredom and yawning so hard my jaw nearly locked up on me. Letters of commendation are okay; but look how many people get them. This had the smell of bigger game.

One day Harry dropped out of sight and nobody seemed to know where he was. I had become popular with the ladies at the switchboard next door and made a point of dropping in to brighten their day. That's not me talking; that's them. One was named Maggie, an older woman, lots of makeup, and really big; some problem with her glands. Tugboat Maggie is what they called her. She was quite the flirt despite that. She called me Adonis.

"Hey, Adonis," she'd say, "what's happening in Handsome Land?"

When she was on a smoke break, I asked if she could put me in touch with Harry.

"He's not supposed to be contacted," she said.

I told her it was important. Very important.

"Okay," she said, "but it'll cost you a kiss."

I puckered up after a look around. She'd eaten anchovies and the peppermint candy she chewed to cover the smell fell short of the mark. I was getting off easy; she could've easily said a roll in the hay or nothing doing. With the best of will, I wasn't confident my pecker would cooperate in that case. I'm giving you the truth, warts and all. Tell me if you want me to ease off.

"Gimme another," she said like she was about to swoon.

One's the deal, I said.

She said go back to your desk and wait for me to put the call through. I was still gargling with whiskey when the phone rang.

"Hello," Harry said, sounding weak.

Sorry to bother you, I said, gasping a little from swallowing the whiskey. That's okay, Harry said, I'm just getting a little rest. Sounds in the background made me think he was in a hospital.

"I'll be back in harness before long," he said. "What can I do for you, Commander?"

I explained what it was about and Harry was silent. "That's very interesting," he said at last. "Who else knows about this?"

Just you, I told him.

"Let's keep it that way for the time being; just the three of us. I'll call the president right now."

I was over at the Navy Building that afternoon gassing with some of the guys when a secretary came in. "Is there a Commander Brady here?"

That's me, I say.

"The White House is on the line for you."

I threw my arm out to check my watch and nodded as if to say right on time. I followed her to the phone.

"Commander Brady?" a strange-sounding voice with a heavy foreign accent asked.

I said yes.

"This is the president," Franklin said in his normal voice. "I want you to come right over and bring that Canadian with you."

A half hour later we were led into Pa Watson's room next to the Oval Office.

The president wants…I started to say.

"Go right on in," Pat Watson interrupted. "I don't want them on the usher's log," he told his secretary. "We didn't see anybody walk through that door."

Memorandum

Dear Toly:

Thank you for thoughtful gift. I would have never thought to buy something that color for myself. As you have said so many times, perhaps I am too stodgy. I hope your family visit goes well. My best to everyone, especially your mother. I hope she's feeling better. The cherry trees are budding here. I'm glad you will be back to see them in bloom.

There has been a development I would like your opinion on. Enclosed are memoranda from SAC Hawley from our Washington office. You will recall the subject, Lowell Brady, because of that misunderstanding. What a time I had convincing you my interest was just official!

He was believed dead in the war, but the possibilityif Donovan is right is that he survived. If he were to go public

with what he knows about Pearl Harbor, I can't say what the
consequences would be. A lot of the old isolationists are
still in Congress, and they could cause trouble. I think the
Bureau is safe, but I wouldn't want to push our luck. This
matter could be a distraction from the search for Communists
in government. Joe McCarthy is drinking heavily again and
when he is like that, he is erratic. I would hate for him to
seize upon this to launch an investigation, particularly
if he thought the Bureau played a role in covering up for
Roosevelt. He gets very morose after a few drinks about
buddies lost in the war. I would not put it past him in a
black mood to telephone Drew Pearson or Westbrook Pegler.
The hyenas in the press are bold because censorship went out
after the war, and there is no will to bring it back despite
Korea.

Here is the strange thing. Our files on Brady have
disappeared from the secret records depository in Bethesda.
Not a scrap of paper remains, according to Hawley. It takes
several clearances, including ours, to examine them, let
alone remove them from the premises. When you come back,
I'd like you to take charge of this. There is no one else I
would trust with it.

All my best,

John

* * *

One night I came home late from transcribing a tape to find my four
roommates sitting around in robes and hair curlers talking about the new
man who rented an apartment in our building. Their consensus was he was
fair game: an eligible bachelor, well-spoken and presentable.

"Not that you would be interested," Mary-Clare jested.

This reference to my mythical boyfriend provoked the usual merri-
ment. I made my dinner and listened to them with only half an ear. They
decided if the man showed a partiality the others should not trespass;
the harmony of our living arrangement thereby being preserved. But I

did not think they really trusted each other, and they were wise not to; Washington is filled with scheming women. I feel men bring out the worst in women, but the contrary is not necessarily true, at least to the same degree.

As the days passed they exchanged reports of chance meetings with the new resident. He was promoted from merely presentable to somewhat handsome if you squinted. One day I met him as I was hurrying down the stairs.

"In quite a rush, aren't you?" he said, pausing on the step. He was slender and had a long head with neatly parted hair, a large nose and Adam's apple. I could not say that I agreed with the promotion to "somewhat handsome."

I explained somewhat impatiently that I was running a little late for work. I expected him to make way, but he stood his ground. "I'm Greg Pearson, the new neighbor." He raised his eyebrows interrogatively.

"Harriet Gallatin," I said. I started to edge around him.

"I'm never one to stand in the way of progress," he said, smilingly stepping aside.

It seemed my roommates had an encounter every day or so. They bumped into him at the grocery store or coming home from work, and they found virtues overlooked at first. I was preoccupied with worry and did not add a thimble's worth to their gushing. Captain Brady was resigned to being taken into custody whenever the FBI chose. He shook his head when I said he should hire a lawyer.

"Even if I had the money, what could one lawyer do? They'd find a way to shut him up; buy him off, or whatever. This isn't small potatoes as I think you're starting to understand. People think Roosevelt was a god. If they find out he tricked us into war, the country would go off the rails. What was it, four hundred thousand Americans dead? You think their families would shrug and say, 'Oh well, that's way it goes'? I don't *think* so. There'd be hell to pay."

I wondered if this was true. Didn't people accept what they couldn't change? President Roosevelt was in his grave, the war was over and a new one being fought in Korea. Nothing would bring the dead back to life.

There would surely be public outrage, but it was more likely to dissipate after a short time than bring on social or political upheaval. If Captain Brady thought differently, I felt allowance had to be made for the solitude he had endured while a vagabond roaming the country. I think there is a natural tendency to brood in those circumstances.

Mr. Markos, who owned the neighborhood butcher shop, liked me and always went to the back for the best cuts when I came in. My roommates had little interest in cookery, and I felt sorry for their future husbands. They ate out or had soup and sandwiches after work. They were interested in my meals (I'm a plain but good cook) when the kitchen smells spread. If they were willing to contribute to my cost and add something for the cook, I was willing to share. If they weren't, I ate the leftovers during the week. Sometimes they didn't like what I'd prepared after they tasted it.

"It smelled so good when it was cooking," Tina said once. "What is it?"

"Ragout."

"It's kind of sickening."

"Don't eat it."

"Can I have my money back?"

"No." That was a firm principle. Once the food was on the plate, it was theirs.

One evening when I had made a roast with potatoes and carrots, Emily came in with our new neighbor. "Wow," he said, "what's that great smell?"

Emily explained the arrangement we had, and Greg said, "Boy, count me in. How much?"

I said a dollar and a quarter, pricing it high because I didn't want to be the cook for the building, otherwise why not just start a restaurant? Everyone was on her best behavior, wanting to show Greg how well they had been brought up, asking nicely for dishes to be passed and not gabbling like geese.

"I'm buying the cook dessert down at the ice cream shop," he announced when we were all finished. "And I won't take no for an answer."

There was really no way to refuse without being rude, so we walked to the corner. He told me he was an archivist at the State Department and asked what I did. I said I worked at the Smithsonian Institution.

"Not stacking books on shelves, I bet, a woman as smart as you."

"How do you know I'm smart?" I said with sharpness. I do not like to be patronized.

"I can always tell when someone is intelligent." Greg was a chirpy conversationalist. He told jokes in a twinkly manner and liked to mock the Senators baseball team.

"I don't know much about baseball," I said.

"Say, how about you and me go to a game sometime? I'll explain it to you."

I didn't really want to go, but once again I didn't know how to say no; it was my lack of experience with men. So that Saturday we drove in his car to the ballpark. After a few innings I knew I could never develop an interest, even though Greg explained what was happening in a lively way and often jumped to his feet over what was happening on the field.

There are times when a pitcher has allowed too many men on base and another gets ready to replace him by throwing practice pitches. During one of these lulls, Greg explained that his work involved looking up treaties and other agreements when there were questions about their provisions.

"And what do you do at the Smithsonian?" he asked.

I told him about my field work and the monograph on Ole Dan Tucker. "That's fascinating!" he said. "I'm going to look it up."

The next time we met on the stairs, he spoke flatteringly about the monograph. "To think there could be so many regional variations within ethnic subgroups. The Arkansas version sung by whites plucking banjos sets the Kentucky mandolin one on its head. And you wrote that the song might have an even earlier derivation."

"Yes," I said, "there are some who think it is derived from the older *Walk Along John*, which is sometimes rendered as *Oh, Come Along John*."

"Do you suppose there actually was such a person as Dan Tucker?"

"Possibly," I said with professional caution. "There is evidence some versions may apply to a farmer and part-time minister named Daniel Tucker who lived in Georgia. He was kind to slaves in his area, and the song is believed to be tongue-in-cheek homage."

"You only hear about the Simon Legree slave owners cracking whips; it's nice to hear there was another kind. Are you working on anything so interesting nowadays?"

I told him about my work with war veterans, and he seemed envious. "It sure beats digging around in old files like me." He wanted to hear some of their stories. "But not here, it's too noisy. Would you like to go to dinner sometime?"

I was by then heartily tired of going out to dinner.

"Or something else," he said, seeing my hesitation. "A Sunday drive?"

CHAPTER 10

NORMALLY THAT TIME OF DAY, THE CLEANERS AT THE WHITE HOUSE ARE running vacuum cleaners and polishing the floors and furniture, but the corridors were empty when Stephenson and I were led to the Oval Office.

Franklin flung his arms up like he was floored that the two people in the world he most wanted to talk to had just walked through the door.

"You fellas are a sight for sore eyes. Welcome, welcome." He wheeled himself around from his desk and gripped our hands like we were long lost brothers.

Stephenson was stunned, but I wasn't fooled. Back when I was a messenger boy I saw him go through that act with the mayor of Paducah. I overheard someone say Franklin never saw the man before in his life.

"Stephenson," the president said, "I've heard a lot of good things about you. How's my good friend Winston?"

"Very well, Mr. President."

Stephenson didn't know politicians here call everybody "my good friend" unless they were blood enemies, and even then they were "my esteemed colleague." Englishmen can know each another a lifetime and that's still not long enough to say they're friends. Yes, we're acquainted; they might go that far.

"And Mrs. Churchill is in fine health as well," Stephenson said.

"Ah, yes," Franklin said. "I think the world of Caroline."

Stephenson stopped himself from correcting Franklin.

The president rolled to a sidebar and looked over his shoulder at Stephenson. "Care for a cocktail?"

"Why, yes, I believe I would."

He was thrown by Franklin's relaxed way and habit of nodding along with what you were saying like he couldn't agree more. "Fine! Fine! Fine!" he'd say.

You'd never see a British prime minister whip up a drink for somebody he never met before. Franklin poured from several bottles, added ice, rattled the cocktail mixer and poured. Stephenson took a swallow and his eyes bugged out.

"Delicious," he said huskily. "May I...may I ask what it is?"

"Brady here will tell you I like discovering new drinks. This one doesn't have a name yet, but it's bourbon, peppermint schnapps, ouzo, blue curacao and a couple of other things. What do you think?"

Stephenson didn't look like he could say anything more at the moment, so I said it was very good, excellent in fact.

I'd had drinks in foreign dives that tasted like paint thinner mixed with something you didn't want to think about. This ranked with them.

Franklin took a sip and shook his head. "No, it still needs something. Drink up boys, and I'll try again."

Franklin got busy again at the sidebar pouring liquor. Maybe he had a method, but it seemed random what bottle he picked and how much went in. Stephenson took out his handkerchief and wiped his eyes.

"Tell me about yourself, Stephenson," the president said.

"Not much to tell, Mr. President. I was in the war and now I'm in business, and I've had a little success. I'm engaged now in helping the mother country in her time of peril."

Not one word about being gassed in the trenches, recovering to fly against the Hun, being captured and escaping; not to mention probably lots more I never heard about. I wouldn't be surprised if he had enough ribbons and medals for two chests. But if he was waiting for me to fill in the blanks, it would be a long wait. Only an idiot leaves himself open to comparison to someone like that.

The president shook the shaker again, poured, and watched like a hawk as we sipped. It might have been my taste buds were shorted out from the first one, but this one didn't seem as bad. Stephenson closed his eyes and took a dainty sip.

"Oh my," he said. "Very good."

Franklin rolled himself back behind his desk, all business now. "Now, Mr. Stephenson, what have you come to see me about? Whatever we say will be considered secret."

"Sir, I have been asked to tell you on an unofficial basis that Britain anticipates the need to work closely with your administration in the critical times ahead."

"Do you mean Mr. Chamberlain?"

"I don't necessarily include the prime minister."

"I have it on very good authority he's said I'm flashy and unreliable." The president smiled not very pleasantly.

"I would be surprised to hear that, sir. But I have no information on the subject."

"Mr. Churchill sent you to see me."

"With the agreement of a number of senior figures who hold important offices in the government or have done in the past."

"I wonder that you've taken so long. You and the French can't stop Hitler and Mussolini without us."

Franklin didn't need to be persuaded. Stephenson looked like he'd put down a heavy rock he had carried a thousand miles. "And I hope you're thinking about what happens if our yellow friends get tired of slaughtering the Chinese and decide kicking the white man out of the Orient is next."

"We're deeply concerned, Mr. President. You're aware we're building up defenses in Singapore."

"You should have done it years ago," Franklin said. "Now let's get down to brass tacks. You're aware my hands are tied."

"Yes, sir; the isolationists."

"I even have some in my own administration, so total secrecy is needed."

"Yes, sir."

"This is going to be a two-way street."

"Of course."

"You can start by helping us with the German spies down in South America. Tell Pa Watson to get Hoover over here on your way out, Commander Brady."

Yes, sir, I said, jumping up.

I saluted and nodded goodbye to Stephenson on my way out. He was pinching the bridge of his nose as if he'd got a sudden headache. The president's cocktails could do that.

I was relieved at getting the heave-ho. Being in on the ground floor of this sounded like it would be shoulders to the wheel with Sunday mornings off if you were lucky. People were already coming in early and burning the midnight oil, and now tons more work was highballing down the track. I needed to do some groveling before the Senator for reassignment before that wave broke.

It was a question of finding the right moment. He slept late and was in bed by the time I got back from the fleshpots. Another reason to move fast was the indignation senior officers felt because I was still outside the chain of command. To them it was like a sin against nature.

"What the hell do you do around here, Commander?" an old sea dog roared in the men's room as I was checking in the mirror to see if my shave was close enough. "I see you coming and going, buzzing around like a horsefly. I asked but nobody seems to know what you do."

Captain Elmont Waite had commanded a destroyer division in the Great War and had a voice like a loud-hailer. He had come out of a stall cinching his belt.

White House liaison, sir, I said.

"One of Roosevelt's spies." Waite was known for his belligerence. He was one of those short, wide men you don't fool with even if you've got a pope and a president in your corner. "Look at him, primping like a woman at her toilette."

I didn't know if this was for the benefit of others in the stalls and didn't stick around to find out. There's no point wasting breath on that type of man. Admiral Bill Halsey was another, but more about him later. He hated to be called "Bull" by the way. He thought it made him sound dumb. He was a sensitive man despite that "Kill the Japs!" act of his, not that he didn't believe in it. I often heard him say he liked killing Japs more than eating pie.

It was one thing to come and go as I pleased, but I didn't want a name for being the president's spy, and from what Captain Waite said things might be trending that way. Nothing would go on paper, but some brass hat would tell another to mark me for dealing with later. If Franklin and the Senator had a falling out, the Navy would take its revenge. The thought sent a chill down my spine.

Everybody knew about the officer who crossed one of the all-powerful bureau chiefs and spent years in charge of bean procurement. The Navy is particular about its beans; have to be grown in the right soil, be the same size, and so forth. Mess up and a ship could go up in a great fart blast. I'm exaggerating, of course, but you get the point. Even if you're careful and do everything right, what glory is there in a job like that? He got the name Captain Farts, of course.

He and his wife avoided social events because after a couple of drinks the younger officers began grinning. Sooner or later someone busted out laughing and everyone knew why. Captain Farts—his real name was Eugene Utz—had a promising career until he crossed that bureau chief. He resigned his commission and was heard from no more.

Mother hosted a reception for the new ambassador from Ecuador a couple of nights later. The Senator liked to wait until all the guests arrived before he came downstairs in his white-haired glory, one hand on the balustrade and his other twirling his red and white cane. He always got a big round of applause. People admire pluck in a blind man, and no one knew that better than he did. After the applause died down, I drew close and said I sure hoped he could swing that transfer.

"Certainly not," he said. "You're finally in a position where you can help me. Europe's a tinder keg as any fool can tell. Who knows where this Sudeten trouble will lead?"

How can I help? I said, meek and mild.

"I talked to the president yesterday. Your name came up but he put a finger to his lips like don't ask any questions. The man loves to be mysterious. What the hell's it about?"

I could have said it was top secret, but I knew the Senator wouldn't put up with it. If I held out on him, I could forget about reassignment or at least until Mother finally made his life not worth living. But he'd dig in his heels as long as he could.

A Canadian, I said in a low voice, has come over from England unofficially to ask if we'll help them get ready for the war that's coming.

"Why send a Canuck? Never mind, it doesn't matter. We'll talk later. Take me to the Ecuadorian ambassador."

Later, after the guests left—Clare Booth Luce whispered to give her a call—we sat in leather chairs before the fireplace in the Senator's study. He took his teeth out for comfort, as he did with no one else but me, and sipped something for his digestion. In the light from the fire, he looked like a shrunken head with big white hair.

"I need to know what Franklin's doing," the Senator told me, "not what he says he's doing. Harry used to let me know sometimes, but there's no telling how long he's going to be out sick. That's why I want you at the White House. He could have told me yesterday about the Canadian and didn't. I don't mind him being devious with the Republicans, but we're on the same side."

He sat in silence for a long time and then gave me one of his mean sideways looks. "If you had any wits about you you'd ask why I'm so interested."

I brought my mind back from Mrs. Luce; a writer or actress someone had said. I said I was just about to ask that very question.

"He's getting rid of Jack Nance. He's been a lousy vice president and doesn't like the job anyhow. Not worth a pail of warm piss, he says. That's Texas for you; the most vulgar people you'll ever see. He gave us a lot of trouble when we wanted to make the Supreme Court bigger. He hasn't said so except to a few of us insiders, but Franklin will be running for a third term."

I said Harry had told me he wasn't interested in running on account of poor health.

"He told you that?" The Senator was surprised. "Seems like you know more than you let on." He sucked his cheeks in and out. "Somebody's going to replace Nance. Why not me?"

Because you're blind? I didn't say it out loud, but the Senator knew what I was thinking.

"Why not a blind man as vice president? No president was a cripple before Franklin. Cleveland was so fat he got stuck in his bathtub. The point is there's a first time for everything. Blind folks might not see, but we're not stupid. Why, there's not an employer in the country who wouldn't hire me over you."

Yes, Senator, I said, there's no doubt about it.

I telephoned Mrs. Luce the next day. She was a woman of "robust appetites," she said over a cocktail in the hotel lounge. Fifteen minutes later, she was proving it. I never saw a woman get out of her clothes so fast.

"A brainless fuck; just what I needed," she said afterward.

The exact words she used, so I hope you'll excuse me.

"I was desperate enough to pick up a stevedore at the loading docks."

She asked if I minded being used as a sexual object—that was a new one for me—and I said I certainly did not. Use away all you like.

"Henry's a dud in a bed and, to adopt a metaphor from your line of work, I'm looking for a safe port to duck into for occasional relaxation. I'm rather famous in my own right, as you probably know, and I have to be careful of publicity."

I asked her what she was famous for and she laughed.

"Did I strike it rich or what? An unthinking hunk of rutting manhood!"

I wasn't sure what she meant by that, but why not take it as a compliment?

The men in her circle were eggheads. They talked about books and ideas and so forth, but they couldn't stand up to all that brains and beauty. They shriveled up like when you put salt on a snail. Most of the wit she was famous for shot way over my head, so I wasn't so impressed that I was struck dumb like them.

"Would you like some money," she said as she dressed. "I've got heaps and heaps."

For what, I asked.

"For screwing me. Don't hold back out from false pride; I would've paid the stevedore a good price for his time. The only thing I envy the Germans for are their blonde beasts. I'm so tired of the timidity of American men in sexual matters. You've been with prostitutes, haven't you? Foreign ones."

Well, I thought, does Mrs. Simpson count?

I admit I was tempted. A gigolo—what man wouldn't like that billet? Grow a thin moustache, oil your hair and you're in business. Stepping into my shorts, I thanked her but said I couldn't possibly take money for what was a real pleasure.

So we made it a regular thing when she was in Washington or when I went up to New York to look in on Stephenson at the British Passport Control Agency.

"See what our friend is up to," was how the president put it.

The FBI must have been keeping track of them, but Franklin liked other people nosing around. He might have had a dozen people checking up on Stephenson, none of us knowing the others were on the job. That's just the way he worked as I mentioned before. Stephenson started small but by the time we came into the war the English had two floors in the Rockefeller Center. Hundreds of their agents at work all over the country and the public didn't know a damn thing.

One time I swung by his office and a well-dressed Jew nodded as we passed. "That was George Backer," Stephenson said. "His wife just bought the *New York Post* and we're going to be working with them. They also have the Overseas News Agency and the Jewish Telegraph Agency. We'll give them money for more correspondents. That'll make the agency more attractive to newspapers. They've only got forty-five under contract now. but watch it go up."

I said what's in it for you guys?

He did a double take and quick-like I said one of my jobs was to ask dumb questions, so bear with me. I recommend it if you ever find yourself in that fix. Worked for me every time.

"England alone is without a bloc of voters in this country. Your politicians cater to the Italian vote, the Irish vote, the German vote and on and on. Perfectly understandable if they want to be elected. But we're not represented in that way, you see, so we have to start from scratch. We'll start planting stories that make us look good and the Germans bad. Tell the president I'm also completing negotiations to buy WRUL. Do you know it? It's a shortwave station with 50,000 watts heard in thirty countries. Highly respected. They get a thousand letters a week from their listeners. Its good will alone is worth what we paid for it. We're going to add all sorts of people to the staff, editors, announcers, translators and whatever else they need."

I used to listen to it sometimes. Their programs sounded like you were getting the straight dope; no way could the average person tell it was propaganda. Stephenson was also starting up committees to fight the America First people. They had rallies and marches and so forth. They were everywhere all of a sudden. The labor movement was on their side except for the Reds in the CIO; they came around in a hurry when Hitler turned on Stalin. I doubt the president would've got Lend-Lease through Congress without those English agents behind the scenes. Seems like ancient history now, doesn't it?

Pa Watson used to call me into the Oval Office for bill-signing when they needed people grinning in the background for the photographers. I was in pictures for the March of Dimes, the new nickel stamp, the levee and dikes law, and plenty of others. The president waved me over as I was leaving one of these publicity shots and I took the opportunity to tell him about Stephenson's deals. He already knew, of course.

"The Schiffs bought the *Post* at my request," he said. "It'll be a great help."

It was around then that the Germans and Russians signed the non-aggression pact. I don't know about the Army's MID—they kept things from us and vice versa—but the guys at ONI couldn't have been more surprised. I stood in the doorway of our little office when a bunch of generals and admirals and J. Edgar Hoover went by. You could tell from their faces that the president lit into them pretty strong.

Garrison was watching over my shoulder. "Boy, those guys are down in the mouth," he whispered. "Hey, did you see that look Hoover just gave you? Jesus, do you think he's a queer?"

I was standing at attention, saluting with eyes straight ahead. When they were gone, I asked if his ass was getting bigger or was it just my imagination.

"I'm not listening, Pretty Boy," he said. "Save it for Hoover."

When he was taking a leak, I snuck a look at a memo he was writing that said the Hitler-Stalin pact wasn't going to go over well with voters. He was already into a second page which guaranteed the president wouldn't read it. Nothing over a page had a chance; Harry told me that. I suppose I should have clued Garrison in.

You'd be surprised how much stuff in our intelligence files was from newspapers or gossip junior attachés heard as they loaded their plates or swilled down the liquor at diplomatic receptions. I bet ninety percent was useless. After the pact was signed, the English sent experts to teach us how to do espionage and counter-espionage. We were babes in the woods compared to them. That's the advantage of a couple centuries running colonies. There are times brute force isn't enough and you have to use cunning. They had to show us simple things, like how to open and close envelopes so nobody could tell.

What I sent the Senator from London was pure gold compared to the regular sources, and I noticed a subtle change toward me as word leaked out as it docs about everything in Washington. I bet Joe Stalin was reading our atom secrets the day after Franklin did. We weren't all that fond of John Bull before the war—never paid back our war loans, they were trade rivals, and don't forget they set fire to Washington—so in a way I was sending my stuff from what was unfriendly territory. Even if it was hand fed to me, hardly anyone knew that and results are results. So on top of the jealousy before, I began to sense more hatred in ONI. Nobody wants someone he doesn't like to do well. It's only human nature.

ONI was run by Admiral Anderson, who had been the naval attaché at the Court of St. James when I was in London. Brass hats get their noses out of joint when an officer operates in their area of command without them knowing. When he became chief of ONI he was cheesed off more that even naval intelligence had been kept in the dark. He came to the White House a lot and his frosty looks told me he thought I was lower than a snake in a wagon rut. I pretended not to notice.

One morning Pa Watson's secretary told me to go out to visitor's gate and see a naval lieutenant who wanted to talk to somebody.

"The general says you're probably not doing anything at the moment," she said.

Lieutenant Stephen Jurika was walking back and forth on the sidewalk in front of the Secret Service booth. I introduced myself and asked what he wanted.

"Can we talk in private, sir?" he said.

It was too early for a drink unless you were Churchill, so I suggested we walk over to the Mayflower Hotel for coffee. He had a springy stride, the eager beaver type that rolled out of the rack early at the academy and studied late to get a jump on the rest of us. They always had their hand up in class and volunteered for jobs nobody else wanted. I hated their guts and so did most of the rest of the midshipmen.

"I was attached to the embassy in Tokyo and got back a month ago, sir," he told me after the waitress brought coffee. "I've been trying to go through the chain of command, but nobody will listen. A source in Tokyo told me the Japs have a torpedo with a huge warhead that goes twice as fast as anything we've got and—get this—it doesn't throw up a wake."

I laughed in his face.

"I know, I know," he said with a pleading look. "It's hard to believe. But the same man got me into an air show where I sat in their new carrier fighter and later I was given the specs. Sir, it beats our Brewster Buffalo hands down. It does 310 miles an hour and climbs to ten thousand feet in three and a half minutes. It's got two cannons and two machine guns and flies for eight hours with drop tanks."

Laughing more, I told him nothing in the air beats the Buffalo. Had paid a call on the Bureau of Aeronautics and they had the same opinion as me.

"They told me I should be more careful about the lies foreign agents feed me."

I'd be embarrassed in your shoes, I said, ashamed to show my face.

"But I got this dope from a high-quality source, someone opposed to their militarism. There are a few of these people left, believe it or not. When I went to the Bureau of Ordinance about the torpedo they laughed like you."

Why wouldn't they, I said.

I told him what I told you, Japan's a country of scarecrows. How could they be ahead of us? But the guy was so sincere I admit he planted a seed of doubt. Much as I hated the type at Annapolis, experience taught me they can make a superior officer look good. Work them like a rented mule and they come back for more. I gave him some vague promise I'd see what I could do.

The morning after Luce flew off to the West Coast to speak at one of those captains-of-industry affairs, Clare and I sat at the breakfast table at their Park Avenue suite, she in her nightgown and me in the striped pajamas she bought for my visits.

"I really don't do this," she said as she buttered my toast for me. "You bring out my domestic side." It wasn't so much a side as a slice, and a small one at that. The woman was tough as nails.

I wondered if Luce knew or cared about our little affair. He was a big shot in the news business, as I had found out, so it was hard to believe he could be completely in the dark. But you just never know. Too much forest to see the trees, as the saying goes. Clare said straight out I wasn't the first and wouldn't be the last.

I got the feeling she shuffled men in and out like we were cards—Randolph Churchill was one, funnily enough—but if she was being straight with me I ranked among the stars. The top five, say. I liked her well enough even though her bon mots were wasted on me. You know the saying "No good deed goes unpunished"? That was hers; and she had plenty more right off the top of her head.

But Lady Cybil was more to my liking. She was jolly and fun and didn't make you feel like you were a dunce if she was in a bad mood. Like other women, Cybil complained about my letters. The usual, too short, not enough detail. She wrote a long one every week until she was killed. Excuse an old man's tears.

As we were finishing our coffee that morning, Clare told me to turn the radio up. "Something bad has happened." The radio announcer was saying Germany invaded Poland before dawn.

You'll recall the English and French drew a line in the sand after the Czech trouble. If the Germans attacked Poland, they'd stand with them. Even people in Churchill's circle thought that was a blunder.

"This means war," Clare said like she was having trouble breathing. "That's why Hitler and Stalin signed their treaty, to carve up Poland."

The Krauts will be sorry, I said. The Poles have the finest cavalry in the world.

CHAPTER 11

MR. PETTIGREW CALLED ME INTO HIS OFFICE AND I COULD TELL FROM HIS jumpiness that he had heard from the FBI. He lost no time confirming it.

"They want to know how the interviewing is going," he said.

"He is very forthcoming."

"Good, good. They'll be pleased to hear that. Where in the chronology are you?" He shook a Lucky Strike from a pack and lit it although one burned in an ashtray.

"The fall of 1939. The Germans just invaded Poland."

"I don't think they're interested in that." Pettigrew stood and began pacing and jingling coins in his pocket.

"What are they interested in?"

"Closer to Pearl Harbor, don't ask me why. Do you know what he was doing for the Navy then?"

"No, I don't. And I don't think I can rush him. He wants to tell his story as it happened, and he's a very stubborn man."

"How stubborn?"

"As a mule, I'm afraid."

"They won't be happy about that. Good Lord, supposing he worked for the Japanese and the Navy hid it all this time. Another thing, why are your meetings in restaurants, fancy ones? The Director doesn't like his agents spending money, and I have a funny feeling he's taken a personal interest. I doubt Hawley is a pleasant man in the best of times, but having Hoover looking over his shoulder makes him worse. You aren't putting these meals on your expense account. Why's that?"

"Captain Brady insists that he pay."

"A man on a pension living in an old soldiers' home?"

"But he's getting low on funds."

"We'll pay," Pettigrew said decisively. "Put it on your expense account from now on. We must keep him talking."

"Who is the Director?"

"Hoover, of course. Don't you know anything about this town?" He took another turn around his office, still jingling his coins. "That means it's big. I spoke to our lawyers. We don't want to be dragged into any scandal in budget season. Hoover has a lot of influence on the Hill. They say he has something on anyone you can name, even Truman from his days with the Pendergast machine." Pettigrew slowed as if he'd just thought of something that Hoover might have on him, and then shook it off. "It would be easy for his friends to blow a hole in our budget at the committee level," he continued, "and it's hard to get that overturned in the full House."

As I wrote earlier, Pettigrew was a steady helmsman. He knew where the rocks and shoals were in Congress as well as the coves to wait out passing storms. It was clear, to continue the maritime metaphor, that he felt bad weather was brewing.

"The FBI wants your recordings and notes, but our lawyers say we should hold on to them unless they are subpoenaed. Cooperation is one thing, but they say, and I agree, we can't allow the Smithsonian to be a floor mat to wipe their shoes on."

It was brave talk but if the Director was as powerful as Pettigrew said, would the Smithsonian submit to *force majeure*? From his jumping eyebrows and his pacing back and forth, I didn't feel confident about the outcome.

"Our Board of Regents is not without power of its own," he said, "but it's a question of..." He didn't finish the sentence. "How much does your supervisor know about this?"

"Doctor Broadbrow knows next to nothing," I said.

"Good, keep it that way. The fewer involved the better."

I went back to my office with a knot in my stomach. This was expanding like a dry sponge in water. If Pettigrew's hunch was correct, Hoover was now involved; a man whose name inspired awe and fear. I am someone who likes stability and predictability, not events shearing off in wild directions. I confess that I wondered again if it was too late to make a clean breast of it with the FBI, but I immediately felt ashamed. Captain Brady had put his trust in me.

I had adopted the practice of hiding the transcriptions behind a pallet of toilet paper in the storage room on our floor. If agents were listening to the spools after the Smithsonian closed, they were hearing the rather dull stories of other veterans I continued to interview. As with all military forces, only a small percentage saw actual combat. It was far more likely for an individual to have served in a support capacity far from the battlefields.

They drove trucks, built base housing, steamed back and forth in safe waters, worked in laundries and kitchens, peeled potatoes, did guard duty, dug holes and filled them in again. Their work was routine and repetitious, and the enemies they faced were boredom and loneliness. These veterans only knew about the foe from reading newspapers and listening to the radio like the rest of us on the home front. It had to be dull work and the agents would have used strong language about my choice of subjects, all of whom were interviewed for at least thirty minutes in keeping with the standard set by Doctor Broadbrow. With ums and ahs and ruminating pauses, this time was usually doubled.

"I guarded Italian POWs in South Carolina. They were nice guys, happy to be out of the war; never gave us a bit of trouble. We had Italian food night one a week and they cooked. Mamma mia, it was great." "I was a clerk for General Bradshaw who was in charge of base logistics in New Mexico, Arizona and Utah. You couldn't believe the paperwork." "I'm a mechanic and I worked on tank treads in Morocco." "I was assigned to mosquito control at the Panama Canal Zone." "I was a sergeant at a tire depot in France." That sort of thing.

I felt exhausted at the end of that day and irritated that I had agreed to go to the pictures with Greg. He was as big a movie fan as he was of the Senators baseball team.

"You seem a little glum, chum," he said as we walked to the theater. He had many rhyming expressions like that. "Anything wrong at work?"

"No, why do you ask?"

"Everybody has a bad patch now and then. Family stuff?"

"There is nothing wrong," I said with firmness. I do not encourage prying into my private affairs, particularly by people I know only slightly.

The movie, *The Crimson Pirate* with Burt Lancaster, was foolish and my attention wandered. I stole glimpses at Greg as he ate popcorn, absorbed by a sword fight or actors swinging on ropes. For all his faults, how much more striking Captain Brady must have been at the same age.

Greg's attempt to feel me out about my day at work could have been genuine solicitude, but it seemed coincidental to a suspicious degree. An inner voice asked what if his interest had another purpose? He had moved into our building a short time after Captain Brady waved at Donovan. From the start, Greg expended great effort to get on our good side. Natural enough, I suppose, but of five roommates why was I chosen for special attention? This was a source of unkind discussion when the other girls didn't think I could hear; not that I cared what those silly geese thought. I was the most intelligent, I gave myself that, but the others were coquettes, livelier and more accomplished in the arts of luring men. They would be thrilled to be asked to baseball games and pirate movies and would easily feign enthusiasm.

"What did you think of it?" Greg said as we walked home.

"Burt Lancaster has awfully big teeth."

"What—you didn't like it?" He was astonished.

"I don't much care for costume dramas. People were dirty in those days, literally unwashed. They smelled bad and their teeth were rotten, even the royalty. Their breath would have been atrocious. Movies don't show that."

"That's real picky."

"I suppose it's because I'm a historian."

"Or a bad day at work." He crinkled his face humorously. "Want to talk about it?"

Despite myself, I laughed. "No, I don't."

He didn't press the issue further, and we stopped at the ice cream shop for cones before returning home. As we parted at my door, he said, "I hope we can be friends."

I said of course we can.

Agent Hawley could never in a million years crinkle his face humorously. It would shatter into a thousand pieces.

* * *

I took the train back to Washington that night and was at the White House the next morning a couple of hours before regular reporting time. When things are popping, you want people to see you putting in extra hours. And make sure you've got a stern look that says you take matters more seriously than they do. Lucky this was my habit because my telephone rang at six forty-five sharp.

"The president would like you to join him in the family quarters for breakfast with Bill Donovan," a female voice said.

A Secret Service agent was already at my door to show the way upstairs to the residence. The president was in his pajamas and robe and waved off my snappy salute as usual.

"This here's Wild Bill Donovan, a real live hero with the medals to show it."

From his looks, Donovan was the last guy you'd call "Wild." He had the smooth Wall Street lawyer look. Pinstripes, quiet tie, thick, neatly combed hair, stocky but not fat—is that detail enough for you? When I asked around later I leaned he won the Medal of Honor in the Great War, so he was a bona fide hero.

"I'm sending him to Europe on a fact-finding mission and I'd like you to give him your contacts over there," the president said. "Tell the waiter what you want for breakfast. The pancakes are good if they're hot."

They talked about the German attack while I wrote down people from my London days, including some not strictly in Churchill's circle like Menzies, Cardigan and Vansittart.

"If you think of others, Commander," Donovan said looking at the list as I laid into breakfast with my stern look, "let me know."

"Are the pancakes hot?" the president asked.

"Not really, but they're good."

To tell the truth, I could barely get them down. If a Navy cook put those pancakes in front of me, I'd have had him before the captain's mast.

"Mine were cold, too," he said sadly, like he was used to it.

I'd heard the White House staff talk about the woman in charge of the kitchen, Henrietta Nesbit, a friend of Eleanor's from the League of Women Voters. A Wall Street big shot named Averill Harriman—the newspapers say he might be president one day—came to lunch one day. They gave him chopped up spinach leaves in hot water, cheese soufflé with more spinach, white toast, and three fat pancakes, cold of course. Harry said he choked down a couple of bites just to be polite. The housekeeping was also crummy; Henrietta Nesbit was in charge of that, too. Run your finger across any surface below eye level at the White House and you came up with dirt.

"Brady is one of my finds," Franklin said, fitting a cigarette into his holder. He was good for forty or so a day even though Eleanor gave him hell for it. "He's done a bit of digging around for me across the pond. Did some very valuable work."

"Is that so?" Donovan said, giving me a look like a livestock appraiser. If the president wasn't there he might have asked about my wind and wanted to see my teeth.

"He's not at liberty to talk about it, of course," the president said. "I haven't even told Hoover."

"He won't like that," Donovan warned. "He wants to run the whole show."

Franklin smiled and tilted the cigarette holder that cocky way he had. "Not while I'm president."

"I'd keep an eye on him," Donovan said. "The man's power mad."

"I keep an eye on all you boys. Don't I, Commander?"

Yes, sir, I said to Donovan. Not a sparrow falls that the president doesn't see.

Donovan reared back in his chair. "Whoa," he said. "I think that's going a little far."

"I agree," Franklin said, frowning.

It was a little embarrassing at the time, but a good lesson on how far to take flattery with him. The president had a mighty good opinion of himself, but he didn't think he was God whatever the Republicans said.

"Stick around a minute after Bill leaves," he told me.

Donovan understood that was his cue to beat it and he stood and dropped his napkin on the table. "Good to meet you, Commander," he said. "Maybe we can get together sometime."

We shook hands on it. A smart man keeps on the good side of people like that, and I suspect he felt the same about me. As far as he knew, I ate pancakes there every morning. It's not what you know, et cetera.

"Our embassy cabled to say Churchill has joined the cabinet," the president said after the door closed. "Chamberlain put him in charge of the Royal Navy."

I said I wasn't surprised and wouldn't be if he was named prime minister before too much more time passed. A coalition government with Labour looked likely. I rattled on as if I was an expert longer than the president usually allowed; he liked to be the one talking as a general rule. He butted in just as I was running out of things you could find in any newspaper.

"Chamberlain is a dead duck, if I'm any judge," he said.

I totally agree, I said.

"I can't see anybody else coming forward except Churchill, can you?"

I thought fast. Halifax? That little fellow, Amery? Who was that up-and-comer I met over a punch bowl in Devon? The man was a pretty fair shot. Bad teeth.

There's Anthony Eden, I said.

"Smart but too young," Franklin said. "No, it'll be Churchill. He and I need to start talking. Tell him I'm writing him a letter. He'll need permission from Chamberlain to answer. Get right on it. Top secret."

I gave him my smartest salute, spun and headed for the door with shoulders back like I was on the parade ground. No better way to leave a room, but you have to practice it. I'm surprised more officers don't work on it.

My first idea was to send a top-priority cable for delivery by the hand of our naval attaché, Admiral Mitchell, but then I remembered the White House switchboard. It had a reputation for being able to get in touch with anyone who had a telephone no matter where they might be.

"Try the Admiralty House in London," I told Ethel Burton, the head operator.

She was a buxom, stern woman with dyed red hair; a cigarette always hung from her lip. There's more colorful detail for you. A couple of hours later my phone rang.

"Go ahead, Commander," said Ethel. I heard the sound of static and then a faint female voice said I was being connected to the office of the First Sea Lord.

"This is Admiral Grantham." It was one of those plummy accents you hear in the Home Counties. "To whom am I speaking?"

"Commander Lowell Brady, United States Navy. Put on Winston Churchill."

"I'm afraid the First Sea Lord is occupied at present." I felt the frost through the static.

The president wouldn't be happy to hear I left a message with a flunky, so I said tell Winston his old friend Lowell Brady is calling.

"As I said, Commander, the First Sea Lord is teddibly busy. A war is on if you have not heard."

That plummy way of talking flattens the average American.

"So, if you'd care to leave..."

"Admiral," I cut in, "don't fuck it up."

"What's that you say?!"

"This is the most important phone call *you'll* ever handle."

I know what was going through his mind. One part said put this coarse Yankee in his place. The other part said but what if it *really* is that important?

"Er...one moment."

Churchill came on the phone. I wish I could do one of those imitations you hear on the radio.

"Lieutenant Brady, I am sitting behind the same desk in the same office I occupied twenty years ago and more."

It's Commander Brady now, sir, I said.

"And Admiral Grantham has just brought me the charts I kept in a box behind a sofa. They were still there after all this time. Are you calling on behalf of someone whose name I will not say aloud?"

Yes, sir. He's going to write you in secret and I think he wants it to be a steady back and forth.

"I am greatly relieved and look forward to receiving his communication.

Tell him I will reply as Naval Person. Commander, did you say? Congratulations and well done. Now if you'll excuse me, there is urgent business."

He hung up without saying goodbye. I called Pa Watson's secretary to have him pass word to the president message delivered; Naval Person will be in touch.

Five seconds later, Pa called, hopping mad. "What's this message and who's Naval Person?"

I knew I was making an enemy, but there was no way around it. Sorry, I said, but the president asked me not to tell anyone.

Call it coincidence, but the next day I got orders from the Bureau of Navigation. I was being reassigned to Halifax, Nova Scotia, as liaison to the Royal Canadian Navy Yard, and I had a week to report. I telephoned the bureau and talked to Captain Boldenwick.

"You got my sympathy," he said, but I had the feeling he was grinning into the phone. "It's a cold, depressing place, a sharp wind most days. There'll be a lot of convoys crossing over and weather up there is brutal. We anticipate ships will have to have to stop in Halifax for emergency repairs, which is the reason for a liaison officer.

"The Canadians generate a lot of paperwork, but nothing compared to our Bureau of Construction and Repair and the Bureau of Engineering. You'll be doing dealing with both, so at a rough guess you'll need thirty or forty forms for the simple jobs. The bigger ones will take more. I'd put in my order now for cargo space. Make sure they don't ship them on the open deck. Those winds peel tarps off like onion skin and they'd be sodden pulp when they off-load. You'll get three seamen clerks with zero experience and a civilian secretary hired locally. I question whether that will be even half the people you'll really need. You'll have to beg the Canadians for help, but they're in the war so good luck with that."

That evening I had dinner with Mother and the Senator. I complimented her on the new mother-of-pearl combs in her hair and mentioned I saw her picture in the society page.

"He wants something," the Senator said suspiciously.

"I don't think that's what we need to hear tonight, Senator," Mother said in her warning voice. Then, turning to me, her tone softened.

"I haven't had the chance to hear what you think of the developments in Europe, dear."

It don't look good, I said.

"My Aunt Fannie," the Senator said. "I heard a man on a street corner yelling that this afternoon. 'Don't look good in Europe.' Over and over again. He was hawking newspapers."

"Oh, stop it," Mother said. "You make me tired."

The Senator seemed to shrivel. He feared making her tired.

I told her the English and French would make short work of the Germans if the Poles left anything for them.

"I'm glad to hear that, dear," she said.

Now I know what you're thinking, Harriet. But like I told you, I wasn't the only one. Nobody knew how good the Germans were, not even Churchill. The French ran with tails between their legs and the English would have surrendered at Dunkirk it Hitler hadn't stopped his Panzers short of the beachhead. We were fixin' to fight the old war, but the Germans were on to the next. That's the plain truth of the matter.

"He's sending *Donovan* to Europe?" the Senator said after mother withdrew to listen to the Lux Radio Theater, her favorite program. "Hell, he's a Republican and a papist to boot. He ran for governor in New York and got walloped so bad they were fainting in the Vatican. What's Roosevelt thinking, building up a man like that?" He was always on the look-out for anyone that was a threat to run for president.

I said it was a secret mission and they gave no details.

"If it serves Donovan's purpose down the road, it won't be secret for long."

He was silent and I knew he was already scheming on how to sabotage Donovan. It was pure fantasy, of course—the man *was* a Catholic for God's sake—but the Senator always said in politics lightning can strike where least expected. Take Harry Truman for example; the Senator said he was a nobody in the Senate. "A mediocrity."

He was a good poker player though, a hard man to bluff. I used to drop by for the weekly game in his office.

"What were you doing there for breakfast anyhow?" the Senator said suddenly.

I explained that I gave Donovan contact information for his trip to London. I made a joke about the pancakes to lighten his dark mood.

"They gave me fried mutton chops as tough as boots and fig pudding last time I was there," he said. "I didn't think you could put figs in pudding, and I still think it's wrong. It's pitiful the food they eat. The president told me they have liver and beans three nights a week. He complains but it doesn't do any good. Some say it's Eleanor getting back for some affair he had, but I think it's just she has queer ideas about food.

"I sat next to her at a political dinner and she told me a quarter of the food we eat is meant to be 'evacuated' otherwise it poisons the blood. She went on about it until I didn't feel like eating anymore. She makes the president drink a spoonful of wheaten bran in a glass of water for his bowels a half an hour before breakfast every morning. She watches to make sure he drinks all of it."

I was listening with half an ear waiting for a chance to bring up Nova Scotia when he suddenly wheeled on me. "Your mind's on the diseased whores you lay with."

I'm listening to every word, I protested. Wheaten bran in water for the bowels.

That quieted him down some. "It's a good thing I got you at the White House watching them. It's things like Donovan that catch you by surprise."

Unfortunately, I said, I'm being transferred.

"Where to?"

Bermuda.

He could have lived with me being sent to some frozen hell, but not white sand beaches and women wearing hardly any clothes. The Senator didn't have eyes to see, but he imagined as well as the next man.

"They can't do that." It was the voice of a man who got his way in everything except with Mother.

I casually said I hadn't mentioned the matter to her.

"Don't," he said quickly. "It would only upset her." He'd speak to the president personally. "He knows what it's like living with a difficult wife."

Franklin's secretary called me at the end of work the following day and said to join him and few others for cocktails, the start of a steady thing for me. Everybody was talking about how good the war would be for the economy.

"A little bird told me they wanted to send you up north," Franklin said as poured me gin and prune juice and a "mystery ingredient" from a shaker. "I'm going to call this cocktail the Run for It. Did that little problem get straightened out?"

Pa Watson, who was standing nearby, looked down at the floor with a red face. I had learned by then that the president didn't care for people messing where he didn't want them.

Yes, Mr. President, I said, my orders were cancelled. I shook my head like it was all too much for a simple sailor.

CHAPTER 12

AFTER MY FIRST AIRLINE FLIGHT EVER, TO LOS ANGELES, I OBTAINED A Chevrolet from National Car Rental and drove to the Castaic Honor Farm two hours north to interview the famous Hollywood producer and director Walter Wanger. He was incarcerated for shooting Jennings Lang, the lawyer and movie agent, because of an affair with Wanger's wife, the actress Joan Bennett. We met in a small, windowless room furnished only with a table and two chairs. He was a short, slim man who looked dapper even in prison garb. He had a restless and impatient manner, and I detected arrogance just below the surface.

"The only reason I agreed to talk is you're with the Smithsonian and working on a book," he said. "My lawyer says absolutely no interviews with the newspapers. Is that an Ampex? Good machine; I've used many. Bing Crosby wanted me to invest dough with him in the company, but like a dope I said no. It's made him even richer than he was before."

I explained that I had been unaware of his trouble until my research on Captain Brady reached his Hollywood period.

"Christ, how could you miss it?" he said. "It was all everybody talked about for months. A man shoots his wife's lover in the nuts and wings him in the leg with the second shot. That should take care of that cocksucker's career in *amore*. A limping castrato: not many women will see the allure. I don't blame the newspapers for playing it up. I would've ate up every word myself. Yeah, I remember Brady from before the war; a good looking guy, on a par with Coop. He could have had a career before the camera if he learned to act. I told him it takes about a month and I'd teach him myself, but he wasn't interested. Not queer enough, I guess. All the women gave him the eye, not just the slutty bitch-whore actress types a dime a dozen in Hollywood. He was pals with a Canadian named Stephenson who was a spy for the English."

I showed him a photograph I had taken with my Brownie and asked if it was the same man. "Still looks good, but put on weight didn't he. Why write a book about him?"

I told him it wasn't about just Captain Brady; he was one of many veterans I was interviewing. I had decided to stick to my cover story to minimize slip-ups. I mentioned some of the duller examples, including the tire depot sergeant and the soldier who served in Alaska. It didn't take him long to lose interest.

"You wouldn't believe the slop they call food in this place. I'm making a movie about prison life when I get out."

In keeping with Doctor Broadbrow's teaching, I drew Wanger out slowly, not shaping the conversation with my questions but allowing it to range where he wanted. He said life behind bars was mental starvation and in many ways that was the worst part of confinement.

"All these guys talk about—nobody wants to listen, by the way, all everybody wants to do is talk—is how they're innocent and their lawyers were stupid or the cops planted the evidence. Or they want to talk about women, and I'm kind of soured on that subject right now."

He asked questions about "the outside world" and the news of the day which I answered to the best of my ability. He wanted to know which movies I'd seen lately. I said the only one was *The Crimson Pirate*.

"Oh, yeah, with Lancaster. Funny, you don't seem like the audience they had in mind. They wanted Errol Flynn for the lead, did you know that? I'll tell you a story about him from the hundreds kicking around the industry. He came in naked on a horse at a party at the Malibu Colony and jumped off and banged out a tune on a piano with his boner. Talk about ice breakers! Everybody was in stitches. This one will kill you about that movie. They were shooting off some island in Italy, and when they looked at the daily rushes they could see the Queen Mary crossing the horizon.

They couldn't go back and reshoot because they were already way over budget so that's how it went out to the theaters. Unexpected shit like that happens all the time in this business. A star goes on a bender for two weeks and you have to shoot around him and hope they can dry him out. You roll with the punches or you end up flat on your back and your head is spinning and some asshole is counting to ten. That's when you get the ticket back to the rag trade or wherever else you came from. You're deader than dead as far as Hollywood is concerned, and you don't get up from the grave and walk again like Lugosi."

Wanger's talk was peppered with profanity and I was thankful Doctor Browbrow's training taught me not to be prudish. Moonshiners had often used bad language or threatened violence when they ordered me off their property. For them it was enough that I was from the government. They made no distinction between what I did and the "revenooers" who took an ax to their stills. Once I was told I'd get a small head start before a farmer let his dogs loose, and I just did reach the car before they caught up. As I sat there with that heavy recording machine on my lap and my heart pounding, a shotgun was discharged as a further inducement to depart. Filing a criminal complaint was pointless, of course. No corroborating witness would have come forth; and with the speed word got around with those clans I would have forfeited all hope of future cooperation. The difference was their profanity was from sudden anger or fear of being discovered while Wanger's seemed an automatic part of his speech.

"I'm an Episcopalian but my parents were Jews, so I was involved a lot earlier in what was happening in Germany and those other rectums. The Nazis refused to show *Blockade*—Hank Fonda was my star—and so did Spain, Italy, Portugal and a bunch of other fascist countries. I say that as a fucking point of pride even though I'll be the first to admit it wasn't the best film I ever made. I founded the Hollywood Anti-Nazi League, did you know that? If you just go by the papers, I'm a no-good rat and crazy on top of it. They never give you the whole picture, only the worst parts. The league had five thousand members, from directors and writers to grips and best boys; the full gamut of the industry not just fairy intellectuals with beards and berets. You know who the biggest pain in the ass was for us? The cocksucking Hays

Office. You expect them to look for off-color stuff. Shit, some of us put it in the fucking screen plays so they could cut it out and feel proud of protecting the country from double entendres. They were also death on anything political. They told us we risked a backlash against Jewish war-mongers if we put that stuff in. Bullshit! Americans don't think? Alfred Hitchcock came over to ask us to put English people in leading and secondary roles. They're better actors anyhow, so it wasn't a big sacrifice. But we could've done a lot more to show what animals the Nazis were if it wasn't for the Hays Office. Boy, don't get me started on that shit."

Wanger's involvement with Captain Brady and Stephenson was brief, ending when he lined up a meeting with the Warner brothers, Jack and Harry. "'Sure, we'll talk to them,'" Jack told me. 'Send 'em over.'"

He had nothing more of material interest to offer about Captain Brady, so I packed up my equipment. As I was going, he said to judge from the snapshot that Captain Brady still had potential for older roles if it interested him.

"The son of a bitch has still got some quality you can't put a finger on. Tell him to give me a call when I get out."

* * *

Yeah, I remember the Warner brothers. Smart Jewish guys, tough as nails. They invited us to the studio for lunch after Wanger put in a word. Funny thing, he wanted me to go into movies. I thought he was kidding, but he swore he was serious. I heard on the radio he shot somebody's Johnson off for messing around with his wife and they threw him in prison. Is that right?

Jealous husbands are a serious risk to life and limb, believe me. I had close shaves where I had to go out the window in a hurry. Climbing down the fire escape with your clothes in one hand is comedy in the movies, but it's a different story in real life. Those bastards who break bottles in alleys should do jail time; I almost lost a big toe from a bad cut. I thought I was going to have a heart attack a few times going over fences with snarling dogs leaping at me. So you're thinking was the game worth the candle? To be honest, I wonder sometimes. Obviously, ending up in an old soldiers' home with a phony name says I made a few mistakes along the way. Shall we ask to see the cheese? And perhaps a glass of their splendid port.

Bill Stephenson was a millionaire, did I say that? His line was construction materials—steel, cement, and that stuff—and he made a bundle after the Great War. He calls one day and says he's going out to the West Coast to talk to Hollywood big shots about making movies where the English look good and the Nazis bad. He didn't come right out and say that exactly, but I knew that's what he meant from when I was listening behind the yellow screen.

"I've talked to people on the telephone, but this needs the personal touch," he said. "It would help if someone from the president's staff went along to show we have support at the highest level. Everything on a strictly informal basis, of course, nothing official. Think you could swing it?"

Who could say no to that? It sounded like fun and we might meet movie stars. I got my chance to ask the boss the next day when a bunch of his pals were having his custom cocktails in the China Room. Harry was on a sofa looking like he was ready for the coffin lid to be closed. The man was nothing but skin and bones.

"The president tells me you did a fine job in London," he said.

I said something humble. Did the best I could, was happy to be of service, et cetera. I mentioned what Bill planned to do out west.

"I think it's a great idea," Harry said, seeming to come to life. "Have you mentioned it to him?"

I said I had just talked to Stephenson the day before and hadn't had a chance.

"Let me talk to him first."

I said okay and went over to listen to Robert Jackson, the Supreme Court justice, talk about the great Mel Ott. He was saying it was too bad the other two outfielders the Giants had, Bob Seeds and Johnny Dickshot—that was his real name—were no great shakes. The president had rolled his wheelchair over to the sofa and he and Harry had their heads together. Later, Franklin called me over and gripped my forearm to pull me down and grin into my face. His breath smelled like a tobacco drying shed, I kid you not.

"I'm going to let you go on detached duty for a couple of weeks with our Canadian friend," he said. "Pa will straighten it out with the Navy. Don't wear a uniform, of course. Say hello to my son Jimmy while you're out there. He has a job with Louie Mayer at MGM, a good friend of mine. I've got a lot of friends and supporters in Hollywood. Who knows what would have happened in this country if it weren't for the pictures. People forget their troubles for a few hours for a dime and a nickel. It helped kept spirits from hitting rock bottom when things seemed hopeless."

I said they certainly did, Mr. President. Many was the time when feeling low about the grave world situation, I'd go into a theater…

He spun his chair and wheeled away. "Don't forget to say hello to Jimmy," he said over his shoulder.

We took the Super Chief out to the coast; now there was luxury travel. A streamliner with terrific service, as good as any fancy hotel. Bill sported for posh compartments and put us up at the Beverly Hills Hotel, a place so swanky it made the Dorchester in London look like a slum. There can't be more beautiful women in one spot anywhere.

A flunky met us at the stroke of noon at the front gate of Warner Bros and led us to Jack's huge office. A bunch of Oscars stood under a spotlight and the originals of movie posters hung on the walls.

On the way we saw a bunch of people in different costumes—cowboy, monks from the Dark Ages, can-can girls, and so forth—heading for the studio commissary. I was hoping we'd see some famous faces, but Jack Warner didn't even let that idea get out of the starting gate.

"I don't need to look at actors when I eat," he said, like the thought disgusted him. Harry Warner, the silent one, nodded as if any decent person would get sick to his stomach.

We went instead to the executive dining room filled with business types in suits and ties where a nervous waiter took our order. Jack sipped water, beady-eyed and all business.

"Let's talk turkey," he said to Bill. "You brought this guy with you to show you've got juice with the White House. Okay, you've got juice; I'm impressed. What's next?"

If Bill was surprised how fast Jack got down to business, he didn't show it. He started to say that the Nazis were doing a better propaganda job than the English.

"Hell," Jack said, "any idiot can see that. Most news or pictures from Europe are from German news agencies. Those guys are circling the track while you're still in the starting blocks. It's time to get your finger out of your ass. What are they in London, stupid or lazy?"

Bill a-hemmed and said they were aware of their shortcomings and working on correcting them and more stuff from their side would get out faster, just wait and see.

"We had a good salesman in Europe, Joe Kaufman, who was kicked to death two years ago by storm troopers. They trapped him in an alley in Berlin; a man with three kids. That shit goes on all the time and the world doesn't know a thing about it."

"Hollywood should make movies that show these atrocities," Stephenson said.

"We got a film coming out later this year called *Confessions of a Nazi Spy* starring Edward G. Robinson. It's gonna be controversial and we'll take a lot of heat, but who cares? The country doesn't know what's going on in Europe. But the Wonskolasers—that was our family name before— remember night-riding Cossacks, houses burned down, women raped; the whole migillah. That wasn't news in Europe; it was business as usual. Our father was smart enough to get the family out and move to Canada, and even smarter, move to the U.S. of A."

Bill went into his routine about screenplays sympathetic to England and so forth. The British government would be happy to put together some of the greatest living writers for story ideas and even deliver scripts if Warners wanted. Their best actors and actresses, directors, film technicians, the works—all free of charge.

"Walk with me," Jack told Harry and they scraped back their chairs and went to a corner for a huddle.

"It would take six months in London to get as far as we have in six minutes," Bill said looking impressed. "There's something to be said for the famous Yankee efficiency."

Jack was doing the talking and Harry the listening. After ten minutes they came back, Harry walking behind like an Indian in single file. "Okay," Jack said when they sat down, "here's the deal. We accept your proposition with one change. We split the worldwide profits on these movies, but you give us all the box office from England."

THE GREAT LIARS | 165

This time Bill couldn't hide his surprise. "You'd put that in writing?"

"Sure we would," Jack said. "I'll have our lawyers draw up the papers this afternoon."

Bill put both hands up in full stop position. "Hold on, I have to speak to London first."*

"Understood." Jack took a forkful of his tuna salad. "You boys fixed up for tonight?"

"Fixed up?" Bill said.

"Yeah, you know, girls."

"Oh, well, I'm a married man."

"What about you, sailor boy?" Jack gave me a man-to-man wink. "Is one starlet enough or would you like two?"

I told him I guess you'd call me old fashioned. I said that for Bill's benefit, not knowing his ideas and all. So just one beautiful young woman knocked on my door at seven o'clock sharp. She was Yvette, one of the can-can dancers. She thought I was an actor, too, strangely enough. I couldn't tell her my real business, of course, so I gave a load of B.S. about roles I'd had on the stage.

"I don't see you as Abe Lincoln," she said. "And I never heard of 'The Rail-Splitter and the Blond Bombshell.'"

I said the scholars had only recently stumbled on that aspect of Lincoln. That's all I'll say about the evening except at the end when I was starting to wonder if I had to pay some money, she asked me to put in a good word with Jack. I said I'd put in more than a good word and meant it, but never got a chance because Bill said he had to go back as soon as possible. He postponed the appointments he had with the other studio big shots because the Warner's offer was such a great deal. But he knew he'd have to fight for it in London. So we left the next day on the Super Chief. Waiter, I'm looking at an empty glass here.

Bill kept busy in his compartment writing telegrams to London and answering replies sent to stations along the route. "The Foreign Office is moderately enthusiastic for them," he said at dinner, "but the Treasury people have stuck their nose in and other ministries are lining up for their say."

Without Bill to talk to, I played a lot of cards. The poker players were a sorry lot and I picked them clean. They didn't want to play any-more, anyways not with me, so I hung out with the gin-rummy crowd and even played acey-deucy. The rest of the time there was nothing to do but look out the window. This is a big country in case you don't know; empty as hell. The train rushed past little towns with boarded-up stores and grass growing in the sidewalks, with lots of scenery in between. Talk about monotonous. Tramps in hobo jungles watched us rip past with air horn blaring. Some shook their fists and yelled at us in our plush seats looking out the windows at them like they were just part of the show. You couldn't make out their words; curses no doubt. Class hatred at work, plain as the nose on your face. There were prob-ably agitators among them.

Feet up in my compartment and drawing on a fine cigar, I noticed that clothes hung out to dry on backyard clotheslines were so thin you could nearly see through them. Yet a businessman in the bar car said there were mountains of baled cotton in warehouses and textile mills had cobwebs on the machines. If you aren't too young to remember, news-reels showed dairymen spilling milk onto the ground and fruit rotting on the trees. Farmers plowed corn under because a bushel wouldn't buy a pack of gum, and ranchers rolled dead cattle into lime pits even though millions went to bed hungry every night. It made you shake your head to think about it, which I admit I didn't do much back then—thinking, I mean. About that sort of thing, anyhow. But if you're not one for books and there's no card game, all there is to do is think. It's a damned boring way to pass time. I was glad to get back to New York.

Have you noticed those two men at the table in the corner? I'll tell you when to look. The FBI must have a factory where they stamp them out. Dark suits, white shirts, clean cut. They might as well wear signs. Okay, look now. Am I wrong?

Remember Jamie Garrison, the fat guy I had an office with at the White House? I thought he was ribbing me about Hoover, but damned if he wasn't right. John—that's what friends call him—asked me to din-ner because he wanted to talk about something. How do you turn down somebody that big? He picked me up in a shiny black Packard big as a whaleboat with a driver on the other side of a sliding window. Like Churchill, he had a bulldog face, but a meaner bulldog. Dark suit, white shirt, quiet tie.

We went to a little French restaurant an hour out into the countryside. The driver stayed with the car when we went in. Dark wood, brass, antlers on the wall, a clubby kind of place.

"You like martinis?" he asked after he told me to call him John.

Doesn't everyone, I said.

"We'll have a pitcher," he told the waiter.

He ordered the *Duck a l'Orange* and I chose the stuffed pork loin roast. Fresh green salad, French onion soup. Pretty good for a joint out in the sticks. We had a couple of pops and shot the breeze about baseball. Who'd I pick for my team, Ted Williams or Joe DiMaggio?

"Tell me about this Canadian you went to Los Angeles with," he said all of a sudden.

I said sorry, John, I'm afraid I can't talk about that.

"The president wants me to meet with him. I know the bare-bone facts but not the way he thinks."

He wasn't someone you wanted to be on the bad side of, but neither was the commander-in-chief. He leaned forward, and his eyes were hard as buttons.

"I like a man to be careful within limit, but I'm the Director of the Federal Bureau of Investigation. There is not a safer man to talk to in the country—make that the world. J. Edgar Hoover keeps secrets."

Yes, sir, I said. No doubt in my mind whatever.

"Well?"

Stephenson is a good man, I said. I'd bet my last dollar on it.

"Oh, I don't care about that, that's immaterial. He's a tool, but whose? Does he represent the prime minister or other interested parties?"

I was about to buy more time by saying that struck me as a damned good question too when Hoover got a look on his face like he'd seen a ghost.

"Clyde!" He stood up and hurried over to a man looking from the door and they had an intense talk. The other man also wore a dark suit, white shirt and quiet tie—the uniform. Hoover waved an arm in my direction like he was explaining something. Then he returned to the table very upset.

"Something has come up, Commander—an emergency," he said. "My driver will take you home when you're ready."

They left and the driver came in as the plates were brought to the table. Just in time, I said, pull up a chair. His name was Stan Larson and had been with the FBI twenty years. Nice guy. Dark suit, et cetera. You could tell right away he was a hard one to surprise. Seen it all.

"I bet that's gin in the pitcher," he said.

Martinis, I said. Help yourself. The duck, too.

"Beats the peanut butter and jelly sandwich I got out in the car. The Director likes to get good looking young guys drunk."

He must not know many Navy men if he thinks a pitcher does the job, I said.

"I wonder how Mother Tolson caught him."

Mother Tolson?

"Clyde Tolson, the Number Two man at the bureau. He gets jealous when Aunt Em is with another man."

So they're homos?

"You didn't hear it from me, pal. Driving the Director around is a good job. It beats going through somebody's garbage for evidence."

A couple of days later I got a call to join Harry upstairs in the White House residence. He was in bed in his pajamas with a glass of milk in reach. I told him he was looking better, but I don't think he believed it.

"I understand you and Director Hoover had a date," he said with a sly smile. A little bird had told him so.

The little bird was right, I said.

"I bet he was dumbfounded when Tolson came through the door."

Just about floored, I said.

"What did he want to know?"

About Stephenson, I said.

"You tell him anything?"

No, sir, I said. Not a word.

"He knows foreign intelligence is a high priority from now on and wants to call the shots. Presidents come and go, but Hoover is permanent. He picks up a little more power with each administration, and the boss doesn't want him to get any more."

Why not fire him, I said.

"He can't be fired," Harry said. "He knows too much."

About the president, even?

"What if I were to tell you he has nude photographs of Eleanor Roosevelt?"

You're joking.

"What if I weren't?"

Who'd want to see them?

"Our enemies." He took a sip of milk. "A lot of Baptists in this country don't believe in taking your clothes off before the lights are off and the blinds down."

No disrespect for Mrs. Roosevelt; she's done a lot of wonderful things for the world and all that, but she was about the last woman you'd want to see without her clothes.

"Remember I said, What if? And don't forget this is strictly off the record."

The president's enemies would have to break every bone in my body before I'd let that out, I said, be it true or false.

"I'll tell the president Stephenson was who Hoover was interested in. He'll bring it up in that casual way he does when he's setting someone up. The Director only suspects we have a friend in the agency, but at that moment he'll know for sure. I'd like to be there to see his face, and maybe I will if I'm feeling up to it. He'll wonder how much more we know about what he's doing behind our back."

Was Mrs. Roosevelt skinny dipping, I asked.

"She was influenced for a while by Bernarr Macfadden and that health faddist crowd. Running around the woods without clothes might have been part of it."

Afterward, I thought about the trap the White House set for Hoover. You have to be sneaky to get ahead in Washington. The Senator said anyone who thought lies and deceitfulness were beneath them might as well stay home.

"The president is smart to trim Hoover's sails," he told me that night. "The man knows too much as it is."

Lucky you've led a blameless life, I said.

"Are you trying to be smart?" His lips pulled back in a snarl.

As far as I know, I said, humble as pie.

"Even the saints might have had a few triflin' things they don't want the whole world knowing about. Not saying I do, but you get my point. Word is Hoover's got a secret department that digs up dirt on people in public office. I wouldn't put it past him to make up scandal when the genuine article isn't available. The way some people vote here they must live in terror of him. Lord, Eleanor Roosevelt naked. I'd be glad I was blind."

Harry knew I would pass the story on to the Senator even though I swore I'd keep it secret, which I did except for him. The Senator was always pressing me for inside dope, and I had to deliver in case Franklin decided he didn't need me anymore. Did Harry tell me about the Director on the president's say-so or on his own? Washington politics is hard work for a simple sailor to understand.

You're probably not as old as you look—no offense—but you'll remember what they called the Bore War after the Poles were finished and the Soviets licked Finland. Except for a few naval engagements nothing much happened for months. The Chamberlain crowd bragged the Germans had missed the bus and England was ready for whatever happened next. But Hitler was only waiting for the ground to dry out, and in April he lowered the boom.

I ran into Adolph Berle around that time at a reception for the new ambassador from Argentina. "Does the president know how many English agents are in this country?" he asked. "It's outrageous. Something must be done."

Absolutely, I said. Couldn't agree more.

I hadn't been spending as much time at the White House because the deadwood at the Navy Building was worse than I let on. Younger officers kept pulling me aside and telling me about which old crocks were gumming up the works. You'd need Paul Bunyan and his axe to clear the place out proper. These senior officers were Captain Bligh types when afloat. Ashore, they were the masterminds behind Form 84 and Form 335 and all the rest. Regulations, manuals, ledgers, logs and the other paperwork in triplicate or more—this building was the headwaters of that paperwork. When the English took those old Lend-Lease destroyers off our hands, they were astounded how many records we kept. They dumped most of them overboard within sight of land.

It wasn't just the paperwork. New ideas that battled up the chain of command got sat on when they reached the Navy Building. Nope, never been done before, not possible. There's no authority for this, greatly surprised this request was passed on, please explain in full with copies to the relevant bureaus. Those fossils were the enemies of progress.

They had to be polite because they feared me, but they hated my guts all right. A word from me would put them out to pasture, or so they believed. The truth was all I did was send in names. Franklin probably had some secret committee that gave thumbs up or down. I admit I evened a score here and there going back to academy days. I suppose it's nothing to be proud of, but they would have done the same to me. What I'd forgotten was how cunning the president was. The enemies I made turned on me when the time came. I had to take my hat off to the old devil.

Admiral Ralston Hughes, the latest chief of the Office of Naval Intelligence, sent one of his aides to the canteen where I was getting the lowdown on the Base Maintenance Division. The admiral wanted to know if he might see me in his office.

He was another of those mean-eyed old bastards with a face that goes purple when their temper blows. A voice like sandpaper from yelling language I can't repeat before a lady. He closed a file he was reading and put it in a drawer. Then he took spectacles off and forced a smile. It had been so long since he'd had to be civil it didn't come easy.

"Take that chair, Commander. Are you a cigar man? I've got some mighty fine Havanas in that humidor. Help yourself. Take a couple for later."

A mighty fine, cigar, Admiral, I said after I tucked away two and lit up the third.

He sat back in his chair and said we hadn't had enough rain, to which I agreed. Been pretty quiet over there in Europe, but that won't last. I agreed with that, too. He asked how Franklin's stamp collection was coming along—he had an interest in that line himself—and I said pretty well. We might have been old pals out on the porch sipping lemonade.

"I wondered if you had any questions I could answer to save you time and trouble," he said.

With respect, sir, I said, that isn't the way I do this.

"Oh, it isn't?"

I'm talking only to junior officers.

They know things the upper rank doesn't, Harriet. I sometimes wondered what they said about me. Nothing good, I reckon. At one time I led the Atlantic Squadron for putting men in the brig for dumb insolence. Looking back, I was too heavy-handed. You don't want to be in the lead of anything, even discipline. That's just begging to be picked off.

"Talking to junior officers?" the admiral said. His face was beginning to get dark. "That's not how we've done things in the thirty-two years I've been in the Navy." He gave me a smile like an ape showing its teeth. "The communists have political officers as co-commanders. Is that what you have in mind?"

I said I hoped he didn't think I favored that.

"Then maybe you'd like to give me a better idea of what you're up to."

Just following the commander-in-chief's orders, I said.

He looked like he was about to say something, but stopped in time.

The best defense is a good offense so I dropped Lieutenant Stephen Jurika's name; what he said about the big torpedo warhead and the Jap fighter plane being better than the Brewster Buffalo.

"Where did you get that crazy stuff?"

I said I considered Jurika a reliable source.

"Why haven't I heard about this?"

A good question, sir, I said. I puffed on my cigar.

"No way are Japs going to build a plane or torpedo better than us," he said. "They're good copiers. I'll give them that. But something has to be invented for them to copy. Now, if you'd said the Germans, I might think there might be something to it."

I said I was troubled we knew about this but he didn't.

Admiral Hughes looked like he wanted to lunge across the desk and crush my throat between his huge thumbs. Instead, he punched a button on his intercom.

"Get in here!"

A minute later a scared-looking captain came in. "This here officer," the admiral said, "says the Japs have a new torpedo and a carrier plane better than the Brewster Buffalo."

The captain—his name was Forbes—had the rolling-eyes look steers get in the slaughterhouse.

"Well?" the admiral roared.

"Um, yes, there were some silly rumors a few months ago."

Hughes couldn't believe his ears. "And I wasn't told?"

"Sir, they were so absurd I didn't think they were worth bothering you with."

"Where'd they come from?"

"I believe a young attaché at the embassy in Tokyo."

"What happened?"

"Sir, he was informed he must be more discerning in the future."

"The man must be an idiot, but I should have been told."

The admiral slammed a big fist on the desk making the lamp, pencils, the clock, the captain and me jump. "Instead, I hear this ridiculous story for the first time from an officer..." He could barely get his words out. "...from the White House."

Captain Forbes shot me a look of pure hatred.

I said Jurika had actually sat in the new fighter plane and read the specs on the torpedo thanks to his connections with the anti-militarist element in Japan.

"Our understanding," Captain Forbes told the admiral timidly, "is that the anti-militarists have all been murdered or put in prison."

"What difference does that make?" Hughes was hollering.

Captain Forbes blew his cheeks out but didn't answer.

"What matters is the White House knows something we're paid to know and apparently don't."

"Well, sir, we *did* know."

"*I* didn't!" the admiral thundered, bringing down his fist again.

I was glad I didn't work for him. Forbes was a nervous wreck; stomach problems, probably.

"Tell the president," Hughes raged, "that we were aware of these"—he took a deep breath—"ah, rumors and thought they were pure bullshit."

Yes, sir, I said, standing for a snappy salute.

I left, striding off head up and shoulders squared for the benefit of the officers in the anteroom. The admiral was shouting even louder at Forbes.

CHAPTER 13

ONE DAY HARRY CALLED ME IN AND SAYS HE'S BEEN THINKING ABOUT THE Pacific. With all the attention going to Europe, maybe it was in danger of becoming an orphan. He didn't trust official channels to give him the straight dope any more than the president did.

Maybe I should go out there and look around, I said casually.

"Good idea."

I dictated my own proceed orders to the Bureau of Navigation, routing me to Honolulu via the Super Chief and the *SS Lurline* with the explanation I was going to study conditions in Hawaii. You couldn't get any vaguer if you tried all day. First class all the way, and not a peep from the green eyeshade boys.

I looked up Yvette when I got to Los Angeles and we had another bit of fun; sorry, no details! Yes, I told her, I talked to Jack Warner, hasn't he got back to you? It was a little white lie, but why take the hope from people?

The voyage to the islands on the *Lurline* was fine. I swam in the outdoor pool and played poker into the wee hours and did pretty well. An American named Foster told me the future was bright for coconuts and the Solomon Islands a good place to grow them.

"But steer clear of the ones where there's malaria that attacks the brain."

He told me that before I had bluffed him out of a big pot with two treys. After I raked in all those chips, he would have said take your time checking those islands out, and don't worry about the mosquitoes. Nobody talked about war. It was a nice change of pace from Washington where that's all they talked about.

We had deep swells the first four hundred miles, but smooth going the rest. I met a woman named Lily at the bar. I sized her up as a possibility the first night, but she had been missing since. The blond and brassy type, rings on every finger. A little on the common side if you want the truth. She nodded when I sat down a few stools away and patted the one next to her.

"I don't bite, Handsome."

I acted like I didn't see the bartender's wink and swapped stools. Up close I saw she had more miles on her than showed from the other stool. She must have plastered makeup on with a trowel. She wore expensive perfume but too much of it.

"My name's Lily. Put 'er there."

We shook hands. Mine's Lowell, I said.

"Where'd you get that wonderful tan?" Her accent was from well south of the Mason-Dixon Line.

I sell farm equipment, I said. It gets me outdoors a lot.

"And I bet you know a few farmers' daughters, too." She had a big laugh, the kind that cuts through the racket in honky-tonks when everybody is drunk. "They must lock 'em up when they see you coming."

I know how to pick locks I says, going along with the joke.

"Do you believe that, Ira?"

Ira the bartender had dark slicked-back hair. He blew on a glass and polished it. "I believe everything I hear."

"Gawd," she said to me, "this is the first time I've been able to get out of my cabin. Seasick or a bug or both. If I'd had the strength, I would've thrown myself over the side. Tell me where you're from, sweetheart."

Georgia, I said.

"We Southerners have to stick together." We shook hands again. "I'm from Mississippi. Just buried my third husband."

Sorry to hear it, I said.

She shook a Camel out of a pack and gave me her lighter, putting her hand on mine as I lit it. "A heart attack got Aaron at the factory. Bedsprings, in case you're interested. He had the biggest company in the country."

I said I knew a Stanhope in the furniture line.

"Everybody knows that man," she said. "Aaron refused to have anything to do with him. He could squeeze a pint of water from a lump of coal. We produced a bed for when you have to live with your in-laws that I named Close Quarters."

Is that so, I said.

"It didn't squeak no matter what people did, and Aaron and I gave it a good workout."

Sounds like he died a happy man, I said.

"You can take that to the bank, buster." She reached over and squeezed my knee. "I'm gonna have another drink, what about you?"

I said the night is young.

Lily sucked in liquor like a fleet oiler taking on bunker fuel, and after five or six asked if I wanted to see the picture of her late husband in her stateroom.

"I told Aaron if anything ever happened to him," she said when she closed the door behind me, "I wasn't going to give up living life to the fullest."

Well, she wasn't kidding about that. We carried on like honeymooners to where the people in the next cabin pounded on the wall. Lily said ignore them, they're just jealous.

"I hope you're not too disappointed," she said the night before we reached Honolulu, "but my first husband is meeting the ship."

That was my cue to say something mushy; I knew that from the deep way she looked into my eyes, but damned if I could think of anything.

"Mel and I are going to try it again."

Good luck to you both, I said.

She dabbed at her eyes but was careful not to mess her mascara. "I hoped you'd take it a little harder." She looked away. "I'm not sure it's a good idea, going back to Mel. We had fun but we didn't always get along." She gave me a crafty look. "I inherited a lot of money, you know."

It'll work out fine, I said. You'll see.

"Yes, I suppose so."

Well, I said, I'll see you in my dreams.

Remember when you couldn't get away from that song no matter where you went? I still hear it on the radio now and then.

"It's been fun," Lily said and then her eyes flashed. "But I've had lots better."

It's best to lift your chin and walk away with dignity when women start that up.

When we docked the band played and confetti flew like it was snowing a blizzard. Every time a big liner comes in it's Boat Day. Boys dive for the coins the passengers throw in the water and brown-skinned hula girls in grass skirts greet you with kisses and hang leis around your neck. Aloha, they say.

Everyone went ashore in white linen suits or dresses and the ladies carried white parasols. Ever been to Hawaii? The air smells like flowers. The warm wind makes the palms rustle. White clouds in blue sky. The green Koolaus Mountains in the background. You're glad to be alive.

I took a taxi to the Royal Hawaiian Hotel, which looked like something from the Moors, and walked over Tunisian carpets past the French art they got on the walls. Young guys on wooden planks rode the waves in the surf beyond the lanai where I sipped a rum drink.

"They call those surfboards," the waiter said.

I changed, swam in the ocean, and worked on my tan some more. I decided I'd learn to ride one of those surfboards to brag about it later. There were women on the beach watching, and who knew what might come of that.

The next day I took a taxi to Fourteenth Naval District headquarters to see Commander Webster Magee, flag secretary to Admiral James O. Richardson, CINCUS. That was short for Commander-in-Chief of the U.S. Fleet, the official name back then for the Pacific Fleet. They changed it after Pearl Harbor and you don't have to ask why.

"Welcome to Hawaii, Captain," Magee said, rising from his desk. He had snowy hair and a square jaw and a direct, honest look that put me on guard. "I see you got a good start on a tan."

If I'd known it was this nice, I said, I would have asked for a transfer a long time ago.

"Honolulu has all the vices of the East and West," Magee said. "This was a windjammer port in the days of sail. Sailors from all over the world dropped anchor to get drunk and satisfy their carnal lust."

You have to be careful with people like Magee. When they drop to their knees and lift their eyes to heaven they're not acting. A normal man is uncomfortable around them.

"I looked you up in the Naval Academy Register for the admiral. I guess meteor-like describes your career...at least recently. And now a captain. The register didn't have that."

I said I happened to be the right man at the right time, nothing more to it than that.

"Uncle Jo is looking forward to a chat."

Like with Admiral Hughes, I said I wasn't interested in high level briefings; that wasn't the way I worked. I'm there for the skinny from junior officers and senior non-coms so you staff guys won't be seeing much of me. Give my compliments to Admiral Richardson. I'll need a car and driver for a week or so if the fleet would be so kind.

"The admiral won't like this," Magee warned.

The White House screens out a lot of the real world, but it comes roaring back the farther away you get. When Richardson was chief of the Bureau of Navigation, I bet he smiled and kowtowed with the best of them. But now that he was a fleet admiral five thousand miles from Washington he was a law unto himself.

I no sooner got back to the Royal Hawaiian and was changing into my swimming suit when there was a knock at the door. A Navy lieutenant was there with two shore patrolmen in white helmets and leggings and pistols in holsters. They were the burly types I led driving drunken sailors back to the ships.

"Beg your pardon, Captain," the lieutenant said trying to hide a smile, "but Admiral Richardson requests that you return immediately to headquarters. My orders are to accompany you."

I could have tried to telephone Harry and after all the usual delays and faint voices on the line, I might actually have reached him. Then he would call Nimitz, and maybe the admiral would be in his office and Harry could straighten this out. Maybe Nimitz would and maybe he wouldn't. But it would be more likely Harry would want to check with the president first, and he'd be tied up in a meeting or something. If I was really lucky, Franklin would be at his stamp collection with the magnifying glass. But he wouldn't go against a fleet admiral for something as petty as this. Or maybe Harry would dope this all out in five seconds and tell me, "Sorry; no can do." So I got dressed again and went with them.

Uncle Jo kept me sitting in an outer office for a half hour before Magee said to come in. He was a bald, jug-eared, stocky guy with a grizzled look. He had skippered torpedo boats, gunboats, destroyers and probably every other ship except subs. Only crazy men volunteered for that duty. I hadn't bothered to check out all he'd done because the plan had been to give him plenty of sea room.

"What the hell is this all about?" Admiral Richardson said; another Texan from his accent. It seemed to me the Navy had more than its share of them.

Remaining standing because he didn't invite me to take a chair, I explained I was conducting an informal study for the White House. It occurred to me that Nimitz sent his old friend a cable with some history about me.

He snorted and gave Magee a look.

"Are they reading the reports I send?" he asked me.

I have no knowledge of that, Admiral.

"They would be fully informed if they do, and you would have been spared a long trip." He smiled sarcastically. "But then it's pretty pleasant at the Royal Hawaiian."

I looked straight ahead.

Richardson opened a file on his desk. "Just to pick something at random, this fleet is short three hundred and fifty lieutenants and lieutenant commanders. Destroyers are putting to sea with crews of a hundred and ninety instead of the full complement of two hundred and thirty-five. Magee tells me from your record you're light on sea duty, but I expect you know what that means. I was notified the other day that my cruisers will get two fewer machinists and the communication watch will be reduced to one lieutenant and an ensign. We're under strength five officers on heavy cruisers as it is."

I wasn't aware of this, Admiral.

"Who's going to man all these new ships we're building, that's what I want to know."

I didn't think I was expected to give an opinion.

"I tell Washington about this and other problems you'd think they would want to pay attention to, but I might as well yell down a hole. I keep two-thirds of the fleet at sea at all times, but I'm informed that will be cut back to a third next year to save on wear and tear. We've already cut sailing speeds to twenty-four knots for destroyers and cruisers and fifteen knots for battleships. We call it a scouting force, but it's doing a damn less scouting than it should."

I shook my head like this was hard to believe.

"The reserve officers I'm getting aren't up to the Great War quality; they're not qualified to relieve regular line officers. They're weak on discipline and initiative and need more supervision. You have to watch them like hawks."

I wasn't aware of that, sir, I said. I'll certainly see the president is told.

"You spend a lot of time with him, do you?"

Mostly with Harry Hopkins, I said.

"I thought he was sick. Cancer, someone said."

He's back to work now, Admiral.

"To protect Pearl Harbor from an attack by Jap carriers I would have to patrol every night out to a distance of eight hundred miles on a 360-degree arc. That's a sixteen-hour flight. Do you know how many PBYs I would need?"

A lot, I said.

It would take two-hundred and fifty. Do you know how many I have right now in flying condition?"

I couldn't guess, Admiral.

"Forty-nine."

He let that sink in.

"Magee tells me you have some asinine idea of going around talking to junior officers and non-coms."

Yes, sir. I've found that questioning the…

"Well, you can forget that. I'll tell you what you need to know, and you can read the cables I sent to Washington. Magee will show you around so you get a sense of the place. A PBY is flying to San Francisco day after tomorrow. You'll be back in Washington the following morning. I'm sure they'll be glad to have an officer of your value back on the job now that the Germans have attacked Norway."

An evil grin spread on that wrinkled old mug of his.

"I guess you were planning on a longer visit to our island paradise. The first thing that will become apparent in your inspection is this is no place to base a fleet. For one thing, we don't have the facilities to maintain it."

He leaned me back in his chair and looked me over. He didn't like my new uniform, nipped in Italian style at the waist against regulations. He said he wouldn't permit it with any officer under his command. He finally let me sit and then let her rip. I was a stand-in for the people in Washington he really wanted to chew out.

"When we brought the fleet out here from the West Coast for the annual exercise, I thought we'd be ordered back to our home ports as usual when it was over. And yet we're still out here with our thumb up our ass. Have they said why?"

Not to me, Admiral.

He ticked off more of what was wrong. Pearl Harbor and the Lahaina anchorage were too small and crowded, reenlistment was down because of no family housing, bottoms fouled faster because of the warmer water, everything had to be imported, and that cost an arm and leg. If war broke out the fleet would have to return to home ports on the West Coast to get fitted out and gather its auxiliary ships, and so on and so forth. I won't bore you with details, but he made a good case. That led to my fatal mistake as you will hear in due course. Waiter, there stands an empty glass. Well, would you look at who just walked in the door? Pay no attention to the FBI agents, dear; they think they're invisible.

"I've heard through unofficial channels," the admiral said, "that the State Department pansies convinced the president that keeping the fleet here has a restraining influence on the Japanese. They're not fools in Tokyo; they're hard-headed military men who have been fighting in China for years. They've got spies throughout the islands, and it's obvious there's no fleet train here. They see it for what it is: an empty bluff with nothing behind it."

As the admiral kept going, I had to force myself to keep my eyes from the windows and the palms swaying like hips and the blue sky and fluffy clouds. Man alive, the Navy had a sweet spot there.

After he was finished, I was parked at a desk to read the cables he sent to Washington. The Orange war plan in effect at the time—Orange was what we called the Japs—called for the Pacific Fleet to move westward to recapture Guam and the Philippines after they fell. But we lacked floating dry docks, ships for distilling water, high-speed oilers, tenders, mine sweepers, mine layers and sub nets, landing boats, equipment for building airfields—it went on and on. Richardson was a great man for the small stuff. Every detail of every detail was explained, more than once in some cases. Well, a lot of cases. It was eight o'clock by the time I was finished and my jaw ached from yawning. Why was I reading this stuff if Washington wasn't interested? Well, I had been ordered to read it; that's the short answer.

The next day Commander Magee drove me around to show the points of interest. He was a New England puritan and didn't care for the lazy tropical pace, but it was right down my alley.

"People come in late and go home early for a drink on the lanai," he said. "The district commandants are elderly admirals who get one last cushy billet to ease them into retirement, and they don't demand much from their staff. Richardson tries to maintain stateside standards, but the whole place is slack. Lazy is not putting it too strong."

We visited the naval station, Hickham Field—Magee said we had blazing arguments with the Army over the tight air space—and then took a launch over to Ford Island and Battleship Row, where *California*, *Arizona* and *Maryland* were anchored.

"Everyone is shorthanded," he said. "They're losing officers and men to the new ships coming out of the yards. You can build a destroyer in twenty-three months but it takes twenty-four months for a fairly bright recruit to be turned into a petty officer third class. Six years for a chief petty officer."

Civilians don't think of things like that, so that was something for Harry to chew on. The training centers were bottlenecks, according to Magee; they were too slow handling the masses of men coming into the Navy.

"The Army is in charge of defense if the fleet is out to sea and we are if the fleet's in," Magee said. "Each ship is assigned a field of fire by the naval district."

I should tell you that naval doctrine says bases protect fleets, not the other way around. Somebody had screwed up, but in military life that's an everyday fact of life.

"The Army has seventy-five three-inch guns but only enough people to crew seventeen. Their feeling is why spend money on harbor defenses when the Navy has all those guns on ships. There are a few machine guns on the ground at Hickham to defend against saboteurs, but none for air attacks. No ditches or slit trenches anywhere, either. The post guards only carry pistols."

That's not good, I said.

Magee gave me a pained look. He probably thought I should say something stronger, but I didn't want to get in the crossfire.

"Another reason to get back to the mainland," he said, "is everything from bunker fuel to toilet paper has to be shipped, and that's expensive as hell."

Big oil tanks that held bunker fuel and aviation gasoline were on the hills around the harbor. I said they sure looked like fat targets.

"It would take a year to replace them, and the fleet would be twirling its thumbs all that time. They ought to be underground, but that costs money."

We got back in the car and drove to the north side of the island to look at airfields, passing miles of sugar cane plantations and pineapple orchards. At Wheeler we watched one of the new B-17 bombers take off on a training flight.

"The Army says they'll be murder against shipping, but I wonder if they realize how much harder it is to hit a moving ship than the stationary targets they use."

Soldiers napped under palm trees or played lazy games of catch. People moved slower than on the mainland. It was the way of life.

"Like I say, it's the tropics," Magee said when I mentioned it. "Nobody pushes hard except the Japs. Hardest working people you ever saw." We stopped for sodas at a small, crossroads country store in a grove of pineapple trees.

"You notice anything unusual about that store?" he asked as we drove away.

I said the pineapples looked really fresh.

"Half the stuff on the shelves has Japanese labels. That's the big worry here. A third of the population is Jap and ten per cent have Japanese citizenship only. When the Imperial Japanese Navy arrives for official visits, the welcome the Nisei gives them looks like Mardi Gras. A district commandant kicked up an almighty fuss when he doubted we could count on them in war. He caught hell from the local politicians, but, hell, that's what everybody says in private. They Japs are a clannish bunch. Their kids go to their own schools to learn Japanese after public school. Figure five per cent with us in a war, five per cent against, and the rest on the fence. Army intelligence thinks the Japs have a fifth column ready to go. We'd like to buy up the land around the bases so the locals don't shoot at us from the sugar cane, but the growers want too much."

From his remarks, I judged that Magee had a pretty low opinion of the Army.

"They go their way and we go ours," he said. "There's not much mixing socially, either."

We drove past a cop on Kalakaua Avenue—that's the main drag—who was wearing a lei and directed traffic like he was doing the hula. I got a laugh out of it, but Magee said to him it was unprofessional.

"The other islanders aren't much friendlier than the Japs. My wife tells me you can be first in line at a store but they wait on their own people first. There's a brawl just about every weekend between sailors and natives. Both sides are drunk on okolehao, which has the kick of moonshine. I suggest you steer clear of Iwelai and Blama; those are the red-light districts. There's still a lot of bad feeling over the Massie case in the early 'Thirties."

Never heard of it, I said.

"A young lieutenant's wife got in an argument one Saturday night at the Ala Wai Club and walked out on him. She was gang raped by a bunch of locals. Feeling here ran high enough that there was talk about imposing martial law. The guys were arrested but a jury let them off.

We put pressure on and another trial was scheduled, but the husband and a couple of enlisted men kidnapped one of the suspects and killed him. The famous Clarence Darrow came over from the mainland and got them off with an hour of detention. They served it right there in the courthouse."

We drove up into the foothills where mansions stood on grounds as green and smooth as a billiard table.

"That's where the *kamaaina haoles* live—'old whites' to you. They're the descendants of the Scottish and English merchants and the Yankee traders and missionaries who got here when they were still called the Sandwich Islands. They grabbed the best of everything."

I'm looking for a rich wife, I said. Which door do I knock on?

"You'd have to ask someone else," Magee said, real sharp.

He was not a barrel of laughs, as I hope you're getting the idea.

The three of us had lunch at the admiral's home and Richardson pounded away some more on the Orange War Plan. Even Walt Disney couldn't match that fantasy, he said. The Imperial Japanese Navy was stronger in the Pacific, especially with so many of our ships gone to the Atlantic Squadron, yet we were supposed to establish bases in the Marshalls and Carolinas as soon as hostilities broke out.

"Do you know how many charts and maps we have of those areas? Tell him, Magee."

"None."

"He's exaggerating; we might have one or two from the Captain Cook days. The Fleet Marines aren't big enough to hold a base against strong opposition, and the Army has zero capability in that regard. And how do we put anybody ashore in the first place, forgetting for the moment what they'd need to build airfields and defenses?"

I cleared my throat. Aren't there plans for...

"The president seems to think passenger liners can be used. They could if it was dock to dock, but it isn't. They would have to be converted to amphibious attack transports with small boats to land troops and equipment on a hostile shore in a ground swell. It would take the shipbuilding industry a year for that conversion."

On and on he went. We were building seventeen battleships; twelve *Essex* class carriers and who knew how many baby flattops; three battle cruisers; forty-eight light cruisers; a hundred and sixty eight destroyers; but—and here he held my eye like a hypnotist—only two repair ships and six destroyer tenders. "There should be one repair ship for every twenty big ships and a tender for every eighteen destroyers."

I thought he'd never wind down. Ah, here's our lunch. That flounder looks very good. I'm glad you're eating more than just salad these days. Rabbit food I call it. More bread, waiter. Tell me, Harriet, should we send a bottle of wine over to our friends? No, you're right, salt in the wound.

Admiral Richardson said something very strange out of the blue that day. "I'm a suspicious man, Captain. I sometimes wonder if we're being set up out here."

For what, I asked.

"There's going to be war with Japan. Hell, that's not news. Roosevelt told people war was inevitable when he was assistant secretary of the Navy twenty years ago. I heard him with my own ears. Seems he had a Jap roommate in college who told him they thought so themselves—just a matter of time. The president must be afraid England will be beaten, the Royal Navy fall under German control, and we end up all alone. The Krauts ruling Europe, the Japs in the saddle in Asia, and South America rotten to the core with fascists—not a very pretty prospect."

I didn't want to say anything for fear he'd think I was speaking for the White House, but he didn't take his eyes off me. I finally asked the question he wanted me to. What did he mean by "set up"?

"It seems to me the president believes the war will be lost before we even get into it. An attack on Guam or the Philippines might not be enough to do the trick, but what about Hawaii?"

I had him there. How would war against Japan help England?

"It wouldn't unless Germany and Japan were allies. Look around, Magee, and make sure there are no listening ears. Check outside too."

As soon as he was gone, Richardson leaned closer. "There's a building not far from here that even CINCUS can't go into. I'd be stopped by armed sentries. Even me! It's so secret my flag secretary doesn't even know about it. That's why I sent him from the room. I believe they're breaking Jap code in that building. You're in the White House so I'm guessing you know."

I said I never heard of such a thing.

"That exactly the answer I'd expect," he said with a wink. "I suspect—and I told you I was a suspicious man—the president knows there's a treaty in the works between Germany and Japan. If one goes to war, the other comes in on his side with the dagos. That'd be a blessing in disguise because it lets us get into the scrap before the British and French run up the white flag. I won't ask you to show me the flaw in my reasoning because you're sworn to secrecy. Nimitz says you're a born liar anyhow, but that's neither here or there. I don't want to hide the fleet to keep it safe, but I do want the means to defend ourselves for when the time comes. We don't at this point have those means and won't for two years. That is the message I want delivered. Tell the president at one of those White House cocktail parties; I understand you're one of the regulars. Ask him to meet with me and I'll fly back there and fill him in on all the details and answer any questions he might have."

You can imagine what was going through my mind. I go to Hawaii expecting to goof off in the sun. Not only am I screwed out of that, but I'm asked to be a back channel between CINCUS and the president.

There was more long silence with his eyes boring into mine. To break the spell, I told him I still didn't get the set up part.

"The first blow will be against the Pacific Fleet. The Japs took the Russian fleet by surprise and defeated it at Port Arthur in 1904, and they'll try that trick again. We'd have a better chance of defending ourselves at our home ports on the West Coast. You see that don't you, Captain?"

There was no dodging it. I had to say yes, I saw that.

He went back to staring, his will against mine. We might have sat there until suppertime except I caved in and said I'd do what I could. He stood and gripped my hand.

"We're counting on you," he said.

The PBY took off at four the next morning for the thirty-hour flight to San Francisco. I made a place for myself among the sacks of official mail—urgent military communications went by air back then and the rest by slow boat. Sometimes they got mixed up, as you might expect. If the Army can't find a way to screw up things, the Navy will do the job for you.

We landed at Treasure Island before noon and a car drove me to the airport where I flew in a DC3 to Washington. That was another fifteen hours in the air, not counting stopovers. You had to be an iron man those days.

I wouldn't mind a nice chunk of Stilton cheese to round off the meal. Port, of course. How about you, dear? Then it's back to the old soldiers' home for my nap.

CHAPTER 14

RENEE PHELPS, OUR ROOMMATE FROM NEW JERSEY, CAME HOME FRAZZLED from work a few days after my lunch with Captain Brady. To hear her talk, her suffering at the Department of Commerce approached martyrdom. She always had a profusion of detail about the latest outrage, and when that was exhausted she reminded us of past injustices she had suffered.

"What a lousy day," she said flinging herself into a chair still in her coat. A trim brunette with features that made you think of a cat, she was impatient for the man of her dreams to take her away from all of this.

"Where's my Mr. Right?" she said as she had many times. "Why's it taking so long?"

These were wrongs with which we were wearyingly familiar, at least I was, the chief of which was her boss had his favorites and she wasn't one of them. As a consequence Renee got the most tedious and boring jobs. She didn't know why he didn't like her, but it wasn't anything she had said or done, of that she was certain. It wasn't only the fractious relationship with her boss. The office was too hot, and the smell of the sack lunches her coworkers brought sickened her. One man brought sardine and onion sandwiches every day and drank sodas that made him gassy. Or the office was so cold people worked in their coats. They sneezed germs into the air or hawked to clear their throats or annoyed her in a hundred other ways. Her new nylons, bought just the day before, already had a run. Did we know what they cost? (Of course we did.)

She interrupted this recitation of woes to say to Denise, "I saw your boy-friend just now. He was talking to two men sitting in a car."

"He's not my boyfriend," Denise said. "We just went to that ball game. A hot dog with that awful green relish on it was our dinner. He's the last of the big spenders."

"I called about the telephone," Mitzi volunteered. "They said they'd send someone to look."

We had all noticed clicks on the line and Mitzi got the feeling someone listened in on her conversation with her parents in Connecticut.

Captain Brady had warned me to expect it. "They'll plant hidden micro-phones too."

So I was prepared for surveillance, but the surprise that Greg was one of them gave me a sick feeling. He pulled his car over as I walked to the bus stop the next morning.

"I've got some interesting news," he said. "C'mon, I'll give you a ride to work. No need to freeze in the breeze."

His sparkling eyes told me he was bursting with whatever his news was. He kept a teasing silence until we turned on Third Street Northeast.

"My friend with the cop shop asked a few questions. Those guys in the car? They're with the federal government, and I bet they're FBI agents. They must be watching someone in the neighborhood."

"Did you talk to them?"

"Yeah, how did you know? I went up to the window and asked if they were on a surveillance job. They were pissed off and told me to beat it. They drove away a minute later."

"What if I told you they're watching me?"

"I'm serious, there's somebody in the neighborhood so bad the FBI has them staked out. Maybe it's a Russian spy." He was as excited as if he saw a home run go over the wall. "So what'd you do, rob a bank?" He laughed at first and then had a look of growing astonishment as it sank in I was serious.

"Here's the Smithsonian," I said.

He put a hand on my arm. "Wait a minute," he said, "you gotta tell me what you're talking about."

I said it was a long story and I didn't have time to explain now.

"Come on, you can't leave me hanging like this. Dinner tonight?" As I hurried away, he called out to me. "I'll pick you up at seven."

I had no sooner taken off my gloves and hung up my coat than Mr. Pettigrew, jittery and smoking furiously, asked me to join him in his office.

"Hawley tells me that last interview was worthless."

After we had returned to his room after that lunch, I persuaded Captain Brady to postpone his nap in order to dilate on various unimportant subjects for the FBI to listen to on the tape.

"Those sea shanties he sang," Pettigrew said with irritation, "who would have thought *Whiskey Johnny* would have so many verses, and then there was *Hog-Eye Man*. How can the man keep it all in his head?"

"He just about has total recall," I said.

"Jesus, what a waste of a brain." Pettigrew walked around smoking and jingling change in his pocket. "Think of it, a man with that mental power in an old soldiers' home. I'm not a philosophical man, still less religious, but it makes you wonder why talents get distributed the way they do."

"If you read the transcript, you know I kept trying to lead back him to the start of the war."

"I have the impression time and patience is running out."

"What do you mean?"

"There is always a period of drift in this town between when an administration is elected and takes office. General Eisenhower will be the first Republican president in two decades. The Democrats deserve what they get for serving up an egghead like Adlai Stephenson, but never mind. There are a lot of loose strings the bureaucracies want tidied up before the new appointees take charge."

I asked what he meant. He lit a new cigarette from the end of the other.

"If the past two administrations can be shamed by unearthed scandal that will redound to the advantage of the general, whose campaign stressed the political corruption of the other party. Matters that could end careers or, worse, lead to investigations and criminal indictments must be resolved as quietly as possible. These are the days when things get swept under the rug. I'm sure whatever they want to know can be discovered by methods other than your leisurely questioning."

I felt my stomach drop to the floor.

"Director Hoover puts a nice face on the FBI, but you are naïve to think the agency doesn't have a dark side. I am washing my hands of this business; I told Hawley so. He didn't like it, but that's hard cheese. I have dictated a memo for the record setting forth what I know to this point and I informed him of that fact. He liked that even less. You and I will not speak of it again."

"But what about me?"

"This now a matter between you and the FBI." His face was a cold mask.

I was being squeezed between forces I had no control over. Captain Brady continued to unspool his past at a glacial pace, and the FBI was running out of patience. That Pettigrew had formally separated himself from further involvement and written a memo for the record, a warning to the FBI that he was prepared to use his considerable bureaucratic savvy to protect himself, was an ominous development. He knew the ropes and pulleys behind the scene, but I did not have that advantage.

I hadn't wanted to bother Dr. Broadbrow, my mentor since coming to the Smithsonian, particularly as I'd been avoiding seeing him and his wife for fear I would inadvertently say something that would draw him into this. But I went straight to his department where his loyal secretary Angelica guarded the inner office.

"He won't be in today," she said. Angelica knew how close we were. "He hasn't been well for a long time. Anne's trying to get him to see a doctor." She lowered her voice. "Haven't you seen him lately?"

"No...I've been very busy."

"He's lost a lot of weight." Her eyes filled with tears.

"Why so glum, chum?" Greg said that night over dinner at Ling's, a chow mein joint with plastic tablecloths and fake flowers. "Got some troubles, Bubbles?"

I laughed despite myself. Greg's silliness had that effect.

"No, seriously, if there's anything I can do."

The dam broke and I started talking and talking and didn't stop until I had told him everything from when the man with the mop led me to Crockett's room to now as I broke open my fortune cookie.

"Expect the unexpected," it said.

"That doesn't have to mean bad," Greg said, "it could be good."

The sympathy that shone in his eyes warmed me. Sharing my burden didn't make it lighter, but somehow more bearable.

"Hey, how could you ever think I was with the FBI? I'd have to be a two-faced son of a gun."

I said I was sorry I doubted him. "I've never been in a situation like this."

"What do you think the big secret is?" he asked.

"It has something to do with the start of the war," I said.

"Let's see," he said, "the Russians were boycotting the Security Council and…"

"Not this one," I interrupted, "World War Two."

"We were attacked at Pearl Harbor. There's nothing secret about that."

"That's what I thought."

He stared into space, his brow furrowed. "And this old guy knows what the government wants to stay secret?"

"He'll tell, but only in his own good time."

"Boy, these are deep waters. You poor kid, it must be hell."

I sniffled and fumbled in my purse for a handkerchief. "Excuse me, I'm *never* like this."

"Golly, who can blame you?"

Greg walked me back to the apartment and surprised me at the door with a peck on the cheek. I struggled against the urge to follow him up the stairs.

Denise was catty. "Did you have onions with your hot dog?"

"We went to Cathay Gardens," I said.

That was the expensive Chinese restaurant with white linen tablecloths, and her face fell gratifyingly. I tossed and turned that night, my mind switching back and forth from my troubles to Greg's kiss. Denise said they had shaken hands at the door. I felt like a cockleshell on a tossing sea, emotion taking me first in one direction and then reason in another.

Captain Brady got blustery when I told him about the meeting with Pettigrew and my dinner with Greg.

"Pettigrew is looking out for himself, the same as I'd do in his shoes. As for this Greg character, I wouldn't trust him as far as I could throw him.

I've fed the ladies a few lines in my time, and this is one—guaranteed. Do you think they'd plant a guy in the building who actually *looked* like an FBI agent? It's your business; be a fool if you want."

* * *

Let's see, where were we? When I got back to Washington I was hoping for a couple of days to recover from travel, but an ensign was at the airport with a message to go directly to the White House.

The telephone was ringing when I got to the cloak room. "Finally," Garrison said. "It's been ringing off and on for an hour. I would have said you were in Hawaii except you told me never to touch your phone."

A woman's voice was on the line and then through the static Winston's came on.

"This is Naval Person speaking," he said. "Tell our friend the storm has broken upon us in full fury, but they have miscalculated. We have the Hun right where we want them in Norway. The supply of iron ore for their war machine will be choked off, and I foresee that the French hesitation over mining the German rivers will now be resolved."

Before I could say anything, he hung up. I called Harry in Lincoln's Study and he told me to come on up. He was in bed in his pajamas with files and teletype messages scattered all around him. I told him about the call.

"What's this about mines?"

I said maybe it was something the president knows about.

"If it is, he didn't tell me. Why did you rush back?"

I said I wanted to be at my duty station at this critical time.

"I'm sure the president will be impressed, but that might have been your last chance for a vacation for a long time to come. What shape are things in out there? On second thought, save it for later. We've got our hands full right now."

Things in Norway went to hell in a hurry, if you remember. The Germans beat the English from start to finish and showed air power was a match for sea power. Seeing that in the first battle action reports, I realized I'd better switch from the battleship to the carrier school. I put it around that I had admired Billy Mitchell's ideas from the start even though it cost me as regards promotion. I see from your face you disapprove, dear, but I'm telling you as honest as I can no matter how it makes me look.

The Germans invaded Holland and Belgium next. A hot knife through butter, that was. Next thing you know Chamberlain was out and Churchill in. Then France fell and the English were alone. People in the White House were worried sick. The Germans had invented a new way to wage war and there we were drilling men with broomsticks on their shoulders because there weren't rifles for them. Trucks had signs that said This is a Tank at military exercises because we didn't have the real thing.

One day the president came up the elevator to Harry's bedroom where I was chained to a telephone taking messages for Harry and passing on his orders to the people on the other end.

"An informant in Jamaica passed word that the Duke of Windsor and his wife are playing footsie with the Nazis," he said.

"What the hell for?" Harry said.

"My guess is he wants to force his brother to abdicate, take back his crown and negotiate an end to the war. Remember that picture of him giving the Heil Hitler salute in Germany? Our papers anyhow; the British press didn't print it."

"Has anyone told Joe Kennedy?"

"I'm not sure I want him to know," Franklin said. "He's in thick with those Clivedon aristocrats. I wouldn't be surprised if they hatched this up. They admire Hitler and think he's the only man who can stop communism. The duke doesn't have the brains to fish in waters this deep."

"You ought to tell Churchill," Harry said.

"I'll send him a note in the diplomatic pouch. When does the next one go out?"

We couldn't use the transatlantic telephone line because you didn't know who was listening in.

"Lowell?" Harry asked me.

They go out to London every day now, I said.

"Harry keeping you busy, Captain?" the president asked.

Yes, sir, I said. Not enough hours in the day.

"Everybody's got to work harder, right Harry?"

"You said it."

A cripple and a sick man running the country; it's amazing to think about it. Harry stayed in bed most of the time and doctors came every day to give him shots. I asked him what they were for.

"To keep me living, I suppose," he said matter-of-fact.

The president wasn't all that hale and hearty himself. A cold could last a month and he had anemia from bleeding piles that made him tired all the time. Harry told me he had headaches and fevers and spent days in bed himself. I trotted from sick bed to sick bed with papers Harry wanted the president to see.

He didn't show him too much, though. Harry said Franklin liked plenty of facts if it was something that interested him, but sometimes he couldn't get them organized right in his head. He'd get overwhelmed and Harry had to nag him to make up his mind.

A barber shaved Harry in the morning and a nurse washed his hair once a week. Eleanor dropped by to see how he was doing and always opened the window even though it was November. He told me to close it as soon as she left.

"Somebody told her a person corrupts twenty-five barrels of air sleeping every night. The lungs get waste particles that poison the blood unless the window is open at the top so the bad air gets out."

Even though he was sick, Harry was sharp as a tack. I'll pick a day at random, April 20, 1940. I remember like it was yesterday. He decided how many airplanes were to go to the Greeks and how many ships to Yugoslavia; talked to a scientist about steel alloys and a union boss about a strike that was stopping propellers for Navy fighters; gave the go ahead for government money for a new process to make aluminum; got briefed on the situation in the western Mediterranean; closed the market for quartz crystals; told the president of a company that made small-arms ammunition they had to work faster; got more copper lined up for Russia; and worked up figures on shipbuilding for the chief. Those are just the highlights. There was plenty more, but you get the idea. In between he talked to people in Congress about keeping the isolationists from putting more sand in the gears.

Every one of these deals involved one to five phone calls and guess who was in charge of that. I had to run down whoever Harry wanted to talk to, even if I had to send someone to get them out of the shower or where they were fishing. People on the West Coast were always asking did I know what time it was when I called. I once had Henry J. Kaiser pulled off the john where he studied the newspaper every morning. I'd no sooner put down the receiver than the phone rang again. Sometimes we were both on two at the same time, one in each ear. Harry usually said no more than yes or no to conserve his energy.

"What did he mean?" people asked when Harry passed me the call. Or they said, "Wait a minute, is that *it?*"

I told them whatever he said is what he meant. And, yes, that was it.

Some wanted to argue about it, but I had my orders and hung up. Forget politeness until we're out of the woods, Harry said. It's all business now.

The isolationists dragged their feet every step of the way, even after the Germans began bombing the bejesus out of England. Senator Wheeler from Montana said if Lend-Lease went through Franklin would bury every fourth American boy before he was done. That brought the president up to Harry's room madder than a hornet.

"Did you hear what Wheeler said?" he said as he rolled through the door in that old brown cardigan sweater he wore all the time.

The Secret Service people always stayed outside. Sometimes I got sent out too and did card tricks to entertain the guys while we waited.

Harry read the same papers, so he'd already seen what Burton said. "Call the press boys in and b last him."

But the president was already starting to simmer down.

He took a piece of paper from his wallet. "When I get hot under the collar, I look at this letter Abe Lincoln got." He read it to us. "'God damn your god damned old hell-fired god damned soul to hell god damn you and god damn your god damned family's god damned hell-fired god damned soul to hell and damnation god damn them and god damn your god damned friends to hell." He laughed. "I'll tell the press what Wheeler said is the rottenest thing I've seen in a generation.'"

Harry said, "That's not good enough. Tell the mothers of America you won't send their boys to fight in a foreign war."

"War's coming one way or another. Everybody knows that."

"The mothers of America don't. They won't vote for you if they think that's what you've got up your sleeve."

Roosevelt thought about it and nodded. "I'll get the speechwriters on it." Sure enough, that was a regular line in the campaign against Wilkie.

Harry said after he left, "Sometimes he doesn't see the most obvious things even when they're right in front of him."

Joe Kennedy was becoming a major pain in the ass judging from how often Harry mentioned him. He kept saying the English were licked. Then he started to put it around that the chief was conniving with Churchill. Some said he was going to run for president himself.

"He won't," Harry said. "He's wants Joe Junior to be president someday, and he knows he can forget about it if he crosses the chief." He smiled. "Nobody worked harder than Joe to get that ambassadorship. The boss called him in and asked him to drop his trousers. True story, swear to God. He'd heard from someone who saw Joe in a bathing suit that he had the worst bowed legs ever. New ambassadors had to present themselves in tights and silk stockings, and Roosevelt said he'd be a laughingstock and so would the country. Kennedy pulled his pants up and said he'd get London to give him a pass on tradition."

I didn't get home before ten on a good day. Mother knew how bad the food was at the White House and had something waiting for me; she and the Senator were in bed by then. Some nights I was too tired to eat and just stumbled up to bed. It didn't feel right to wake up in my clothes without even a hangover to show for it. This was seven days a week by the way. Harry spent Sunday mornings with his daughter and let me come in at noon like he was doing me a big favor.

To be honest there got to be a time when I was glad he was feeling poorly. If he'd been healthy he would have worked me to death; he was like Roosevelt in that regard. Fortunately, every four hours or so his head fell back on the pillow and he was out like a light. I'd tell the switchboard no more calls and go out for some fresh air. Or maybe I'd chat up the talent in the secretarial pool if I had the energy, which I didn't a lot of time. Man, was I dragging. I'd be back when he woke up. Now where were we, he'd say, and we'd pick up where we left off.

As the weeks passed he got better and began dressing and going downstairs for meetings, but he went back to bed right away and spent the rest of the day there. One morning he came from the president and told me he was going to London for a couple of weeks to talk to Churchill.

Send me a postcard, I said.

"You're coming with me."

We flew under assumed names on a Pan Am Clipper to Bermuda and on from there to the Azores and then on to Lisbon. After a day's layover, we flew to the south of England, making a loop far back out into the Atlantic to avoid the German fighters in occupied France. The Clipper was big and slow, the civilian version of the one from Hawaii. But it was the difference between night and day, the very lap of luxury. It had air conditioning, berths, and tables with linen napkins and china service, and even a lounge. The crew had nautical ratings and blue uniforms with silver epaulets and buttons, and they rang a ship's bell on the hour. The captain was called the master like in the days of sail, and sat at a desk behind the pilot on the upper deck. The navigator, a guy with a big can on him, climbed a ladder to take celestial sightings from a transparent dome.

Harry was feeling poorly and stayed in his berth after takeoff. "He's very neglectful about his medications," Eleanor said before we left, "so you have to do the remembering for him. He has pills for his stomach pain, pills to keep him going when he runs out of energy, and pills to help him sleep." She gave me two heavy quart bottles of what looked like motor oil. "Make sure he takes two spoons of this twice a day."

Harry flared up when he sniffed the bottle. "Christ! Throw that out."

Harry, I said, Mrs. Roosevelt...

"I don't give a damn what she said. Did you smell it?" I said I had. "What does it remind you of?"

A swamp, Harry. We have them back home so full of snakes that...

"No, it smells like a cesspool. What's it for, digestion?"

That's what she told me.

"It smells like it was digested by somebody else before it was put in the bottle. Throw it away before I puke."

He rolled over in his berth and I went forward and took a stool at the tiny bar.

"You are traveling with Mr. Hopkins?" asked a man who joined me.

He had jowls like pork chops and a roll of fat on the back of his neck. Big belly and fat hands. He made you think of a butcher shop on legs. Kraut accent, jolly way about him. A guy from naval intelligence had warned me Lisbon was a hotbed of espionage and spies traveled back and forth on this flight.

"Ja, from the newsreels I recognize him. My name is Otto Heidel. He is under the weather, yes?"

Put 'er there. Call me Mort. Who'd you say?

"Harry Hopkins."

I said Harv would sock somebody if they said that to his face. He was a Willkie man and voted for Landon and Hoover before that. I laughed like I thought what a funny thing to say. I asked where he was from.

"I am from Austria."

He said he was a commercial traveler in shoes and belts. I said we represented Stanhope furniture featuring the Close Quarters queen-size bed.

"Before you ask," he said, "like most good Austrians I was to the Anschluss opposed."

I said I seemed to remember bands and parades when the Germans marched in, and weren't people throwing flowers?

He shook his head sadly. "Your press emphasized that unfairly. Most were opposed, but the loud get the attention. Is it not so in your country as well?"

He bought me another and we talked about beer. "I like your country, but your beer? Nein, too weak. The English ale is good, but you have to give the honors to the Germans. Their beer is top of the mountain."

I figured from his age he must have been an officer in the Great War.

Ja, he said, he had fought under Emperor Franz Josef and then the great-nephew after the old man died. The Hungarians and the rest of the rabble in the empire were useless. He had used the flat of his sword on the cowards; better they should have been on the other side. He gave me a nudge with his elbow.

"How the stewardesses look at you. Women must be easy for you, no?"

I said modesty forbids. That got a laugh from him, actually more a bellow with wheezing and coughing. We were already buddies.

"Why does your friend, who is not Harry Hopkins, stay in his berth always?"

He thinks it's a bad cold, I said, but my hunch is the flu.

"Gott im Himmel. He should not be in public with such germs."

Herr Heidel said he nearly died in the big epidemic that killed who knows how many. Millions and millions. They were dying so fast the grave-diggers couldn't keep up. They had to close schoolhouses back home for room to stack the bodies. Funny how nobody talks about that anymore.

Otto held thumb and finger an inch apart. "This close I came to death."

I said Harv's symptoms came on in a hurry.

"That is the flu, ja."

Harv's a friendly guy even sick as a dog, I told him. Want to say hello? Just keep a handkerchief over your mouth and nose. It seems to work, except my throat is a little scratchy. I got up like I was saying let's go.

"Nein, nein," he said. "I won't bother your friend."

I coughed into my hand and he shifted his stool to put a little more distance between us. It was madness for the English and Germans to be fighting, he said. Why? Why?

"The true enemy is to the east. He has many faults, Hitler, but he agrees with Churchill that the Bolsheviks must be stopped."

Harv and I make a point of standing clear of politics, I said; that stuff's no good for business. He agreed and dropped the subject, and didn't seem to have any more interest in Harry. Otto was a pretty nice guy for a spy, which I'm fairly sure he was. It would have been quite a coup for him to report that the president's right-hand man was traveling to Europe in secret. We could have got along under other circumstances, but then you can say that about a lot people you really don't know. He got off the plane in Lisbon and waddled across the tarmac ahead of us, and I never saw him again.

CHAPTER 15

GREG WAS IN A STATE OF HIGH EXCITEMENT, TELLING ME THAT I WASN'T going to believe what he was going to say when we met for coffee around from the Treasury Building.

"*I'm* being followed," he said when we sat down. He acted like it was a tremendous honor. "I lost them with a trick from a Humphrey Bogart movie. You walk through the front of a restaurant and out the kitchen."

"Oh no!" My hand went to my mouth.

He laughed at my alarm. "No big deal."

"Being followed by the FBI isn't a big deal?"

"My world?" he said with scorn. "My world is looking up old documents to clarify if clause 27, parenthesis Section B parenthesis means what Treasury says or the way Commerce interprets it. This is like the movies!"

I wish I could say looking back this made alarm bells go off, but tragically I was not that percipient. For most of us, picture shows are merely an interruption of mundane reality that fades when we leave the theater, but I came to see that for Greg it was life as he wished it to be. I dreaded being the object of an investigation, but for him "having a tail," as he put it, charged dull existence with glamour and excitement. He had gone from just a fan rooting on the sidelines to being part of the action.

"You've got to let me read these transcripts, the real ones, not what you gave to the FBI. Whatever he knows is giving the government conniptions."

I reminded him that Captain Brady had not, as yet, given me any proof of anything.

"But don't you see, the way the FBI is digging into this is all the proof you need," he said.

I acknowledged that was a logical inference, but said that it fell far short of proof, historical or legal. There was another not-so-small point to consider. "He says he will be killed or confined until he dies because of what he knows. Why wouldn't a similar fate await us?"

"That's crazy talk," Greg said, grinning. "This isn't the Soviet Union or someplace like that. They couldn't get away with that here, not in a million years. We're a nation of laws, not men."

He was reciting something he heard in a civics class. I too had absorbed that belief as well as teachings about separation of powers and other aspects of our form of government. But this structure, devised to restrain the worst in man, depended in part on consensual behavior. The law could punish aberrant behavior but not prevent it. That required self-restraint or fear of retribution. Hoover, according to Pettigrew, was a law unto himself with the power to depart from consensual beliefs with impunity when circumstances warranted.

"You notice we're both sneaking looks to see if we're being watched?" Greg said. His eyes sparkled with delight. "Isn't it the greatest?" He reminded me of when he was watching *The Crimson Pirate*.

I agreed to let him look at the transcripts, and when darkness fell we left the apartment building by the rear door and slipped over a low fence to the neighboring street. The night watchman knew me from my late hours in the Smithsonian and admitted us. It took Greg a couple of hours to read through them all, avidly at first and then more slowly. His disappointment showed.

"I see what you mean by no evidence. But look, you can tell he was obviously in the thick of things. Is there any way you can get him to go faster?" He made one of his funny faces.

"Now you sound like the FBI," I said, vexed at myself for laughing.

"Well, I see their point."

"He knows the fancy meals come to an end when his story does. He lived as a hobo for years; I imagine he was hungry a lot of the time and dreamed of food, so how can you blame him?"

I was too shy to reach for his hand after we alighted from the bus that took us back home. He was so caught up in our "adventure" that he gesticulated frequently.

"We've got to get him out of that place before the FBI snatches him," he said. "My folks have an empty rental in Dover. I could say I have a friend who wants it."

I said I doubted that Captain Brady could afford to pay rent. That's okay, Greg said, we'll cover it. "It's only fifty bucks a month. Like you said, we owe it to History. And it will be exciting as hell."

My earlier idealism about History had been tempered by actuality. I knew now it was naïve to believe that it existed in a state of latency, indisputable facts waiting to be discovered through diligent research. The truth was coarser: the past was clay shaped by whoever had the power. Rival narratives had to be slain, smothered in the crib or cut down in their first baby steps. What I was slowly uncovering would be a thunderclap that shook the staid world of historiography. Instead of a thin layer of sediment, an incremental addition to our understanding, I had come across a colossal up thrust whose existence could not have been imagined. It would revolutionize what we knew about America's entry into the war. I admit I was aware my status as a scholar would be magnified immeasurably when this became public.

Memorandum

April 2, 1953

To: Clyde Tolson

From: The Directorr

Subject: Lowelll Brady

For: File 24898

If the cIA has inittiated a domestical operation in violation of their charteer, as we surmise, the Bureauu will be in the bedst positi)on since before the ware to subordiinate that agency and assumeed many of its duties with a correspponding increase in our budgrget and perrsonnel.

We will continuue quidwt efforts to understand wwhat the Agency is up to in regard to LOWELL BRADY. Why igniete a public debate about Peall Harbor after all these time? Defaming the memory of President Rooseveld tserves nooo interest but the Communists. The paralysis of our political orgaans by the ddebate //that would follow seems a stroyng possibility. Thus, it seems likely the CIa has been infilttrated by Reds at a hieh level.

If that is the ccase, HARRIET GALLATIN is an Agency ooperative whose cover is the Smithsonian. ARNOLD PETTIGREW's membership in the left-wing "Scholars for a Seconnd Front" raises the possibility that he is a molee and GALLATIN's conntrol agentt. The Memorandum for the Reecort he gave to Hawley copy to me is in my view mere blauster to throw us off the scent. We will put a tapp on his telephone and coduct surveillance of his movemants. At some pint we might have to threatenn he with exxposure to gain his cooperation. I dout he is the only Communisst at the Smithsoonian.

GALLATIN is quiete friendly with GREG PEARSON, a low-level State Departmenty employeee. /He approached twe agents on surveillance duty, effectively endingg their usefulnesss for this operation. He telephone will be tapped and aactivities and moveements monitored. There are known Communists still at State aand it is possible he is part of the conspiracyy that SENATOR JOSEPH MCCARTHY claims went as high as Secretary of State GEORGE MARSHAL. The Bureau has given MCCARTHY information on occasion, but wee don't want to get involved in what I personally think are drunkken ravings about MARSHALL.

Remind the agentss about expensing costlly restaurant meals when keeeping BRADY and GALLITIN under observaation.

They do not need to make a show of who they are, but a quiet
word to the owner or mmanager should aallow them to drink
coffee a/t a table rather than orderingg expaensive meals.

Ir been awwhile ssince I used a TYPEweTer , Iknow we
agred we shld keep thiss between the two of uss , bnt this t
ook me alll afternoon .to do. tHAT is not acceptable.

/Hoover

* * *

I don't know what mental image Greg had formed of Captain Brady.
I had mentioned restaurant eating so often that he may have pictured a
jowly man like Sidney Greenstreet in *The Maltese Falcon*. That was one of
his all-time favorites.

His cocksure manner lasted up to when Captain Brady opened his door
to us. As I have written, he was still handsome, remarkably so, despite the
inroads of age, and had an impressive physical presence. The domineering manner he assumed with Greg probably went back to his whip-crack-
ing days at the Ironwood School for Boys. His handshake made Greg do a
quick two-step and cry, "Ow!"

"Sorry," Captain Brady said jovially.

Greg was put to work lugging his possessions to the car. We drove sepa-
rately to Delaware. After he helped me unload, he drove back home. Despite
being ordered around like a coolie, Greg was full of admiration for Captain
Brady when we talked next.

"Boy, what a guy," he said. "I can hardly wait to hear the juicy part the
government is scared of getting out. Do you think he'd let me sit in on
some of the Q and A?"

Captain Brady had been clear on this point. He didn't want any addition
to me and the recording machine. He sometimes seemed unaware of me as
he spoke to future historians. He almost seemed to be working his charm
on the tape recorder itself, smiling and dropping his voice as if drawing it
into his confidence.

* * *

This isn't a bad place, quiet neighborhood and all. That stale smell will go away with the windows open. Looks like nobody's lived here for a while, but a woman did at one time. You can tell from the curtains. Back when I was a tramp I would've knocked at the back door for a handout. Look, even a Kelvinator in the kitchen. Nice of you and your friend to set me up here. But, you know, it would be a lot easier to put the collar on me here than in the old soldiers' home. My old buddies would help me, hitting them with canes and ramming wheelchairs into their legs. Your boyfriend? He's a Nancy boy. He's trying to hide it, but it's as plain as the nose on your face. I can spot them a mile away; a million made passes at me over the years. They think every good looking guy must be one of them. Don't go getting all mad. I'm just setting you straight.

Okay, where was I?

We holed up in a hotel in Lisbon the embassy booked for us that was posh and private—that last being the most important because of all the spies. It was where rich men took their young mistresses for afternoon fun. The place was set back from the road behind lots of thick bushes, a former monastery they told us; thick walls and arches. The kitchen sent some sort of gruel to the room which Harry pushed away after a couple of spoonfuls.

"I can't eat it."

He sat up in bed as pale as his sheets. I gave him the pills for after meals and reminded him Eleanor said he had to drink the whole glass of water. Nagging is not in my nature, so I let it slide when he didn't.

A fair young lass promenading with her elderly sponsor gave me an encouraging wink while I was looking around. The liver-spotted duffer had hair combed over bald spots and a wide belt to keep his gut in. He glared to warn me off, but I just grinned. I was looking forward to cutting down to the bar later on and hoping something turned up, namely her.

"We're entering a dark time in history," Harry said, "and it's going to get worse."

Yes, Harry, 'deed it does look that way. Can I fluff the pillows up a little? Big day tomorrow. You want to be rested.

"Any man who's an optimist about the future is a fool."

Harry was usually pretty upbeat—debonair is what the president called him. That means happy-go-lucky, right, or is that another word? That night it was like a dark raincloud hung over him.

"Unless Hitler makes some terrible blunder, I don't see how Germany can be beat. I hope Churchill gives me hope they can hang on until we get into the fight."

I pointed out that the president promised he wouldn't send our boys off to a foreign war.

"Oh, that was just campaign talk," Harry said like he was waving off a fly. "Nobody believes that stuff."

Growing up around the Senator, he didn't need to tell me. But to hear the president's right-hand man say people who believed what politicians say are idiots—well, let's just say you don't get honesty like that every day of the week.

"You're authorized to read top secret stuff, right?"

If I'm not, I said, someone's neck ought to be on the chopping block seeing as how...

"Look at this," he interrupted. He tossed me a file with the name Estimate of the Situation in the Pacific and Recommendations for Action.

To boil it down, German, Italy and Japan were against us and the Russians were on the fence but leaning toward Hitler, who wanted to keep us on the sidelines. We ought to keep the British Empire on its feet until we got in the fighting, which should be ASAP. The Germans were causing trouble in Central and South America and egging the Japs on in the Far East. That crowd would declare war on us if we came in on England's side; even if we stayed neutral they'd turn on us once the English were licked. God help us if their fleet fell into German hands. We had to get the Japs to attack us before it was too late and that could be done by cutting off oil and trade and helping the Chinese and so forth.

Harry was giving me a sharp look when I finished reading, probably because my jaw had dropped. Hold on, I said, didn't the newspapers just say ninety percent of the people don't want a thing to do with Europe and its wars?

"They'll change their mind when we're attacked," Harry said. "That'll happen when the Japs walk into this trap and see there's no way out short of war. What do you think Churchill's reaction will be?"

Old and fat as he is, I said, he might try a cartwheel.

"We had it worked up so we could get going as soon as the chief won his third term."

You count on Hitler coming in on the Jap side?

"To honor their treaty, yes."

Hitler wipes his ass with treaties.

"Then we'll think up something else." His eyes narrowed. "Say, you *do* agree we have to get into this war?"

Of course, Harry. I can't wait to ride to the sound of the guns. They say you're never more alive. It's just you caught me by surprise.

"For a second it looked like fear on your face."

I forced a laugh as it sank in what a bad mistake this job was. Senior officers had me pegged as a shirker with political connections, but civilians like Harry believed I was at the White House because of qualities their untrained eye couldn't see. In a way, it was like when I was passing on what I heard behind the yellow screen. As time went on, people began to think I was a great spy, and of course I did nothing to discourage that. At Georgetown dinner parties I put on a faraway look as if weighed down by secrets that would flatten an ordinary man. I was a terrible showoff in those days, little knowing what was in store.

But that's off the track. Harry had shown me something in that Lisbon hotel room so shocking maybe only half a dozen people in the whole world knew about it. If it got out, Franklin would be wheeled into a prison cell for the rest of his life. If I told the Senator, they'd trace it to me as soon as he started tipping off friends so they could put their money in the right companies. On the other hand, when he found out I hid the biggest secret in history from him, I could forget about his help no matter how much Mother nagged. So it wouldn't be a shore command in some safe backwater when the shooting began, I'd be in the thick of it as much as the greenest Reserve officer. No, even more because of my enemies at the Navy Building. "A suicide mission behind enemy lines? I think Brady's your man for that."

Harry was silent and I thought he was getting ready to say more to say on the subject when he commenced to snore.

Slipping out of his room, I fell into one of those moods preachers put you when they rattle away about hellfire. As Harry didn't give much thought to security, I took the file to my room and put it under the mattress. I lost interest in going downstairs to see if that old man's mistress showed up—that's how bad I was feeling. I went to bed and tried to stare a hole in the ceiling. The Hindus or Mohammedans, one of them groups, say your life is written out before you're born and you can't change it no matter how much you might squirm. It makes you think, don't it?

There were just a few other passengers on the Dutch airliner the next day, and they looked sick with worry. You had to have almighty important business to risk Messerschmitts coming at you with guns blazing. To stay clear we took that long loop out into the Atlantic. We landed at Poole in the south of England after turbulence rattled us around like dice in a cup. Harry was pretty well wiped out; he was collapsed into his overcoat and his head lolled when the plane came to a stop.

Churchill's friend Brendan Bracken was first aboard and gasped. "My God," he said, "is he dead?"

He's just a little under the weather, I said as Harry's eyelids fluttered open.

"Mr. Hopkins," Bracken said with relief. "I'm the prime minister's parliamentary private secretary."

"This is my aide Captain Brady," Harry said struggling up in his seat.

We've met, I said.

Bracken was a tall guy with pale freckles and frizzy red hair I'd seen a lot of over there. He was actually closer to Winston than Randolph, and there were many who thought he was an illegitimate son. Even Clemmie supposedly asked if that was true.

We got Harry down from the airplane with me ahead in case his legs gave out, and Bracken hauling on the belt of his overcoat from behind. A bunch of Scotland Yard detectives and motorcycle police waited next to a tall, black Rolls Royce.

"Do you need a doctor?" Bracken asked in the car.

"No," Harry said, "I'll be all right after I rest up."

"A special train is waiting," Bracken said.

We followed the motorcycles to a small station where a panting locomotive was guarded by soldiers in battle dress. The train shot out of there like a scalded cat as soon as we climbed aboard. Bracken said the tracks were cleared all the way to London.

"The engineer has orders to pour on the coals so we get there before the nightly blitz."

Harry went to the sleeping car to rest while Bracken and I settled on a green leather banquette with drinks brought by a waiter in a tuxedo and white gloves.

"Does Mr. Hopkins need to go to a hospital?" Bracken said.

He'll be right as rain, I said, a touch of stomach trouble is all.

"But he's so thin."

When he saw I wasn't going to say any more on the subject he dropped it. I'd see that London was a much changed place, he said. Whole blocks turned into rubble, glass crunching underfoot, smoke stinging your eyes.

That's the Hun for you, I said, either at your feet or your throat. The leopard can't change its spots and so on, making light conversation like you do. Had he seen Lady Cybil around by any chance?

"I'm afraid the social scene is quite inhibited. I heard she's in Scotland. Not a bad place to be all things considered."

The train clickety-clacked through rural country, our car swaying like a ship at sea; fastest one I was ever on. A police car sat with headlights off at every crossing. We flew past silent, dark villages.

"The blackout," Bracken explained.

Under other conditions it would have been fun sitting there with our tumblers of whiskey and going like the dickens. But he was grim and nervous, and of course I had my own worries thanks to Harry.

"I've been told an astonishing thing, Captain Brady. Our embassy in Washington cabled us that we must consider Mr. Hopkins the most important visitor ever to set foot on our island."

The president practically does everything he says, so, yes, I reckon that's so.

"Astonishing that I'd never heard his name before."

Harry thought about running for president himself, I said. Roosevelt wanted him to until he changed his mind about running again.

"My God!" Bracken was quiet for a minute. "Lindsay seems to have kept us in the dark about a good many things we should have known. Look here, Captain," he said suddenly. "We've got a bit of a sticky wicket and Winston told me to take you into our confidence if the moment seemed right."

I didn't want to be taken into anybody's confidence after the latest reminder Harry gave me that ignorance is bliss. Bracken talked on anyway.

"We need American aid, a massive amount, and as fast as possible. The situation is critical, but Harry mustn't get the idea we're about to go under. That's the problem, getting him to see the difference. Winston is afraid you'll leave us in the lurch if he gets the wrong impression."

I almost said I was only the guy who carried the medicine bag, but that meant demotion to flunky and I couldn't bring myself to do it. I was hoping to see Lady Cybil and I wanted her to still think of me as a big shot. Man's pride, you see.

"You lived among us and you know what kind of people we are, and you know Winston would never give up the ship. Yes, there are defeatists after Dunkirk, I won't deny that. But they're a small minority and we'll put as many people behind bars as we have to. Give us the tools and we'll fight on to victory, I promise you that."

I'll see what I can do, I said. I must have sounded grudging because that's how I felt. He was like a drowning man thrown a life preserver.

"Thank you, Lowell." He gripped my hand with tears in his eyes. You don't expect to be embarrassed like that by an Englishman and we quickly pretended it hadn't happened.

After a while Harry felt better and joined us. Looking out the window, he said: "You're not going to let Hitler take this pretty countryside away from you are you?"

"Never!" Bracken said.

We moved to the dining car and a candle-lit table with linen and heavy silver. The waiter gave us a gilt-edged menu.

"The lobster's awfully good," Bracken said as he studied the menu. "I had it coming down."

Sounds good to me, I said.

Harry didn't feel like eating. "The reports of food rationing appear exaggerated," he said in a dry way as the waiter poured Champagne.

"Newspapers always make things seem worse than they really are," Bracken said. "Mountains heaped up from molehills of facts."

"But there *is* rationing?" Harry persisted.

"Yes, but fortunately, the finer things of life are holding steady."

We sped through the night and when we reached the industrial area near Clapham Junction, Bracken looked tense. Loud explosions behind made us all jump.

"What's that?" Harry asked.

"Bombs," Bracken said. The lights went out on the train. "No use giving them a target."

We picked up even more speed and train whistle shrieked. I felt my way to the rear and watched the flash of hundreds of incendiaries on factories we had passed minutes before. Luckily, the bombers finished their run and peeled off as we pulled into Waterloo Station in a cloud of steam. Leave Poole a minute later and we would've been right under those bombs. The thought made me break into a cold sweat.

Bracken hoped Harry would go straight off to see Churchill, but he wanted a good night's sleep first. "You go ahead and say hello to your old friend, Lowell," he told me.

Bracken said the streets of London were darker than in the Middle Ages. "You might see a flaming torch or an open fire back then."

How the driver found his way beats me; a candle gave more light than his hooded headlights. The anti-aircraft guns began banging away in Hyde Park as we crept along.

"They don't do much good, but Winston thinks they help morale," Bracken said.

We stopped outside a sandbagged building and an officer shined a pen light in his face and asked for credentials. A door led to a dimly lit staircase that went down several flights. Another door with an armed guard opened onto a corridor as busy as a beehive. Every room we passed had maps with pins on the walls and staff officers hard at work. The tempo had stepped up back home, but nothing compared to this. Having your back against the wall does that.

Winston was in an office pacing and dictating to a secretary. He wore a blue one-piece outfit with a single zipper, his "siren" suit which I guessed was based on Mountbatten's get-dressed-quick theory. He was pulling on an eighteen-inch Havana and the air was blue from smoke. He broke off what he was saying and stuck his pudgy hand out.

"So good to see you again…I was about to say Commander Brady, but I see I must congratulate you on that new stripe, Captain. War is not an unalloyed curse. You will have a professional interest in something I just discovered. Very nearly half of the captains and commanders on the Admiralty's active list have desk jobs here or in Bath. I already ordered a severe reduction in the number of rearward positions for our army in the Middle East. A longer tail means smaller teeth at the point of attack, but you would be surprised how many generals didn't grasp that truth. We're taking food from the mouths of our civilian workforce and shipping it around the Cape of Africa to feed men who are not fighting. I would be remiss not to do a similar cull at the Admiralty. Every naval officer capable of it is to be sent to sea unless it can be proven that his duties ashore are more important. Sea duty is what they were very elaborately and lengthily trained for, not occupying a desk and chair."

Put a deck 'neath my feet and I'm a happy man, I said. But I can't let my selfish feelings…

"Yes, yes," Winston interrupted, reading a dispatch an aide handed to him. "Hmm. Tell General Ismay no. It's a bad idea to reinforce the Hong Kong garrison. There's not the slightest chance we could hold it against the Japanese, so it should have only symbolic value. Yes, Lowell, we all must make sacrifices in war, and I'm sure Mr. Hopkins leans heavily on you for advice. I'm told you had a close call on the train. Shall we take a glass of whiskey for our nerves?" A flunky did the pouring and we clinked glasses.

"Air bombardment takes getting used to," he said, "but we are adjusting." There was a little pause. "Our guest…is not well?"

He might not look that great on the outside, I said, but all the lights are on upstairs. The same old Winston—he did the talking and Bracken and I did the listening.

"Brendan," Winston said after a while, "I wonder if Captain Brady and I might have a word alone." When he was gone, he said, "Will you allow me to prevail upon our friendship?"

Prevailing on our friendship seemed a little strong, him being the prime minister of England and me the man who carried Harry's medicine bag, but I said yes sir, wind 'er up and let 'er go.

"I learned only by accident of Mr. Hopkins' relationship with the president. It would not be going too far to describe him as assistant president would it?"

That's exactly what he is all right.

"Had it not been for that accident I would have fobbed him off on junior ministers for the tour we give visiting firemen from the Commonwealth. It would have been a most grievous snub."

Oh, I said, Harry would have found out what he wanted one way or another.

"And can I ask you what that is?" Winston's blue eyes were sharp.

If y'all will stand up to the Germans or turn tail like the French.

"And if there is no possibility we will"—Winston smiled—"turn tail"?

Harry says the president will do everything to keep you going.

Winston let out a long breath. "Then Providence smiles for we shall never submit to that villain. Never. Never. Never. Icebergs will rise from Hell's fiery purlieus before that. Thank you, Captain. Now, if you'll excuse me, there is a war to be fought. Brendan will show you around our headquarters."

We looked at more rooms full of people shouting into telephones, poring over maps and so forth. Everybody looked tired but determined. A porter pushed around a cart with sandwiches and coffee.

"It's what they live on," Bracken said. "That and cigarettes. There are cots where they can catch a few winks when they reach the point of collapse."

Say, I said, isn't that Araminta Hallam-Peel?

The beautiful young woman with those green eyes I met at Adsdean was in a Wren's uniform passing out papers to men around a table.

"Do you know her?" Bracken said.

Not nearly as well as I'd like to.

"Let me have a word with her," he said.

He entered the room, spoke a word to an officer with red tabs and then to Araminta. She gave me an odd look, nodded to Bracken and followed when he left the room.

Third Officer Hallam-Peel gave me a smart salute. "Good evening, sir," she said crisply. "Nice to see you again."

I didn't think you'd remember me, I said. We only spoke a few...

"Oh come now, you're too modest. You are quite the handsomest man I have ever seen."

That sounds like I'm bragging on myself, but those were her very words. But her tone wasn't nice. On the bitchy side wouldn't be going too far.

"And now we're to have a drink," she said, "that's the schedule, is it? Well, come along. There's a place not too far, and I have my torch."

We went out outside where her flashlight was so dim we could barely make out the sidewalk. I mentioned what Bracken said about it being darker than the Middle Ages.

"Not very original, I'm afraid," Araminta said. "I'd say as dark as a mental condition."

It seemed like a strange thing to say, but I let it go so. We reached a sandbagged building and she led the way in. Beyond the blackout curtains men and women in uniform were eating dinner. We made our way to the bar where she ordered champagne. I said I didn't think it was a good idea to put bubbly on top of the prime minister's scotch.

"Order what you want then." She pushed some money across the bar.

No, no, I said. I reached for my wallet, but that seemed to irritate her more.

"Thanks, but I insist."

I wondered if she was wound tight because of the Blitz. Overwork and so forth.

"I suppose you're staying at one of the nicest hotels," she said.

Claridge's, I said.

"Do we go to your room after we finish our drinks?"

That put me back on my heels. A beauty like Araminta generally takes a good deal of work; you ladies probably aren't aware how much. Flowers and candy, that sort of thing. Compliments and fawning. Begging if that don't work.

But her eyes blazed. "Tell me, Captain, why does a man like you need the British government to procure women? I would think it would be easy to find what you need. The bombs may fall but the streetwalkers are still out. You can do it standing up on a street corner; a lot of men and women do. It's called Marble Arch Style."

I reared back like a horse. *Procure?* I didn't know at the time what the word meant, but it didn't sound good. I laughed because I didn't have my bearings with her, which normally is a smart thing to do when you're not sure of your ground. But that just made her madder.

"That toady Bracken told me you're part of some official party from Washington we must impress or England dies. Even though I'm just a female, I can add two and two. You Yanks sat on your fat bottoms last time before coming in at the last minute like knights in shining armor, and you've been raking in the spoils ever since. It doesn't seem fair now that we must beg you to save us and furthermore that I sacrifice my virginity to the cause."

She was talking loud and people turned to look. I admit I'd be cupping an ear myself if I was one of them. I lowered my voice, hoping she'd take the hint. I said what we have here is a misunderstanding.

"Oh," she said even louder, "I think we understand ourselves very well indeed."

Men were scraping chairs back from tables and it was a matter of time before one decided he must defend a lady's honor. I was with a jolly bunch in Boston once, Irish mostly, everybody drinking and roaring away, having a fine old time except for one woman sitting there not saying anything. All of a sudden she cuts loose with a scream that made the blood run cold. You could hear a pin drop when she finally stopped. When people asked what's wrong, she said all the talking and laughing made her feel like she was disappearing. A nutcase, in short. It took all the fun out of it because people were afraid she'd rip off another scream if the party picked up again. That's the power one woman has.

I was afraid that Araminta would throw her drink in my face and I'd feel a hand on my shoulder and somebody would say, "See here, old man." I've had to talk my way out of that sort of thing more than once. You look yellow, but it beats getting a punch in the nose. I said goodnight and made for the door at a good speed, half expecting her purse to catch me on the back of the head. It was so dark outside I had to feel my way like a blind man. I reached a row of taxicabs with faint blue lights showing and rode one back to the hotel. Harry had asked me to wake him when I got back. He sat up in bed and asked how it went. Pretty good, I said. No need to bring Araminta into it.

"Did you see Churchill?" Harry didn't look like sleep had helped any. He kept the covers up to his chin because the heat was out.

Winston looked good, I said, and he's in full charge. He said send everything from beans to bullets.

"He already wrote to the president saying that. I'm more interested in mood. Did you see any quit in him?"

None I could see, I said. He told me Clemmie is learning how to fire a pistol to pick Germans off if they come over the garden wall.

"When do they expect the invasion?"

The spring, I said.

"Did he get drunk?"

He drank but was sober as a judge, I said.

"What did you tell him about me?"

You're here to see if they'll run up the white flag if things get too bad.

"And?"

He said icebergs would float up from Hell first.

"It sounds like we're going to hit it off just fine."

CHAPTER 16

"**D**O YOU KNOW WHERE LOWELL BRADY IS?" HAWLEY SAID.

He and a silent man every bit as big loomed over my desk. At my request, we stepped into the corridor to get away from staring co-workers. They stood close to me, thick, meaty men who gave off body heat like stabled animals. I felt small and weak with their mass towering over me.

I said I hadn't seen Captain Brady since I dropped him off at the old soldiers' home two days ago. My face burned and I knew I must look guilty. I have never been able to lie convincingly.

"It was right at eight o'clock," I said, hoping precision made me sound more believable. "I'm afraid he still hasn't gotten around to anything you might find interesting. He merely..."

"He's gone with all his things," Hawley said. "Nobody saw him leave."

I made my eyes go wide and batted my lashes. "Where did he go?"

"We're hoping you'd tell us."

Unable to meet that ice-crystal gaze of his, I looked down at my toes curling in my shoes.

"This is your last opportunity to play straight with us," he said in a flat voice. "Tell us where he is and no harm done."

I said I didn't know. "Why do you want him?"

"As I explained before, this is a national security matter."

"In what way?"

"Do you read the newspapers, Miss Gallatin?"

"Of course I do."

"Then you know our country is in great danger, at home and abroad. There are people who would like to see us fighting the old quarrels over again. They want to see disunity sapping our will to fight the Red menace."

"What does that have to do with me and him?"

"So you won't cooperate?"

"I didn't say that. I just don't know where he is."

My heart was thudding in my ribcage. They glanced at one another—there was so much silent menace in that look!—and turned away without another word.

"Oh, wow," Greg said excitedly when I told him. "I hope they come to see me at work."

"Why would you wish for that?" I said. "It's nerve racking."

"C'mon, we're having a battle of wits."

"It's not a fair fight in that case." He looked insulted. "They have the whole *government* behind them," I explained. "We're just two people."

"Two very smart people," he boasted. "If they don't know that, they'll find out."

"How will they find out?" I asked.

"When the secret gets out, whatever it is."

"But what if it *shouldn't* get out?" That had begun to nag at me. What if it had to do with atom secrets or something like that?

Greg looked surprised. He had never considered the possibility he might not be on the side of the angels. That is what picture shows do to thinking.

"What if it would hurt the country?" I said.

His cocksure manner returned. "In that case, we don't let it get out."

I reminded him that Captain Brady wanted his story told. "That's why he's talking to me."

"Hmm."

In the movies Greg liked best the choices were always clear cut, the path straight and narrow. "That's not something we have to think about now." He smiled. "We can trust ourselves to do the right thing."

"Because we're smart people?"

He pointed his trigger finger at me. "Check."

Greg was sure of his ability to "shake a tail" and liked to show me.

He parked his car one Friday night on a street where friends lived, and I drove us home. The following morning we took the bus to their house, striding through the front door without knocking. Two young men on a sofa with a chintz cover that matched their curtains were stroking a yellow cat between them.

"Hello and goodbye," Greg said cheerily. We went out the back door and down an alley to his car.

"The FBI will be waiting all day for us to come out," he said gleefully.

* * *

The next morning we were driven to the embassy where Joe Kennedy and a bunch of civilian and military aides waited in a big office. Kennedy and Harry knew each other, but I didn't get the feeling they were bosom buddies.

"What you and the president need to understand," Kennedy said getting down to business, "is the English are finished. The army left most of its equipment behind in France. They're scrounging up shotguns and old fowling pieces for when the Germans come across the channel. It would be funny if it wasn't so pathetic."

Harry said we can make good all their equipment losses.

"Yeah, by stripping our military of what we need to defend ourselves."

Kennedy wore round spectacles that made him look like a wise owl, but his eyes behind them reminded me of a terrier that sinks its teeth into your ankle when you're not looking.

"We've got to keep them in it," Harry said. "They're fighting as much for us as them."

"Everything we send will end up in the hands of the Germans," Kennedy said. "Isn't that right, Colonel?"

An officer with a bottle nose nodded and the others around the table took their cue from him. Joe liked Yes men and I didn't hold it against him. Speaking from my own experience, there's no easier duty than telling the man above you what he wants to hear. Did you ever heard of a No man who climbed to the top rung of the ladder? Of course not; they're weeded out early. The last guy you want around when the shit hits the fan is the one who is in a position to say I told you so.

"You're wasting your time over here," Kennedy said. His look said Harry should be more careful how he spent it, considering how little was left to him. "I sent the president a cable before you left telling him that. No reply, of course. I don't know why I'm here." He said the German war machine was a steamroller that would flatten anybody who got in the way.

"What about the people?" Harry asked.

"What people?"

"The common people."

"What about them?"

"Are they going to fight?"

"I'll tell you this: the Blitz is scaring hell out of them."

"It scares hell out of me."

"Nobody can stand up to this night after night. We sleep in the basement. I wake up every morning with a headache from the bad air."

"So they'll throw in the towel?"

"No question about it," Kennedy said. "Churchill's government will fall and they'll bring in someone to negotiate peace."

"What do you think, Lowell?"

Every eye turned to me. Kennedy's glared through those owl glasses. "Who did you say this man is?" he said.

"Lowell Brady." Harry looked at me. "Lowell?"

I reckon they'll fight to the bitter end, I said.

"Ridiculous," Kennedy said. "He doesn't know what he's talking about."

Heads nodded up around the table. Mine would have been doing the same if I was on Kennedy's staff.

"He spent more than here a year gauging public opinion from all levels of society," Harry said. Kennedy looked like he was working up something scornful to say when Harry added, "He's Senator Brady's son."

Kennedy swallowed whatever sneering thing he was about to say. No Democrat got crosswise with the Senator if they had sons to push along in politics.

"Is that so?" Kennedy said to me sweet as honey. "Why, he's never mentioned a son to me. He's a fine fellow, the Senator is, none better. Give my warmest regards when you see him."

The briefing went on for an hour about how the English were whipped but didn't know it or couldn't admit it to themselves. They were short on everything because of the U-boats.

"The U-boats dive in an emergency," said a lieutenant commander named Farley, "but they're really surface attack boats. They'll do seventeen knots to the six knots the English get out of some of the old rust buckets they use. The U-boats surface in the middle of a convoy and let fly. A wolf pack picked off twenty out of thirty-four ships in a convoy between dusk and dawn."

"Churchill is giving you lunch?" Kennedy said when he saw us to the door. "I'll tell you right now he'll be spreading lies about me."

"What kind of lies?" Harry said.

"Whatever ones pop into his crooked mind."

"Why would he do that?" Harry said.

"Because I'm Irish. They hate us."

"I'd say that's a two-way street," Harry said.

"The difference is we didn't starve a million of them to death," Kennedy said.

"Well, I think we need to set that one aside until the Germans are licked."

"We don't want to tie ourselves to a drowning man and get pulled under."

Harry was down in the dumps on the drive to Downing Street. "He makes it sound hopeless. But I wonder if it's half as bad as he says."

Good question, I said.

We passed through bombed-out neighborhoods where building fronts were blasted away. Their insides looked like a bunch of stage sets ready for the actors. Fire hoses in the streets out front were like big ole snakes and streams of water were still being poured on the fires of the night before. The embassy driver told us he got flat tires two or three times a week from the broken glass.

Harry craned around to look at the workmen digging. "They're joking as they're shoveling—that's a good sign."

Harry got a big welcome at Ten Downing and they gave us the guided tour. The Cabinet Room was long and narrow with a high ceiling. It had chandeliers, rose-colored walls, a long table with leather chairs and a marble fireplace with an oil painting of some big shot in a wig.

"Lord North conducted the war against your revolt from this room," the guide said.

I would have liked to hear more but Bracken kept whispering he was sorry about Araminta's scene, and what could he do to make up for it? I guessed Winston had taken him to the woodshed.

"I don't know how she got the impression I was suggesting anything improper," he said. "Her commanding officer did say she has been working very hard. He ordered her to take a week off."

No harm done, I said, water off a duck's back and so forth, then he switched to my forgiveness reminded him of a saint. I like being buttered up as much as the next man, but there comes a point. I broke away and asked the man giving the tour questions about a prime minister name of Disraeli whose picture also was on the wall.

Really, sir, he said, you've never heard of Mr. Disraeli?

"Of course he hasn't!" Bracken said with fury. "Americans have their own history. They can't be expected to bother about ours."

Winston showed up at that moment and quietly stuck out his hand to Harry. He nodded to me and then they went downstairs for lunch and a private powwow. Bracken and I ate with four Royal Navy officers in an oak-paneled room with blast curtains at the windows.

We talked shop for a good while. Every sailor has stories about bad weather and we swapped them back and forth. Mine was when we cleared Cape Mays in heavy weather and turned north. Out of the lee of the island we got hit by the big wind that had been blowing for days. A huge wave swept the bridge and knocked us down like pins in a bowling alley. Orders from fleet headquarters were to plow ahead regardless of conditions.

You drank coffee from the spout standing watch otherwise the wind blew it in your face; and you dreaded the call of nature. The ship climbed to the top of the waves and dropped like a rock. When it slammed down, water shot out of the heads like geysers; lifted you right off the seat. The flap on the outboard discharge was ripped away and a good two feet of sewage and seawater washed back and forth. Did I mention this was a destroyer? Whenever we were alongside a bigger ship and they saw how we rolled, they thanked their lucky stars their weren't with us.

I mentioned that convoy where they lost so many ships. Sounds to me like a royal screw up, I said, and the room went quiet.

"I'm sure we can trust you to be discreet with that information," Captain Feversham said. "We've managed so far to dismiss Jerry's boasting as crude propaganda lies."

Mum's the word with me, I said.

"How long before you're in the fight?" Feversham asked. He seemed to think timing was the only question.

Those guys were living in a dream world. All Hitler had to do with the Germans was give them a light touch of the spurs and they were off to the races. Franklin was pulling at a mule with hooves dug in.

I have no idea, I said.

"Many thought when you let our warships use your ports it would push Hitler into declaring war," one of them said, "but it seems he was too smart."

I gave them nods they could interpret any way they wanted.

After lunch some deputy assistant of something or other let me have his office until Harry and Winston wound up their lunch. Two o'clock, three o'clock. I stretched out on a sofa and the next thing I hear is Harry's voice.

"Lowell, wake up," he said.

Just resting my eyes, I said.

"Let's go."

It was already getting dark and people carrying their gas masks were hurrying to get home before the blackout. Harry was in good spirits.

"He's a great man," he said in the embassy car. "Maybe even as great as the boss."

My feeling exactly, I said. When I was over here...

"There's no quit in him, by God."

Back in his hotel room Harry said, "I want a copy of that evaluation of the Japanese situation to show to Winston tonight. I can't give him the original because the chief said not to let it leave my possession."

I said I doubted the embassy had a secretary with the clearance. I had to raise my voice because anti-aircraft batteries opened up somewhere close by.

"Send down for a typewriter," he yelled back. "You'll have to do it yourself."

I'm a hunt-and-peck man and Harry was picky. When he got up from his nap he looked over my shoulder.

"Too many typos and crossovers," he said. "Are the other pages like that? Let me see. Look at that! You have to do them all over, and better get a move on."

It took *hours* to finish. I know how the Japs in the Washington embassy felt sweating over that fourteen-part message from Tokyo. The Pacific Fleet was already blasted to bits by the time they pulled the last page out of the typewriter. I just had time to change into my dress uniform for the reception in Harry's honor. You look kind of doubtful now and then about how good my memory is. I'm going to show you. I quote:

> The United States today finds herself confronted by a hostile Germany and Italy in Europe and by an equally hostile Japan in the Orient. Russia, the great land link between these two groups of hostile powers, is at present neutral, but in all probability favorably inclined toward the Axis powers, and her favorable attitude towards these powers may be expected to increase in direct proportion to increasing success in their prosecution of the war in Europe. Germany and Italy have been successful in war on the continent of Europe and all of Europe is either under their military control or has been forced into subservience. Only the British Empire is actively opposing by war the growing world dominance of Germany and Italy and their satellites.

> The United States at first remained coolly aloof from the conflict in Europe and there is considerable evidence to support the view that Germany and Italy attempted by every method within their power to foster a continuation of American indifference to the outcome of the struggle in Europe. Paradoxically, every success of German and Italian arms has led to further increases in United States sympathy and material support of the British Empire, until at the present time the United States government

stands committed to a policy of rendering every support short of war with the chances rapidly increasing that the United States will become a full-fledged ally of the British Empire in the near future. The final failure of German and Italian diplomacy to keep the United States in the role of a disinterested spectator has forced them to adopt the policy of developing other threats to U.S. security spheres of the world, notably by the threat of revolutions in South and Central America by Axis-dominated groups and by the stimulation of Japan to further aggressions and threats in the Far East in the hope that by these means the United States would become so confused in thought and fearful of her own immediate security as to virtually preclude U.S. aid to become so preoccupied in purely defensive preparations as to virtually preclude U.S. aid to Great Britain in any form. As a result of this policy, Germany and Italy have lately concluded a military alliance with Japan directed against the United States. If the published terms of this treaty and the pointed utterances of Germany, Italian and Japanese leaders can be believed, and there seems no ground on which to doubt either, the three totalitarian powers agree to make war on the United States, should she come to the assistance of England, or should she attempt to forcibly interfere with Japan's aims in the Orient and, furthermore, Germany and Italy expressly reserve the right to determine whether American aid to Britain, short of war, is a cause for war or not after they have succeeded in defeating England. In other words, after England has been disposed of her enemies will decide whether or not to immediately proceed with an attack on the United States. Due to geographical considerations, neither Germany nor Italy is in a position to offer any material aid to Japan. Japan, on the contrary, can be of much help to both Germany and Italy by threatening and even attacking British dominions and supply routes from Australia, India and the Dutch East Indies, thus materially weakening Britain's position in opposition to the Axis. In exchange for this service,

Japan receives a free hand to size all of Asia that she can find it possible to grab, with the added promise that Germany and Italy will do all in their power to keep U.S. so attracted as to prevent the United States from taking positive aggressive action against Japan. Here again, we have another example of the Axis-Japanese diplomacy which is aimed at keeping American power immobilized, and by threats and alarms to so confuse American thought as to preclude prompt decisive action by the United States in either sphere of action. It cannot be emphasized too strongly that last thing desired by either the Axis powers in Europe or by Japan in the Far East is prompt, warlike action by the United States in either theater of operations.

An examination of the situation in Europe leads to the conclusion that there is little that we can do now, immediately, to help Britain that is not already being done. We have no trained army to send to the assistance of England, nor will we have for at least a year. We are trying to increase the flow of materials to England and to bolster the defense of England in every practicable way and this will undoubtedly be increased. On the other hand, there is little that Germany or Italy can do against us as long as England continues in the war and her navy maintains control of the Atlantic. The one danger to our position lies in the possible early defeat of the British Empire with the British fleet falling intact into the hands of the Axis powers. The possibility of such an event occurring would be materially lessened were we actually taking measures to relieve the pressure on Britain in other spheres of action. To sum up: the threat to our security in the Atlantic remains small so long as the British fleet remains dominant in that ocean and friendly to the United States.

In the Pacific, Japan by virtue of her alliance with Germany and Italy is a definite threat to the security of the British Empire and once the British Empire is gone the force of Japan-Germany and Italy is to be directed against the United States. A powerful land attack by Germany and Italy through the Balkans and North

Africa against the Suez Canal with a Japanese threat or attack on Singapore would have very serious results for the British Empire. Could Japan be diverted or neutralized, the fruits of a successful attack on the Suez Canal could not be as far reaching and beneficial to the Axis powers as if such a success was also accompanied by the elimination of British sea power from the Indian Ocean, thus opening up a European supply route for Japan and a sea route for Eastern raw materials to reach Germany and Italy.

While as pointed out paragraph (3) there is little that the United State can do to immediately retrieve the situation in Europe, the United States is able to effectively nullify Japanese aggressive action, and do it without lessening U.S. material assistance to Great Britain.

An examination of Japan's present position as opposed to the United States reveals a situation as follows: Japan has a geographically strong position, but a million and half of her men are engaged in an exhausting war on the Asiatic continent. It has a highly centralized strong capable government, but its economy and food supply are severely straitened. She has rigid control of the economy on a war basis, but a serious lack of sources of raw materials for war. Notably oil, iron and cotton. It has a people inured to hardship and war, but it is totally cut off from supplies from Europe and dependent upon distant overseas routes for essential supplies. It has a skillful navy about two-thirds of the strength of the U.S. Navy, but is incapable of increasing manufacture and supply of war materials without free access to U.S. or European markets. It has some stocks of war materials, but major cities and industrial centers are extremely vulnerable to air attack.

In the Pacific the United States possess a very strong defensive position and a Navy and naval air force at present in that ocean capable of long distance offensive operation. There are certain other factors which at the present time are strongly in our favor, viz: A—Philippine Islands still held by the United

States. B—Friendly and possibly allied government in control of the Dutch East Indies. C—British still hold Hong Kong and Singapore and are favorable to us. D—Important Chinese armies are still in the field in China against Japan. E—A small U.S. naval force capable of seriously threatening Japan's southern supply routes already in the theater of operations. F—A considerable Dutch naval force is in the Orient that would be of value if allied to the U.S.

A consideration of the foregoing leads to the conclusion that prompt aggressive naval action against Japan by the United States would render Japan incapable of affording any help to Germany and Italy in their attack on England and that Japan itself would be faced with a situation in which her navy could be forced to fight on most unfavorable terms or accept or accept fairly early collapse of the country through the force of blockade. A prompt and early declaration of war after entering into suitable arrangements with England and Holland would be most effective in bringing about the early collapse of Japan and thus eliminating our enemy in the Pacific before Germany and Italy could strike at us effectively. Furthermore, elimination of Japan must surely strengthen Britain's position against German and Italy and, in addition, such action would increase the confidence and support of all nations who tend to be friendly toward us.

It is not believed that in the present state of political opinion the United States government is capable of declaring war against Japan without more ado; and it is barely possible that vigorous action on our part might lead the Japanese to modify their attitude. Therefore, the following course of action is suggested:

Make an arrangement with Britain for the use of British bases in the Pacific, particularly Singapore.

Make and arrangement with Holland for the use of base facilities and acquisition of supplies in the Dutch East Indies.

Give all possible aid to the Chinese government of Chiang-Kai-Shek.

232 | JERRY JAY CARROLL

Send a division of long range heavy cruisers to the Orient, Philippines or Singapore.

Send two divisions of submarines to the Orient.

Keep the main strength of the U.S. Fleet now in the Pacific in the vicinity of the Hawaiian Islands.

Insist that the Dutch refuse to grant Japanese demands for undue economic concessions, particularly oil.

Completely embargo all U.S. trade with Japan, in collaboration with a similar embargo imposed by the British Empire.

If by these means Japan could be led to commit an overt act of war, so much the better. At all events we must be fully prepared to accept the threat of war.

* * *

Harry got a lot of odd looks as we were being introduced to the guests in fancy uniforms, which are way better than ours by the way. He wasn't what you'd call a sharp dresser at the best of times, and now he looked like a refugee in that overcoat that looked like it was about to swallow him. He didn't take it off all evening; the man could never get warm in that climate. Of course, he wasn't pouring down wine and whiskey and getting red-faced like the rest of us.

Winston held forth in the Small Dining Room, where we had saddle of lamb and roasted potatoes, and kept it up afterward over brandy and cigars. He told us he wanted the Italian forces in Libya destroyed and Tobruk captured by March. He expected the Italians in Abyssinia would give up by then and forces could move north from Kenya to act as reserves for future developments. Spanish spines had been stiffened by English success in the eastern Mediterranean. Hitler wouldn't invade Spain to take Gibraltar because he already had more occupied countries with sullen populations than he could manage. England could promise six divisions with air and naval power if Marshal Petain took up arms in North Africa. The naval blockade of France would go into effect from time to time to maintain the fiction of hostility, but also to remind the Vichy government it shouldn't expect life to be a bed of roses if they did nothing to help against Germany.

The Greeks were fighting well and valiantly against the Italians—any general would be happy to have Eyeties as the enemy—but unfortunately it looked like the Germans would come in against them through the Balkans, in which case the possibility of the Greeks making a separate peace could not be ruled out and this would influence Yugoslav opinion, and not for the good. But all of these were sideshows to the main event. That was defeating the invasion of England because Hitler could never win so long as she was free. If they used poison gas on the civilian population, the English would do the same against them.

He asked one of the guests, a general named Alan Brooke, what the plan was if the Germans landed amphibious tanks ashore. Brooke didn't hesitate.

"Light forces would surround them and follow closely, preventing the crew from refueling or getting food or drink or even leaving the protection of their armor. That is apart from anything that artillery, mines and tank traps do."

Well said, Winston said with a big smile. Meeting over. He ordered up the record player—the gramophone they call it over there—and did a few dance steps to the music.

I've given you just a rough idea of what he said. On every subject Winston had plenty to say. Lord, how the man could talk. Words flowed like he'd opened the floodgates. You might think there'd be some slow patches now and then, but you'd be wrong. He was like a performer and had us in the palm of his hand. The high strategy stuff got broken up with stories like the time a Boer's bullet clipped a feather from his hat.

"When it sang past I felt elation impossible to describe," he said. "Life is never sweeter than at moments of supreme peril."

It turned out Winston saw a lot of war before he went into politics. You probably never heard of the Battle of Omdurman; I know I never did. To make a long story short, which is not Winston's style, in 1898 the English sent an army into the desert after some religious nut that had cut off the head of one of their generals and was giving them lots of other trouble as well.

"What a blunder in that battle," Winston said, "the sort of miscalculation for which Lord Kitchener gained unenviable fame as his career ripened. In the beginning of the action, the defensive position he took was textbook sound. Infantry soldiers two deep were behind thorn fences thrown up overnight to guard against infiltrators. In the Nile behind them gunboats and cannon on barges augmented the regimental battery, bringing seventy artillery pieces to bear.

"I was ordered out before dawn's light with a small patrol of 21st Lancers to scout the dervish horde marching to battle sixty thousand strong, three times greater than Kitchener's waiting army. The Mohammedans, followers of Kahlifia, advanced across the sand with medieval pomp and splendor. Standards aloft, these modern Saracens wore helmets and chain mail and were armed with sword and spear. I scribbled a note to Kitchener saying the enemy would reach him in an hour. As the messenger spurred off at a full gallop, I turned my field glasses to the approaching army. It stretched four or five miles long and filled the horizon. A roar reached us like a wave breaking on the shore when they cheered and quickened their pace. What a moment to be alive, I thought.

"They paid us no attention until I ordered my lancers to dismount and fire. They returned our bullets and we withdrew out of range. Kitchener's artillery began to arc over our heads and we watched the explosions tear big gaps in their ranks. A patrol made for us, dark, figures like monks in cowls on horseback with long spears. I fired a few shots and they turned away as a messenger arrived on a lathered horse with an order to return to camp.

"The carnage of the cannons was so satisfactory that Lord Kitchener was led into his error. He gave orders to abandon our riverbank redoubt and advance on Omburdan seven miles across the desert. Kitchener didn't know the left wing of the dervish army had marched too far and therefore escaped being pounded by the artillery. It was intact and in position to attack the undefended rear of his strung-out army as it marched in echelon. Two hours later the 21st Lancers felt the consequence of this misjudgment as we cantered toward what looked like demoralized spearmen with the intent of scattering them. Instead, they were riflemen who began to blaze away at us.

"Orthodox tactics called for wheeling in retreat, but we had no time to do anything but charge them. We had no way to know that hidden in a waddie behind the riflemen were more than two thousand spearmen, ten or twelve deep. The dervish knew how to fight cavalry. The Lancers who slammed into their center were stopped cold and their horses swiftly hamstrung by scimitars. The men were then pulled from saddles and hacked to death. My squadron had the luck of reaching the waddie toward one end where they were not packed so tightly, but even so it seemed I was surrounded by dozens of them.

"I couldn't use my saber because of a shoulder injury and this turned out to save my life. I pulled a Mauser pistol I bought to use for close-in skirmishes in place of my sword. The melee broke up into slow, dreamlike individual combat and I fired into the furious faces around me, killing three for sure and wounding others. When two riflemen dropped to their knees and took aim, I decided it was time to take my leave. There was no way both could miss but somehow they did.

"Back with my troop as it regrouped, a wounded dervish suddenly appeared in our midst with a spear. Stabbed repeatedly by the others, he staggered toward me hoping to kill an infidel to cushion his ease in paradise. I shot him a yard away. What would a man in such a situation expect but to die, and yet there was utter astonishment on his face. Horribly wounded lancers began to make their way back, gasping and crying or looking straight ahead as silent as the shallow graves soon to be dug in the sand for them. Some had fish-hook spears through them, others had arms or faces cut to pieces or were dying in the saddle as they held their intestines in. Kitchener's rear guard meanwhile was in hand-to-hand fighting as he desperately wheeled his army round to meet the threat. The men in the rear guard had an average of two bullets left when the battle ended. It was a close brush with catastrophe."

There were glazed eyes around the table, even some closed. I guessed they'd heard Winston's war stories before and maybe more than once. Or it could've been all the liquid refreshment. Harry seemed to wilt as time went on, and when Winston broke for a pee he waved me over.

"Look, I've got to get back to the hotel or they'll have to make up a bed for me." He took the report I had typed up from his overcoat. "I'll make my apologies and tell Winston you have something for him to read and we'll talk tomorrow. Bring it back when he's finished."

Harry intercepted Winston as he came back from the loo and they shot me looks as they talked. When I came back from walking Harry out to the embassy car, Winston was laying the law down. The reports he was being sent could have been said in a third of the space. His time was valuable and he didn't need to know every last bloody detail.

"I want only the pith."

He glared around the room and waved at me to follow him. He shooed away the hovering aides. We went a small room with a fire.

"What is it Harry wants me to read?" he said.

I gave it to him and he put reading glasses on the end of his nose. A servant knocked at the door and came in with decanters of brandy and water on a tray.

"A weak one, Ames," he said. "Help yourself, Captain."

After he finished, Winston read it again, more slowly this time. "It takes my breath away," he said finally. "Are you the author of this, Captain?"

I said I had a hand in it.

"Your modesty does you credit," he said. He tapped one of the pages. "This here is the key. 'Germany and Italy expressly reserve the right to determine whether American aid to Britain is a cause for war after they have succeeded in defeating England.'"

He looked over his glasses. "We didn't think you quite understood that, but clearly the president does. This document is worthy of Machiavelli."

I didn't know who that was, so I kept quiet.

He puffed on his cigar. "But risky, too. It is predicated on the Japanese rising like a trout to take the bait. Attacking America while engaged in a major war in China would be sheer madness, but history brims with lunacy."

That's the pure truth, I said.

"The thing is to box them in so they feel they have no choice but to act in the spirit of the samurai with everything to gain or lose. Like the gallows, cutting off their oil will concentrate their minds wonderfully. They have reserves, of course, but not enough for more than a short war." He sipped at his drink. "Exposing your Pacific Fleet at Pearl Harbor will tempt the Japanese to attack as they did the Russians at Port Arthur. It is brilliant! Here's to you, Captain."

Thank you, Winston.

"That single act would overnight nullify the isolationist movement in your great country and unite the population in a spirit of wrathful vengeance. We've been puzzled by your decision not to return the fleet to its home ports given what we understand about Pearl Harbor's limitations. It seemed to make no sense, but now I see the thinking behind it."

He doffed an imaginary hat. "Well done, Captain Brady."

Others helped, I said. I didn't want him to take this too far.

"False humility is tedious after a point. Tell Harry I well understand the need for complete secrecy and won't confide in even my top people until I have his approval. And now you must tuck this away in an inside pocket. I will have you escorted back to the hotel and armed guards will be posted outside your doors."

I got up to go, but he wasn't done yet.

"Brendan is appalled that President Roosevelt would send so ill a man on such a vital assignment, but I know a heart of stone is needed in these dark times. A leader must be willing to sacrifice even his closest friends without the blink of eye. I ordered a brigadier I knew very well to fight a hopeless, last-ditch battle at Calais to give the men at Dunkirk a few more days to get away. The ships that had gathered offshore to take off his soldiers were ordered to leave lest doubt linger in anyone's mind. No word has ever been received on the fate of my friend and his gallant force. You may ask if I ever have second thoughts about that decision, and I will tell you I have not."

Harry met with Winston for breakfast. "He told me I could see anything I wanted, so we're going on a tour," he said afterward. "He also had some interesting news. The boss sent him a cable agreeing to secret talks between their military and ours. Winston is sending people over immediately."

It was clear things were moving fast as that express train that brought us to London, and I did some mental looking about. Even if I didn't get that stateside billet with palm trees I was aiming for through the Senator, I was in a pretty good position as Harry's naval aide. There would be shortages and rationing, but Washington wouldn't be as bad off as the rest of the country; not even war bothers the folks with connections. We'd be eating high on the hog and the common man would have pig's feet. You're shaking your head; I know you think less of me for saying that straight out, Harriet, but that's the way of the world.

Harry paid a call on the king and queen next day while I sat outside with royal aides. They had cleared out all the nice things and Buckingham was as bare as a high school gym. On our way back, Harry said he forgot to give the king a letter Franklin sent special. It was delivered the next day by someone from the embassy. Harry said it was no big deal anyhow, just the standard standing-by-you routine.

The Germans were gathering Rhine river barges in French ports for the invasion, so we inspected the coastal defenses going up for a hot welcome. The country was evacuated for miles and miles inland. Pill boxes were being built and barbed wire strung on the beaches. All the road signs were taken down so the Germans couldn't use maps from the Royal Automobile Society to find their way around.

We also visited a dozen or so factories converted to war production. Winston got cheers wherever he went and lifted his homburg or gave that V-for-victory salute. Sometimes he asked Harry to give a little talk, and he got cheered too. Reporters began showing up at our stops, telling us the government had given up on keeping our mission secret. Or they wanted the Nazis to know. Harry played along and answered questions at the press conferences that started up as we walked from factory gates to the cars.

Q: Can you tell us the number of planes we are likely to get from America by, say, March?

A: I could but I wouldn't.

Q: Have you any idea how long the war will last?

A: I have a good idea who's going to win.

Q: What impression have you gained from your first experience of the Blitz and your first view of air raid damage?

A: I don't think there could be anything less important than my emotional response to such things. I haven't seen much of the damage, but I don't like what I have seen.

"I bet I've talked to a million reporters over the years," Harry said in the car.

"It must be two million for me as I am much the older man," Winston. "I believe ours are cheekier."

Although Harry was frail as a chick just out of the shell, Winston treated him like he lifted barbells and drank raw milk like Bernarr Macfadden. It was windy all the time and colder than a witch's...cold enough that Harry put on a bomber jacket under that overcoat—lucky it was so big—and fur flying boots on his feet. It was when we went to inspect the home fleet at Scapa Flow that I saved Harry's life.

We were transferring by ladder from a battleship to a destroyer and a step weakened by Winston's heavy load gave way under Harry. He looked up with terror as the gap between the hulls opened and closed. I lunged to grab the ladder a second before a petty officer did and together we pulled him up. Sometimes you just do things without thinking; I'd have had second thoughts if there had been time to think about being mashed between steel hulls. I'm being as honest as I can.

We laid him out on the deck and a vein in his forehead showed how fast his heart was pumping. "Thanks, Lowell," he said when he got his breath. "I don't think I could have held on much longer."

Some instinct whispered in my ear that modesty was the line to take. I couldn't have done it without this fellow here, I said. I heard the quiet murmur of approval in the crowd of officers around us.

Harry was helped up and gripped the sailor's hand, too choked up for words. The guy's name was Hitchens. Later, he got Winston's promise to send him over to be thanked in the White House. Sadly, no happy ending. His ship was torpedoed going back to England and went down so fast nobody survived except a cook. We kept it from Harry because his heart would have broken and he would've thought it was his fault, which it was in a way. No good deed goes unpunished, as Clare was the first to say. But that's not always true as Harry owed me as much as he did Hitchens. I looked at it as a check I'd cash down the road.

We flew home by flying boat and Harry met with the president, just the two of them, for an hour. He called me up to his bedroom where a Navy doctor was just leaving after ordering Harry to stay in bed for a week.

"We're in it with them all the way," he said with a smile. He gave me Churchill's V-for-victory signal.

Memorandum

April 7, 1953

To: Clyde Tolson

From: The Director

Subject: Lowell Brady

For: File 24898

I have given Edna clearance for this project even though
we agreed knowledge of this case must be limited to as few
as possible. Having your office just a door away facilitates
communication and decision making, but there is a tendency
to forget that oral communication has disadvantages as to
maintaining a record we can consult to refresh memory. She
is loyal and trustworthy and I think you will agree her
typewriting skills greatly exceed mine.

Welcome aboard, Emma! Enjoy the flowers.

I lunch next week with ALLEN DULLES. If they are mixed
up in this it complicates matters. As you foresaw, he declined
my suggestion that one sweep of the private dining room for
listening devices was sufficient. So his people will do it as
ours watch, to be repeated with roles reversed. They are very
wasteful with tax money at the Agency.

There is a strong network of Roosevelt loyalists in
and out of government fanatically devoted to the memory of
the late president. It is a bread and butter issue for most
of them. To dim his luster is to diminish their power and
influence. AVERILL HARRIMAN has presidential ambitions and
he is not the only one. It is possible they are working hand-
in-glove with the CIA.

Hawley is having difficulty drawing HARRIET GALLATIN
out about her conversations with BRADY. She claims he is
taking his time relating his wartime experiences and has not
yet reached the period leading up to the war. Hawley listens

to her tapes after the Smithsonian closes. This is time
consuming as she also is interviewing other veterans.

She traveled to California to interview WALTER WANGER,
the movie producer active in left-wing causes before the war.
He is presently incarcerated for assault with a deadly weapon.
They spoke about a visit BRADY made to Hollywood in 1938 in
company with a British spy William Stephenson. (File attached).

Instruct the Bureau's source in the CIA to try to find
out whatever he can without compromising his position there.
Emphasize that. He will become ever more valuable to us as he
climbs the ladder and we want to guard against blowing his
cover.

/John

                        Memorandum

                                                April 8, 1953

    To: Clyde Tolson

    From: The Director

    Subject: Lowell Brady

    For: File 24898

    As I think about this, the conviction grows that it
wasn't by accident that WILLIAM DONOVAN alerted us about
LOWELL BRADY. DONOVAN knew it would be brought to my
special attention because of our past relationship. He
was foremost among those who turned ROOSEVELT against my
proposal to consolidate all intelligence gathering under
one roof. (Attached file). We had many frank exchanges, once
nearly coming to blows at the Mayflower.

    Does DONOVAN know we knew of the clandestine efforts
made to silence BRADY during the war? Those frequent
transfers to hazardous theaters of war, known to me

personally at the time, would have been proof even if we
hadn't had this confirmed by confidential sources within the
Navy. That file too is among the missing.

I personally do not think DONOVAN is a Communist, but
it is possible he is being used by them without his being
aware of it. Put a tail on him to see where he goes and who
he talks to.

Memorandum

July 7, 1953

To: The Director

From: T.E. Hawley, SAC

Subject: Lowell Brady

We are 100 per cent satisfied from records obtained in
Annapolis that LOWELL BRADY and COLONEL CROCKETT are the
same.

The tap on GREG PEARSON's telephone shows a heavy
pattern of calls to two known homosexuals, FRANK KELLY and
SAMUEL KATZ. They are clerks at the Bonny House of Threads
in this city. PEARSON said he is in on a "big secret" that
will create headlines across the world but hasn't told them
what it is.

We have been unable to advance the investigation of who
took BRADY's file from the depository. On re-interview, EZRA
KLEINSTADT said the credentials shown to him may have been
CIA, but he could not be certain with so much time having
passed.

/Hawley

Tolson _____

/John

CHAPTER 17

"I FOUND OUT SOMETHING EXTREMELY INTERESTING." GREG'S VOICE SHOOK with excitement on the telephone. "I went to the FBI building and asked to speak to Hawley."

I was aghast. "Why did you do that?"

"If they weren't going to come to my place to talk to me, I was going to theirs."

"Oh, Greg, that's so dumb."

"Maybe not when you hear what I found out. There is no Hawley at the FBI. How do you like them apples?"

It took a few seconds to sink in. "Who is he with, then?"

"They want to know, too."

My mind whirled. "What if they weren't telling the truth?"

"Why would they lie?"

"Why does anybody lie? Because the truth is not in their best interest. Anybody who doesn't know that is sleepwalking."

"There's a law against impersonating an FBI agent. They're going to talk to you."

"I don't want to talk to them," I said angrily.

"Well," he said in a hesitant voice, "I'm not sure you have a choice. They asked a lot of questions."

"Maybe that's just what they want us to think."

"What?"

"That he's not with them."

He was silent for a minute. "Why would they want us to think that?"

"You are such a child."

I could think of two reasons straight off. They didn't want to Greg to know Hawley was with the FBI. Or whoever he had talked to didn't know that he was. Actually, there was a third: Hawley was with another agency that dealt with secrets the government didn't want out, one that operated off the books and was not fastidious as to the means employed. I was sure I could come up with more possibilities if I put my mind to it.

"I think you put us in more danger," I said.

"What do you mean?" The excitement was gone from his voice.

"You showed them what the captain knows is starting to leak out. They only suspected it before, but now they know."

"Of *course* it's going to get out because the people have the right to know."

"There are lots of things the government doesn't let the people know. Senator McCarthy is in the papers every day saying they're hiding something."

"He's on the crazy side isn't he?"

"The Gallup Poll says he's the fourth most popular man in the country."

"Yeah, well." I could hear traffic noise.

"Where are you?"

"In the first phone booth I could find. World War Two ended years ago. Hell, it's been ten years now since Pearl Harbor. There's no need for secrecy anymore."

"Obviously, the government disagrees."

After he hung up, his spirits dampened quite a bit from my pail of cold water, I wondered if McCarthy *might* be a factor in this. Maybe they were afraid he would hear about the captain's story. Bingo, another conspiracy to investigate. His political ambitions were said to have grown. Maybe he could ride this to the White House.

Later in the day Angelica called. "He wants to see you," she said. "Very upset."

"Do you know what it's about?" I asked.

"No, but he just got off the phone with the Secretary himself."

Angelica had told me he had lost weight, but I was not prepared for what

I found. Dr. Broadbrow was clearly gravely ill. His face seemed too small for his eyeglasses.

"I have just been given the most confounding news," he said. "I've been ordered to tell you you're fired."

I sank into a chair.

"The Secretary did not explain why. You're to be out of your office before the end of the day." He peered at me through a haze of pain and fatigue. "Do you know why?"

I shook my head. I didn't want to add to his burdens.

"Have you been doing anything that would come under the Hatch Act?"

I told him I didn't like politics and didn't even vote.

"It must be a mistake then, but when I called Arnold Pettigrew for clarification he said never to mention this again and hung up." Dr. Broadbrow put his hand to his forehead. "It's so upsetting."

I felt so sorry for him, and tried to ease his worry. I said don't worry; I'll find another job easily enough. He was right, a mistake had been made and it would be cleared up. I'd continue my work at home until then.

"Remind me again what that is, dear."

I told him it was battle fatigue.

"I remember now." He shook his head. "So many of our veterans are mentally disturbed."

The people in my office were dumbfounded when they found out. Nobody got fired by the federal government, certainly not with the speed I had been. Old Mr. Butler, the security guard who had a smile for everyone, showed up with a stricken look.

"They say I have to see you out, young lady," he said apologetically.

Fortunately, I'd had the presence of mind to collect all of the transcripts. He watched as I packed my things and helped me carry them out the door to the parking lot.

He shook his head. "I never had to do this before, except with Fenwick who they caught stealing from purses because he was a drug addict." I assured him that wasn't the case with me. "No, no. I'm just saying it's not right, a nice young lady like you."

FBI special agent Tim Burress was camped out on our stairs when I got home. A lean, fit man with dark hair touched with gray at the temples. He said he was looking into the case of a man who falsely represented himself as being with the FBI.

"I don't think I can help you." I said when he showed his credentials.

"A man you know, Greg Pearson, said you have had conversations with this individual."

"I gather you've never heard of him."

"No one by that name works for the FBI."

"He showed me a badge in a little wallet the same as yours."

"It was a forgery."

"How do I know yours isn't?"

"Feel free to telephone the agency. I'll wait while you do." He sat in a chair and crossed his legs.

"I'll take your word for it, just like I took his."

"Would you mind telling me what he said?"

You have the transcripts, I said.

He looked as if he sensed deep water best avoided. "And this Captain Brady, where can he be found?" he said.

"I won't tell you."

"But you seem to think he's in danger." He wrinkled his forehead. "Why not tell me if that's the case?"

"I think he's in danger from the government."

"Oh, come, Miss Gallatin." He smiled.

"Even if I didn't think so, he asked me to keep his whereabouts secret. I won't break my promise."

Agent Burress closed his notebook. "If this man Hawley gets in touch again let me know." He gave me his card. I telephoned Greg when I got home, but he wasn't at his office. I was too humiliated to say anything to my roommates and stayed in my room. A job is an anchor and if you lose it your life is turned upside down. I kept trying to reach Greg until I went to bed, but the phone just rang.

The next morning, still ashamed to tell the others, I said I wasn't going to work because of a headache. Renee wished she could stay home, too.

"I don't know how much more of that place I can take," she said, putting on her lipstick. Mr. Right was still taking his time.

I listened for Greg coming down the stairs and telephoned again with no result. When my roommates bustled off in a cloud of chatter and clashing perfumes, I tried to master my thoughts. I had to be practical now. I had accrued vacation pay and my savings, somewhat depleted by entertaining Captain Brady at fancy restaurants, so I was all right financially without any need to tap into my inheritance from a maiden aunt. Dr. Broadbrow had encouraged me to file an appeal with the civil service commission, but that would take a long time. I would have to find another job, and having been fired from my last one would not make that easier.

Unfortunately, my uncle was no longer the mayor of Helena and I couldn't count on his influence projected from afar. I could always go back to being a secretary. I went out to get a newspaper for the want ads and saw that Senator McCarthy was back in the headlines about Communists in government. When I came back home, I telephoned Greg at work. The voice on the other end said he hadn't been seen since lunch yesterday and did I know if he was coming in? I went upstairs and knocked on the door but got no answer.

That night Greg's two friends with the cat came by, worried that they hadn't heard from him. I went with Frankie and Sammy to get the key from the landlord and we let ourselves in. Nothing was amiss; it was as if he had just stepped out. The bed was neatly made and dishes were in the drainer.

"It looks like all his clothes are in the closet and his suitcase is here," Frank said. "There's food in the Frigidaire."

"I think we ought to file a missing person report," Sammy said. He glanced at Frankie. "We have a friend who works there."

* * *

He's most likely dead. Look, crying over it is no good. Here's my handkerchief; it's clean. My mother taught me never go anywhere without one. I warned you this was serious business but I never really thought it sank in. Your friend stuck his nose where it didn't belong and paid the price.

The question is what we do now. I don't like the thought of going on the road again, but maybe we don't have a choice. They'll come for you before long; you know that, right? They might even be waiting now for you to come home. Call your roommates and see if there's anything that doesn't look right. Pack light and come back. I know you're careful about being followed, but be extra sharp. You can have the sofa until we figure out what to do. I'd sleep there myself, but I don't want to screw up my back.

So where were we?

Okay, I got into the swing of things when we got back to Washington. The government was renting every building they could and covering every inch of open space with Quonset huts. Everywhere you went you heard sawing and hammering. Carpenters were subdividing offices, making three or four where there had been one. You breathed sawdust everywhere you went.

The deadwood in the Navy Building was mostly gone, shipped out or retired, but I still spent a lot of time there because I didn't want it to look like I was hanging around the White House with nothing to do. Garrison had been moved to party headquarters and I had the cloakroom all to myself. Unfortunately it was too small for a sofa to stretch out on.

The schedule was just right because my interest in female companionship often got me home late at night. I found my mother waiting up once. She had fallen asleep on a sofa, a book in her lap.

"Oh, there you are," she said when I touched her arm. "Are those birds I hear outside? Why, yes, it's dawn. They're working you young men too hard." Mother always put the best light on things. "The Senator said just the other day that he hasn't seen you for weeks."

What about it, I said.

I already had a hangover, which doesn't put a man in the sunniest mood. A secretary I met at the Willard had a wooden leg, and I took on a pretty good load myself.

"It's just that he misses his little chats with you," Mother said.

That would be the ones when he pumped me for inside information, I said.

The country was going flat out to build up its war strength, and the Senator's powers of persuasion with the Republicans weren't needed so much. Mother said he was being eased out of the president's inner circle.

For a man who liked being in the middle of things this was bad news. Just another face in the crowd was a role the Senator didn't care for.

"Do you think you could spare him a little time this week?" Mother said.

I said I'd see what I could do, but he shouldn't count on it.

"Thank you, dear," she said.

Harry worked day and night even though the docs had him confined him to bed with two secretaries taking his orders and working the phones. I dropped by morning, afternoon and evening, always pretending I was in a hurry. The Navy thought I was working for Harry and he thought the Navy had me hopping. I could've have kept that up through the war if Harry hadn't mentioned "the codes" one day. He threw me a look when he said it.

"You know about that, right?"

I said sure, but not in a lot of detail.

A cagy answer, I thought: Enough to show I'm in the know but not so much that I could answer a specific question. That was another of my big mistakes.

I walked into Harry's room a couple of days later and Admiral Hughes, the purple-faced bastard who ran ONI, was in mid-sentence. He shut up at once.

"That's all right," Harry said, "Brady knows about the codes."

"He's not on my list," Hughes said, forcing his surly features into a smile.

"Carry on, Admiral," Harry said. The glass of milk he was sipping told me he was having one of his bad days.

"Yes sir," he said with a black look at me. "As I was saying, we've cracked another Jap naval code; that makes four. And we're reading their diplomatic code nearly as fast as they are."

So Admiral Richardson was right, I thought.

"Purple is their diplomatic code?"

"Correct," Hughes said. He said nothing stood out except transmissions were way up from last year.

"I don't know that I need to be briefed about this on a regular basis. Captain Brady will tell me what he thinks I should know."

That went down like castor oil with the admiral.

No need to tell me everything, I told him as we left. Just the highlights will do.

"You heard what the man said, and I take it as an order from the commander-in-chief himself. You're going to see everything I do from now on."

There were cables and decrypts to read and daily meetings with code breakers and analysts to make sense of them. A concrete structure on the roof of the Navy Building was off limits to everyone except The-On-the-Roof-Gang, as they called themselves. It was like the one at Pearl Harbor that even CINCUS couldn't get into. Thousands of radio interceptions and decrypts flooded in every day from listening stations in Hong Kong, Corregidor, Seattle and a bunch of other places.

One evening before the president's daily cocktail party, I looked up to see Admiral Richardson in my doorway. "At ease," he said, "continue with your game of solitaire." He closed the door behind him. "It's nice to see an island of calm amid all the frenzy."

I pretended not to notice the sarcasm. He took off his hat and sat in the chair where Garrison's desk had been. "No danger of developing delusions of grandeur in a room like this. Did they keep brooms in here?"

Coats, I said.

"I'm having lunch tomorrow with the president, and I wanted to have a word with you. Did you deliver that message?"

About leaving the fleet at Pearl Harbor?

"That's the one."

Yes, I did.

"And?"

The president didn't say anything, I said.

In fact, he had given me one of those looks people got from him when they stuck their nose where they didn't belong. Harry told me later not to make that mistake again.

"I'm told he still thinks we're having a 'restraining effect' on the Japs," Richardson said, "and that's still hooey. Nothing has changed. They still know we have to go back to the West Coast to get those ships ready for war, and that'll take weeks and more likely months. Have you seen the new war plan?"

I said no.

"The Orange Plan said war could begin without warning after strained relations with Japan. That point is missing in Rainbow. Also, Pearl Harbor isn't mentioned as a target or that steps should be taken to guard against a surprise attack. Why were these taken out do you suppose? It might just be sloppiness, Lord knows there's enough in the best of times, but it looks suspicious to me. We were promised a hundred and eighty B-17s, and we've got a dozen so far. They said they'd send a hundred PBYs to watch for the approach of an enemy fleet, and none have arrived. We're still sitting out there ripe for the plucking, so I guess the president doesn't see it as a problem. Am I right? And it would also explain why we're getting only a trickle of the intelligence we did before."

I couldn't say, sir.

"Is everyone around here a Yes man?"

I said pretty much.

"Betty Stark is one for sure. That's why the president made him chief of naval operations. I don't trust him and neither does the Navy. He's a ventriloquist's dummy like Charlie McCarthy. I'm going to say so at lunch."

Admiral, I said, I don't think you ought to.

That was going out on a limb I didn't have to, but you had to respect Richardson. He was a fine man, honest as the day is long and sound as a dollar. Maybe I didn't have his qualities—well, okay, I didn't—but I could still admire them.

"The president isn't getting good advice because you people are afraid he won't like what he hears," he said.

He put his hat on, nodded and walked out.

He spoke his mind at lunch like he said. He was relieved as CINCUS and spent the war in charge of the Navy relief league. A career studying the Japs and when the time comes all that was wasted. Well, can't say I didn't warn him.

Months passed as our diplomats and theirs talked in circles. In July our listening stations heard the order go out that all Jap cargo ships were to return home. That put an end to all their trade, of course, which is what they lived on. You didn't have to be a genius to know what those marus were needed for. Franklin closed the Panama Canal—for repairs he said—meaning those in the Atlantic had to take the long way home around Cape Horn.

That order to the commercial fleet looked promising if war was what you wanted, but the White House still didn't know what it would take to push the Japs into striking first. He and Harry figured that was necessary if the country was to pull together. Getting into a war isn't as easy as you might think. A German sub sunk one of our freighters even though a big American flag was painted on the side, but Congress and the public acted as if it was no big thing.

The Senator's office called about that time to say he wanted to meet with me ASAP. I hung up and forgot about it a minute later. Between running back and forth to the White House, it was meetings, meetings, meetings. Sometimes I was so tired I lay my head down on the desk and fell sound asleep. I believed all this work made me a cinch for job far behind the lines when hostilities broke out. Harry was way more important than the new vice president. Harry Wallace was to the left of the White House, and Franklin didn't trust him any more than he did Jack Nance. Harry told me Wallace went to séances where ghosts rapped on the table.

"The boss put him on the ticket for the farm vote, but he won't give him much to do."

Hoover came to the White House to say Wallace was a Communist sympathizer. Franklin said yes, he had been wondering about that himself. Agreeing was his favorite way of getting rid of somebody. Hoover put on his hat and left.

Why wouldn't I think I was in like Flynn? Harry was the work horse more than ever and I was his Navy man. The way I looked at it, the Senator wasn't that important anymore.

"Didn't you see my message," he snarled at me Sunday morning as I was having breakfast. He had got up early and threw on a robe to catch me before I went to work. That thick snowy hair looked like a tornado got at it during the night, and he hadn't put his teeth in. Little kids would have been scared.

I've been busy, I said. It was as if I'd smote him with an axe handle.

"Too busy for *me?*" He couldn't believe it.

We're getting ready for war you know, I said.

"Why," he said in a voice that tried to sound friendly, "that was my question. How soon do you think the ruckus will start up? I've got friends who'd like an idea when."

The spring of next year, I said. That's what we thought at the time.

"That's the best estimate is it?"

Best I've heard.

Having got what he came for, he went back upstairs. Money was to be made on Wall Street regarding when the shooting was to start. There's nothing in life you can't bet on. He lost life-long friends passing on what I told him.

They didn't let on to us at the time, but the English were reading German codes the way we were reading the Japs, and doing an even better job. They tipped us that Hitler was fixing to invade the Soviet Union. That had us scratching our heads. Why look for more trouble?

Churchill tried to tell Stalin they were coming, but got no answer. Joe probably thought he was trying to stir up trouble with Adolph. So the Russians were caught with their pants down when the Panzers rolled across the border. A couple of week into Barbarossa and you wouldn't give a plugged nickel for their chances. I was offering ten to one the Reds would give up by July. Lucky for me I didn't get any takers.

They were throwing down their weapons and surrendering by the hundreds of thousands. We heard reinforcements were rushed to the front by train and slaughtered to the last man within hours. Some went into battle without guns and had to wait for one of the comrades to fall to get one. A single rifle went through many hands that way. The Soviet soldiers were brave, no doubt about that, and probably didn't need the political commissars with machine guns behind them to make sure they kept moving forward. The fighting suited us just fine; we hoped they didn't run out of bullets before everyone was dead on both sides. I mentioned it to Harry.

"Winston thinks we ought to think about helping them if they can somehow survive," he said. There was the usual mess of telephones, cables and newspapers on his bed.

That's an about-march for him, I said.

"The funny thing is I think he's right, but Franklin might need some convincing."

Well, I said, they're licked so there's no point wasting time on might-have-beens. We'll see Hitler walking around Moscow with them taking his picture like in Paris. Maybe he'll put Stalin on all fours at the end of a leash. That got a laugh from Harry. I had a knack for breaking the tension; I think that's why he liked me around. That and how good I looked in uniform. Harry was kind of a slob himself and I made up for that. He didn't want the country's image hurt with the foreigners.

The president decided that Harry had to go back to England and work out Lend-Lease details, and I was to go along again to carry the medical bag. We flew over in a flight of twenty B-17s we gave to England. We stopped in Newfoundland where the weather kept us on the ground twenty-four hours.

"This is where they wanted to put you?" Harry said as we looked at the sleet blowing sideways. "Good thing you've got friends in high places."

I didn't say there are worse places the Navy can send you. To certain death being one of them.

Those bombers cruised at a hundred-and-seventy-five miles an hour and it's twenty-three hundred miles to England, so you can calculate yourself how long it took. Man, the time dragged. There was nothing but ocean to look at. Or the sky when you got tired of that. Harry spread out on the floor in his overcoat with a parachute for a pillow and slept. I pulled rank and took the radio man's seat. I would have charged him with dumb insolence for the look he gave me if he was under my command. I gave it up when he needed the seat to twiddle the dials or key in something in Morse. Those planes are full of sharp edges that are dammed painful when the air gets bumpy.

England was far different than the last time. The Germans hadn't been dropping bombs for a couple of months, and people looked more cheerful now that the Russians were in it with them. There were so many Americans in uniform in London you'd think we were in it ourselves. They spilled out of the embassy into annexes around Grosvenor Square, and crowded the bars and restaurants at the better hotels. Sometimes you couldn't even get a table. The few well-heeled locals looked at us with disgust. I thought they would almost rather see the Germans.

Our people—we called ourselves "observers"—were there on all sorts of missions, from food and shipping to ordinance. You name it and we had an expert on the subject with a staff. Compared to last time, Churchill was upbeat. The weather was beautiful and flowers in the little garden behind Number Ten were in bloom. He now had a glimmer of hope the Russians might hold out through the fall.

"Then the Germans, like Napoleon, will learn what the Russians mean by General Winter," he said.

"Captain Brady is offering ten to one the Russians are finished," Harry said.

"He might be right; a glimmer of hope is still only a glimmer. The bad thing is the longer the fighting goes on the more battle experience the Germans get."

As usual, I was junior to everyone wherever we went. The English brass hats we saw most often were Pound, Dill, and Portal. Ours were Ghormley, Chaney and Lee. From the freezing look Admiral Ghormley sent my way, he'd got an earful from the Navy Building at 18th and Constitution.

The only reason I was in the room was Harry didn't like to draw attention fishing around in a pill box. When he felt himself fading, he gave a signal to pass a Dexedrine tablet hidden in a sheet of paper. We had got so good it looked like I was sending notes with ideas. Even Ghormley was impressed.

Winston dominated as usual. He gave a strategic overview, talked about tactics in Libya, and called on people to explain details. His words were like a river rushing to the sea.

"The Soviet government in response to our offer of materiel in continuing their fight has expressed more interest in talking about boundaries and spheres of interest after the war. This might be said to be putting the cart considerably in advance of the horse." There were chuckles around the table.

"The president instructed me to say we're not going to talk about any of that stuff," Harry said in a pleasant voice. "Win the war, that's our priority."

"Our feeling exactly," Winston said.

"That brings up reservations we have about this here emphasis on the Middle East," Lee said. He was a Southern gentleman who mixed with wealthy magnates and titled folks over there like he was one of them; I'd met him at weekend shooting parties a few times when I was passing myself off as a hog man. "We feel most efforts should be turned to the Battle of the Atlantic."

"We say the Middle East is just a sideshow," said Chaney, He was a jowly man from Missouri as subtle as a ballpeen hammer. "We put it behind the defense of the United Kingdom and the Atlantic sea lanes, Singapore and the sea lanes to Australia and New Zealand, and the trade routes in general."

The Battle of Crete showed that the Germans had figured out a way to beat the RAF, and Hitler had sixty thousand parachutists they weren't using on the eastern front that were available to drop on England.

"Hell, we understand some of your airfields are defended by men who are armed only with pikes, maces and hand grenades," Chaney said. His nod said what about them apples?

I'll give those English officers this, they knew how to hide what they were thinking. They looked at the ceiling or out the window, but I had a pretty good idea what was going through their minds. They had picked up a little military know-how over the centuries. Who was this son of a farmer or shopkeeper to tell them their jobs?

"Some of us in America don't understand the importance you place on the Middle East," Harry said diplomatically. "Maybe it's our lack of information."

The brass hats turned to Churchill to explain. It took a lot of words, but what it boiled down to was that what kept the Moslems and the other natives in line was they believed the British Empire was invincible. If they lost that fear the whole thing fell apart. Withdrawing from the Middle East would be the first domino and the rest would soon follow.

"One English officer armed only with a swagger stick can walk into an angry mob and disperse them with a few shouted words," Winston said. "I saw it myself in India when I was second lieutenant in the Queen's Own Hussars. Perhaps you remember Sir Charles Napier, the British Commander-in-chief there nearly a hundred years ago."

We Americans shook our heads. Nope, never heard of him.

"He signed an agreement with local Hindu leaders that he would respect all their customs with the exception of the practice of suttee whereby widows were forced to burn themselves to death on the funeral pyres of their husbands. When the Hindu leaders protested, Napier said so it is your custom to burn widows. Very well. We also have a custom. When men burn a woman alive, we tie a rope around their necks and hang them. Build your funeral pyre, and beside it my carpenters will build a gallows. You may follow your custom. And then we will follow ours. As you might expect, a thoughtful silence fell. Lose moral authority and the single man with a swagger stick is powerless; they go back to burning widows on funeral pyres."

If anybody at the table was against bringing civilization to the savages, he kept quiet. Harry did say colonialism was something Franklin had strong opinions about, but that discussion should be postponed until the two met.

"It can't happen too soon for me," Winston growled. "Many things must be decided."

One of the big problems we faced was nobody knew what the Soviets were thinking. They were backstabbers and murdering thugs; everybody knew that. They were Hitler's enemy now, but were they our friends? That was the question nobody could answer.

"We can get nothing from Ambassador Maiskey," Winston said. "He is either stupid of terrified of his masters in the Kremlin, and I strongly suspect it is both."

"Maybe I should go to Moscow and talk to Stalin personally," Harry said. It looked like the idea had just popped into his head and surprised him as much as Churchill. "I'd need to get permission first."

"By the heavens, Harry, it is a stroke of genius," Winston said, slamming the table with his fist. "You have the full confidence of President Roosevelt and mine as well. There is not another man on the planet that can make that claim. Fifteen minutes of conversation between you two would be worth three months of jabbering and *aide-mémoires*. But it is an arduous journey, my friend. Is your health up to it?"

"Oh, Captain Lowell and I have logged a lot of miles together, haven't we?" Harry said to me.

My heart sank. What little the world knew about Stalin and the Kremlin wasn't good. I could pick a hundred places I would rather go without getting up from my chair.

"Have the Foreign Office cable Stafford Cripps in Moscow to find out if they will receive Harry," Churchill said. "General Portal, can the Royal Air Force get him there?"

"Humph," Portal said, drawing on his pipe. "A PBY from Scotland to Archangel. A long journey, fifteen or sixteen hundred miles off the top of my head. Bitter cold that far north even this time of year. The Russians could fly him from there to Moscow."

A dinner was laid on at the Admiralty and we were invited to bring a wife or someone else of the female persuasion. Lady Cybil was up in Scotland but wasn't home when the post office sent someone to say she had a phone call. Out gunning down the game, I supposed. I doubt she could have found a seat on a train anyhow; they were all packed with soldiers and sailors.

So I decided to invite Wanda, the art student from the Fitzrovia days. I asked the embassy to track her down and the job went to a young Foreign Service officer named Archibald Crawford from Phillips Andover, Yale and Harvard Law. I got most of the following from a report he wrote. A skinny guy with eyeglasses and neatly parted hair, he had thought of going into the missionary field. Not your worldly type is what I'm hoping to get across.

The building where Wanda lived was bombed out and he went to the neighborhood police station where they kept a record of who died in the Blitz and where survivors could be found.

Oh, yes, the sergeant behind the desk said, we know Wanda quite well. And what might your interest in her be? Crawford sensed he was close to being in trouble. When he announced that he was with the American embassy, he was told to "hop it" if he knew what was good for him.

I had said the Wheatsheaf pub might know where she was and he went there after leaving the police. A bartender directed him to the Royal Arms where Wanda had worked as a living statue. He eventually found himself in a bad neighborhood. After he paid a bribe for directions, his search led him to a squalid—his word—building where he walked up three "noisome" floors—I think he meant noisy—and knocked on the door.

Wanda opened up and it was the rare man who wouldn't see that she was a prostitute; and not high grade, either. Crawford was that rare man.

She put up a little fuss when he said I wanted her as my dinner companion. She required more notice as a rule, love, but seeing how it was me. Crawford said a tough looking man came out of another room, barefoot and shirtless.

"'ere, what's this then?" He had a broken nose and a knife scar over one eye.

Crawford had read about "villains" but had never seen one in real life. My guess is he was one of those types always with his nose in a book.

"You want to talk to Wanda, you talk to me first," he said.

"Leave him be, Charlie," Wanda said. "Can't you see he's just a lad? He's come to take me to dinner with an old friend of mine."

"Old friend is it?" He put his face an inch from Crawford's.

"Oh, Charlie," she said. "Can't a girl have a friend without you making something of it?" She had to change and do something with her hair and left the two of them nose to nose.

"Money's going to change hands before she goes anywhere," Charlie said. "Ten pounds and not a ha'penny less."

Crawford said the man's breath was so bad he bent backward as far as he could. Can you imagine this prissy, fancy-pants guy in that situation? Makes you laugh. He said he would have left immediately if the Hopkins mission wasn't so important. He gave Charlie the money.

Charlie got a couple of tumblers and wiped them with the sleeve of a shirt from a pile of dirty clothes under a table and poured gin from a bottle.

Not for me, Crawford said.

"When Charlie Smoots drinks, everybody drinks." He was back in Crawford's face. "Bottoms up!"

The cheap gin burned all the way down and Crawford felt drunk almost at once; too drunk to demur—as he put it—when Charlie poured another. Bottom's up again. The room spun and when he raised his head from the table—he didn't remember putting it down—it seemed that Wanda had been taking a long time. He felt an aggression foreign to his nature. That's the way he put it.

"Say," he said, lurching from his chair, "what's the problem?"

"Yeah," Charlie said, "get yer arse out here, Wanda."

Crawford didn't recall trading blows with the taxi driver in front of the embassy. Holding Wanda by the arm, he pushed his way into the building. Buttons were torn from his jacket, his shirt was hanging out in front, and his hair stuck up from the headlock the taxi driver had him in. Wanda was tarted up in streetwalker finery—low cut, tight fitting. Between the two of them, it was quite an entrance.

Crawford shouted, "Harry Hopkins's guest, clear the way."

We were late arriving because of my slow typing and Harry had to send off cables to Franklin, skipping the State Department because it was as useless as tits on a boar hog. An embassy flunky met us at the side entrance.

"Excuse me, Mr. Hopkins," he said, "a woman named Wanda Burke?"

Is she here, I asked. The weariness from being a clerical drudge lifted on the spot.

He gave me a queer look. "Well, yes."

Harry said, "Is there a problem?"

"Not at all, sir, but she does seem a little worse for wear. The young man we sent for her had to be carried to his bed."

"This must be some broad," Harry said.

Senior officers in dress uniforms with medals and decorations and wives in evening gowns were staring at Wanda with a kind of shock when we went into the reception.

I couldn't believe my eyes. She was a fallen woman, all right—about a mile I'd say. A mistake has been made, I said to Brower. I don't know that woman, never seen her before. She had just planted a big wet one on Admiral Selby's cheek and he was going for his handkerchief.

"I moved my head otherwise she would have caught me full on the lips," I heard him say later. "Extraordinary to find a woman of the streets at such a function. To their credit they ushered her out without fuss except for that one scream."

Well, young lady, I suggest we call an end to it for the day. I've worked up an appetite and I'm thirsty. I'm told there is a chop house up the road a piece. Probably nothing fancy, but we'll have to get used to things being different now.

CHAPTER 18

ONLY RENEE PHELPS WAS AT HOME, THE OTHERS HAVING GONE TO A BAND concert in hope of meeting men. "Well, you're late," she said, her cat-like features expressing surprise. I said something vague about work and it had the predictable effect.

"Lord, what a day I had," she said. "I am seriously thinking about giving my notice. I'm not appreciated and never will be."

Renee trailed after me, elaborating on her mistreatment. I pulled my big suitcase from the closet and began packing. "Going somewhere?" she asked.

I said I was being sent to Lexington for a long weekend to assist in setting up a traveling exhibition.

"Mr. Hazelwood just about stood over me as I typed the page over again. Well, of course I was nervous and made mistakes. You would have thought the world came to an end."

She paused for breath—your only chance of breaking in—and I asked if anyone had been asking for me.

"Yes, a couple of times on the phone. He didn't leave his name. Is he very big?" She had seen a big man standing by the tree in front when she came home from work.

She followed me into the bathroom and watched as I packed my toiletries. When I was finished, I wrote out a check for my share of the next month's rent. Renee pointed out it wasn't due for another week, and I said I wanted to get it out of the way. She hoped I had a good trip and went into the living room to listen to Baby Snooks on the radio.

I slipped out the back way, heart in throat. I watched my rearview mirror, thankful no headlights followed. It was then that I gave way to tears; feeling regret for the life that I was certain was now over. Maybe it had been too quiet and uneventful for most, but it suited me. Now it was receding with each mile and I had a terrible certainty I would not return to it. And what had I exchanged it for? Captain Brady was used to knocking around with only a pack on his back; his stay at the old soldiers' home had merely been an interruption of his vagabond's existence. Before, he had been a naval officer with no fixed abode.

But I was different. I liked to send roots down deep, not be blown about like frothy spindrift on the sea. My brothers in Montana were not likely to take in a spinster sister they had not seen for years. If they did, the wives would not be welcoming. Two women cannot live under the same roof; that is one of nature's laws.

When I reached Devon, Captain Brady was sleeping heavily, his few possessions gathered by the door for quick departure. He had folded a blanket on the sofa for my use and I lay down feeling waves of panic.

"General quarters."

I opened my eyes to find him standing over me with a mug of coffee. "All lines are cast off and I've signaled the engine room for flank speed. Drink this and we'll get going."

And so began our long passage into the unknown.

Memorandum

July 27, 1953

To: The Director

From: T.E. Hawley, SAC

Subject: Lowell Brady

By the time we were able to win GREG PEARSON's cooperation by interrogation during extrajudicial detainment, LOWELL BRADY had disappeared with a woman whose descriptionsmall, wearing glassesmatched that of

HARRIET GALLITIN. They are believed to be driving a 1947 Plymouth (License Plate 143-297). I have sent teletypes to local law enforcement agencies asking them to detain the couple for questioning.

/Hawley

Tolbert _____

Memorandum

July 28, 1953

To: Clyde Tolson

From: The Director

Subject: Lowell Brady

For: File 24898

Tell T.E. Hawley to purge his paperwork of the phrase "extrajudicial detainment" regarding GREG PEARSON and not use it again in this or any other case.

/John

* * *

We drove west with no destination in mind. Pennsylvania and Ohio, Indiana, Illinois and Iowa—ever westward he drove and talked as I took notes. The vast country revealed itself to us from highways and farm-to-market roads, fruited plains to timber-clad mountains. I sometimes thought of Greg and wept, but I hid my tears from Lowell.

My shorthand skills lost their rust as I filled notebook after notebook, and we stopped at stationary stores along the way to buy more. I wound rubber bands around the growing stacks and kept them in the trunk. At nights we stayed in auto courts and shared a bed, at first platonically and then more—so much more. I had fallen in love with him as he had with me. A good-natured country parson married us in a little South Dakota town. His laughing wife threw handfuls of rice at us when we left. Their small town seemed to cower beneath the vast sky that stared down with blank indifference at mankind and his works. Without city rooflines to bring your eye down, you felt like you could be swallowed by the emptiness. But strangely it didn't bother me with my new husband at my side.

"That was the simplest of my three weddings," Lowell said. "To date, that is." He winked and I punched him on the arm.

"It's a little like being on the ocean," he said as our car crept across the prairie that stretched to the far horizon. "More silent, though. You heard water against the hull in the days of sail even if you were becalmed. There's zero sound out here if the wind is down. It'll make you mournful if you let it."

He wasn't worried now that we were on the open road; I would say blithe described him best. He had been battered and besieged by life and come through it all with good humor. He had dodged his pursuers for years and had a low opinion of them. If he hadn't sought shelter at the old soldiers' home, they wouldn't even know he was still alive.

"It was my teeth," he said. "I started having toothaches. I didn't want them to fall out and be one of those guys gumming his food. Yeah, I was tired of running like I told you, but the real reason was I needed a dentist."

I learned more about his years on the road. He could always find jobs because of the many skills he possessed. He had worked as a short order cook, auto mechanic, shoe salesman, gas pump jockey, farmhand, tractor driver, factory laborer and what have you. Employers asked him to stay on unless the work was seasonal, but instinct kept him on the move. He hinted with sideways glances at one-night stands. He was a man with a man's needs, as he put it.

"I won't have any trouble finding work when your money runs out," he said. "I've seen lots of help wanted signs."

My fear of capture slowly ebbed and I adapted to this nomadic life, and even began to like it. Each day was a new adventure, an experience far from my constrained life where I always knew where I would be and what I would be doing. We rose early and breakfasted at a local café or on bread and fruit from a grocery. We never had any set destination, and stopped whenever we were hungry or tired of driving. We bought a tent and camping gear and liked to pitch a camp in a park or pretty place alongside the road. There aren't many fine restaurants in the hinterlands, and this was a source of disgruntlement for Lowell. The food was plain but substantial, and that is the most that can be said for it.

He was the commander and I the crew. He determined the grand design, where we would go and when, and it was my job to take care of the details. Getting maps and directions at the filling stations, cleaning the windshield as he pumped the gas, running into stores for soda pop, tuning in radio stations when there was a signal, checking out the rooms at auto courts before we registered; all of the small, subordinate jobs, the wifely jobs, were mine, and I did them without complaint. I was happy to bask in the warmth of his large presence and to reflect on how small and cramped my previous life was as a historian learning more and more about less and less.

* * *

The next day we drove to Chequers with a flock of Winston's aides. An old pal of Harry, a big guy with curly hair named Quentin Reynolds of *Colliers Weekly*, came along to write a speech for Harry to go out on the BBC.

"Hell, Quent," Harry said when he woke up from a nap and read it, "you have me declaring war on Germany. The boss would hammer my scalp to the wall."

Take a look, he said to me. Tell me what you think.

I agreed that "Nazis beasts" and "foul monsters" was on the strong side.

Harry took a pencil and toned it down considerably. They had a little radio studio right there at Chequers and Harry read the speech into the microphone as we sat around the radio in the drawing room. He sounded more Midwestern than ever compared to the announcer who came on before and after, speaking in that clipped ruling class way. If you just listened to the BBC you'd think all English talked that way, but they have lots of other accents.

"Our people will be very reassured by that speech," Winston told Eden, lighting up one of his big cigars. He and Harry walked on the lawn afterward talking. When they came back inside I heard Winston say, "Tell him, tell him. Tell him that Britain has but one ambition today, but one desire—to crush Hitler. Tell him that he can depend upon us. Goodbye, God bless you, Harry."

They laid on another special train for us and we shot out of Euston Station going lickety-split for Invergordon up in the north of Scotland. We passed long trains on sidings. Men in uniform filled the windows to see who was so important that they had to pull over. They probably thought it was the king and queen. I gave them friendly waves and got the middle finger back from a good many. I didn't blame them; those wartime trains were no picnic. You were crammed in like sardines and the toilets were horrors. You don't want to hear about it.

Harry was quiet on the train ride. When I was giving him one of his pills he said, "You know, Brady, right now I think I'm the most important man in the world."

I laughed but there was not the ghost of a smile from him. As I look back, he wasn't kidding. He was the trusted friend of both Franklin and Winston and was going to Moscow to try to talk Stalin into throwing in with us. Remember, it wasn't so long before that we'd thought Stalin was as bad as Hitler and probably worse, and he didn't think much of us capitalist stooges, either. So one way or another three of the four most powerful men in the world depended on this skinny guy who should have been in a hospital bed.

We arrived in Inversgordon in foul weather—I'd say the only kind that part of the world has—and had drinks at a small hotel with the base commander and his staff. They didn't know who we were, only that we were *very* important. So there was a bit of stiffness; people afraid to make a mistake and so forth. But they began to relax thanks to the Harry's charm. The liquor didn't hurt, either. I found myself alongside Commander Goodsail. A fitting name for a sailor, I said.

"You'd be surprised how many people say that," he said.

He was a jolly fellow, but shrewd; you could see that behind the smiles. I asked what the flight to Archangel was like.

"We've just begun to patrol up there in your Catalinas—thank you, by the way—but I suppose the best word for it is awful. It's above the

Arctic Circle, you know. Gets frightfully cold and the light off the snow is blinding. Nothing below but emptiness, hours and hours of emptiness. In the back of your mind is what if we're forced down? It would be better not to survive the crash. If you managed to get off an SOS before going down and somebody heard you—nobody would, of course—it might be days before they got to the wreckage and that would be more or less by luck. That's if they spared somebody to search for you, which they wouldn't."

He glanced around to see if anyone could hear his next words. "I see Butler is assigned as your navigator. I'd ask for another, Mr. Hopkins being as important to the war as seems the case. Butler's dead-reckoning skills are not what I'd call the best."

Who's the man I talk to, I said.

"That fellow over there with the impressive moustache, Tommy Byrne-Worth. Good luck with him; he enjoys saying no. He thinks it tones moral fiber for men to hear it. It goes without saying that none of this came from me."

Captain Byrne-Worth was standing ram-rod stiff with a couple of respectful junior officers taking in his clipped conversation. Like the rest of the flyboys, he had come up through the Royal Navy. That generally meant old family with old money and a high opinion of yourself. I told him who I was and asked if for a few words.

"Yes, of course," he said. "Good job you chaps are getting on board at last."

I told him I wanted another navigator. "Afraid not." His brushed-up moustache bristled. "The schedule is up."

Does your pencil have an eraser, I said.

"Pilot Officer Butler is the only navigator we've got."

If you'd rather get the order from higher up, I said with a smile, I'll get Winston Churchill on the blower.

The starch went right out of him. "Look here," he said, "what's wrong with Butler?"

I said I heard he couldn't find his butt to wipe it.

"My God!" he burst out. "What a disgusting thing to say."

We come to the point where I'm from.

"Who have you been talking to?" he said.

A little bird.

We had a staring contest.

"Very well," he said, now a brick red. "I'll assign a different navigator, but it will take a day to get him here."

Maybe the weather will improve, I said.

"This is northern Scotland."

I've had to eat more than my share of crow, so I knew how he felt. Then a couple of hours later, we're told London wants us to leave that night because weather on the way could ground us for days. I was aware on the tarmac that Byrne-Worth was grinning and trying to catch my eye, but I didn't give him the satisfaction.

As we were getting ready to board a small boat to take us where the PBY rode at anchor on a choppy sea, Goodsail drew me aside.

"I did this rough drawing of the coastline on our first flight up there. If any charts exist they're secret. It's probably not worth a glance, but take it just on the off chance."

We crossed the North Sea flying low and slow. We had so many extra people on board—a few of our Army officers came along to answer technical questions—that I sat in a machine gun blister. I had permission to blaze away if Germans attacked, but luckily we didn't see anybody. After a few hours the monotony was so bad I almost would have welcomed a Kraut. PBYs don't grow on you, and it seemed I was wasting years of my life on them.

You wouldn't believe how cold it was. Harry was on a canvas cot with blankets piled high. We made landfall and I noticed the coastline didn't look anything like Goodsail's map. I squeezed out of the blister and went to Butler at his tiny desk next to a wheel well and asked where we were.

"Below is the entrance to the White Sea," he said.

I think you're north of there, I said, maybe a long way. I showed him Goodsail's sketch.

"What's this?"

What's it look like?

"A coastline." He was a younger guy, weak looking; the kind women like to mother.

It's not the one we're looking at, I said.

He went to a porthole to look out. "Where did you get this?"

Goodsail drew it when he was up here.

"Oh."

I went up to the pilot's compartment. "Trouble?" said Flight Lieutenant D.C. McKinley.

We're probably lost, I said.

"What!" he said in a voice like thunder. "Butler, get up here. What's he talking about?"

"I don't know, sir."

We haven't seen the Cape of Norway, I said. Goodsail says it has a sheer cliff a thousand feet high. Hard to miss something like that. This could be Cheshskaya Bay you turned into, not the White Sea.

"Christ Almighty! What about it, Butler?" he said.

"I'll recheck my calculations, sir. The wind might be pushing us more easterly than I allowed for." He scuttled away like a kicked dog.

"This map is rather crude," McKinley said.

Goodsail didn't think anybody would ever be looking at it, I said.

"We could be off a hundred miles or more." He thought for a minute. "Still, plotting a course is the navigator's business. I don't know that..."

If he's made a mistake, I said, we'll fly on this heading until we run out of gas.

"Hurry it up, Butler!"

The co-pilot was taking this all in. "If I may make a suggestion, sir: why not have the radio operator see if he can pick up Archangel."

Fifteen minutes later as Butler still sweated over his calculations, the operator took off his earphones and called out, "I got a faint signal southwest of here."

McKinley made a sharp turn and followed the direction finder until we put down at Archangel two hours later. Butler probably spent the rest of the war brewing tea in the mess. I hope so anyhow.

Harry later said he never shook so many hands in his life, and I got the same routine. The Russians threw a big banquet for us when we landed; so many toasts to friendship that I lost count. Cold fish, caviar and vodka, cucumbers and radishes. The next day we flew another four hours over endless forests to Moscow. Christ, what a hangover. I never made the mistake of trying to keep up with the Russians again. The secret is to eat a big chunk of bread and caviar with each toast.

Our ambassador, a little round man with a small moustache named Steinhardt, met us at the airport and we drove to the embassy. Harry said he was there to find out the facts of the situation.

"Good luck with that," Steinhardt said. "The Russians are so suspicious and secretive they'd be considered mentally ill in the rest of the world. Everybody with a brain is afraid of his own shadow, and for good cause. Stalin rules like Ivan the Terrible except for the impaling, and that's probably because he hasn't thought of it. Say or do something he doesn't like and you disappear in the night." He put a finger to his head like a gun.

The long and short of it, he said, was if you wanted to find out anything it had to come from him. Steinhardt said it was in the Russian blood to want a strong ruler, thanks to centuries of czars. Stalin means Steel in case you don't know. It's a name he picked so people knew who they were dealing with.

"Don't let on if you're put off by his appearance," Steinhardt said. "There's as much human feeling in those narrow eyes as in a wolf. The talk is he relaxes at night drawing up lists of people to have liquidated; and he's got the memory of an elephant for anybody who ever crossed him, even his old schoolteachers and the people who declared him unfit for military service because of his rotten teeth. They're all gone, they say. God knows where he finds new people for his lists."

We got a guided tour through part of the Kremlin. It's a huge place behind a high wall with four palaces and four cathedrals and a bunch of other buildings. It's a gloomy place and silent as the grave. They showed us through one enormous, beautiful room after another with fancy chandeliers and polished floors, every one empty, until Harry got tired. We went back to the embassy for him to rest up. No way could you keep all those rooms heated. You'd have to wear all your clothes and a blanket over your shoulders in winter.

I went with Harry and Steinhardt for the first meeting. After that it was just the two of them and a dumpy female translator.

Stalin was a short, blocky guy—five foot six and around a hundred and ninety, just as a guess—with a moustache like the old-time barbershop singers. Red Army uniform and boots polished like mirrors. I'd say more cunning looking than scary, but I wouldn't argue the point. He was standing in front of a bunch of what Steinhardt called *apparatchiks*, gray-faced guys with blank expressions.

Stalin chain-smoked and did all the talking, and I bet that hasn't changed a bit. His way of shaking hands was to grab the end of your fingers and let go almost right away. Steinhardt was right about the eyes.

"The czar had strong, handsome officers like you," he said to me through the translator. "They waved swords as they rode into the mouths of the cannons that made them *varen'e*."

I think I don't want to know what that is, I said.

"*Varen'e* is jam," she told me.

Stalin spoke again. "What you spread on bread," she said.

His flunkies burst into robot laughter but stopped when he glanced at them.

"You won't catch Captain Lowell on a horse," Harry joked, "with or without a sword."

Everybody sat down and Harry told Stalin how much Franklin and the American people admired their brave struggle and so forth, and what could we do to help?

Stalin was all primed for it. He said I want anti-aircraft guns, aluminum to build planes, fifty-caliber machineguns, and thirty-caliber rifles as fast as you can get them to us, and we'll let you know later what else. A million of those rifles.

Harry nodded. I guess he didn't remember how our troops were drilling with broom sticks on their shoulders.

"We won't lose this war, but we and the English can't win without you," Stalin said. "You must find a way to join us before Hitler can use the secret weapons we know he is developing."

Harry said afterward he was struck by how down to earth Stalin was. Not a word wasted once the diplomatic guff was out of the way. The Russians had already lost maybe a million soldiers by then, but if it bothered him it didn't show. No emotion whatever, not a flicker. Harry said he reminded him of an intelligent machine—his exact words.

The Russians had 180 divisions on the front when Germany invaded with a 175 divisions. Now there were 231 German divisions on the front versus 240 Russian divisions. Stalin said they'd have 350 divisions next spring and he guessed the Germans could mobilize up to 300.

Harry was writing this down, showing Stalin the top of his head most of the time. I was watching the apparatchiks watch Stalin like their lives depended on it. I don't think it took much to get on Stalin's bad side. A cough or sneeze might do it if he was in a bad mood. It sounds like I'm exaggerating, but you had to see those people. Deathly afraid, every last man jack of them.

Captured prisoners told the Russians that Hitler was already pulling some of his best divisions off the line to send to the Western front. The Germans were digging tanks into the ground which told Stalin they were already planning to go on defense even though there were months to go before bad weather closed up shop for everybody.

"It is one thing for mechanized forces to travel on the boulevards of Belgium and France," Stalin said with a little smile, "but it is another question in our country." Seventy-ton tanks were too heavy for Russian bridges, is what he meant.

Harry said he was impressed Stalin put aluminum so high on his priority. "A man thinking of giving up wouldn't be planning to build airplanes." He had another meeting with Stalin, but I wasn't invited. It was just Harry, Stalin and the translator.

Nobody knows what was said except Stalin, Harry and Franklin and that woman, unless she was strangled for what she knew. He kept coming back to the Japs when I was there. He was worried they'd make it a two-front war for Mother Russia. He didn't come right out and say it, but I got the impression they might sue for peace if that happened; give up the land they'd already lost and call it a day.

"We've moved so many of our troops from our Far Eastern Military Districts that we worry about the army Japan has in Manchuria," he said. One of the flunkies stepped forward to light his latest cigarette. "But if you could say America would come to our assistance if they attacked..." He left the sentence dangling. Those cunning eyes were on Harry.

"Only the president can make that decision," Harry said. Then, like an afterthought, he said, "And Congress, of course."

As we left that meeting, Steinhardt told us in a low voice. "Remember what I said. Assume your room is bugged and they're listening to every word." He gave me a sharp glance. "And if a beautiful woman takes an interest in you, don't assume it's innocent. They're great ones for blackmail."

The Moscow black-out was so complete it made London look like Broadway. German bombers came over along about midnight, and from the racket the Russians must have blazed away with thousands of guns.

Harry's room was for the princes they used to have; a fireplace big enough to walk into and a four-poster bed with a canopy. As I was doling out pills, he whispered, "Do you ever think about evil, Brady?"

Not much, I whispered back.

"It's like it's even in the walls here. You've seen the way people look. And the silence. Everyone is afraid to talk."

I said I'd noticed all right. Hard to miss.

"The world's a wicked place. Do you ever wonder why God allows evil?"

There's a deep one, I said.

"Everybody is born with good and evil and most of us spend our lives trying to keep the bad side down."

You have to drink down the whole glass of water.

"Isn't that what you do?"

Try to keep the bad side down? I guess so.

"I told him Hitler is an enemy of mankind and that's why we want to help. But do you think Stalin's any better?"

Seems like apples from the same rotten barrel, I said.

"Churchill said Stalin is the lesser evil."

I guess you have to go with that.

"It's hard to keep clean hands in these times." He was quiet for a minute. "Maybe it's always been that way."

They took me to inspect anti-aircraft positions around factories while

Harry was having his *tete ta tete* with the head man. Colonel Baryatinsky of the KGB then drove me to a huge tractor factory being taken apart down to the last bolt. What a job! I asked where it was going.

He thought about how much he could say without getting in trouble. At last he came to a decision. "East."

Harry didn't volunteer a word about what he and Stalin talked about and I didn't ask. They had a farewell feed for us in a huge hall. Dozens of people there, everybody drunk and red faced. There was music by a military band and a guy with a deep voice sang soulful songs that made the Russians cry. We got to bed late and while I slept somebody stole the medical bag from the room.

"Hell," Harry said when I told him, "I need that stuff."

We were talking to the KGB colonel about the theft when Stalin himself was in the door with a thunderous look. Stalin said something in Russian and Baryatinsky sagged like he'd taken a bullet in the belly. The translator with her hair in curlers hurried in tying the sash to her robe. Stalin barked something at her.

"The general secretary expresses his regret and says you may be sure all parties responsible will pay."

He said something else, just a few words. He wasn't a man who wasted them.

"If you will give the names of your medications our doctors will replace them."

"What are they called, Captain?" Harry asked.

Search me, I said. All I do is pass them out. I didn't think Harry should be taking Russian pills.

Stalin told Harry through the translator—she was stuttering from nerves by now—that the foreign ministry could send an urgent cable to Washington to find out. Or our embassy could, she added.

"Tell him thanks but we've got to get the show on the road," Harry said.

As we drove to the airport, he said there was going to be a secret meeting off Newfoundland between Franklin and Winston and he had to be there as a buffer.

"They're both prima donnas," he said. "If they don't get along history could be changed." He gave me a sad smile. "I'm still the world's most important man for just a while longer."

It seemed that Russian trip was cursed. Back at Archangel, Lieutenant McKinley had a long face and not just because the Russians had kept him and the crew confined while we were gone.

"I recommend that we delay our departure for a day or two, sir," he said. "We'd fight heavy headwinds all the way back."

Harry was bent over from stomach pain. No, he said through gritted teeth, I have to get back as soon as possible. The Russians had given him a fur rug and he lay on a canvas cot. I crouched alongside like a slave at his master's foot. The German agent in the Kremlin knew the pills kept Harry going; we were lucky he was so slow in pinching them. Harry got weaker on the flight and his pain was worse.

At one point we were only doing a hundred knots over the ground because of the headwind. The white nothingness was passing below at half the speed as the inbound leg. Every now and then we hit an air pocket and Harry and the cot were lifted off the deck. I tried to cushion the fall but sometimes he landed hard. Never a word of complaint from him.

"A ship is firing on us," the co-pilot said after we cleared the Murman Coast. I looked out the porthole and saw a destroyer banging away below. They had a pretty fair bead on us because the flying boat rocked from flak bursts.

"Flash the recognition signal the Russians gave us," McKinley said.

The co-pilot used the blinker light but they kept shooting anyway.

"Maybe they're Germans," McKinley said.

They kept it up until we drew out of range. Harry didn't stir while this was going on, and I checked to make sure he was still breathing. The Orkney Islands were on the horizon at last and then we saw the Home Fleet at Scapa Flow. Foul weather, of course. The water was covered with whitecaps.

"No one has told us where to land," McKinley said.

He picked a spot with the fewest ships and set her down. The co-pilot used the blinker light to signal an armed trawler. The answer came back that the admiral's barge waited for the pickup a few miles away.

"I'm not going to taxi in water this rough," McKinley said.

So we turned into the wind and took off again and landed a few minutes later in a narrow lane between ships at anchor. Harry was awake but looked like death.

"The admiral's barge is coming alongside," McKinley said. The PBY reared and plunged like a bronco. "I don't see how Harry is going to make the jump. The man's too weak."

I looked at the crew. They were all small men, and I damned them for it to myself. I was the only one big enough.

I'll carry him on my back, I said.

Believe me, I hated the thought of it. Transferring to a bobbing boat in rough seas? If there'd been even a middle-sized man, I would have ordered McKinley to make him the mule. They jury-rigged a harness and strapped him on my back in his life jacket. Harry didn't weigh that much, being skin and bones, but it was still awkward as hell with the PBY pitching like it was.

Harry, I said over my shoulder, try not to choke me when we jump.

I staggered to the hatch with their help and stuck my head into the wind and spray. My cap blew off and went sailing away like a seagull. The crew had maneuvered the barge close enough that they had to use boat hooks to keep it off the PBY.

I waited for the right moment. And waited and waited. The barge and plane rose and fell and the distance between them kept changing. Now close and then yards apart. I decided no time would be perfect and jumped as the barge was going down and the PBY rising. Incredible pain in both knees when I landed on the deck. I thought I had broken or at least dislocated them, but it turned out they were only sprained. *Only.* I would have cried like a baby if I was alone. They peeled Harry off me and the barge headed for shore.

Harry sailed on the *Prince of Wales* to Argentia and the secret conference. They put me in a naval hospital until I could hobble around with canes. The nurses were very accommodating, but ask me no details. That was my old life.

Memorandum

August 19, 1953

To: Clyde Tolson

From: The Director

Subject: Lowell Brady

For: File 24898

A teletype from our office in Pierre, South Dakota, said LOWELL BRADY and HARRIET GALLATIN were married two weeks ago in Rogersville, a small town in Moody County.

I don't think our source at the CIA should push his queries any further for fear of raising suspicions.

Our surveillance of the three people he thinks most likely to be involved has yielded nothing except that Assistant Director MELVIN CROSBY frequents theaters in seedy neighborhoods that show European films featuring nudity. There is a good photograph that shows him buying a ticket below a marquee that says "Hot Danes Show it All." (File attached). The time may come when we can put this to good use.

/John

CHAPTER 19

FROM TIME TO TIME I TRIED MY NEW LEVERAGE AS HIS WIFE TO HASTEN THE narrative. My husband—how wonderful it felt to say that—always gave a look of playful amusement.

"Hold your horses, pretty lady. I had plenty of time to think about all that happened during my years on the run. I added two plus two and connected the dots. If I jump ahead you might have gaps to fill in if I'm not around."

"Why would you not be around?" I felt my eyes fill. The man was so dear to me.

"You never know what's around the corner in this old life," he said. "Look at the curve balls thrown my way."

"We must never be apart now that we have found each other." I put my hand in his and he gave it a squeeze.

"Took a while, didn't it?"

It was impossible to think of life without Lowell. He filled all the lonely places in my heart. Ours was not a May and December romance, more like July and November. But mine was an old soul and his was a young heart.

The qualities that must have been so insufferable in Lowell when younger, the caddishness, the shirking and low cunning, had been transformed in life's crucible. He was not a saint—who among us is?—but the base metals had disappeared in the refining process. He had been humbled and hounded and known hardship. The years had mellowed him the way a rough young wine ages into a distinguished vintage.

His love turned the desiccated wasteland of my life into verdant garden. I thanked God every night for joining us together through the unlikely agency of that humble janitor. Life before was only reedy prelude compared to the full symphony that struck up when I woke each morning.

Lowell was so much fun to be around, which I believe was the true nature of his charm, not his handsomeness or noble bearing. He liked to joke and talk and silences did not last long around him. His conversation mixed what he saw on the road—"Look at that old bat in the DeSoto—is she blind or drunk?"—with his inexhaustible fund of recollections.

"The most shameless guy in the Pacific war was Lyndon Johnson. He's a senator from Texas now but he was just a congressman back then. When he came out on a fact-finding mission, MacArthur let him fly on a bombing run over New Guinea. They turned back with generator trouble way before reaching the target, but he convinced MacArthur he deserved a Silver Star because the plane he was *supposed* to be on got shot down. The story got pumped up so that he was cool as a cucumber and laughing in the face of danger when the Zeros attacked." He chuckled knowingly.

We were as comfortable as old shoes. Some nights we danced at honky-tonks after dinner. He knew all the steps and was surprisingly light on his feet. But he was red faced after a couple of dances and we sat down.

"Not as young as I once was," he said as he mopped his brow.

I was beginning to think we were safe. Then one day I sat in a public library in Iowa looking up the dates of some events during the war.

"They're on to us," he said in a low voice.

The Classical Revival library was one of the seventeen hundred built in this country through the generosity of Andrew Carnegie; they all have a stairway to the entrance to symbolize how libraries elevate the individual. This feature was responsible for the view down on Main Street where a policeman was walking around our car.

"What do we do?"

"Improvise," Lowell said.

The library had a public phone booth. "This'll do," he said scanning the Yellow Pages. He called the police department and said in a whisper, "I'm a teller at the Farmer's Bank. There's a man with a gun."

The policeman lifted his head at the radio call that went out seconds later. He ran to his car and sped away.

"Quick," Lowell said.

We drove out of town, my husband carefully observing all the traffic laws. We turned off on a farm road and parked.

"We'll wait until after dark," he said.

He looked glad to be back in his element as a fugitive. We traveled all night on back roads bound for Kentucky where I had made many friends in my field work.

* * *

Washington gave me convalescent leave for my knees, the Royal Navy coughed up a car and driver, and I went to Scotland to see Lady Cybil. To say she was glad when I walked through the door was the understatement of the year.

"Darling," she cried, rushing into my arms.

The old girl and I picked up where we left off and spent the next forty-eight hours in bed. Now, now, dear, I see your look. She's long gone now, just a memory. Nothing to do with us. There were already food shortages—butter, eggs and sugar got scarce in a hurry—but I pulled a few strings and London sent up hampers with an armed guard. A lot of food got pinched before it got where it was supposed to, so I gave the guard a hard look and checked off each item before signing the receipt. We rode to the hounds, blazed away at game, pulled salmon from the river and generally had a grand time.

She was sad on our last day together. "Will we beat the Hun?" she asked me.

Like a bass drum, I said.

"But the world will be changed."

I said I supposed so, maybe even for the better.

Lady Cybil cried a river of tears at the train station like she knew we'd never meet again. Go on, I said, we'll see each other plenty before this is over. But she wouldn't be comforted. Woman's intuition, I suppose.

When I got back to Washington I still had a week of leave coming to me, but I reported for duty early. I limped a bit more than was necessary when I went in to see Harry. Nature hates a vacuum and they had already squeezed a vice admiral into the cloak room with me. Fredericks was his name. He was a beaky old salt with snapping eyes.

"I've heard of you," he said when I introduced myself. You could have cooled a pitcher of lemonade on a summer day the way he said it.

Things were still going to hell just about everywhere you looked. People who were worried before were scared now. The first couple of convoys with guns and ammo got to Russia all right, but the Krauts had Leningrad surrounded and were slicing toward Moscow like a hot knife through butter. A German U-boat fired torpedoes at one of our destroyers, and then sank another two weeks later.

Harry told me each time Franklin slapped his desk and said by God there's the spark. "Watch the people rise up."

But the people shrugged them off like mosquito bites. The president was flabbergasted.

"He just doesn't get out enough," Harry said. "Most people would do about anything to keep out of another war."

A couple of weeks later I got a call at quitting time from Admiral Richardson. He asked if we could meet for a drink. Against my better judgment I said yes. There was nothing he could do to help or hurt my career, but like said before I admired the old coot. He said to meet him in a bar in an out of the way place and hung up. He was at a table in street clothes with a hat pulled low. He waved me over.

"Do you have a machine that plays recording tapes?" he said when I sat down.

I said the Senator had one for practicing his speeches.

"Good," he said and passed me a spool of tape.

He said few knew that Roosevelt secretly recorded conversations in the Oval Office. Sometimes he forgot to turn it off when a visitor left. "Give it back tomorrow."

I played the tape that night when Mother and the Senator went to bed. The two voices were Franklin and Admiral Ernest King, one of the orneriest men you'll ever meet. He got things done, though. He shaped up the Atlantic Fleet like nobody's business. He put a lot of old friends on the beach without blinking an eye.

"Good morning, sir," King said.

"Good morning, Ernie," the president said. "Take the weight off. The chief usher doesn't begin logging visitors until ten so this conversation never took place—savvy?"

"I understand, Mr. President."

"You did a swell job shaping up the Atlantic Fleet. You stepped on a lot of toes."

"And put my shoe up a few asses," King said.

I pictured Franklin throwing his head back, but his normal roar of laughter sounded like it was forced.

"But we're still a long way from being ready," he said.

"War may come faster than we think," Franklin said. "Our ambassador in Tokyo has a source high in the government. I'm reading from his latest dispatch. "Action by Japan which might render unavoidable an armed conflict with the United States may come with dangerous and dramatic suddenness."

"So the talks have broken down?"

"Not yet, but the Japs are getting impatient. They know we're playing for time. The moment is coming when we tell them flat out the only way we'll sell them oil is if they get out of China and tear up their treaty with Germany and Italy."

"They'll never go for that," King said.

"Have you got a good second-in-command?"

"Good enough."

"I'm going to make you my chief of naval operations. You're a tough man and tough times are coming."

King's long silence said he was stunned.

"Admiral Stark is a fine man," the president said. "But I need a ruthless son of a bitch, Ernie."

"I've been called that."

"I mean a real bastard."

"They say that, too."

"This man must consider the big picture and be willing to sacrifice American lives, and not torture himself about it afterward. I need to know before we go any further, are you that man?"

"If it's for the country."

"Good. The Japs are going to hit Pearl Harbor."

"Admiral Kimmel is a good man. He'll be ready for them."

"I don't want him ready, Ernie."

"Sorry?"

"I want it as big a surprise as we can make it. It's the only way it can succeed."

"*Succeed!?*"

"We have to get in the war before the English throw in the towel, the Russians and Chinese get beaten, and we're all by our lonesome against the Germans, the Japs, and God knows who else—probably half of South America. Did you see that Gallup Poll? I'd be thrown out of office if I tried to take us into the war. You showed Pearl could be attacked by surprise three years ago."

"Sure, it's a stupid place to base the fleet."

"That's why I got rid of Richardson. He just wouldn't shut up about that. I have no doubt Kimmel feels the same."

"So we have to let them attack us?"

"It has to be a bad bloody nose, Ernie. It's the only way this country is ever going to get unified. We have to get caught by surprise and get knocked on our ass. Then we'll get up and wipe the floor with them."

"So we'd know in advance they were coming?"

"We'll know, Ernie."

"There are spies who'd pass the word?"

"Better than that—far better. I'm going to let you in on the biggest secret in the world and it must not go beyond this room. But first let me ask you, are you still on board?"

"So far, yes sir."

"We broke their naval codes last fall and we're also reading their top secret diplomatic code. We know what they're thinking as soon as they think it."

"Jesus Christ!"

"We've got some pretty smart boys working for us, Ernie. One is your own intelligence officer."

"Bob Weeks? He hasn't said a word."

"I wanted him in the picture so things go smooth as glass when the time comes."

"Who else knows?" King asked.

The Secretary of State, the secretaries of navy and war, Betty Stark, General Marshall and a couple of dozen communications and intelligence officers. The people in the know have to be kept as small as possible. General MacArthur is getting the word. Churchill knows."

"But not Kimmel?"

"That would be defeating the purpose. I nearly sent you out as Richardson's replacement, but nobody could've fooled you. You'd know something funny was up. Don't take this the wrong way, but Kimmel is too honest and decent. You've got a devious mind like me."

"What about Betty Stark?"

"A lot of reputations will be ruined, and his will be one of them."

"Does he know?"

"Yes."

"There's no other way?"

"I've tried everything I can think of. The Germans aren't going to give us another *Lusitania*. Even if they did, Congress wouldn't buy it this time around. But I've worked the Japs into a corner where there's no way out except war."

"This won't stay secret for long."

"After we're in the war, it won't matter. Our people will be crazy mad and all they'll want is revenge. It has to be a bad bloody nose, Ernie; a little pin prick won't work. We know from ship movements and radio direction finders that the Japs are assembling a fleet to hit us. We're going to have to play chess with Kimmel—feed him crumbs so it doesn't look like we kept him in the dark, but not enough that it spoils the surprise."

There was a long silence and I thought it was over, but then Admiral King spoke. "I'm with you, Mr. President." Another pause. "But we've got to get the carriers out before it happens."

I poured down three fingers of the Senator's finest scotch and hoped I got it wrong, missed a key word or something. The president of the United

States and the next chief of naval operations keeping Pearl in the dark about an attack? Ridiculous. So I played it again. What finally convinced me was what King said about the carriers.

He had made no bones in speeches that battleships were finished and carriers the coming thing. More and more senior officers—they were getting a lot younger, by the way—looked down on the big guns crowd. As I told you, I made the switch myself and told people battleships were as out of date as the Monitor in the Civil War.

King could steel himself to losing a few older battleships, but not the all-important carriers. We were building a hundred more, but right now all we had was a pitiful handful for both oceans. As for the human side of it, they didn't count. Oh, you would mourn them afterward, fellow human beings and so forth, but you had to think of them as units you replaced. Sounds hard-hearted, but that's the way it is.

I was tempted to pour another drink, but I needed to think this out. I didn't know why Richardson passed on the tape or who gave it to him—some FBI type or maybe a high-up civilian shocked at what he heard—but I wanted to give it back as fast as I could. I'd deny I knew anything about it if, God forbid, anyone asked. You see why, right? If Franklin and King were willing to let who knows how many die at Pearl, Richardson and I were just as expendable—more so because we'd heard this. I put the tape in a bureau drawer in the attic and spent a sleepless night.

The next morning I turned my overcoat collar up and walked in chilly weather to the Navy League building where Richardson saw to the widows and orphans. What a come down. Roosevelt didn't just demote men who crossed him, he stomped them into the ground. The admiral who had commanded the Pacific Fleet now was in charge of an office full of gray-haired ladies with large bosoms and glasses on chains around their necks. You know the type, bossy biddies with eyes as sharp as their tongues. After some trouble about not making an appointment, I was allowed to see the admiral.

Richardson sat behind a big desk bare except for a brass chronometer. Our eyes locked as soon as I came through the door. He didn't look like he had slept very well either.

"They say we'll have an early winter," he said. "Snow by Thanksgiving,"
I said I didn't appreciate being put in this position.

"I felt the same way," he said. "The tape was given to me by a trusted
friend. I didn't see how I could refuse. The question is what are we going
to do about it?"

You didn't tell him you were giving it to me?

"No," he said.

Good, I said, keep it that way if you don't mind.

"You have a reputation for looking out for yourself, but even you see
this for what it is. They have to be stopped. What about Harry Hopkins?
He's always seemed like a decent guy. Can you talk to him?"

He and Franklin are like peas in a pod, I said. You can bet Harry agrees,
and I wouldn't be surprised if it was his idea in the first place.

The admiral shook his head as if he couldn't believe treachery like this
was possible. A lot of those old-timers believed as much in the honor code
as when they were midshipmen. Naïve is the word for them.

"We can't send Kimmel a warning through official channels. They'll be
listening on the long distance lines and monitoring Western Union and
RCA. Someone has to go out there and tell him so they're not caught with
their pants down."

Why not you, I said.

"My travel is subject to approval. They'd never let me go to Pearl. You're
not under that restriction."

One of Robertson's gray-haired ladies poked her head in. "Captain
Blevins to see you, Admiral."

I knew Blevins to nod at when I was cutting away at the deadwood at
the Navy Building. He was a leathery sort with jug ears and a bald head
the color of mahogany.

"Hugh sees the intelligence we're giving Kimmel," Robertson said.

"More important, what we're not," Blevins said. "The naval and diplomatic cables to and from Tokyo are being withheld. One of our decryption stations is a half mile from him as the crow flies, but it might as well
be on the moon. Hell, even the Asian Fleet is reading this stuff, and they're
ordered to run like a scalded cat when the balloon goes up."

Give him an example, Richardson says.

"The Japs have a spy at their consulate telling Tokyo about ship movements at Pearl. The FBI and ONI are watching him, but Kimmel doesn't know a thing about the guy. He'd be getting ready for action if he did. Instead, he's devoting full time to training all those greenhorns we're sending him. Three quarters of the officers and men never heard a gun fired before they got there."

What about the Army, I said. Is General Short getting this intelligence from MID?

"Nope," Hugh said. "General Marshall is keeping him on short rations as well." He gave me a wintery smile. "You might call it a conspiracy."

This is all very interesting, I said, but it's got nothing to do with me. I put on my hat and coat and walked out the door.

Memorandum

November 27, 1953

To: Clyde Tolson

From: The Director

Subject: Lowell Brady

For: File 24898

Hard luck that we just missed capturing BRADY and GALLATIN in Sioux City. It is encouraging, however, that police departments are watching for them. As we know, they are not always that cooperative. I credit your Operation Handshake for the better rapport we have now with local law enforcement.

The descent of MELVIN CROSBY into moral depravity is now well documented. The photograph of him opening his raincoat and exposing himself to passing cars establishes that beyond a doubt. (File attached). What is more important is the man on the opposite corner who also was also taking a picture. He has been identified as ANTON MOROZOV, an NKVD operative who has consular cover at the Soviet embassy.

There are different ways to interpret this. One is CROSBY is already working for the Soviets and photographing him in an act of deviance is to ensure he remains under control. A second is the NKVD has been tipped off about his flaw and plans to blackmail him into cooperation at some point in the future.

If it is the latter, how did they know learn about CROSBY not long after we did? That again raises the specter of a high-placed traitor within our ranks whose goals are the Kremlin's goals: the disunity of our nation and the paralysis of our foreign policy. Apart from you and me, I don't think anyone should be above suspicion.

If CROSBY is under Soviet control, it may be that he used WILLIAM DONOVAN as a tool to bring LOWELL BRADY to our attention. How else to explain the "coincidence" of their meeting at the restaurant? There are deep currents that we do not understand. For example, it is possible BRADY remained in the Soviet Union after the war and was brainwashed?

CROSBY and DONOVAN know each other at least casually from social events hosted by the Agency, our source there informed us. This raises the possibility of employing guilt by association if DONOVAN proves troublesome down the road.

If the Soviets mean to stir up ugly division in the country to weaken our will to oppose them, as I believe is the case with BRADY's sudden reappearance, we must stop them by every means at our disposal.

/John

CHAPTER 20

"**I**F THIS ROAD GETS ANY WORSE," LOWELL SAID, "WE'LL HAVE TO GET OUT and walk."

He fought the wheel as the car bounced and lurched over deep ruts and pot holes. The road climbed as darkness fell through hardwood forests in Hart County, Kentucky, a passage so daunting that federal agents were seldom seen.

"It's not much farther," I said.

We arrived at the clearing where the Monroe family had lived for generations. They eked out a living on stony soil from a few cattle, hunting and fishing, and selling white lightning prized by the connoisseurs of that intoxicant. That last gave them a modest prosperity even in bad times, which accounted for most years in that region. A big tumbledown house dominated the clearing. Outbuildings slumped as if they were tired of it all.

"Sounds like a party," Lowell said.

Fiddle music with banjo, harmonica and washboard poured from inside, and the shades in windows showed the black shapes of people dancing. I told Lowell to honk the horn so they didn't think we were sneaking up. The music stopped at once.

Jake Monroe, the stooped, elderly and bearded patriarch of the family, came out on the front porch with a shotgun.

"Declare yourself if'n you don't want to be chawing birdshot. This here's private property and more so after dark. Armed men is spreadin' out in the woods as I speak."

"Mr. Monroe," I called, "it's Harriet Gallatin. Do you remember me?"

"Lord above, Harriet. You get over here and bring that big fella with you. Put your guns down, boys. We were hopin' we'd hear from you again someday."

He leaned the shotgun against the wall and gave me a big squeeze as women and children pushed outside and men came in from the trees. I judged there were three or four dozen Monroes, toddlers to ancients, all with welcoming faces. Backwoods people can be as warm as they are standoffish, and I found myself passed from one embrace to another. The teacher at the one-room schoolhouse three miles west had read my monograph on Ole Dan Tucker to everyone within a twenty-mile radius after it was published. The music I recorded by the Monroes during my visit was played on the radio. They had basked in the limelight.

"What smells so good?" Lowell asked.

We had arrived at a birthday party for Lorna, one of Jake's daughters, who was turning fifty. A fine Appalachian spread was on the tables pushed against the wall to clear room for dancing. There were platters of squirrel stew, fried rabbit, venison sausage, roasted quail wrapped in bacon, whistle pig pie, possum and sweet potatoes, chestnut and cornbread dressing, and lots of other savory dishes. A pitcher of cold buttermilk was brought from the cellar for us to drink.

Lowell sampled the white lightening after he shook hands with everybody. "Woo!" he said, stamping his foot. "I'll go easy on that."

The Monroe men grinned at one another. They disapproved of women drinking, so I wasn't offered a taste.

The music and dancing struck up again and we joined in ourselves after eating. When one musician tired, another took his place. Couples collapsed into chairs flushed and perspiring. After they fanned themselves and got their breath back, they were up and dancing again. The party lasted long into the night and ended with a prayer that everyone would have a safe trip home.

"Y'all stay here tonight," Jake Monroe said to Lowell and me. "We got plenty of room."

I thanked him and he led us into a wing of the rambling house built in the early days. The room was primitive but clean, and we sank gratefully into a feather mattress under an eiderdown comforter. The family was as welcoming at breakfast as the night before.

"What brings you and your husband back to these here parts?" Jake asked as he poured our coffee.

"We're running from the law," Lowell said matter-of-factly as he tucked into a steak and roasted potatoes. "I haven't had bear meat for years. Strong flavor, isn't it?"

Jake studied him for a moment. "Nothing violent, no murderin' or thievin.' No takin' advantage of others?"

"He knows something about the government it doesn't want people to know," I said.

"Well, that bein' the case," the old man said with a nod, "yer among friends and stay as long as you like."

At Lowell's insistence, we came to an arrangement for room and board. His many skills were put to good use around the farm, and the early autumn days passed happily. We felt secure because no one could approach by car unheard. The Monroes and their neighbors were always out hunting and fishing so snoopers on foot would be spotted.

At night after supper was over we returned to our room and he lay on the bed with arms crossed behind his head, dictating by lamplight until he got sleepy. It was an idyllic time, the best of my life as I look back. But even the sunniest day was shaded with worry. Our pursuers were thorough; they would get around to my monograph in time; they would comb through the footnotes for clues, and question everyone I had interviewed.

* * *

Something funny happened after I left Richardson's office I can't explain to this day. I was walking to the White House thinking I'd eased myself out of another jam, but not feeling good about it, when I came on a long column of seamen marching in pea coats. I seemed suddenly to see things in amazing detail. The bark on trees, a bird sharpening a beak on a limb, even the tiny sparkle of minerals in the sidewalk—all of it leaped out sharp and clear.

Looking into the faces of those young men was as if I was looking into their lives. No more than a glimpse because there were so many and they passed so fast, but enough to know them. Their hopes and dreams and fears, that kind of stuff; they were clear as glass to me. They were decent guys mostly—there were some bad apples and I saw that too—who were filled with love of country. I'm not going to compare myself to Saul on the road to Damascus, but it was like that in a way. When the last detachment passed, I felt like a different man. I turned around and went back to Admiral Richardson's office and told them to count me in. They were surprised to put it mildly. I think they had been saying hard things about me.

I asked Harry when I got to the White House if I could take a few days off.

"You've earned it."

I flew to Hawaii on Pan-American and paid for the round-trip myself. The Navy would want to know the reason for the travel and make me go the cheapest way if it didn't have priority. I carried a letter from Richardson telling Kimmel I had sensitive information that couldn't go through official channels.

It was the rainy season and we landed in a squall. I took a taxi to naval headquarters, glad to see security was tighter. Even though I was in uniform, the guards at the gate looked at my ID and telephoned somebody before they let me in. No one was manning the new machine gun emplacements because of the weather, but at least they were there. Tarps covered new slit trenches.

"What's this all about?" Admiral Kimmel said when he put down the letter.

Richardson's old office had one more potted fern, but otherwise was the same. Kimmel had thinning sandy hair, wore glasses and looked honest as the day is long. Men of integrity were pigeons for Franklin. I believe I've mentioned that.

I asked him to promise he'd keep our conversation strictly secret.

"What the hell for?"

I said I couldn't continue without his promise.

He thought for a moment. An officer flying all this way had to have something important to say. "Well, all right," he said crossly.

Word of honor?

After a struggle with his temper that turned him pink, he said, "Very well."

I had to go slow. Spill all the beans right off the bat and every ship in his command would get steam up within the hour and head for open water. Then he'd get on the blower to Washington demanding to know what the hell was going on.

You know the games they play in Washington, I said.

"What about it?"

There are people like Admiral Turner, I said, who want to restrict intelligence to fewer commands. Need to know and so forth.

Turner was head of the war plans division, but had muscled into naval intelligence and put Admiral Hughes on the sidelines. The man was a champion empire builder. Bureaucratic politics might explain Turner's control of ONI, but Richardson believed there was a darker reason.

"I'm glad I'm not in Washington. The CNO told me last month to make preparations for war without saying what he meant, and then a couple days later said to forget what he said. I assumed he was under mental strain."

Some of us don't think you're getting all the intelligence you need, I said.

"Funny you should mention that," Kimmel said, his manner changed. He turned to look out at the wind and rain lashing the palm trees. "We stopped getting the radio direction finder reports on Jap ships. Turner said he didn't want to bog us down in detail."

How long has this been going on, I asked.

"Since the first of the month," he said. His eyes snapped. "What business is this of Richardson? Why is he going behind backs?"

It's not only Richardson, I said. There are others.

"Who?"

I'm not at liberty to say.

"This seems like a lot of tomfoolery."

Tomfoolery. A word from when people wore powdered wigs.

It isn't, I said. Nor, I wanted to say, is it piffle or shenanigans. This tells you better than a whole book who I was dealing with.

I asked if he thought it was a good idea to base the fleet at Pearl Harbor.

"Of course not, he said. "The only ones who do are the president and toadies like Stark. It's pure craziness."

Especially, I said, with war so near.

"If you believe the newspapers, war could start tomorrow. They're whipping up hysteria. Some way ought to be found to shut them up, the Constitution be damned."

I studied my fingernails.

"Tell me what's on your mind—you and Richardson and the others. You didn't come all this way just to drop mysterious hints. Tell me what you're driving at."

You know the global situation, I said.

"Only what I read in those damned newspapers. I figure every other word is false, and that's being generous."

We're running out of time to get into the war, I said. That's what the White House thinks. The Russians are on the ropes and the English are starving.

"It's that bad?"

I nodded.

"Christ!"

You might think it strange that Kimmel wouldn't know the big picture, but like most he was an official-channels man. If something wasn't his business, it wasn't his worry; he had enough work to keep two men busy. Strategic thinking was somebody else's job; if he got that assignment, he'd do it as well as anybody. But his job was getting the Pacific Fleet ready for war, and that took all he had.

"How can the president get us into war soon enough to help the English and those damned Soviets?" Then a light bulb went on. "A surprise attack by the Japs? He thinks that would get us in because of the Tripartite Treaty?"

His eyes went to the big map of the Pacific on the wall. "Our war games always assumed they'd come down from the north and launch their planes from the Prokovief Seamount."

That's a submerged volcano, dear, one of a bunch named after long-haired composers. It's about a hundred and eighty miles from Honolulu.

He walked to the map. "Weak as we are right now, they could take the Philippines, Indochina and the Dutch East Indies and not even break into a sweat. Presto, their oil and other natural resource problems are solved."

They know we'd come after them, I said.

"True enough," he conceded. "But it might be a year or more before we were ready, whatever the dreamers say. They could get a lot of defense built in that time."

Word is we're going to tell them pretty soon that they have to get out of China.

"Where'd you hear that?" Kimmel said. He couldn't believe it. "They'd never do it in a million years, the kind of people they are. They've lost tens of thousands of men in that war, maybe hundreds of thousands by now."

An unimpeachable source, I said. That was a word the Senator used that I rolled out now and then to impress people.

"That's just asking for it," Kimmel said, shaking his head.

There's also a rumor we're going to tell them to tear up that treaty with Hitler, I said.

"What's in it for them?"

Maybe we'll give them a discount on rice balls and fish heads.

Kimmel glared. "I do not find humor appropriate under the circumstances."

I said sorry and asked if a taxi could be called to the main gate as that was all my business and I had a seat on the noon flight to Los Angeles.

"That's it!?" Kimmel said in amazement. "A few hints and rumors?"

I'd feel cheated myself, but I couldn't tell more without the risk he'd think the situation was so grave he could go back on his word of honor.

On the drive to the airport from the Royal Hawaiian where I changed out of my uniform in the suite they kept for officers, I told myself Mission Accomplished.

Kimmel had no doubt heard of me and believed the stories, but the fact I came at Richardson's request made him pay attention. He knew Uncle Jo got the shaft for asking questions he thought about himself. I guessed he'd start questioning the intelligence Washington was sending him.

"That is the shortest Hawaiian vacation ever," said the red-haired stewardess who had been on the flight over.

I beat my old record by fifteen minutes, I said.

I had a few drinks to encourage a philosophical frame of mind and talked to the man in the next seat. From his haircut he was a hundred per cent Marine. Jack Nipper was his name.

"Are they fugazi back there or what?" he asked.

Definitely, I said.

"I'm glad I'm going back to the mainland."

I don't go that far. The weather, for one thing.

"Screw the weather. I'm ready for something different."

Like most Marines, he believed it was government policy to make life as hard for as many people in his uniform as was possible, regardless of expense.

"They're sending Army troops to replace the jarheads on Midway and Wake," he said. "The big brains sent twenty-five-thousand fully trained and equipped Marines to the east coast in May, just about all we had in the Pacific. Now all of a sudden they realize we might be a little light on real fighting men out here."

I remembered that was the same time a carrier, three battleships and eighteen destroyers were transferred to the Atlantic Fleet, a fourth of the available fighting force. More dots for Kimmel to connect. But he might decide Washington wouldn't dare order deployments like that if we were going to war.

"There's no harbor or anchorage at Wake and you have to unload ships in the open seaway," Nipper said. "Waiting a week for conditions to calm down is pretty standard. Sometimes it takes a month."

Definitely fugazi, I said.

I called Richardson the next day from the Washington airport. He stopped me at Hello.

"Don't say anymore," he said. "I'll meet you at that same bar."

He waved at me from the table in the corner. "I think my phone line is tapped," he said. "I hear clicks and breathing."

We'd better make this our last meeting.

"I agree."

I told him about my conversation with Kimmel.

"Do you think he gets it?"

He sure had a thoughtful look, I said.

"Blevins was told he's being transferred to Great Lakes. He won't be able to help anymore."

Sounds like they're onto you, I said.

"We did all we could," Richardson said sadly. "This thing is just too big and deep."

I don't say it's to my credit, but I was relieved it was over before I got in any trouble. We shook hands and parted.

Two weeks later as Harry and I were shooting the breeze in his bedroom, Admiral Turner came busting in with a message ripped from a teletype. He wore steel spectacles and had thick, dark eyebrows that were always jerking up to full mast at the stupidity of people he worked with.

"The shit's hit the fan," he said. He looked at me and stopped. "Is he okay?"

"He knows about the code stuff," Harry said.

I guess Turner assumed Harry was saying I was in on the even deeper stuff so it was okay to talk.

"Kimmel is off the reservation," Turner said, sinking into a chair. "He sent the fleet to the Prokofiev Seamount. His order says assume they could encounter an enemy force at any time."

He read from the message. "He's got forty-six ships out there, including *Lexington* and five battleships. Twelve PBYs are searching a sixty-five degree arc six hundred miles out from Oahu's north shore. Orders are to signal by flag instead of breaking radio silence if the enemy is sighted. Kimmel told them that could happen at any minute."

"How did this happen?" Harry said. He was really mad.

"He didn't say a word to us," Turner said. "He did it on his own authority."

"Where's the Japanese fleet?"

"It's just leaving Hitokappu Bay. Yamamoto is probably two weeks from where Kimmel has his ships."

"Tell him to get his ass back to Pearl Harbor," Harry said angrily. "He's going to screw up everything."

"Does the president know?" Turner said.

"I'll tell him when he gets back from Bethesda. He's being entertained by the crown princess of Norway." He formed a circle with forefinger and thumb and poked his other forefinger through it.

"I'll be damned," Turner said. "So he can still do it?"

"His legs are the only parts that don't work. Get going Admiral. You stay here, Lowell."

He was quiet for a moment after the door closed. "I'm sorry," he said. "As my naval aide and the guy who saved my life you should have been in the picture, but the president wanted this held as tight as possible."

Harry was *apologizing* to me for not telling me we were going to let the Japanese attack our own people! Good thing my face was trained from poker.

"The president and I hate it, but it's the only way we can get done what has to be done. We've looked at the situation from every angle. The Japs have to hit us with a baseball bat before the American people will react."

What about—my throat was dry all of a sudden and I swallowed—the men on the ships?

"Turner says we're taking in enough new recruits every day of the week to cover what we're likely to lose in the attack." Harry got a funny look. "You know, I was a social worker before I got into politics. Every life was important to me. But you guys in the Army and Navy think different. You don't blink at losing ten men today to save a hundred tomorrow. Turner says the carriers and our newest warships will be gone before the Japs get there," Harry said.

So it won't be a total loss, I said.

I guess Harry heard bitterness.

"This is hard for me," he said, tears suddenly in his eyes. "I can only guess how bad it is for you guys in the know—old shipmates and all."

I didn't say anything. Couldn't.

There was a tap at the door and a Navy doctor came in to give him an injection. I felt Harry's eyes follow me out. He wasn't faking how bad he felt.

I started to see a difference at the Navy Building. Everybody was grim and tense, but some guys looked like they had a fox chewing at their guts. I guessed they were the ones who knew what was coming. I may have had the same look for all my bragging about a poker face.

There was a floor in the Navy Building with armed guards where no one could go unless Turner personally approved. I was called up there one afternoon a couple of days later. I was escorted by officers with pistols.

Turner was furious. "I don't want to go through the switchboard with this. Get over to the White House as fast you can and tell them Kimmel is at it again. He's sending Halsey north with a task force of twenty-five ships. It's like somebody here tipped him off. I'm sending him a signal to pull Halsey back to Pearl forthwith. Make sure Harry understands that."

Pa Watson popped out of his office at the White House when he heard I was there. "What is it?"

Sorry General, a message for Harry's ears only.

"Is it okay if the boss hears?" he said sarcastically. "They're in there together."

If you could tell him Admiral Turner sent me.

Watson went to the Oval Office door, tapped lightly and went inside. A few seconds later, the door opened and he motioned me in.

"Well, well," Franklin said cheerily, "Captain Brady as I live and breathe." He acted happy to see me, but like I said I had wised up to that BS long ago. "It's too early for the cocktail hour, so what's up?"

I repeated what Turner said and the blood drained from his face.

Then he exploded. "Jesus Christ! Doesn't anyone in the Navy obey orders?" He pounded his desk with a fist and all the donkey figures jumped.

Admiral Turner is ordering him to return the task force to Pearl, I said. Forthwith.

The president turned to Harry. "Tell Turner to get off a message to Kimmel saying he is very close to a court-martial. No, wait a minute. Phrase it so the possibility of a court-martial is *implied*. Kimmel will get the message."

"Yes, boss," Harry said, picking up a phone.

Franklin was giving me a hard stare and his face was flushed. "You know about this, do you?"

Not much.

"Who told you?" he demanded.

You hear things, I said.

Harry hung up the phone. "Turner's getting right on it."

"I'm appalled Captain Brady knows this. I never authorized him."

"I told you it would get out," Harry said coolly. "No way you could stop it."

"But so soon!" Franklin said. "What if the Republicans get hold of this? They'll file articles of impeachment so fast our heads will swim."

"We've got the votes in the Senate to stop them cold."

"*That* doesn't matter, Harry," Franklin yelled. "It would unify the country against *me*."

"You can trust Captain Brady."

"But who else knows? I want an investigation and I want it now. Find the leak and plug it. But don't get the FBI involved; I don't want to give Hoover something to hold over me. Bring Romano in."

Halsey and his task force returned to Pearl. To make sure Kimmel didn't get any more bright ideas, the two carriers and their escorts were ordered to ferry pursuit planes to Wake and Midway. You want to know how fouled up we were? Army pilots were assigned at first and then someone realized they didn't know how to work off carriers.

You remember I told you the Navy had the responsibility for defending Pearl Harbor when the fleet was in? Well, the biggest piece of that defense wasn't going to be there, the carrier planes. The Army's fighters, the half that the carriers didn't ferry off to Midway and Wake, were lined up in neat rows for the Japs when they came tearing in. That supposedly made it easier to protect them from sabotage. Pitiful, wasn't it?

I met General Short, the commander of the Hawaii District and the man who gave that order. The word on him was you wouldn't find a more henpecked husband if you looked for a year. His intelligence officer spent most of his time keeping Mrs. Short out of the general's hair—running errands and so forth—instead of doing his job. That's part of the public record. You can look it up if you don't believe me.

CHAPTER 21

THE DAYS WERE SHORTER AND THE WIND THAT TOSSED THE BARE TREES brought in rolling mountains of gray clouds. We kept a blaze going in the fireplace, and Lowell chopped wood two or three times a day. That part of the building was not insulated because the early Monroes built it in a hurry with rifles close at hand.

"They never knew when those red devils would come whoopin' and hollerin out of the trees,'" Jake Monroe said. "But it shore beat the cave and dugout they lived in before. Brrr. But it's *cold* in here, ain't it?"

"Whew!" Lowell said after staggering in with a big armload of wood. "Not as young as I was." He sat down, his face cherry red. He gasped for breath and rubbed his chest.

"Don't carry so much at a time," I entreated him.

"Nobody likes a nagging woman," he said, attempting a smile.

"But you said it yourself; you're not as young as you were."

"I was just saying it. I'm fit as a fiddle except for my feet and knees giving me grief."

We had lived among them so long that the Monroes began to treat us like family. Unfortunately, this meant exposure to a Scots-Irish bluntness that in other parts of the country would be construed as boorishness. Lorna Monroe was a sandy-haired woman with bright blue eyes who had assumed the role of domineering matriarch as her intransigent mother declined in health. She was scathing about my spoon bread.

"The men won't eat it like that," she said, scraping it from the pan into the garbage pail. "We'll have to give it to the pigs. Pay attention this time and I'll show you the right way."

She didn't like the way I prepared liver mush or souse meat, though I followed the steps she showed me. "It's a sin to waste good ingredients that way," she muttered, meaning for me to hear. Our styles in the kitchen did not mesh. I liked precise measurements and she preferred the pinch method. She said I didn't use enough salt.

Most of the men were gone hunting or out on the road delivering white lightening to loyal customers in the three adjoining states. It was packed by mules across the mountains to paved highways where they met up with drivers and fast cars. The Monroes were careful people unlike many of their rivals who talked too much or were too trusting of strangers. They served long terms in prison and it was axiomatic among the womenfolk that they did not come home improved by the experience. Some were coarsened and brutal, quicker to anger. There was talk of this when the wives and children came to dinner at the big house when the men were away; there were never less than a dozen adults around the table. I sometimes wondered if they had a choice.

"That man of yours looks like he's going to fall over from apoplexy from how red he gets," Lorna said one afternoon as we fixed the evening meal.

I don't think she meant to sound so heartless; it was just that direct way of speaking they had. If it was a choice between a hard and a soft word, the hard one was picked because to them it was more honest. Life was hard so they must be. She was astounded when I fled from the room in tears.

The other women in the broad-hipped, fecund tribe took Lorna's thoughtless outbursts stoically, their expressions unchanging except for a tightening of lips. I was reminded of flowers that bent before a gust of wind and bobbed back up when it passed. The difference between us was they'd grown up with Monroe harshness or had got used to it after marrying into the family.

Lorna's words crystalized the fears I had been denying about Lowell, his frequent chest pains and the red-faced puffing when he did something strenuous. My heart turned to ice at the thought of losing him. I wiped my tears away before I went into our room where he lay in bed under the comforter.

"It's colder here than even the old soldiers' home. Everything all right?"

"Oh, just a silly argument over cooking," I said.

"What's for dinner?"

"Chicken and dumplings."

"Your style or hers?"

"Hers, of course," I said with bitterness.

"I like yours better."

Ridiculously, that made me so happy that I kissed him. We snuggled under the comforter until he said drowsily, "Okay, all hands on deck. Got your pad and pencil?"

*　*　*

"Dutch Harbor has picked up a message from Admiral Yamamoto to the First Air Fleet." Lieutenant Al Crenshaw had to yell over the teletypes.

It was early evening and I was half blind from reading translated decrypts of Jap navy transmissions. There were a dozen of us—eleven geniuses and me. We were rummy from the long hours, but that sure got our attention.

Kettle scanned the message. "Let's see, the fleet is to advance into Hawaiian waters and upon the opening of hostilities shall attack the U.S. fleet and deal it a mortal blow. The first air raid is planned for dawn of X-day. That date will be given in a later message. Upon completion of the air raid, the task force, keeping close coordination and guarding against the enemy's counterattack, shall speedily leave the enemy waters and return to Japan. Should the negotiations with the U.S. prove successful the task force shall hold itself in readiness forthwith to return and reassemble."

"Well," somebody said into the silence—even the teletypes stopped as if they were listening—"there you have it."

"That puts the boys at Station Hypo in a bind," somebody else said.

That was the listening post at Pearl Harbor, the one that kept Kimmel in the dark on Washington's orders.

"What's the bind?" asked Commander Alfred Mueller as he shook a Lucky out of a crumpled pack. He was a stocky guy with no neck and a head of dark hair that started about an inch above his eyebrows.

"They'll get pasted along with everybody else."

"They're too valuable," Mueller said. "They'll move them to the other side of the island."

The teletypes started up again. "Corregidor is sending us Yamamoto's message," said the operator as he watched it coming in.

Admiral Turner burst into the room. "What've you got?" He read Yamamoto's message. "Send a car to the front entrance." He rushed out.

Nobody was surprised the Japs weren't willing to cut off their nuts just for the sake of better relations with us. They weren't exactly creampuffs, those people. Their officers had beheading contests in China to see who could make the biggest pile. One lopped off a hundred and twenty-six before his arm got so tired he couldn't go on; the Tokyo newspapers covered that stuff like sports events. They buried peasants to the neck and galloped horses over them and nailed people to walls by their tongues for the fun of it.

Word got around that General Marshall told a bunch of newspapermen who agreed not to print it that there'd be war with Japan within the first ten days of December. All Kimmel got was what they called a war warning saying the Jap attack most likely would be on the Philippines, Thailand, or the Kra Peninsula where Singapore is.

The next morning as I was shaving, Mother's butler knocked on the bathroom door.

"There's a gentleman here to see you, suh," he said.

I dressed and walked to the kitchen where Lieutenant Hoople was having coffee. He stood and saluted.

It's damned early, I said.

He handed me an envelope. The district commandant ordered me to report to QH W317 to meet with Commander Sergio Romano.

Hoople drove me to the rows of Quonsets that filled the open space at the Washington Monument. Lights were already on in most of them; the country was getting up earlier than it ever had. Romano was as thin as a dagger and had bushy eyebrows and one of those beards so heavy his jaws were blue an hour after shaving. He welcomed me into his bare office and offered a hard chair to sit on.

"A little about me," he said. "I was an assistant U.S. Attorney in New York before I got called up by the naval reserve. Now I'm with the Naval Intelligence Investigative Service. I know the president from some work of a political nature I did for him. He has promised I'll have an adequate staff and clerical support. He is very serious about discovering who is leaking. I hope I can count on your cooperation."

Staff and clerical support. That froze my guts.

I said naturally, I'd be happy to help any way I could.

"Do you have any theories as to who it might be?"

I said I wondered about Pa Watson.

Romano's bushy eyebrows rose. "Really?"

You didn't hear it from me. I have to work with the man.

"Care to explain why you think that?"

Knows everybody, knows everything. Even more than Harry.

"Does he?"

He's never more than just a few steps from the president from morning to night.

"Why would he leak this information?" He was alert, a man willing to entertain all possibilities.

Pa thinks a lot of himself, I said. It's only natural he would want to make a few things happen so he could tell his grandkids.

He asked a few more questions in an easy-going way. Getting a feel for me, you know. I didn't kid myself that I was convincing him, but I knew Pa Watson would point me out as a likely suspect. This would throw dust in his eyes; he'd think it was office politics. With the huge shit storm headed our way, this was headed for the back burner. That's what I was counting on anyway, and nine times out of ten I would have been right; but I misjudged Romano. The man mixed bloodhound and bulldog. I learned later in civilian life he was the nemesis of the Mafia and they tried to kill him twice.

"These are busy times for all of us, Captain," Romano said, standing up at his desk. "I won't keep you any longer. I just wanted the chance to introduce myself."

I said it was a real pleasure.

He was right about being busy. Serious as the investigation was, it got pushed out of my mind as soon as I walked into the Navy Building. People on the secure floor were discussing a cable from the English that said the attack could come in three days.

"It seems an English airplane mechanic bumped into a drunken Jap engineer in a men's room in Cambodia," Commander Mueller said. "Thinking he was talking to a Vichy Frenchman, he said he'd helped modify racks on carrier planes to carry armor-piercing bombs and shallow-running torpedoes. He was so full of the secret he had to spill it. He even drew a map showing the fleet's route to Hawaii. We cleared those waters of shipping last week so no shipping will report it. The English reckon they'll launch their attack Sunday morning at daybreak."

"Shallow running torpedoes, that's what the English used at Taranto," somebody said.

"How many carriers?" someone else asked. "We haven't pinned that down."

"Six, according to the mechanic," Mueller said. "That would give them roughly 400 planes."

"Tokyo told Berlin war with the Anglo-Saxon countries might come sooner than anyone dreams," Lieutenant Crenshaw said. "Consulates have been told to burn their codes and secret papers."

"Kimmel doesn't know any of this, right?" Mueller said.

"No," said Crenshaw. "And he doesn't know the spy in Honolulu is telling Tokyo where the ships are berthed."

That report by the airplane mechanic would have gone first to Churchill; the president had probably seen it hours ago. Turner would deflate like a balloon when he rushed in and Franklin calmly said, "Yes, I know all about it." The president lived for those moments.

I admit at times I was starting to get with the program. Under the right circumstances it was okay to keep life and death intelligence from field commanders. I see from your face I should explain that.

What did Richardson and them know about world strategy and public opinion and so forth? They only had pieces of the puzzle, not the big picture like we did. All they had to worry about was the Pacific Fleet. But Pearl Harbor was just one of the balls Franklin had in the air. Letting the Japs attack solved his biggest problem, which was getting the country unified before it was too late. It was like he said to Harry and me that time, the people needed someone to do their thinking and he was that someone.

"You look worried all the time," Mother said one night when I got home early enough that they were still up. "It's going to spoil your looks."

"Him worry?" the Senator snorted. "His only worry is whether to go out with a blond, a brunette or a redhead."

"Ignore him, dear," Mother said. "The isolationists are giving him fits."

"They won't listen to reason and they won't be bought," he said. "I can't get the president to understand that. 'Offer them a dam or a highway,' he says. He thinks it's still the old days. Well, I've got news for him, times have changed. I'd tell him myself but I can't even get a five-minute appointment. It's been like that for weeks."

The Senator knew Mother had eyes only for me, so he tapped out of the room with his lower lip hanging.

"It's looking bad isn't it, dear?" Mother said. "Eleanor says it's just a matter of days now."

Even my mom knew what Kimmel didn't.

"Do you know what you'll be doing when it starts?" she asked.

Don't worry, I said. No way will I be in danger.

I've thought about that a lot. That was tempting fate, and fate doesn't hold back when it has its turn at bat—as you'll hear.

Franklin and Harry were reading the cable from Tokyo breaking off the talks the afternoon before the attack. This means war, he told Harry. But somehow (wink, wink) the word didn't get to General Marshall for another fifteen hours. When a colonel finally reached him to say there was something really, really important he needed to know about, Marshall strolled into the office an hour and a half later.

He took his sweet time reading it as the colonel kept pestering him about the Jap deadline. He finished after a half an hour and said it was okay to warn Pearl Harbor by Western Union; he must have forgot he had a telephone on his desk. The telegram was being delivered by a boy on a bicycle as the bombs were falling. Everybody knows this stuff. What they don't know is what went on before, what I'm telling you.

They're ringing the dinner bell so we'd better get in there before everything's gone. They're big eaters, these Monroes, fast too.

* * *

Lorna was contrite when we got to the big table in the kitchen, and the other women gave me soft-eyed looks. She was sorry she made me cry and fussed over us, touching my arm as she dished up the chicken and dumplings. Their hearts are good, as I said; it is just their harsh way of talking. Living in their isolation they never hear more polite modes of address.

After we cleared the table and were doing the dishes in water heated on the wood-burning stove, Lorna said, "I don't want to worry you, but two men dressed as hunters were at Scatter today asking questions."

"Scatter?" I asked, my heart lurching.

"That's a country store and filling station fifteen miles from here as the crow flies. People around here notice strangers, especially ones who ask questions. A friend came to tell us while you were in your room."

"What were they asking?"

"If anybody new had moved into the area. We don't think they're hunters though they're trying to look like it. Their clothes and boots were new."

Lorna saw the fear in my eyes.

"Now don't you starting thinking the worst. Nobody will give you away, none of us anyway. But it might be a good idea for you and the captain to move farther back into the woods for a time." She explained that the early Monroes had lived several seasons in a cave a few miles east.

"A *cave?*"

"I know it sounds bad to folks nowadays," Lorna said, "but it's only for a few days, I hope. We'll take blankets and pillows and the other things you'll need. With a little fire, it's cozy enough."

By noon the next day we were watching the Monroe clan disappear over the near ridge headed home. Carrying the comforts and necessities we'd need, including a mattress and two rocking chairs, they had led us to a room-sized cave. Lorna was right; it had a flat dirt floor and was comfortable enough once a fire was going and a lantern lit. But it was still a cave.

"My momma wouldn't believe this," Lowell said as he looked around, "but the Senator would. He always said I'd end up like this, only without rocking chairs."

Vexed, I said, "It's not the end of anything. It's only for a few days." It was frightening to hear him talk like that.

"I wonder if the G-men are offering bribes. There are a lot of poor people, and some surely would be tempted. We'd better get back on the road soon as we can."

"It's so muddy," I said.

"Yeah, it'll have to dry out some. Or the Monroes can come along to pull us out of the worst spots with their mules."

He was tuckered out and was soon snoring. Lorna had given us enough smoked meats, biscuits, preserves and jams, and other victuals for a week. I prepared something for when he woke and then slipped under the comforter with him.

* * *

Is that lantern enough to take dictation? Good, let's get started.

It didn't take Romano look to finger me as the leaker. He called me back to his Quonset hut the following week.

"How's it going out there?" he asked, meaning the Pacific Theater of Operations.

Not so good, I said.

He got right to the point. "Did you pay a visit to Admiral Kimmel in mid-November?"

Yes, I did.

"What was the purpose of your visit?"

It was just a courtesy call.

"You left that afternoon on the flight to the mainland. So you traveled roughly ten thousand miles for a courtesy call?"

Well, I did see a woman while I was there. I winked man-to-man, but he paid it no mind.

"And then when you returned did you make a telephone call to Admiral Richardson?"

I don't recall, I said.

"We recorded a voice like yours that day with sounds like an airport in the background. The call was made at about the same time the flight you were on arrived from San Francisco."

He knew I was the one.

But instead of a coming across as a prosecutor, his manner was sympathetic. "I think I have a pretty good idea why you did it."

My money is still riding on Pa Watson, I said. He...

"I'd do the same thing in your shoes," Romano interrupted, "at least I hope I would."

I hadn't talked to Harry because I was spending all my time at the Navy Building, but one of the White House switchboard ladies told me the president took the casualties hard.

"Someone saw him crying over the pictures in the paper," she said.

My guess was there was a lot of crocodile in those tears. The country got the bloody nose he wanted and was raving to get back at the scrawny buck-toothed monkeys who stabbed us in the back.

Knowing the White House as I did, that glimpse of Franklin sniveling was a set up. A big blow of his honker when the door closed and back to business.

"The reason why you did what you did doesn't matter in the context of my investigation," Romano said. "One of the first things we did was check the passenger manifests for ships and planes going to Hawaii. Your name came up right away. It's amazing the simple mistakes people make. I see it all the time. Turned out the only staff I needed was the secretary who looked through the passenger manifests. Then there was your voice on the Richardson phone tap. I've never tied anything up so quickly. I have an appointment to tell the president this afternoon."

He shook my hand warmly and wished me good luck. "And I mean it."

Just before we broke for dinner at the Navy Building, Turner called me to his office. "Pack your sea bag," he said, "you're heading for the Pacific."

Before I could ask what I'd be doing, he said, "Dismissed."

Mother wept like her heart was broken when I told her. "You said you'd be safe no matter what happened." When the Senator told her there wasn't a thing he could do, the maid had to help her to bed.

"She's taken a sleeping pill," the Senator said when he came back downstairs. "My life won't be worth living."

CHAPTER 22

THEY SHIPPED ME OUT FROM SEATTLE ABOARD AN OLD RUST BUCKET HAULING airplane parts to Manila. An armed detail met me at the airfield and escorted me to the foot of a gangplank pulled up as soon as I was on board. A shortwave broadcast we heard from a Manila station said half the Army Air Force in the Philippines was destroyed on the ground eight hours after Pearl Harbor was hit.

"How in hell could that happen?" said Perrine Therize the swarthy skipper from New Orleans.

He pulled off his cap to scratch his wooly head—a touch of the tar brush as we'd say back home. "MacArthur is in charge out there. Do you suppose they'll fire his ass?"

There's no doubt about it.

As you know, dear, he got the Medal of Honor instead. If the general wasn't the luckiest man in the world back then, he was no worse than number two.

I told Therize he better get a few more knots out of his floating junk-yard or the Jap fleet high-tailing it back home might catch up.

"I have to check with the company," he said. "They don't like us wasting fuel."

They'll have a screen of submarines out ahead, I said.

He increased speed to twelve knots, all *Susie Q* could manage; she shook from stem to stern, and he worried a boiler would blow. We steamed without lights at night.

"I don't know why they got caught on the ground," Admiral Hart told me when I reported for duty. "They're hushing it up, but I heard MacArthur went into some kind of catatonic trance when the Japs bombed Clark, and it took a while for him to snap out of it. He had convinced himself Divine Providence would protect the Philippines. He hoped the Philippines would be able to sit out the war like Switzerland. The man has his dreamy side. Or it may be he felt bound by Roosevelt's order not to fire the first shot. The flyboys were begging to bomb the Jap airfields in Formosa after Pearl got hit, but he said no. They landed from their morning patrol to gas up and have lunch just as the Jap bombers arrived overhead. They were lined up wing tip to wing tip. To me it's worse than Pearl Harbor."

Hart was a wiry, little guy with a reputation as a strict disciplinarian. He always had a toothpick in his teeth that he worked from one side of his mouth to the other.

"These orders of yours that came by special courier are damned strange," Hart said. "What I get," he said, "is the Navy wants you on the griddle because somebody's got a high opinion of you but wants to see how you do under fire."

That's when it sank in that the president wanted me shut up for good. He couldn't order me murdered outright—Hoover might find out and use it against him—but letting the enemy do the dirty work would work just as well.

"I'd consider that pretty flattering if I were you," Hart said. "They must be grooming you for bigger things."

I said sort of casually that Admiral Nimitz told me every flag officer should have someone like me around so they could focus on the important stuff.

"Chester told you that?" Hart would never get around to checking with all the fur that was flying. "You know, I need a good man to liaison with the Dutch."

I held my breath.

"But no," he said with a shake of his head, "these orders are clear. We're shifting the fleet south to get out of the range of the Jap bombers. They're going to hit Manila harder, and that army they landed up north won't be long getting here. I'll leave you as my in-between with General MacArthur. What do you know about him?"

Only what's in the papers.

"Then you know only the good things; he's got a publicity staff he keeps busy shining up his reputation. I've known Douglas for forty years and haven't liked him a day of that time. I don't know what's worse, that monstrous ego or his sneakiness. The story goes he believes he's been chosen by destiny to do great things. But he also knows the value of a dollar. He talked President Quezon into giving him field marshal rank with an enormous salary, and designed his uniform himself. A white sharkskin tunic with filigrees and a gold cord, black trousers, and a cap loaded with gold braid. It makes him look like a drum major. You'll see the man talks about himself in the third person. 'General MacArthur thinks this' or 'General MacArthur will do that.' Napoleon was like that."

He took the moist toothpick out of his mouth and put in a new one. "But the man has charm, no denying that. I won't let any of my officers talk to him. They gave him everything he asked for until I put my foot down. He sees the Asiatic Fleet as only a flank of his pitiful army. He thinks we might be useful from time to time, but wars are won on land and the rest is a sideshow. Keep that in mind."

I'm going to start skipping back and forth, dear; tell you things that stick out. You can arrange them in the right order later. My orders stated I was to be detached from MacArthur's HQ and reassigned as conditions warranted to put me in the thick of whatever hot spot they could find. I escaped the Bataan Death March by the skin of my teeth; MacArthur picked me to go with him from Corregidor to Australia because he thought my White House connections would help him. That was some of the fastest talking I ever did. The Army didn't talk to the Navy, so he didn't know I was on the shit list.

"Two captains serving on a cruiser at the same time is unusual," Captain Gus Wheeler said when I joined *Vincennes*. I'd put back ten of the thirty pounds I lost on Corregidor, but Mother would still have fainted if she saw me. "We've got an Aussie commander aboard as liaison," Wheeler said. "Maybe it has something to do with that?"

I'd tell you the truth, but you wouldn't believe me.

"What do you mean?" he said with a half-smile. He was short and balding with a dimpled chin. He was as taut as a terrier, wired really tight.

I told how I'd tried to warn Kimmel that Washington was keeping intelligence from him.

"Wait a minute," he said when I finished, "are you saying King and the rest knew Pearl was going to get plastered?"

And then a grin spread across his face. "Okay, you're seeing if I have a sense of humor." He slapped me on the back, but got serious again right away. "Not everybody would think that was funny. Hell, there are flag officers who'd have you court-martialed. But seriously, why did they ship you out so fast?"

I said I'd got on the wrong side of Admiral Turner. That was something he could understand.

"I heard he's a foul-mouthed bastard," he said. "You know, your posting might actually be a blessing in disguise. My executive officer can split his job with you and spend the rest of the time whipping this green crew into shape."

The *Vincennes* was part of the escort for Marines from the First Division bound for the Solomon Islands where the Japs were building an airfield. The big thinkers figured that was part of their plan to invade Australia.

Austin Morgan of the Royal Australian Navy was a cheerful guy, but he lost his smile when I asked about Guadalcanal, which is where we were headed. I looked it up in an atlas another officer carried in his sea bag.

"It was discovered by the Spanish in the 1500s and nobody went back for two hundred years," Morgan said. "Does that tell you something, mate?"

Task Force 61 came up on Guadalcanal at night, so we smelled it before we saw it. The Senator's hogs would have thought they were in heaven.

"What in God's name is that stench?" Wheeler said on the bridge. It wasn't as bad as that freighter with the hides, but it was close.

"Rot," Morgan said. "Guadalcanal gets a hundred and sixty inches of rain a year. Go beyond the coconut plantations and you're in jungle like a wall. Unbelievable insects and rats the size of rabbits."

It was our first amphibious landing since 1898, so you'd expect a few things would go wrong, but the operation was a total mess. For one thing, Washington wanted every gun and bullet sent to Europe. Admiral King had to fight for anything we got.

The supply ships weren't combat loaded when they left home, so everything had to be taken off in Wellington and reloaded. Every minute counted, but the dock workers wouldn't give up their tea breaks and didn't work at all when it rained. So the Marines did the job, and what an unholy screw-up. Boxes turned to pulp in the rain and labels peeled from cans. Cornflakes from broken boxes heaped up like sand dunes. The Marines shipped out in the clothes they stood in with only ten days of ammunition. Sixty days of food instead of ninety. Three-quarters of the tanks, trucks and bulldozers were left behind and all of the 155mm howitzers, which was the Marines' favorite artillery piece.

The command structure was just as fouled up. Admiral Ghormley was supposed to run Operation Watchtower, but he never left his tender moored in New Caledonia, a long way from the action. If Admiral Turner wanted an air search, he had to radio Admiral Fletcher to ask Admiral Ghormley to order Admiral McCain to put the planes in the air.

The Marines were a fine body of men, the first to rally to the colors. They were full of piss and vinegar, but green as grass. Only five weeks of training for most of them. Luckily, General Vandegrift scrounged up some of the Old Breed to stiffen the ranks. Those were lifers who were recruiting sergeants or perpetual privates with disciplinary records as long as their arms. Rough as tree bark, those men. They had brawled with soldiers and sailors in bars from Manila to Peking. They preferred hair tonic to postexchange beer and could live on goat jerky. But they were crack shots with rifles and pistols and had expert badges for machine guns, grenades, mortars and bayonets and just about every other weapon you could name. You didn't want to mess with those ol' boys.

Nobody knew how many Japs were on the island. Some guessed up to eight thousand, but none showed up when our guys went ashore at Lunga Point. While General Vandegrift moved inland and work parties started to unload the supply ships, our screen of cruisers and destroyers steamed north to intercept Japs sure to be racing to the scene. Admiral Turner needed five days to offload, but Admiral Jack Fletcher said he was hauling ass in three days to keep his carriers safe. A very nervous guy, Jack.

The *Vincennes* crew was pretty cocky despite Pearl Harbor and Corregidor. They expected we'd make short work of the Japs and go on to the next victory. We had scorn for them just like Bywater said they did for us.

It's hard to take dictation wearing gloves, isn't it? That wind is damned cold.

* * *

The temperatures had been falling for days and dropped below freezing at night. I kept the fire going strong but we felt the wind that sent gales of leaves flying past the slice of pewter sky at the cave entrance. The trees seemed to cringe before it and their bare limbs jabbed the air like frenzied music conductors.

For all of the comforts the Monroes brought to the cave, you couldn't help but feel desolate at being reduced to so primitive a state. Even Lowell's bluff, cheery nature clouded over. He developed a deep, hacking cough.

"Tell them to bring more blankets next time they come," he said. "I can't seem to get warm."

The Monroe men usually visited us just as dawn broke. They were accomplished woodsmen who moved through the trees as silently as the creatures they hunted. One frosty morn the old patriarch himself showed up with a haversack of smoked meats and a jug of spring water. Huffing and puffing, he sat down and caught his breath. From his look, he was greatly troubled.

"A traitor has brought us shame," he said. "The government money was too much to turn down for folks living to the west of here. The strangers aren't searching just anywhere now, they're looking at this side of the mountain and they're sure to find the cave." He paused, "Unless you'd like us to arrange a little accident."

"Oh no!" I burst out with horror. "We don't want anything like that."

"I judged you wouldn't, but it never hurts to ask. How are you feeling, Captain?"

"Right as rain."

"That's a bad cough," the patriarch said with a look at me.

"Think you could bring us some more blankets next time?" Lowell said. "You can see your breath in here."

"It might be a good idea if we make this your last night. The Hickeys have offered to take you in, and there's forty more families we can depend on. We'll keep one step ahead of them boys 'til the spring thaw."

The idea of slogging from one place to the next with Lowell feeling like he did was not an appealing prospect. "Could you pull our car to where the paved road begins?" I asked.

"A couple of teams of mules might get the job done. Mud this deep, it would take a while."

Memorandum

November 20, 1953

To: Clyde Tolson

From: The Director

Subject: Lowell Brady

For: File 24898

Further kudos to you and Operation Handshake for the valuable tip from that sheriff in rural West Virginia. The fruitcakes that agents give to chiefs of police at Christmas have more than justified their cost.

I think it is a matter of time before Bureau agents combing those hills find LOWELL BRADY and his wife. If more manpower is needed send in additional personnel from here and from the adjoining states.

At my regular briefing today with the PRESIDENT I did not mention our suspicion of Communist infiltration in the CIA. He informed me in the early days that I had his full confidence and not to bother him unless a presidential decision was necessary. That time may be approaching, but it is not now.

We must be careful how we present our evidence to MELVIN CROSBY. We want to win him over, not drive him to suicide. Our agent must appear firm but sympathetic. The line to take is we will not give the Agency the photographs if he cooperates with our investigation.

He must tell us during a lie-detector test if he is being blackmailed by the Soviets. If he is betraying the country, he must tell us what information has been passed to them and who else in the Agency is involved. This will be to our advantage and the Agency's disadvantage when and if I speak to the PRESIDENT regarding this.

Assuming he is not the one, CROSBY is in a far better position to identify who the subversive(s) are at the CIA than is our mole. It may be he is who is running BRADY, but something tells me that is too easy. He is a paper pusher with minimal experience in the field.

Our agents have twice observed the presence of men who also appear to be seeking BRADY. These are almost certainly CIA personnel being guided to the scene by their mole at the Bureau. We must find BRADY and his wife before they do.

/John

The mud was as thick and gooey as chocolate frosting. The mules struggled going uphill and the Monroe men pushed the car from behind. We followed slipping and sliding in a light wagon with Lowell wrapped up in blankets.

"If this road wasn't so bad, I reckon they'd have you by now," old Monroe said. "The country offered to pave it, but we like how it discourages visitors."

They had been such good friends to us that it was hard to say goodbye. When we reached the paved road, Lowell insisted on driving, but soon saw it took more than he could manage. We hoped to get as far as South

Carolina, but had to stop at a little town at the state line because his breathing made me afraid.

I saw a sign that said Hospital and pulled in front. It was a private one in a white clapboard house. An elderly doctor with a bony nose and a gray moustache came directly from his dinner when the nurse telephoned.

"Hi, doc," Lowell said, "my wife's worried about my cough." That set him off on a long spell of hacking.

"She has a right to be," Doctor Winger said. "You belong in bed."

While he was examining Lowell, I moved the car behind the hospital. As I returned, I glimpsed three black Fords traveling fast in the direction we had been headed. Some animal instinct fugitives must develop told me they were our pursuers. They would have caught up a few miles down the road.

My knees were shaking when I went back inside. Lowell was breathing in and out as the doctor listened with his stethoscope.

"It's not as bad it sounds," he told me, "but he shouldn't be outdoors in weather like this. A few days in bed with some medicine I'll give him and he'll be worlds better."

I filled out forms and gave fifty dollars as a deposit and a handyman brought in a cot for me to sleep on. When I told Lowell about the black cars, he said, "We hoist anchor in the morning."

* * *

Nice fella, that pill pusher. Okay, get the steno pad and let's get going.

The night was pitch black as we did our box patrols looking for the Japs we expected down from New Georgia Sound. Everybody was worn out from being at battle stations in our heavy helmets. I told Wheeler the best thing would be for me to rest up so I was in tip-top shape when I was needed. He got a funny look, but said okay. I drank coffee, napped and batted the breeze in the ward room with whoever was there. I couldn't get my mind off those torpedoes Jurika told me about. A twenty-mile range with no wake versus fourteen miles for ours. And ours tossed up a wake, not to mention they were duds half the time. The Navy Building kept the lid on the hell the submariners were raising on that subject. I'd have taken that approach myself while I looked for someone to blame. They were too cheap to give them enough testing in peacetime, was the problem.

Wheeler flat out didn't believe what I told him about the Jap fish, and told me not to pass on bilge like that because he had enough to worry about. The new-fangled radar was giving him fits. When they got it working, it was supposed to give us an edge at night, but half the time echoes from islands and squalls looked like ships. The Japs picked lookouts for their night vision, and they always seemed to spot us before we did them.

I was in the CIC—combat information center, dear—when a voice on the TBS radio shouted "Warning! Warning! Warning! Plane over Savo headed east."

Wheeler had been asleep in his sea cabin off the bridge and got there a few seconds after me. "That might be one of ours," he said. A couple of Long Lances were coming through the water straight at us at that moment. Then a searchlight blinded us. "That fool," Wheeler said. He ordered the colors run up so they'd see we were one of them.

We were spoiling for a fight but we weren't combat ready. It sounds funny, but it was the truth. Combat ready means shooting first in that situation and asking questions later. Like a lot of commanders that night, Wheeler couldn't believe this was it. He was so afraid of hitting one of our own ships that he ordered star shells fired to see what was going on.

If he had called up flank speed and ordered a change in course we might have ducked the torpedoes, but war is full of what-ifs. The gunners were loading the star shells when water spouts bracketed us. Then the first fish blew up the number one fire room and the second hit a few seconds later.

What the average person doesn't know is how loud war is. A five-inch shell smacking a quarter inch of steel shocks the hell out of you, and we were taking hit after hit. It freezes people solid, the noise does. You just want to hit the deck and cover up. If you don't have training to fall back on, and, remember, this was a young crew without combat experience, you're turned into a zombie. One minute we were a proud warship and the next somewhere between a mad house and a slaughter house.

"Jesus Christ!" Wheeler shouted; the last words I ever heard him say.

I left the bridge with a flashlight to inspect the damage below decks. The power went out after the first few hits and the only light was from the bonfire of float planes on the stern. It was like a scene from Hades, people screaming and shouting. I was pretty steady through it all, and it might sound like I'm saying I was cool and collected. It wasn't that at all; it was like a switch was thrown in my mind and I was watching myself in a dream. I went through passageways until the heat and smoke in the engineering space turned me back. I slipped on blood and stepped over bodies coming and going. When I climbed back up the twisted ladder to the bridge every single man was dead or dying from what had been a direct hit, body parts were…It still gets to me, as you see.

I ran dozens of Abandon Ship drills when I was a junior officer, so I knew what to do. We got boats and rafts in the water, but hundreds went overboard with only lifejackets, and some not even that. Our forty-man raft had sixty guys hanging on, most of them covered in bunker fuel.

Dark ships going fast passed twice and tossed us in their wake. I ordered the men to keep quiet because they might be Japs and they'd come back and finish us off with machinegun fire when they had time. Sometimes we heard the cries of other sailors in the darkness. We answered back, but they couldn't find us. The night seemed to last forever, but dawn finally broke. I did a headcount and saw we had lost seven men to the sea.

We were spotted by a search plane and a few hours later got dragged aboard a destroyer. They gave us breakfast and hot coffee with a good lacing of brandy from the sick bay. Rank has its privileges, and I used mine to bump the executive officer from his bunk. He hadn't slept for thirty-six hours, but I pointed out at least he'd been dry and warm. He was about my size so I talked him into loaning his spare uniform as well. I felt like sleeping a hundred hours after a shower and shave, but a tapping finger woke me up after only six.

"Are you Captain Brady?" a lieutenant asked.

Never heard of him, I said.

"We have a high priority message from Pearl asking if you got off *Vincennes* before she went down."

Tell them no. I was worn to whatever is after the nub.

The lieutenant gave an embarrassed laugh. "I think they're serious, sir."

They put me ashore at Lunga Point with orders from Turner to report to General Vandegrift. I rode one of the LSTs ferrying supplies from the attack transports. The scuttlebutt was we lost five cruisers and a bunch of destroyers, and Admiral Fletcher and his carriers were already gone. The transports were sitting ducks and ready to hightail it at the first sign of trouble. I wondered if I could talk my way into skippering an empty one back to Australia. I'd been lucky to survive Corregidor and then the sinking, but luck gets used up fast in war.

Marines were unloading the LSTs as fast as they could, making messy piles on the beachhead that they hauled inland to make other messy piles. The sun beat down and everybody was sweating gallons. A cheer went up when rolls of barbed wire came off a boat.

"I was hoping they'd find that," General Vandegrift said. His headquarters was under a pair of old tarps strung to two coconut trees. It had a desk and two telephones and a few sticks of furniture from a grower's home.

He was one of those leaders that men follow to the gates of hell. He was unshaven and wore dirty fatigues, but looked as squared away as if in his dress blues. A high forehead and cleft chin. He was another one who had a way of sizing up people at a glance. Like I said, I was never felt comfortable with that type. I got the feeling his glance didn't rate me that high.

"Heard of you; the White House and all that. Did Turner say what I'm supposed to do with you?"

I said I supposed the admiral wanted me as his eyes and ears, sending him updates as to conditions and so forth.

"Every man on this island is expected to work his ass off. You got a degree in engineering at the academy, right?"

Yes, I said, but my ship was sunk under me just last night, and I'd been with MacArthur on Corregidor and was still feeling a little peaked from that. I'd appreciate light duty just until I got back on my feet. A week or so sounded right.

"I'm going to put you in charge of building the airfield. Major Morgan will give you the details."

I stood to go and he asked how it was on Corregidor. I wouldn't want to go through it again, I said.

"They shouldn't have surrendered."

Morgan was an Old Breed sort with the usual contempt for the Navy.

Fletcher leaving them high and dry confirmed their belief we had a yellow streak.

"You'll never see Marines running from a fight," he said.

The Japs had begun work on the airfield, but progress was slow; they must have thought they had all the time in the world. Bulldozers were knocking trees flat and scraping vegetation down to the dirt. They did in an hour what took the Japs a day using hand tools.

Like on Wake Island, the construction crew included a bunch of civilians nobody mentions, fifty or so older guys who worked for the Morrison-Knudson Company. The supervisor named Lochner was a bad-tempered Missourian who got a lieutenant's stripe after getting eight medical waivers for everything from missing teeth to flat feet. They were relaxed about saluting and other Navy ways, but they got things done. I sat in the shade of a tree and gave them a loose rein. I sent a man down to the beach every day with a report for Vandegrift. "Work going well," I wrote.

Jap bombers came every day at noon to plaster us, meaning more hard looks my way from jarheads. I had my bunker dug deeper with extra sandbags and timbers and a canvas roof for the rain. I calculated it would take a direct hit for the curtain to drop for good.

I double-timed it from the shade to the dugout when we heard planes overhead. Men piled into the dugout on my heels; you could hardly breathe in there, we were packed so tight. The bombs bounced us around like gravel in a miner's pan, and if we didn't put fingers in our ears we would have been deafened. The civilians started grousing they weren't idiots and didn't sign up for this. When I said they could look forward to the thanks of grateful nation...well, I won't repeat what they said. I'm glad they didn't know at the time what came out later, that the Japs killed all those civilian workers at Wake on grounds they were spies. I hope people never forget how those bastards operated. Their commander was hung after the war.

We were swimming in sweat by the time the bombing was over. Worse was when a Jap cruiser or sub started slinging shells that came in sounding like subway trains. Talk about hairy. It took an hour or so a day to fill in the craters from the bombs and shells.

When the first Catalina landed in a cloud of dust on Henderson Field

you should've have seen the whoopin' and hollerin'. We hadn't been abandoned after all. Then when the Wildcats flew in people were laughing and
crying; even Vandegrift had tears in his eyes.

But we weren't out of the woods yet, far from it. If the Japs got the
upper hand the plan was we were going to melt into the jungle and conduct guerrilla war with what food and ammunition we had. Good luck
with that, I thought.

Complaints from the flyboys began almost as soon as the propellers
stopped spinning. The runway was too short and the dust fouled the
engines. When it rained the strip turned into a thick gumbo. One pilot
called it the only place on Earth where you could stand up to your knees
in mud and still get dust in your eyes. Guess who they blamed; that's right,
the Navy. On the island, that meant me.

Henderson Field probably put more fighters out of action than the Japs.
The dive bombers dug furrows like plows with their wheels, and a lot
ended ass up with props bent or snapped off. Pretty soon we had a bunch
of wrecked planes to cannibalize for parts. I told Vandegrift the solution
was to haul in crushed coral. Make it happen, he said, like all it took was a
phone call. I got the horse laugh because of the priority all the other jobs
had, but I heard they used my idea after I left.

Turner claimed he'd left fifty-one days of food, but when the Marines
counted it was only fourteen, meaning extra-short rations. A scoop of oat-
meal in the morning, and dinner was rice the Japs left behind. A dash of
ketchup if you were lucky; and maybe two prunes. Whatever was in that
rice besides the insects you trained yourself not to see gave the trots to one
in five jarheads. I heard about a poor bastard who had to run to the latrine
thirty times a day. Needless to say, the corps didn't get much work out of
these individuals. We were down to ten days of food when they finally got
a captured Jap shortwave radio going and begged headquarters for more.

My memory of the rationing on Corregidor was all too fresh, so I'd
filled my sea bag with canned food from the destroyer; Christ, it was so
heavy I could hardly lift it. The trick was to open a can and bolt down as
much as you could before the look in some guy's eyes made you give it to
him. Luckily, people were so tired they slept like the dead at night, so I

sneaked my food then. I know what you're thinking, but a man does what he must. It's amazing how good even cold Spam tastes if you're famished. You didn't dare try to warm it up because a dozen guys would spring from foxholes and look around with wild eyes. Hunger gives you a nose like a bloodhound and seems to sharpen hearing, too; opening a can stopped people in their tracks.

Scary as the food situation was, we had a far bigger worry. The Japs landed on the north end of the island were headed our way. A brigade of engineers was scouting in the jungle for possible landing strips when a Catholic priest in a village told them a Jap radio station was just ahead. The Marines came back the next day with a stronger force and ran into a patrol. They wiped out everyone except a few who lit out back the way they came. Maps and orders and other stuff taken from dead officers made it clear they were part of a much bigger force.

Captain Moran was a Quaker—don't ask me what he was doing in the Marines—and First Division's intelligence officer. He was a gray-haired guy in his fifties who used to run a church school in Japan and knew their lingo. A bunch of us were called to Vandegrift's headquarters for an after-battle briefing. Loud buzzing flies flew around and the place stank of body odor. I stood to the side with a handkerchief to my nose; I heard later that made some think I was too hoity-toity. I guessed the general invited me to these meetings out of courtesy, but I wish he hadn't bothered. They chewed the fat about routine matters down to the platoon level.

This one was gut-churning. Moran said the patrol was from the Seventh Army's 28th Infantry Regiment. "This is bad news, gentlemen. It's the best the Japanese Imperial Army has. It earned fame at the siege of Port Arthur, which in their history is like our Battle of San Juan Hill. They've been kicking the Chinese armies around for years; and General MacArthur's more recently. This regiment has never known defeat. A diary from one body said they are certain of quick victory. Each man is carrying just two hundred and fifty rounds of ammo and a week's worth of rations. That bespeaks a high level of confidence."

Moran unfolded a pamphlet spotted with blood. "They like night attacks because it eliminates any edge the enemy has in weapons, fortifications, heavy artillery, airplanes and what have you. Speed, mobility and stealth defeat all of those advantages, and the bayonet is better than the bullet. That is their doctrine. I'm going to give you a rough translation of this publication. The title is 'Read This Alone—And the War Can Be Won.' This is what it says: 'Westerners being very haughty and effeminate and cowardly intensely dislike fighting in the rain or mist or in the dark. They cannot conceive of night as a proper time for battle, though it is an excellent time for dancing. In these weaknesses lie our great opportunities.'" He tossed the pamphlet on the table. "That's what they think of us."

"We ain't the Russkies or the Chinks," a major commented in a southern drawl. "As they're gonna find out."

"What they've found out to date," said Moran, "is they could beat a British army three times bigger at Singapore, and seventy-five thousand Americans and Filipinos surrendered at Corregidor."

The major smiled. "Yeah, well, they weren't United States Marines."

Vandegrift was waving away bluebottles as he studied the Jap maps. "Look at this," he said. "These show our positions and where the artillery is sited. They even show where our defenses are manned and where they're not."

"How come their maps are so good," someone said into the silence that fell, "and ours aren't worth shit?"

Considerable bitching commenced; and then there was more blaming the Navy for no food and lack of air cover, a regular part of every discussion. The usual hard looks were shot my way. Vandegrift let them get that off their chest and then announced that he was moving headquarters from the beachhead to the airfield because it was quieter.

"I need a good night's sleep," he said.

"The Raiders and Parachutists have been worked hard and also wouldn't mind moving where the bombs and shelling aren't as bad," Colonel Twining said.

I learned later that he and some others thought Vandegrift set up the defense wrong. He had the Marines ready for an amphibious attack or along the coastal road whereas they thought the Japs would strike at the airfield because capturing Henderson was what it was all about.

Vandegrift could be stubborn and wasn't about to change his mind, but he did agree to let the two regiments pull back to Henderson to rest up some. That saved our bacon as it turned out.

As much as we swore at the heat and humidity, they were on our side when all was said and done. The Japs had to hack a road through that wall of jungle, and were exhausted and starving by the time they reached our lines, some not getting there in time for the attack. We didn't know that at the time, of course; all this came out later when the campaign histories got written up. I'm thankful they didn't get there rested and rarin' to go, because the story might have turned out different.

We were wound tight as a windlass waiting for things to start. The Japs did launch a night attack along the coastal road, the worst place for them but the best for us, but the main push was aimed at Henderson where those two regiments had been moved. Once the probing began every able-bodied man, even the ones with the running shits, was ordered to hike up to the grassy ridge and reinforce the line. I strapped on a .45 and led a pack of civilian workers up there. They didn't have to go, and strictly speaking, they weren't even supposed to according to international law, but bless 'em they volunteered after I gave a pep talk where I threw in Mom and apple pie and everything else I could think of.

The Marines handed out weapons when we reached the line and put us where they wanted. A miserable rain started and stopped and started up again. We began to hear rustling in the jungle below, but word was passed to hold our fire until the command. The humidity made you feel like you were in the mouth of some big animal with rotten breath. And the insects never let you alone.

The Japs were great at tactical movement; you had to give that to the little bastards. They made no more noise than a crawling snake; not that I could hear all that well thanks to the quinine buzz in my ears. Then one of them cut loose with a warrior's cry I heard very clearly and the fight was on. Up to that point, Japs won their battles by sneaking close and using their bayonets in a mad rush. Being superior to all other races, how could they lose? That was their philosophy.

Our fire and howitzer rounds cut down wave after wave, but, Jesus, they kept coming. Bodies rolled down the slope and were stacked twelve feet deep in spots at the bottom the next morning. About a hundred got over the barbed wire and then fighting was hand to hand. That was when I nailed the Jap coming at me. There was enough light from muzzle flashes to see his ugly mug clear enough. The .45 slug knocked him back on his heels when he was three feet from sticking me with his bayonet. He had the same look of surprise Winston saw on the Arab at Omdurman. What do these people expect, a kiss on the cheek?

Jap soldiers carried opium in their knapsacks and got high as kites before an attack. Shoot them six times with thirty-odd-six Garand rounds and they still kept coming; one crawled toward our line dragging his guts behind him. A .45 slug settles them right down, however. I blazed through three clips before the last was killed in our little piece of the battlefield, but I doubt I hit anyone else; .45s kick like a mule, but they aren't all that accurate. How does it feel to shoot another man; you're thinking that, I can tell. In battle, it doesn't cross your mind. You might think about it afterward if you're the sensitive type, but I never was. He was going to dig out my guts with his bayonet. Him or me, simple as that.

When the shooting stopped, the silence was worse in a way. Your blood cools and you start thinking again, and I can tell you they're not pleasant thoughts. A man on our side went crazy, and he started screaming until they tied him up and stuffed a gag in his mouth.

A corporal crawled along the line calling my name in a whisper and was directed to where I had my face in the dirt trying to dig deeper with a teaspoon. If you lifted your head to see if a Jap was sneaking up, chances were you'd get your hair parted a new way.

"The general wants to see you," he said.

I never heard sweeter words and don't expect to until that heavenly choir sings me through the pearly gates. We belly crawled toward the rear until it was safe to walk.

"Tell them we need ammo fast," said a gunny hustling up to the line with a box of grenades.

The story got around that after leading those civilian workers into battle, I withdrew to the rear and was seen with my feet up eating pie. I didn't blame those old guys for being bitter. They didn't sign up to fight hand to hand, and that night cured them of any curiosity they might've had on the subject. Then comes the dawn and they look around for the man who talked them into it, the craven coward had left them lying in wet long grass with bullets ripping overhead. I'm telling you in case you hear that story. Like the saying goes, a lie travels around the world while truth is still getting its boots on. I didn't desert them, I was ordered to leave the line.

Parachute flares and tracers lit our way to Vandegrift's new HQ a hundred yards from my sandbagged hole. The corporal kept calling out "Apache," the code word, so we didn't get mowed down by someone with an itchy trigger finger, which was everyone.

The general was on a field telephone when I got there; a candle was the only light. He was asking if they could get a plane in the air to see if Jap troop transports were unloading off Lunga Point.

"No," he said, "never mind then."

There were four or five other men in there, but I couldn't make out who they were. While I was up on the ridge, a submarine had shelled Henderson.

"They don't know where the craters are unless they turn some lights on," Vandegrift said. "That would make a nice target." He noticed me. "How's it going up there?"

They're holding on, I said.

"The phone line to the ridge has been cut for an hour, and I haven't got any news. The main attack is on the road, and we're kicking hell out of them."

I said they broke through where I was, but we turned them back. Ammo is low, though.

"They attacked up a steep ridge through artillery and machinegun fire and still got over your barbed wire?" an officer said. Someone lit a cigarette, and in the match's flare I saw Colonel Twining looking at me. "How the hell many are there?"

As many as we can handle and maybe more, I said. It's hand to hand fighting in places. I personally...

"General," he interrupted, "the attack on the road is a diversion. You have to send your reserves up to the ridge before it's too late."

To his credit, the general saw his mistake. "Okay," he said after some quick thinking. "Go ahead and release them, and get more ammo up there fast as you can."

Twining left on the run while the general was barking orders to the others. When they were gone, he drew me away so the radioman couldn't hear.

"We got a high-priority message from CINPAC. You're flying out of here tomorrow."

I was glad it was dark. No matter how well-trained you have your poker face, a royal flush out of the blue is going to show. It was Harry Hopkins, paying me back for saving his life. He would know how dangerous Guadalcanal was from the reports they were getting. He'd have to work his magic without Franklin knowing, but that was easy for him.

I thought of saying if it was up to me I'd stay until the Japs were licked, but I had a hunch Vandegrift just might call that bluff. The radiogram from CINPAC could be made to disappear—fog of war and et cetera—and I'd be humping back up the ridge bent double by bandoliers of extra ammo. From the crackle of gunfire coming from there, the fighting was hammer and tongs again.

"Nice to have friends in high places," Vandegrift said.

It was enemies in high places that put me in those death traps, but how do you explain that to a general in the middle of a battle? The radioman said a company commander wanted him.

I don't think his opinion of me could be any lower, and yet a few minutes later he was saying he would recommend me for the Navy Cross. That's how fast things can change in life.

Thinking it would be a good thing to make myself scarce in case Vandegrift changed his mind, I eased out. I figured my bunker was the safest place to hole up until I flew out. I had only gone a few yards in the darkness when I heard men laughing.

That's the last thing you expect under dire circumstances. They were loud laughs like men having a jolly old time over drinks. Another red flare went off overhead, and I slipped into the shade of some stacked boxes. Just then one of them casually tossed a grenade into a shelter. I had my .45 racked by the time it went off.

They were loose-goosey, grouped together; they probably thought it had been so easy slipping through a gap in our line that the hard work was over. Or maybe the opium made them full of good thoughts. Their rifles were pointed to the ground or slung over shoulders.

"Them .45s shoot straight enough if you hold 'em with two hands," one of the Old Breed sarges had told me up on the ridge. "Most guys won't do it because they think it ain't manly."

The Japs spotted Vandegrift's headquarters because of the candle. I thought about letting them pass and shooting them in the back, but I didn't want to be firing in the general's direction. I had the element of surprise when I stepped out in front of them. The sarge was right; hold it with two hands and a .45 delivers the goods. I went down them left to right, *Bang! Bang! Bang!* It was like shooting ducks in a row at the county fair. *Bang! Bang! Bang!* I bagged all six, and then had to hit the dirt when our people opened up. They may have been slow off the mark, but they made up for it. Somebody cut loose with a machinegun and the stack of boxes was ripped to pieces.

When they got that wild shooting under control, Vandegrift himself gave me a hand up. "If they'd knocked out the HQ, we'd have been royally screwed. I'm going to recommend you for the Navy Cross."

It probably stuck in his craw some to say that, but no one could say he wasn't a fair man. The Navy Cross had just gotten a promotion, by the way, going from third to second after the Medal of Honor. There were probably a hundred men who did braver things than me that night, but you have to be seen being a hero to win a medal. That takes several reliable witnesses, or one general will do.

CHAPTER 23

OKAY, I'M GOING TO SKIP TO BACK TO BEFORE GUADALCANAL. ADMIRAL HART sent me to introduce myself to General MacArthur at his headquarters at No. 1 Calle Victoria. Manila was a beautiful city before the Japs blasted it to bits. It had neighborhoods hundreds of years old; I wish you could have seen it.

The old fortress called Intramuros was the heart of it. Narrow, crowded streets held the heat so you didn't want to be there in the afternoon. Horse-drawn taxis clopping along, lots of shops selling religious stuff. Churches with stained glass windows all over the place. They were full of incense. and candles by the dozens flickered under the statues of Jesus and Mary and the saints. Men and women with shawls dipped holy water and kneeled in the pews; a steady stream day and night. Very religious people, the Filipinos

Intramuras had a long history. It was captured by the Spanish in the 16th century, attacked by the Chinese in the 17th, occupied by the English in the 18th century, and we took it over in the Spanish-American War, but were fixing to give them their independence.

MacArthur's headquarters were in a thick-walled white building that used to be a cavalry barracks. Major Dwyer was nearly floored when I walked in and asked to see him.

"You must be new," he said.

I said that was true enough, and explained that Admiral Hart sent me.

"If you were the governor-general himself you couldn't just walk in off the street and expect to see General MacArthur. The way it works is the

Navy Department officially asks the War Department in Washington, D.C. for an appointment. If approved, word comes down through channels to the military mission and we take it from there."

I asked how long that would take. It wasn't like they were all that busy. A corporal typing with two fingers was the only thing going on that I could see.

"The general is a very busy man."

Then MacArthur himself walked through the door. "Major Dwyer, have you...Why, who do we have here?"

He had on a gray-checked tropical suit straight off the hanger. He changed clothes three times a day, so he looked fresh as a daisy while everybody else was wrinkled and sweaty by noon. They say he caught flak from Chaumont in the First World War for ditching his uniform for jodhpurs, a leather jacket and silk scarf. He took the wire out of his cap like the flyers because it looked more dashing. He was begging for a sniper's bullet in that get-up. When I met him he had taken to combing his hair over from the side to hide baldness. I don't know who these guys think they're fooling.

I saluted and explained why I was there.

"Times have changed," he said to the major. "Flexibility is the thing now; the bamboo not the oak."

"The bamboo not the oak; yes, sir," Dwyer said.

MacArthur led me into a room fit for a king. A huge Chippendale desk had family pictures in silver frames, and inlaid Oriental cabinets from the Spanish occupation stood around the room. Flowers were everywhere, and fans turned overhead.

The general kicked off his shoes and put feet up on a chair. He was very interested when I said my last billet was the White House, and impressed that I had been with Churchill. That was to pay off for me later. He asked about Franklin's health and what the mood was back home. We were getting on so well after a while I asked how his bombers got caught on the ground. He got a faraway look.

"They telephoned to say Pearl Harbor had been attacked," he said. "I dressed and came here at once. After orders were issued, I withdrew to compose my thoughts. Feeling a strange weakness, I sank to the floor.

Contemporary accounts say Napoleon was confused and uncomprehending at Waterloo. I never understood before how so great a commander could become a sleepwalker at such a supreme moment, but in his defense it seems not uncommon. Washington was in a daze at the Battle of Brandywine, and Jackson similarly afflicted at a critical moment at White Oak Swamp where he sat on a stump with eyes closed. Matters take on a phantasmagorical aspect. You barely grasp one idea before another takes its place. One is overwhelmed, drowned by the melee of fact and supposition and the emotions they release. Given a few more months, General MacArthur could have put these islands in a position beyond any aspiration of success by an aggressor. There is brandy in that cabinet. Pour a good measure for me."

I poured myself a stout one as well and we clinked glasses.

"Brandy was the soldiers' great comfort in the trenches," he said. "Hell almost certainly is a place of cold and mud rather than the fiery pit warned of by ecclesiastical authority."

We sipped in silence while he thought. "I had hoped my dear Filipinos would be spared the mailed fist of Mars, but it wasn't to be. Such are the exigencies of Fate."

He went on in that regard for a while, man proposes but God disposes, and et cetera. It looked like Hart was right; some say he was a military genius and maybe they're right, but at the same time the man was a mystic. He knew a lot of big words, too.

The general slipped on his shoes and our little chat was over. He said he looked forward to working with me as a representative of our nation's great Navy. He made me feel like an ambassador from an another power, which to him I guess I was. Like the rest of the Army, the general didn't know much about the Navy except they didn't like us.

* * *

We drove on to the North Carolina coast and stopped at a small auto court near Myrtle Beach that had seen better days. The cabins were weathered from exposure to the Atlantic, and there was a faint smell of mold. The owner, a sweet white-haired gentleman named Dovecote, gave us a very good rate as it was off season and most of the cabins were unoccupied.

His wife, when we met her later, could not have been more different.

Irma Dovecote was rail thin with mousy hair pulled back with a tightness that looked like she was punishing herself for sins. There was bitterness in her mouth, and the anger in her dark eyes was on slow simmer. She came to our door the following morning on the pretext of seeing if we needed anything. I didn't invite her in to snoop as I gathered she thought was her right.

"My husband is such a nice man," she said, "too nice to be a businessman. We have to raise your rate when the weather turns nicer." Her manner implied this could come in a day or two although she clutched her coat to her throat against the wind.

I said we were already thinking of moving on and she back-peddled in a hurry.

"Oh, I mean late March or April when people are traveling again." She said she noticed our car had Maryland plates. "We get a lot of visitors from there."

I was silent and when she saw was not welcome, she gave me a sour smile, turned, and walked quickly back to the office.

Mr. Dovecote came later in the day to clear a drain in the bathroom. "Has Esther been pestering you? She was born wanting to know everybody's business."

She wasn't all that bad, I said sweetly.

"Her brother is the chief of police and she thinks she's supposed to be eyes and ears for him. She lives for the day when she can collect a reward for turning in someone running from the law."

Lowell loved smelling salt air again, and we walked under a lowering sky to the deserted shore where beach grass shivered in the blustery wind. An onlooker would have seen a small woman huddling close to her shambling companion for protection, but I was the strong one steadying his stumbling gait.

* * *

Major Dwyer turned out to be perfect guy for getting me into MacArthur's thinking, which is what Admiral Hart wanted. He was a born bureaucrat who lived to get orders and pass them on; a top-down, by-the-book man; a skinny guy, all elbows and knees like Ichabod Crane. The general had ordered him to cooperate with me and that's what he did.

MacArthur's staff was as loyal to him as his wife. Hart told me they were second raters whose job was to feed the general's ego, and they did remind me of the ring-kissers around King Edward. The exception was his chief of staff, Richard Sutherland, a brigadier general who was a surly bastard as arrogant as MacArthur could be himself. The difference being Sutherland was that way around the clock. He was mean-eyed with a long head and a face as sharp as a butcher knife. Not a day went by without him reaming somebody out in front of people. I've done that myself plenty when called for, but not every blessed day like him. You could tell he enjoyed it.

Like me, he was related to a senator, except the voters threw his pa out after one term. That might be why he hated our system. He said the public were fools who elected other fools.

No argument from me, I said pleasantly.

"Plato had the right idea," he said, "a society of producers, warriors and rulers, each doing what he's told, except the rulers."

The man had it all figured out.

He was hoping to crush me with book learning, but I wasn't falling for that trap. Never argue with someone who knows more than you about something. I always change the subject to women and poker.

Dwyer introduced me to everyone who counted and got me on the invitation list to the Blue Hour at the swanky Manila Hotel where the big shots lived. Man, its air conditioning was heaven when you walked in out of a hot and muggy afternoon. At five o'clock on the dot Dwyer and I rode the elevator to the penthouse.

A tiny woman with hazel eyes opened the door. "You must be Captain Brady." She was the general's wife, Jean. "Hello, Major."

"My husband said you were a big, handsome fellow," she said to me, "but my, oh my. A fellow Southerner as well! Come right in. He's dressing, but you can meet the others."

We got drinks at the bar and she took us around the room to introduce me to people from the High Commissioner's office, senior Army officers and various others. There were no women because wives and families had already been sent home, Jean being the exception. It turned out Dwyer couldn't hold his liquor; one drink and he was unsteady on his feet. That had to be why he was still a major.

It looked like Jean was used to it. "Maybe you two ought to sit down," she said. "I'm sure the captain has many questions."

When she left us, he took my lapel and pushed his bleary eyes close to mine. "Look, you wanna understand the general you have to know his family." He was already slurring words. Amazing, just one drink.

What about it, I asked.

"They go back to the Knights of the Round Table, and I'm not shitting you. King Arthur and all that. His father Arthur won the Medal of Honor at Missionary Ridge with the 2nd Wisconsin. Braxton Bragg's, ah, Confederate Army of Tennessee was dug in above them, and General Sherman ordered the ridge seized. Ah, the first color-bearer was bayoneted and the second had his head taken off by an artillery shell. *Hick!* Arthur seized the standard and shouted 'On Wisconsin!' He carried it to the top and the Rebels were routed. That was the key to Sherman's march through the South."

I said I remembered it well. The truth was we didn't spend a lot of time on military history at Annapolis. I didn't anyhow.

"He rose in rank and was ordered to put down Aguinaldo's insurrection. He was getting the job done, but not fast enough for President McKinley. Arthur thought the Philippines needed a decade of military rule to be shaped up proper. That's Colonel Broderick coming through the door. Asshole! Ah, where was…the commission that McKinley sent out here said there had to be an easier way, and of course they won in Washington."

I'm telling this without all the stops and starts. Dwyer kept blowing his cheeks out and losing his train of thought. "Look at that sunset" or "There's that cocksucker Sutherland." He hummed or said "Whew." One drink! He was starting to fall asleep when Jean turned up.

"Oh, dear," she said, "I was afraid of that." She gently shook Dwyer's shoulder. "It's time for you to go home, Major. Betty will have dinner ready."

He pulled himself to his feet and walked to the door in that over-dignified way people get when they're smashed but don't want it to show. I've done it myself more than once; better than Dwyer, I hope.

"The Gin'ral would like to see you," she told me.

That was her way of talking. Hello, Gin'ral. The Gin'ral says this; the Gin'ral thinks that. The other thing she called him was Sir Boss. MacArthur had an almighty high opinion of himself, and there was nobody at home to bring him down to earth like a lot of husbands have one step inside their front door.

She led me out to a balcony where he was pacing and twirling a light cane. "A visitor, *mon* Gin'ral." She left us.

He wore a blue and gold dressing gown with a big letterman's A sewed on. I got the feeling I was expected to ask about it.

"I played right field in the first baseball game between Army and Navy, which we won four to three, and I had the honor of scoring the winning run. I drew a walk in the third inning and was singled home and the lead held up."

I said Major Dwyer told me only Robert E. Lee and one other cadet beat his marks in their four years at West Point. Dwyer had given me a sheet of paper with other highlights. While on recon in the war with Mexico, MacArthur shot and killed seven men to get back to friendly lines. In the Great War he won more medals for bravery than anybody, and was the youngest chief of staff in Army history. There was a lot of other impressive stuff, command assignments and so forth.

"Poor Dwyer," the general said. "Another commander would fire him for his weakness and he'd rust away on the retired list. But the man is loyal to me, damn it, and I set a high value on that."

It turned out he had his people do some fast digging and decided my record wasn't good enough for a captain's stripes. He figured I must be smart at the inside game; Harry pushing me along was the proof. He was too noble for that kind of low scheming himself, but could understand it worked for people like me.

We stopped pacing for the general to address the setting sun. "God blessed this simple land," he said. "Look at that view."

Purple clouds, green trees, thatched roofs, the harbor stretched out below. The air was turning blue, the reason for the name of the cocktail hour. You'd have to go some to beat that sight.

He asked if Dwyer had mentioned his father.

Medal of Honor winner, I said promptly.

"He was a far greater man than I could ever hope to me. His valor and service to our nation could not be exaggerated. He was military commandant during the Filipino insurrection. Washington saw fit to send out a commission whose chairman was a grossly fat hack politician. Father did not gladly suffer civilian intrusion and there was strife between them. The chairman sweated profusely in this climate and was continually mopping his brow with handkerchiefs that he passed to an aide when they were sodden. My father said it was disgusting. He was fastidious in his own habits, and I like to think I follow his example. You know the politician of whom I speak. He was William Howard Taft, who denied my father his rightful promotion to Army chief of staff when he was president."

I said I was sorry to hear it.

"Yes, my father had made an enemy of a future president. But he would not have changed anything even if he had the gift of prescience such was his fealty to principle. Congress made him a lieutenant general, only the twelfth man to attain that rank since the founding of the Republic. Do you know how my father died?"

MacArthur's eyes locked on mine. "The survivors of my regiment had met in annual reunions since the Civil War, but by 1912 their numbers were reduced to ninety infirm veterans. The governor of the state was scheduled to address them but was forced to cancel. My father, who was ill, rose from his sickbed against the advice of his doctor and my mother to go in his place on the hottest day of the year. 'Your indomitable regiment,' he began to say at the conclusion of his speech. Then he swayed and fell to the floor. The man who had been the regimental surgeon rushed to his side. After a brief examination, he said the general is dying. They all knelt around him to recite the Lord's Prayer. When it was over, a captain who had been with him on that heroic day of battle rose and took the flag my father had flourished on the ridge and wrapped his body in it. That act completed, he fell over my father's body and died."

I'm embarrassed to say I started to snivel; the man sure could spin a tale. He could have had a career on the stage, he was that good.

He got gruff to hide how pleased that I was wiping at my eyes. "It's something all our school children should know."

I said I couldn't agree more.

We went back inside and he changed into a blue blazer over tan slacks with a razor crease. "His trousers are pleated, ah, to hide the paunch he's got from his hernias," Dwyer had said. "Four of them."

He was a fountain of information like that. I thought God help us if a spy ever poured him a drink.

"Jean is his second wife you know," Dwyer said. "The first wife was very rich and quite a bit older. They came out here after a big wedding in Palm Beach. Whew! Where's the...She was Black Jack Pershing's mistress before that. Pershing was chief of staff and for revenge sent the general out here from West Point where he was the commandant. *Hick!* She was used to rubbing elbows with high society, so Manila was quite a comedown. Her stuff filled so much of the ship coming over that the other Army families were limited to a single trunk. You can imagine how mad the wives were. I hate that bastard over there. Look at him shoveling food into his big mouth. Ah, where was I?"

The wives, I said.

"She didn't think much of them as they were so below her station, and she disliked the heat. *Hick!* The general walked on eggs around her. They were late to something and she was still at her dressing table. When he stood behind to hurry her up, she broke a hand mirror over his head. Their divorce was in all the papers."

Admiral Hart wanted me to find out what Army plans were for when the Japanese invaded. He could never get much out of official channels; that's how bad it was back then.

"My Filipino army of forty thousand brave patriots, supported and advised by American forces, will meet them at the beaches and drive them into the sea," MacArthur told me. "You may have noticed the trucks going north from Manila. We are establishing depots to supply them."

General Sutherland flared up when I casually asked where they were training the Filipinos. "Why do you want to know?"

I said I drove around the country in my spare time, and I'd like to drop by if he didn't mind.

"Permission denied," he snapped. "That base is top secret. If you have any questions, write them down and I'll see if the general wants them answered."

Early the next morning I parked a car outside the military warehouse district. When the trucks began to rattle past I followed on the dusty farm-to-market road after the pavement ended. We passed sugarcane and banana plantations and rice paddies cut from the jungle. A couple of hours north I turned off at the sign to Camp Aguinaldo. I showed my I.D. at the gate and was taken to the camp commander's thatched hut. I recognized Colonel Thornburgh from the cocktail party.

"Nobody told me you were coming," he said getting up from his desk to shake my hand.

He was fat and soft like most of them in the peacetime army. Lazy too, if I was any judge. The war thinned their ranks in a hurry.

I said I hoped to get an idea about how things were going; a fresh set of eyes and so forth. I kept it vague and low key. Sure, he said with a yawn, have a look see. He called for Sergeant Lewis and told him to show me around. Lewis was a Mississippian as tough as rawhide. He kept a bulge of tobacco in one cheek and turned his head to spit brown juice.

He drove me around to see the training. "If you want to call it that," he said with disgust. "Look at that." A row of small Filipinos lay on the ground firing rifles that kicked up dirt around targets on a berm. "Some of them old rifles are bigger than they are. If they hit the target it's pure accident. We can't teach them how to march neither. They jaw away in eight languages and about a hundred dialects, and they can't read or write in any of them. I tell you it's the Tower of Babel."

General MacArthur says they'll drive the Japs into the sea, I said.

"Just between us," the sergeant said, "goes no further?" I nodded. "The general is nuts. A few will stand and fight, but the rest are gonna run for it."

He was right. The Filipinos bolted when the Japs came ashore; the Frenchmen of the East you might say. MacArthur had done some rethinking before then, and the plan was back to retreating to Bataan and Corregidor and waiting for the Pacific Fleet to break the siege.

"The Army thinks we'll be here within six months; that's the pipe dream we've been feeding them for years," Hart said when I told him what I'd seen. "Two or three years are more like it. The big Japanese base in Formosa is only two hundred and seventy miles from our airfield on Luzon. The Japanese can get a troop convoy here in a day or two and in four days from their home waters. It's just a *little* tougher for us. Manila is sixty-two hundred miles from San Francisco and forty-eight hundred miles from Honolulu. For two thousand miles of that distance our ships could be attacked from planes from the Marianas, Carolinas and Marshalls." I don't have much appetite, but think I could take a little soup if it's ready, dear. The way that wind is blowing makes me glad we're not still in that cave.

CHAPTER 24

MR. DOVECOTE WAS THE NICEST MAN, LIKE AN OLD FRIEND ALMOST FROM the start. He had sharp blue eyes, ruddy cheeks and sparse white hair under the deer hunter cap he wore with ear flaps down. He asked after Lowell's health and offered to go to the grocery store for me so I did not have to leave him alone. I reminded him of the daughter who would be my age if she hadn't died with his first wife in a car accident. She wore glasses like mine.

"She doesn't like me to talk about Lucy or her mother," he said. Woeful and downcast, he turned his faded blue eyes away. "I'm supposed to be over it after all these years."

He didn't have to say who. I felt her jealous eye on us from the window when I bumped into him in the parking lot or emptied trash. Mr. Dovecote spent a lot of time pottering around outside or just looking out to sea with his hands in his pockets. It took no great feat of mental penetration to deduce that it was to get away from her.

"A lot of women are like that," Lowell said. "They can't stand to think of their husbands talking to another woman unless they're putting in their two cents at the same time. He probably married on the rebound; lots of ex-wives in Las Vegas were like that. The ink was barely dry on the divorce papers before they were pawing the ground to get married again. Loneliness, I suppose."

Loneliness and fear that they were walled off from happiness for the rest of their lives. Their marriages had gone bad, but there must have been times when they were as deeply happy to have a husband as I was. They wanted that feeling again even it meant closing their eyes to the risks. To gamble was better than folding one's arms and declining the game; the six months I had been with Lowell convinced me of that. They seemed as rich and full as all of my years before put together. And it was not just the roller-coaster life of a fugitive, though the intermingling of our fates had sealed the bond between us in a way that I would not have believed possible so soon. I was determined that they would not take him from me even if it cost my life, however melodramatic it sounded. Learning how to use guns when I was growing up, I did not have the usual female fear of them. I slipped away one afternoon while he slept to buy a Smith & Wesson revolver at a pawn shop. I did not tell him.

Mr. Dovecote tapped on the door the next day, his kindly face troubled. "I ran into a friend of my wife, a nurse at our little community hospital. They've been told to be on the lookout for a sick man and a woman in a car with Maryland license plates. She knows it's Irma's dream to get a reward and her picture in the paper, so she wanted me to tell her. My wife will be hopping mad when she finds out I didn't." He smiled a little. "But we've both noticed I've been getting kinda forgetful."

He clearly knew we were the couple in question. "They didn't say why they wanted them, but they're giving this number to call." He handed me a folded piece of paper.

I told him we hadn't killed anyone, robbed a bank or anything of that nature. "It's about something that happened in the war the government doesn't want to get out."

"You're too much like my Lucy to do anything bad. I bet those crooks in Washington have a lot of dirty laundry they don't want aired."

I thought of the gun in my suitcase. Perhaps I wasn't as much like Lucy as he thought. Or maybe if she had lived life would have changed her like it did me.

He put a gentle hand on my arm. "Maybe you'd better get on the road again. This is a small town and there's no telling when Irma will bump into that nurse."

"This here is one rolling stone that wouldn't mind gathering some moss for a change," Lowell grumbled as I quickly packed. We drove to Charlotte and checked into a motel. I got him settled in bed, and went to an outside telephone booth and dialed the number on the paper.

"Hawley," said the voice on the other end of the line.

"What department is this?"

"Agricultural price supports."

"I think I called the wrong number. I'm calling about that couple you're looking for."

"No, this is the right number."

"I'm with the Baptist hospital in Stillwater."

"Oklahoma?"

"Yes."

"A big man and a small woman? Maryland license MB461."

"I can see the car from here. What does the Agriculture Department want them for?"

"We're cooperating with another agency. Can I have your address and phone number, please."

"Is that other agency the FBI?" I asked.

"No."

"Is this Mr. Hawley?"

A small silence. "Somehow I doubt you're in Stillwater, Mrs. Brady."

"So you know we're married."

"We also know your husband is pretty sick. You better let me send a doctor."

"So he can put a pillow over his face?"

"I started off on the wrong foot with you from the beginning. I should have explained we're just interested in clarifying a few facts."

"Facts about how President Roosevelt and a lot of famous men still alive committed treason?"

"Is that what your husband is claiming?"

"You know it is," I said.

"It's his word against a lot of others."

"You might think you've removed everything from the files and archives, but take it from a researcher something always falls between the cracks.

People will begin turning over rocks; newspaper reporters, and then scholars."

"We've thought of that, believe it or not."

I pictured him leaning back in his chair in some anonymous government building; his cold eyes, his heavy body giving off that well-fed animal heat.

"All it will take is one loose string someone pulls on," I said. "Whoever it is will start to ask questions, and pretty soon people will step forward and tell what they know. Then the whole thing unravels."

"A lot of people think Admiral Kimmel and General Short were fall guys. So far it's their word against the people in charge back then, but your husband could change that. He could be the rock bouncing downhill that starts an avalanche."

"You think Captain Brady wants big headlines in the newspapers, but he doesn't. He just wants the historical record to be correct."

"Years from now, when it doesn't matter?"

"Yes."

"If we could just be sure of that."

His kind of man had a low opinion of women; they believe we can be out-thought and they can manipulate our emotions. Even knowing that, I admit part of me wished to be persuaded. Lowell was near the end of his strength. If we didn't stop running, I didn't know how he could ever get better.

"It's not just a question of reputations," Hawley said. "Communism will conquer the world if we don't stop it. The world looks to us for moral leadership, and we're fighting for hearts and minds. If the generation that led us to war looks like it was no better than the commissars, why would other countries choose us over them? We're locked in a life-or-death struggle with the Reds in case you haven't noticed."

"I wish I could believe all you want is to talk to him."

"You must be dead tired. You're a long way from your quiet life. You had regular habits, kept your head down, and didn't make waves; nothing suggested you were capable of this."

"I didn't have a husband I loved."

"After we talk to him, you and the captain can do what you want. We'll have no further interest, I promise you. I'll go out on a limb and say you might even get your job back. That was interesting what you wrote about Ol' Dan Tucker, by the way. The research that went into it. Very impressive."

His promises were so patently false and his playing to my vanity and hunger for praise, which it must be admitted even the smallest writer craves, was so transparent that I was close to laughter.

"If I were to give you transcriptions of all the interviews with my husband, would that satisfy you?"

"That would certainly be very helpful; for sure it would, and thank you very much for the offer. We're starting to get somewhere at last. But we'd still have to go over questions you might not have gone into, or not deeply enough. And there is a non-disclosure contract we'd like signed."

I reminded myself what he was like in person. The intimidating, bullying him, the true him.

"What happened to Greg Pearson?" I said. "You remember him."

"Nothing. I have his number here somewhere. Call him yourself." He gave me Greg's work number.

I said I would talk to Lowell about what he said.

"Fine," he said, "you've got my number."

When I told Lowell, he groaned. "And they've got the one you called from. They'll have a tap on his phone, and it will lead them straight here. They're probably talking to the local cops right now. They'll tell them to hold us until they can get their own people here."

I put the bags in the car and helped Lowell into the passenger seat. I drove for a half hour to a seedy place off the main highway. I took change out to the payphone by the manager's office and telephoned the number Hawley had given him.

Greg Pearson's voice was steely. "I don't think we should be talking."

"I'm so glad you're still alive," I said.

"Look, I'm serious. They told me not to have anything to do with you."

"And you're going to let them tell you what to do? Where's the Greg Pearson I used to know?"

"He's...I'm going to hang up now. Byeee."

* * *

This place isn't as nice as the other auto court, but I'm not complaining.

If the local flatfoots had been on the ball, they would have collared us for sure. Hawley must have given somebody an earful when he found out how close they came.

So let's see, going back to Manila. When Admiral Hart steamed south to the Dutch East Indies, he left Vice Admiral Rockwell in charge. He was the commandant of the Sixteenth Naval District and commander of the Philippine Coastal Frontier. That might sound grand, but it wasn't—not anymore. Put it this way, he was in charge of the smoking rubble, and there was more of that by the day. Rockwell appointed me as his deputy, pending Navy Department approval, and gave me five hundred bluejackets and Marines to move supplies to Bataan and Corregidor. MacArthur's army was retreating there, blowing up dozens of bridges as they went.

We used fishing boats, schooners, ferries and anything else that floated. We could count on at least one per day being shot up or bombed to the bottom of Manila Bay. Our anti-aircraft shells were mostly duds. Those that weren't exploded two thousand feet below the Jap bombers. No air cover, of course.

That was Sutherland's fault. You went through him to get to MacArthur— if you got past Major Dwyer. When the general was in his swoon or whatever you call it, Sutherland kept the world out. One of the people milling around outside was General Brereton, who ran the Army air force in the Philippines. He showed up before dawn after Pearl Harbor was attacked to ask MacArthur for permission to send his B-17s to Formosa where the Japs were loading troop ships at that very moment.

Sutherland told him the general was too busy to see him; I got that from Brereton himself after he'd had a few. Dwyer told me he had resigned from the Navy because of seasickness a day after he graduated from Annapolis. Then he joined the Army air corps, but tried to get out after a couple crashes people died in. No wonder he liked the sauce. There was a big party in his honor at the Manila Hotel the night before the Jap attack. Those B-17s were supposed to be flown down to Del Monte so they were out of reach, but the pilots hung around for the party. Imagine what those bombs did for their hangovers, the ones who survived.

When Brereton said he would send the bombers to Formosa on his own authority, Sutherland nixed it because it might get the boss in trouble with Washington. Hours later he said it would be okay if Brereton wanted to send up planes to take some pictures of what was going on over there. Three B-17s fixing to do that were taxiing on the runway at Clark when they were blasted to pieces by the Jap bombs. Stalin would have hung everyone involved.

A petty officer told me about a sergeant who said there was a depot on the central Luzon plain that had a lot of food stored for war. I had my driver take me to Colonel Thornburgh at Camp Aguinaldo.

"I don't know if I should be talking to you," he said. "I caught hell from Sutherland for letting you look around. He told me not to let you in again."

He was pale and puffy and his hands shook; a classic case of the whips and jingles. Some of those older officers were drinking hard and paying a hellish price the next day. War is for the young, and so is hitting the bottle that hard. Those guys were lonely and worried, and their wives weren't around to put on the brakes. Hell, who could blame them? I sure didn't.

My letters to Mother asking her to get me out of there hadn't been answered, but war screwed up the mails, and I wasn't sure they even got to her. Official channels were overloaded, and anyhow they didn't transmit personal stuff even if you were the deputy commander of the smoke and rubble. I had got a nasty call from Admiral Rockwell for trying to "bully" a lieutenant commander into sending a short message home. I said there had been a misunderstanding. Make sure there isn't another, he told me.

"Screw Richardson," Thornburgh said after he thought about it. "Somebody ought to tell MacArthur how his fuck-ups got us in this mess. That depot has fifty million bushels of rice, enough to feed every man we've got for four years."

I went over to see for myself and sure enough buildings with bags of rice stacked to the ceiling as far as you could see. Depots like that were in the war plans for years, but then MacArthur had decided his untrained rabble would stop the Japs on the beaches. Plans had changed back again, like I said, and the rice still sat there.

When I got back to Manila, I went to see Sutherland. Major Dwyer shot a look over his shoulder in the outer office and dropped his voice. "He's in a shitty mood. The general is giving everybody hell." He picked up the phone and told Sutherland I was there.

Sutherland was abusing a captain with some choice language when I came in. Leaving off from that, he gave me a look that could've froze a side of beef and said, "Well?"

I said I'd just come from a big warehouse full of rice up on the Luzon plain.

"What about it!"

What are you going to do with it?

"Blow it up. Next question."

I said it looked like lean times ahead. If he could spare me the loan of ten or twenty trucks, I'd get that rice to the Bataan Peninsula and...

He cut me off. "No transport is available. We're pulling back to the next line of defense. Anything else?" There wasn't, and I left him abusing the captain some more.

We left Manila for Corregidor on an inter-island steamer on Christmas Eve. The smell of burning oil and cordite rose from what was left of the naval base. Gangs of looters were already prowling the darkened city, and the Japs were at the outskirts. Someone began to sing a Christmas carol and a few other fools joined in, but they knocked it off.

One look at the Malinta Tunnel was all it took for the general to decide that wasn't for him, his wife and little kid, and he bumped the island's commander from his bungalow on top of the rock. The Japs bombed that to rubble after a couple of weeks, and they had to rough it with the rest of us in the tunnel. It shuddered from direct hits, and fine dust sifted down after each one. Everyone went around looking like they had frost on their eyebrows.

The lateral tunnels began filling with the wounded. And the sick, too. Packed in like that and drinking brackish water when the filtration plant went out, fevers began to spread. Typhus, cholera, dengue, you name it. And malaria, of course. You began to forget the whites of eyes aren't supposed to be yellow. Every time I looked at a thermometer it was ninety-five degrees.

MacArthur and his people were bucked up by the radiograms from Washington saying hang on, relief was on the way. He showed me one from Marshall that said 125 P-40s and fifteen B-24s would join them soon.

I said was there any mention of how they're going to get here?

He told Sutherland, "This man's a Doubting Thomas." MacArthur showed me one of the radiograms from General Marshall. Hang on, he said again, help is on the way.

"Maybe he knows something he's not saying," Sutherland said.

"Marshall wouldn't be making these promises if he didn't mean it," MacArthur said. He had lost about twenty-five pounds by then and looked as seedy as the rest of us.

You had to poke a new hole in the belt once a week to keep your pants up. I worked the story about the rice into just every conversation I had. Actual hatred for Sutherland instead of what somebody called "instinctive dislike" was pretty general in the inner circle, but when that got out it spread fast. Junior officers heard it from senior officers and passed it on to non-coms who shared it with the grunts. I see from your face you're wondering didn't I have better things to do? The answer is no. You took cover in the tunnel when the Japs were shelling or bombing, but otherwise there wasn't anything to do but scan the water for our rescuers. People hoped to be the first to spot the fleet on the horizon, and there was a pool with thousands of dollars for the winner. I knew it was all hogwash, but kept it to myself, even from the general. People have to have hope or they give up, as they finally did there.

You might call it petty, but I passed that story around because it had been one screw-up after another since before Pearl Harbor and nobody even got his wrist slapped that I could see. In fact, it was the opposite. The people who *did* their jobs got it in the neck. Sutherland was to blame for our air force getting bombed to bits on the ground, and his blundering left us the choice of blowing up the rice or letting the Japs have it.

In the Malinta Tunnel you went to bed hungry and woke up hungrier and thought about nothing but food. Sutherland was roughed up a couple of times when he left the tunnel for his morning squat. It got to where he had an armed escort everywhere he went. He had a pretty good idea who was behind his unpopularity, and gave me the fish eye when we passed. Being that everybody was jammed into such a small space, this was several times a day.

The senior officers gathered in the communication lateral of the tunnel at ten in the morning to listen to the shortwave broadcast from San Francisco. The radio announcer hurled defiance at the Japs. Is this the best you got, he asked on behalf of the Battlin' Bastards of Bataan. We looked at each other uneasily. That generally inspired the Japs to give us a little something extra. Another fifteen minutes or so over target or a few dozen more rounds of artillery before the morning haze lifted. I suppose those broadcasts bucked up morale on the home front. The workers on strike at the defense factories probably cheered and pounded backs. But I don't feel bitter anymore.

Nobody knew until years later that Marshall called Eisenhower in for advice about it. He'd been MacArthur's chief of staff in the Philippines; the best clerk I ever had, the general jested. Write them off, Ike said; there's no way we can save them. The general would have to go down fighting, but it was better than being hung in Imperial Square in Tokyo, which is what Tokyo Rose was promising on the radio.

But that was the problem. Our holding out at Corregidor was the only bright spot the country could see. Everywhere else there was defeat and surrender. Franklin was the first to realize how fast MacArthur had become a hero. Before he had time to prepare the country for the general's noble sacrifice, the American people were demanding that he be saved.

MacArthur paced back and forth in the tunnel for hours when Franklin ordered him off Corregidor. Disobeying an order from the commander-in-chief was a court-martial offense, but on the other hand he didn't want to and lose his reputation as the country's greatest soldier. Major Dwyer told me he even thought about resigning his commission and fighting on as a private soldier. Franklin and Marshall convinced him in the end by saying he would take command of the great army forming in Australia to take back what we'd lost. It didn't exist, of course.

"Roosevelt never told the truth when a lie would serve just as well," I heard him tell Sutherland when we got there. He had commanded more troops on Corregidor than were in all of Down Under.

Sutherland picked who was going to get off the Rock, and I wasn't on the list. The bastard grinned at me now when we passed, which was my tip off. Dwyer, who wasn't on the list either, got me in to see MacArthur when Sutherland was off somewhere with his armed escort. You could locate where he was from the jeers and swearing.

I knew it was probably a waste of time to plead, but I was willing as a last resort; fall down weeping and pluck at his trouser leg—a man does what he must in that situation. Instead, I told him how valuable I could be to him from my connection to Harry Hopkins. No man is closer to Franklin, I said, and no man is closer to Harry than me.

"Hmm," MacArthur said, "I hadn't thought of that." He paced back and forth with a shrewd look. "Every eye in Washington is turned to Europe. There is no voice speaking on behalf of the Pacific theater in the highest councils of the land."

We might as well be the bastard red-haired stepchild, I said.

"You would go home to present your views, of course. You would press our cause upon the president and Mr. Hopkins with the greatest urgency?"

I came to attention and saluted.

"I'll speak to Dick Sutherland," he said.

I heard that when Sutherland started to argue about it, the general cut him off. You know the saying he who laughs last? But I was careful not to rub it in. A merry whistle as we passed was as far as I let myself go.

What I said about destroyers being too small for comfort? They were the Queen Mary compared to the PT Boats. They weren't built for comfort; their role was to cut in at high speed, fire torpedoes and zip out again. Our four boats had seen heavy service without their ordinary overhauls. The rust and carbon build-up in the engines slowed them to a top speed of twenty-four knots. A cruiser or destroyer could run us down with no problem.

The Japs hadn't missed the talk in Washington about saving MacArthur. They tripled their surface patrols, and coast watchers radioed that a division of destroyers was headed our way. The feeling was we had one chance in five of escaping, but I reckoned that beat the zero chance of the ten thousand people we were leaving behind.

We shoved off at sunset on a March night in heavy seas with twenty-foot waves. Our eyes stung from the seawater from the regular duckings.

I went below from time to time to rub the life back into my hands and wash my eyes in clear water. The general was dry heaving in his bunk as Jean massaged his rigid arms and legs. Little Arthur lay in a bunk and his nanny cooed over him. I have to admit I wasn't feeling too good myself.

You would normally take seas like that at lower speeds in a boat that small, but we had to cross the open water as fast as possible to find a place to hide in the Cayo Islands before sunrise. So we battered through the waves with Lieutenant John Buckeley at the helm. Crashing to the bottom of a crest and then rising again was like being in a cement mixer. It took three days to reach Del Monte and another three days before the Army Air Force flew us to Australia.

MacArthur probably forgot me a week after we got there, and didn't know the White House ordered me to Guadalcanal for another try at knocking me off. When that failed, they sent me off via Vladivostok to liaison with the Russians. It was in the dead of winter, of course. I came close to buying the farm over there, maybe closest of all, but I don't think I'm going to get around to those stories until I get better, darlin'. Just too damned weak from this coughing. Can't seem to catch my breath.

CHAPTER 25

Memorandum

November 20, 1953

To: Clyde Tolson

From: The Director

Subject: Lowell Brady

For: File 24898

ALAN DULLES and I agreed there was nothing either side gains by taking this matter to higher authority at this time. One of their agents shot dead and one of ours mortally woundedit couldn't get much worse. Fortunately, the Bureau and Agency have experience in keeping matters from the public and we are cooperating. If it reaches the PRESIDENT's ear, of course, it will be dog eat dog.

I'm sure Sheriff Dutworth's son will make a competent agent after some dental work and instruction in personal hygiene. If I'm wrong, he can be employed cutting newspaper clippings for the files. It is a small price for silence even considering the new Chrysler for the sheriff. I don't know why a Ford or Chevrolet wasn't offered. The price difference is considerable.

DULLES denied knowing anything about this business and blamed a rogue operation that was kept from him. It is possible he is telling the truth and does not want to believe the Agency is riddled, a word I chose with care for our meeting, with Communists and traitors, but he will act in future on the basis of where there is smoke there is fire. We will be watching to see if he abides by his promise.

He asked if I would surrender our photographs and negatives of MELVIN CROSBY and was put out when I refused. He evidently doesn't have a high opinion of my intelligence, or perhaps he is just naïve.

When LOWELL BRADY and his wife are in custody at last, I think your plan is best. They will be transported to our containment facility in Alaska. His health what it is, they would not be able to escape by traversing hundreds of miles of rugged country with bears, wolves, etc., and they could not communicate with the outside world. When he dies, she will be returned to society on the condition that she surrenders all written and recorded material and signs a confession that we will draft.

If you have a better idea, I'm open to it as always.

Also as always:

/John

I was watching at the window as usual when I saw the first man, who I recognized even at this distance as Ted Hawley of the FBI, in a thick cable-knit sweater. He was coming with swift strides in the early dawn across the long grass in the meadow adjoining the rear of our auto court. He suddenly reared back at someone who lay concealed. The second man rose to his feet and both reached for their weapons.

The gunshots were almost simultaneous, *Pop-Pop*, and both fell to the ground.

"What the hell was that?" Lowell said, emerging from the bathroom as the toilet flushed.

Our luggage was already in the car; he had wanted a last bathroom visit before we drove away, having no destination in mind as usual.

I was unable to speak from the shock.

His arm was around my shoulders. "What is it, darlin'?"

Then the words came. "Two men. They shot each other in that field."

"We're on our way," he said and grabbed my arm.

As we drove away we saw men running toward the meadow from several directions. One of them slackened his speed and put up a hand for us to stop.

"Not on your life, buddy," Lowell said.

I wept with my hands held to my face.

"Some royal screw-up," Lowell guessed. "One hand not knowing what the other was doing. It happened all the time in the war." I kept sobbing. "Look, maybe they only wounded each other."

But I knew that couldn't be true. It was as if the puppeteer had snipped their strings and they dropped to the ground with a strange and terrible suddenness, life gone in the blink of an eye. I will never forget it; the scene is seared in my memory. I later threw away the gun I had bought because I knew I could never take someone's precious life.

We drove all that day and night, ending up in western Kentucky. We had discussed the shootings ceaselessly as we drove, considering it from all angles to try to fathom what happened.

"It was probably a lack of communication between the FBI and the local cops," Lowell said as we turned out the light at the Cloverleaf Auto Court. "Somebody in the wrong place at the wrong time."

He was at last getting over his chest cold and was looking and sounding better, his old loquacity returned. The next day we traded in our car for a newer one and continued our lives as gypsies, my husband talking and me taking down his words, words, words. So many of them. I hope one day our gypsy life comes to an end and we will find a home to call our own. It is nice where we are now. The magnolias are in bloom.

Dearest Toly:

I can't tell you how much it meant to me to have you at the meeting with Ike. Only you know how vulnerable I am beneath my tough and gruff faade. Whenever Ike turned up the heat I looked at your calm face and took heart.

The investigation will be low level and in time will fade away. The CIA has its story and we have ours.

Ike was impressed when you pointed out the CIA has no authority to discharge firearms on domestic soil except for training purposes. Dulles dropped his eyes at that point, and Ike took note of this with a cold look.

I'll end this brief note and slip it under the door while the light is still on. Pleasant dreams, dear. I believe the worst is behind us.

All my love,

John

ABOUT THE AUTHOR

 JERRY JAY CARROLL is the author of the acclaimed *Top Dog, Dog Eat Dog,* and *Inhuman Beings.* A Pulitzer-nominated journalist and J.S. Knight Fellow at Stanford University, Carroll worked for the *San Francisco Chronicle* before turning to fiction.

EXCERPTS FROM NOVELS BY JERRY JAY CARROLL

From _Top Dog:_

Just running at first. Nothing before that. No memories of childhood and family. No early struggles. No career. No friends. No opinions. No country, city, neighborhood, no home where I laid my head at day's end. No idea how I spent those days. Running. One minute oblivion and the next I'm in a forest, shafts of the dying day falling through the trees and dappling the ground with patterns of light and dark. Quail scurry, small animals freeze as I pass. I have no question about my place in the scheme of things. The wind is in my face and nothing seems more natural than running. It's the beginning and the end and everything in between.

From _Dog Eat Dog:_

I was strictly a red-meat guy before. There was nothing I liked better than a two-pound slab of rare roast beef on my plate with a baked potato and sour cream. A good cigar and cognac swirled in a warmed snifter afterward to release its fumes. That was living. But when you have to run down prey, rip out its throat, and snatch a few mouthfuls of hot flesh before some more powerful carnivore shows up, believe me, you lose your taste for meat.

From _Inhuman Beings:_

Mulhenny kept a bottle of scotch in a glassed-in bookcase filled with books he had bought by the yard in the hope clients would think he was deep. He smoked a pipe for the same reason. I found a glass that wasn't too dirty and poured a stiff one, just like Sam Spade. I felt rotten about Princess Dulay. I had kept her alive for a few days, but she still got it in the end. Tired as I was, the alarm bells should have gone off when I saw Alice with the cat.

CPSIA information can be obtained at www.ICGtesting.com
Printed in the USA
LVOW06s2102071014

407680LV00004B/268/P